LADY HELENA
INVESTIGATES

To Diane,
with love

LADY HELENA
INVESTIGATES

JANE STEEN

There's nothing left of what she was;
Back to the babe the woman dies,
And all the wisdom that she has
Is to love him for being wise.

— COVENTRY PATMORE, THE ANGEL IN THE HOUSE (1891)

1

THE BEREAVED

*S*ussex, 1881

"The point is," said my brother Michael, "Helena can't possibly manage the estate now that Justin's dead. And this house is far too large for a widow with no children."

He put his teacup down on the ornate marble mantelpiece, shoving a Dresden shepherdess to the side. The porcelain figurine wobbled dangerously. Michael shot out a steadying hand, glaring at the offending piece for getting in his way.

Julia, Michael's wife, rose from her perch on a gilded bergère by the crackling fire. She retrieved Michael's cup and set the figurine back in its proper place. "Really, Michael, this is hardly the time to browbeat poor Helena. She's been a widow for precisely nine days. Was there a crowd for the burial, by the way? I really don't see why we women should be excluded from such affairs."

My glance met Julia's as she passed me, cup in hand, and I could see the sympathy in her eyes. I swallowed back a threatening tear. Nine days was certainly not enough time to adjust to the death of a beloved husband. I bent down to put a hand on my terrier, Scotty, who was lying at my feet with his head on his paws. The movement allowed me to dab surreptitiously at the corners of my eyes with the handkerchief I held crumpled in my palm.

"The gentry turned out in force, as I'd have expected." Michael fidgeted with his watch chain. "It was a decent enough show. Julia, I wish you'd pour me more tea."

"I'm sure you did a splendid job as head of the family, darling." Julia, who had anticipated Michael's request, handed her husband a fresh cup of tea, smiling up into his eyes.

Poor Julia. Michael was tall, handsome, and well-built, with the thick shock of corn-blond hair and brilliant blue eyes that distinguished the Scott-De Quincys—well, most of them. At twenty-three, he carried his position as the Earl of Broadmere and head of the Scott-De Quincy family well. Or at least well enough that people generally overlooked his lack of social graces, kindness, and empathy. Perhaps I alone noticed the slight downturn in the corners of Julia's mouth as Michael took the cup from her without a word.

"Ned helped with the formalities." Michael waved a hand at where Sir Edward Freestone, our brother-in-law and senior by a good thirty years, dozed in one of the larger armchairs by the fire. He'd forgotten to take off the decorative chain, donned for the funeral, that proclaimed his status as mayor of Littleberry. It was slipping to one side, its heavy gold links reflecting red flickers of flame as Ned's chest rose and fell. "And Thomas made himself useful, of course."

Our sister Geraldine—Lady Geraldine Freestone—sniffed delicately at the mention of her eldest son's name, and her lips tightened. Thomas had been a chief mourner at Justin's funeral by my insistence. Gerry clearly disapproved, but just as clearly felt she should indulge my wishes as a young widow. So she refrained from speaking, communicating her scorn for her son by a straightening of her back and the angle of her blond head. Thomas, always sensitive to his parents' feelings, had taken himself off to the nursery to amuse his nephews and small cousins.

I listened to Michael's terse, factual description of my husband's funeral with half an ear, staring down at my dull black bombazine skirts. If only there weren't quite so many people in the room. As the sixth daughter, I'd spent my youth surrounded by other people, but since my marriage to Justin, I'd grown accustomed to the peace and spaciousness of Whitcombe House. Our world had revolved around the two of us, and we'd been happy. For me, that happiness had been all the more precious since I'd already lost one love, my cousin Daniel—and now my darling Justin had followed him to the grave. I forced out a small cough to dispel the painful lump threatening to form in my throat.

Seeking distraction, I twisted a little in my seat to look out of the tall windows to the sea. The English Channel showed on the distant horizon as a band of glittering silver blue. In the near distance, the River Ealy reflected the intense sky of a late October afternoon. Justin had been found in that river, floating facedown under a dense layer of yellowed willow leaves.

No. My mind skittered away from the thought, as it had been doing for days.

"Don't you agree, Helena?" Michael's harsh voice brought me out of my reverie. "This house is much too large for a woman alone. It's not logical that you occupy a twenty-four-bedroom house by yourself. Hyrst has only twelve bedrooms and houses Julia and me, our children, and Mama—who has four rooms, remember. And since Alice and Annette are unlikely to marry, I, as their brother, must always support them at Hyrst."

"I suppose I could take Mama." I heard my own voice, small and uncertain, and cursed inwardly. Justin had been my defender against my family's attempts to manage me, but now that he was gone, I was all too easily slipping back into my childhood role. A wren among peacocks, my father had—affectionately—said, and I looked the part. I alone among the Scott-De Quincys was small, brown-haired, and gray-eyed, traits inherited from a line of ancestors whose portraits were inevitably hung in the darker corners of Hyrst's dark rooms.

"You certainly won't bully Baby into taking charge of Mama at such a time." Odelia, the sister closest in age to me but still a full decade older, slid an arm across my shoulders, patting me with an elegantly beringed hand. "Really, Michael. The very idea."

She touched my cheek with her other hand, her lean, handsome face close to mine. "Are you feeling quite well, Baby, dear? You don't have to do anything you don't want to do, you know. You're your own mistress now."

"I don't want to be." I stifled a sob and then stiffened my back. Michael wouldn't understand my tears and would draw attention to them in a loud voice. "It's all right, O. I have a headache, that's all. I've done quite a bit of weeping, on and off, in the last few days."

"Justin would not want you to weep." Michael's handsome brow contracted at my reference to my grief. I saw Julia roll her eyes behind her husband's back.

"Don't listen to Michael." O's voice was soothing. "He may be the earl, but to the rest of us he's still the Dreadful Infant. Michael, go away and talk to someone else." She met our brother's blue glare with a hard stare of her own, dark blue eyes narrowed to menacing slits. "Baby's had quite enough of being worried and upset."

Michael, who was argumentative more out of a desire for logical outcomes than from a wish to win, shrugged and moved off. Dreadful Infant indeed. A recurring theme of my childhood memories was drawing or reading quietly while Michael embarked on his fifth or sixth tantrum of the day. And yet I, a year and a half older than Michael, was always called Baby. The Dreadful Infant had received a noble title and an important status at birth. From the moment he first drew breath, Michael was Viscount Overhey, the precious son, the future Earl of Broadmere, my father's hope. Now the title of viscount had passed to his eldest son, as Michael had become an earl at eighteen and a father at nineteen.

Justin had made me forget the slights of my early years by giving me a position of my own. Now that he was gone, the weight of my family settled back over my shoulders like my father's—now Michael's—heavy coronation robes with their three rows of ermine spots.

Odelia wrinkled her nose at Michael's retreating back and returned her attention to me. "Do you feel up to walking to Hyrst, Baby? I was just discussing the possibility of a walk with the others. Lady Ambition is against the plan"—she jerked her head at our sister Blanche—"but naturally Tweedledum and Tweedledee wish to walk. They always do."

I looked over to where Blanche, the widowed Marchioness of Hastings, and our twin sisters Alice and Annette sat eating cucumber sandwiches and making desultory small talk. O waggled her fingers at the twins as their identical faces turned toward us. "I'd like to see Mama, today of all days, and she'll be a comfort to you, I'm sure. It's perfectly unfair that Michael didn't even have her brought here. The poor woman's a prisoner in her own home."

I sighed, unwilling to contradict my sister. Mama was far too ill to leave her rooms, but I wasn't about to provoke an argument by expressing my own opinions. My family had enough opinions of its own and didn't need mine. So I smiled and squeezed O's hand.

"A walk to Hyrst would be splendid."

I rose to my feet, still smiling. After all, I was the mistress of Whitcombe House, and I had a hostess's duties to perform. Scotty yawned and stretched, pricking his ears in a hopeful manner as I crossed to the fireplace to tug on the bellpull. Sensing a walk was imminent, he came to stand close to me, white-streaked tail wagging furiously.

I addressed Gerry, giving my oldest sister a chance to assert some authority in the face of Michael's overbearing assumption of his own importance.

"Would you walk to Hyrst with us, Gerry? The fresh air will do me good." I smiled fondly at Ned as he became conscious of his wife's stony gaze and opened one eye. "Ned will have a chance to shake off some of the cobwebs."

"You try being mayor." Ned affected to sound cross, but his eyes twinkled as he disentangled himself from his chain of office, dropping the heavy thing on the floor beside his chair. "I always seem to have to get up early or retire late because somebody wants to see me. I fall asleep as soon as I'm sitting still." Seeing Scotty, of whom he was rather fond, he clicked his tongue at my little dog. "You understand, don't you, Scotty? These women—if only they'd leave a fellow alone."

I grinned at my brother-in-law, noting that the whole mood of the room seemed to lighten. Insignificant as I was within my family, they were still prepared to defer to my feelings as the recently bereaved—and that was something.

I could almost hear Justin saying, "Chin up, my dear. Think of the county." Those encouraging words, always accompanied by a broad wink, had never failed to make me laugh. *Oh, Justin.* How I would miss my husband's steady, unassuming, *sane* presence.

~

A large family has its disadvantages. It took an hour to get the children ready and to cajole the adults into stopping their chatter and dressing for the outdoors. We arranged for my lady's maid, Guttridge, to travel to Hyrst in the brougham. With her went my evening dress and those of Odelia and Blanche, who were staying at Whitcombe House.

Blanche characteristically made an issue of having to walk. She, of course, would have preferred to occupy the brougham even if it meant making Guttridge carry the dresses over on foot. She made a terrible fuss over how our black dresses would show the dust of the lane, and it took a stinging remark from O to silence her.

And then Geraldine tried to issue an edict that Thomas would slow us down and should go in the brougham. Fortunately, Ned fought in Thomas's corner for once and insisted his eldest son would walk with the rest of us.

"I'm quite sure M-Moses led the Hebrews out of Egypt with less bother than this." Thomas eyed the assorted governesses and nursemaids in charge of Julia and Michael's three small children and my niece Lydia's sons. Lydia was the oldest of Gerry's children—older than me, in fact. Petey, Gerry's youngest, was showing off for his younger cousins by trying in vain to make Scotty perform tricks. My niece Maryanne, not yet married, carried on an intense and audible conversation with her sister Lydia about how soon they could introduce some ornamentation into their mourning dresses. We were at the rear of the procession, of course, because of Thomas's slow pace. Petey, a good-natured child, had walked with his brother for a while until the lure of the dog and the other children proved too strong.

"I daresay you're right." I smiled at Thomas, who was only two years younger than me and more like a brother than a nephew. "Look at Blanche. If I were a betting woman, I'd say

7

she's complaining about the stones in the lane hurting her feet through the soles of her shoes."

"She'd be perfectly happy if C-Cousin Dederick were here."

"Dederick's visits to his mother are rarer than those of royalty since he inherited his title. I suppose you're right, Thomas—part of Blanche's problem is loneliness. You're so much kinder than I am."

"N-nonsense. You're one of the k-kindest people I know. So was Uncle Justin. I'm so sorry about him."

"So am I." I threaded my hand under my nephew's arm, which happened to be his bad one. It was fixed in a bent position, its hand twisted and claw-like, but I was used to its strange frailty and rigidity. Thomas's good left arm, strong and muscular, with the huge hand of a young man not yet done growing, swung at his side. My nephew always refused to use a crutch, saying he didn't want his best limb occupied in bearing him up. His lame foot dragged a little through the dusty gravel of the lane, but he moved easily enough, forcing his pace to keep up with the others.

"You know," I said after a few minutes' silence, "Justin was so very fond of you. Said he wished he had a son like you."

"Not entirely l-like me." Thomas gave me a rueful smile.

"Well," I said, feeling for my words, "I don't suppose I'd wish a disability on any child. But on the whole, Justin and I would have cheerfully accepted your disadvantages to have a son with your goodness and intelligence. And good looks, if they matter at all. In point of fact, any child at all would have been wonderful."

I sounded more wistful than I'd meant to. That chapter of my life was now definitely closed.

"You're r-right of course. I have l-life and comparative good health and a r-roof—one of the best in Littleberry—over my head. I have three good meals a day, warm clothing, and employment. Don't think I c-curse the day I was born, anything like that."

Thomas looked like an angel when he smiled. Tall and fair, a true Scott-De Quincy, he should have been his parents' pride and joy. As things stood, Gerry and Ned had difficulty seeing past the bent arm and shuffling gait to their son's beauty and courage.

"P-Petey's going to school soon, did you know?" Thomas continued. "W-Westminster. Papa thinks he should try for C-Cambridge later. Pursue a political career. No grubbing around in the wine importation business for *him*."

"I'm sorry." I gave Thomas's arm a gentle squeeze. "Petey's far behind where you were at his age as far as intelligence goes, although he's a nice boy. You'd make a much better scholar. Clerking for your father's beneath your position in life."

Thomas's mouth twisted up at the corner. "What position?" He stared ahead to where my brother and sisters formed a straggling diagonal across the lane, a black wall of backs that excluded us completely. "Cripples have n-no position."

"Neither do widows, at least not in Michael's way of thinking," I sighed. "Michael doesn't think I'm capable of looking after Justin's—*my*—land and properties."

"But you own everything, don't you? Not like Aunt Blanche, who has to live on a widow's jointure and watch Dederick squander all the money. If you'd had a s-son—"

"—I'd be in Blanche's position. But yes, I'm the sole owner of all that was Justin's until I marry again. And yet Michael is still trying to wrest control of my life from my hands. And my husband's barely—"

I had to stop and swallow hard. I could feel the emotion I'd been refusing to acknowledge all day building up inside of me, liquid and treacherous. My husband was barely cold in his grave, as the expression went. But he *was* cold, enclosed in the chilly clay of a Sussex autumn. My spouse had been my best friend, a warm and constant presence at my side, snugly encased in the countryman's tweeds he wore whenever he could get away with it. He had smelled of the outdoors and wood smoke and sheep's wool because he was a gentleman farmer who worked for the love of the work and not because he needed the money. He had been a vigorous man—twenty-two years older than me to be sure, but hale and healthy in almost every respect. And now—

"Are you all right, Auntie? You're looking a bit green."

"Yes." I took a very deep breath. "I'm going to have to visit Justin's grave tomorrow. The thought upsets me." My voice sounded brusque to my ears. The threatening onslaught of tears altered its timbre, making my throat hurt again.

"Death puts everything else into perspective, doesn't it? I'm s-sorry I bothered you with my petty jealousies." Thomas looked contrite.

"Don't mind me. I'm fighting the urge to howl and weep like a lunatic." I dashed a furtive hand across my eyes. "Please talk to me about Petey and your father for as long as you like. Remind me that I'm rich and nominally independent. That, unlike you, I can legally and morally do what I jolly well please. I just have to get over this—this *shock*—and learn to find a way to stand on my own two feet for the first time in my life. It's what Justin would have wanted."

2

A PRIDE OF LIONS

*I*n the time it took for Thomas and me to make our way up the grand approach to Hyrst, country seat of the Earls of Broadmere for the last hundred years, the rest of the family had entered the house. Scotty had abandoned me altogether, no doubt still romping with the children.

Our feet crunched on beechnut shells from the overarching allée of trees that marked the entrance to my family home. We passed into its formal courtyard garden under the eyes of the young lad who opened the tall iron gates. The boy's clumsy words of condolence, accompanied by much tugging of his forelock, were kind but served to make the gray cloud over my head seem heavier. Still—*Chin up.* I had another problem to face.

"Come say hello to Grandmama," I urged my nephew. "I don't suppose they'll bring her downstairs. I doubt they've even tried to explain Justin's death to her."

"Why do we let them behave this way?" Thomas asked as he made his laborious way upstairs. "It's like living in a pride of lions. The moment anyone in this family weakens, they're shoved to the margins and forced to feed on the scraps of attention the rest deign to throw their way."

"Probably a legacy of our warrior ancestors." I tried to force a note of cheerfulness into my voice. "The Scott-De Quincy tradition of heroic aggression. All those effigies on tombs and grand paintings of men on rearing stallions are a terrible burden to carry, even given the loss of two castles and a mountain of debt. I've certainly never tried to carry this family's glory on my back."

"Haven't you?" Thomas looked curious. "You used to be quite d-different. I remember the year you were presented at court, you know. Mama said you were so sought after as a d-debutante you could have married a duke. She was quite cross with you for insisting you were going to be an herbalist like G-Grandmama and rushing back to the country earlier than you needed to. You were only forgiven because of your understanding with Cousin D-Daniel. Everyone seemed to approve of the m-match."

I felt the heat rise to my face, and a spark of anger mingled with my grief. "I allowed myself to become arrogant and headstrong because my first Season went to my head. And I was very much influenced by Mama. She was so insistent on the importance of a vocation, however fulfilling one might find being a wife and mother. And much good her teaching did me."

"But you only lost interest in it because Daniel d-died," Thomas said softly. "I'm sorry but I can't help remembering, today of all days, that this is the second love you've lost. It isn't fair."

"Perhaps there's no such thing as 'fair.'" I forced the words out through a tight jaw and turned away from Thomas, dismissing the painful subject.

We had reached Mama's rooms, which were at the end of a particularly musty corridor. I breathed deeper as I turned the door handle, taking in the mingled scents of lavender and furniture polish. Fresh, salty air dominated, rising from the marsh to the wooded promontory on which Hyrst stood. Belming, Mama's attendant, believed in fresh air and cleanliness.

It was Belming who greeted us as we entered, her pleasant, sensible face lighting up as she rose from her sewing. I waved her back into her seat with a murmured greeting and looked around for my mother.

"Have you sent for the gardener?" My mother, Alix, Dowager Countess of Broadmere, announced her arrival with her usual question. She wore a nightgown and robe, but Belming had managed to twist her long white hair into a becoming bun. She shuffled toward us with the peculiar, hesitant gait she'd adopted of late, almost as if she were imitating Thomas. Her faded blue eyes took in each of us in turn with the odd blank stare that seemed to hold anger as well as puzzlement.

She and my father had been third cousins, and Mama had the Scott-De Quincy looks. Once, she had been tall and well-built, with a crowning mane of thick dark blond hair and piercing blue eyes that made people quail before her gaze. Now the long bones of her arms and legs were thin and fragile-looking, her back curved between shoulders that seemed so much narrower now, the strength gone from her face and figure. When I held out my arms, her own frail limbs lifted in response, and she allowed me to hug her.

I closed my eyes for a second, trying to recapture the mother who had dominated my early years. She had seemed to tower over me before her illness. Now it felt as though we were almost of equal height, small as I was. I kissed her cheek, the skin of which was as soft as velvet yet somehow a little clammy, not quite alive.

"Have you sent for the gardener?" she asked again. Nowadays it took all Belming's powers of persuasion to induce Mama to take a five-minute stroll in Hyrst's formal gardens. She completely refused to visit the herb garden that had once been her pride and joy, but she never stopped asking to see the gardener. We'd tried bringing the head gardener and even some of the under-gardeners to see her, but she invariably told them to leave immediately—so we had just resigned ourselves to her strange obsession.

"Of course I've sent for the gardener, Mama," I reassured her, wishing I could see one tiny spark of the mother I'd known in this woman's eyes. "He'll be here directly."

"Be sure to tell him to tie in the dahlias." Her expression shifted to one of deep anxiety. "Do I know you?"

"I'm Helena, your youngest daughter. And this is Thomas, your oldest grandson."

Thomas bent down to salute Mama's cheek with a quick peck of a kiss. He was the only one of Gerry's children who would visit his grandmother. Lydia and Maryanne found the experience "too trying." Petey looked so scared whenever a visit to Grandmama was suggested that we'd stopped asking.

"I don't have any grandchildren." My mother paused for a moment to break wind loudly and then looked at Thomas again. "What's wrong with his arm?"

"It doesn't work, Grandmama." Thomas grinned. "Never has."

For a moment, the clouds in Mama's mind appeared to part, and an answering grin spread across her face, almost sly. "I've become a silly old woman, haven't I?"

"No, Mama." I led my mother to her favorite armchair and seated myself nearby. I felt Thomas lower himself a little awkwardly onto the sofa next to me. "You've never been silly, and you're not silly now."

"Where's the other one? The one—him—the one who goes with you. That nice man."

"Justin?" I felt my throat constrict. Today of all days Mama would remember I had a husband. "He died, Mama. We buried him today."

My mother's brow creased. "You must be very sad."

"I am." To my consternation, my voice broke on the last word. It was no good—all the grief I'd held at bay during the day overwhelmed me afresh. I slid to the floor, buried my face in my mother's lap, and howled like an infant for a full five minutes.

I came to my senses to find Thomas offering me a clean handkerchief.

"Belming's gone to make tea," he said.

I took the handkerchief with a nod of thanks, blew my nose, and wiped my face. I breathed deeply until the urge to cry some more had passed.

"Better now," Mama said.

"Much better. Sorry, Thomas."

"Cry all you like, Auntie. I don't see why we all have to go around pretending nothing important's happened. Widows should be allowed to scream and wail, rend their clothing, and wear ashes on their heads."

"Steady on there." I felt the ghost of a smile twitch at my lips. "Think of the county."

"Damn the county. Kill them all."

Thomas and I looked at each other in surprise as my mother, having delivered this verdict in a ringing voice reminiscent of her old self, rose to her feet. "I want to use the commode," was her next remark, provoking something of a flurry. My mother no longer had the patience for bodily continence and could just as easily use the furniture to relieve herself if not taken in the right direction in time.

Belming's arrival with a tea tray spared me that particular task. Thomas and I were left to drink the restoring beverage while I recovered my equilibrium. I was sure my nose was shiny and my face blotchy, but Thomas and I were easy in each other's company.

"Michael was more than hinting earlier that I should take Mama off his hands." I stared at the window, where a thick strand of ivy had broken loose and was flapping against the panes in the wind off the marsh. "O said he was bullying me."

"So he is."

"But it would make sense. Whitcombe House is so much bigger than Hyrst."

"Wouldn't the twins object to losing her? I thought they liked being in charge of everything."

"The twins have their charity work and looking after Hyrst in general. I concede that Mama doesn't create a whole lot of extra work for them—Belming's an absolute marvel—but then she wouldn't create an awful lot more work for me either. It's just that—" I was suddenly as weary as if I'd spent the whole day riding. "Oh, Thomas, the thought of doing anything right now wears me out."

Thomas leaned in and kissed the top of my head. "Of course it does, Auntie. You can make Grandmama one of your worries once you're feeling more like yourself."

"I keep thinking of how *she* would have taken charge, back before Papa died. And she would have done it cheerfully too. Nothing ever seemed to upset her for long. The perfect wife, mother, and hostess, and on top of that she did so much good with her herbal remedies. A happy and useful woman."

Thomas was silent for a few moments, watching me. "You're not useless, Aunt Helena," he said eventually. "No more than I am. We may both think it at times, but what do *we* know?"

He stood up and held out his good hand to me. "Come along. Let's join the rest of the family. After all, it's not often we're all together."

~

I slept better that night than I had for days, no doubt from sheer exhaustion. I awoke hungry—widowhood had not stolen my appetite—and decided to take breakfast in my pleasant morning room.

I was lingering over the last few mushrooms on my plate when I heard Michael's loud, plangent voice ascertaining my whereabouts and ordering coffee for three. I heaved a large sigh, popped the last mushroom into my mouth, and wiped my lips on my napkin just as the footman swung open the door.

Of course Michael had brought the odious Brandrick with him. The man entered the room close behind my brother and removed his cap with a respectful "M'lady." Michael gave me his version of a brotherly kiss, a bare touching of his nose to my cheek.

Joshua Brandrick performed the functions of steward, land agent, and private secretary for my brother when Michael was in the country. When Michael was in London for parliamentary business, he employed another secretary. Such help was vital since Michael, a highly intelligent man in all other respects, had never acquired the ability to read or write.

Brandrick had befriended Michael when the latter was an awkward, unhappy boy of fifteen, an odd duck returned from his private tutor in Somerset at our father's insistence so he could be trained for his future title and responsibilities. Michael found the burden of these responsibilities unbearable. The strain of them compounded the anger born of frustration at his inability to grasp skills other people took for granted.

At that time, Brandrick had been a gardener at Hyrst, a young man of fierce ambition and an appetite for learning.

His smoldering resentment of his lowly position had somehow struck a chord with Michael. Brandrick's ability to calm Michael's temper had earned him our father's gratitude in the form of education and promotion. Now, at thirty, Brandrick was a constant, taciturn presence at Michael's side. Although good-looking, he had taken no wife, preferring to devote himself to Michael's interests body and soul.

"Sit down and stop standing around looking servile," was Michael's instruction to Brandrick when the coffee arrived. "Lady Helena won't mind."

Lady Helena *did* mind, and Brandrick knew it. He complied with a flick of his gaze toward my brother and the ghost of a smile on his lips. His "as m'lord wishes" held an unmistakably sardonic edge.

"I have been giving your position the most careful consideration," was Michael's opening salvo as soon as Brandrick's chair ceased moving. "Now that you are a widow, your most logical course of action is this." He leaned forward, using his finger to count off the points of his argument on his other hand.

"First, you should hand the running of the Whitcombe estate over to me—and Brandrick, of course—until you marry again."

I sat up straighter. "Michael, I've only just lost my husband. Why would you even mention my marrying again the day after his funeral?"

To my annoyance, my tone was placatory. What was wrong with me that I couldn't simply tell my little brother to stay out of my business?

"Because it is the logical step. Please do not interrupt. You must marry again to provide yourself with an heir to the estate. You must not delay this step; you are no longer a young woman. Naturally, your new husband will wish to have a say in the running of the Whitcombe estate, and that is why he must be chosen with care. Your holdings are considerable."

And how could Michael be so certain about the extent of my wealth? I looked at Brandrick, but the dreadful man lowered his gaze to his coffee.

"Of course," Michael continued, "there's a strong possibility you will produce no heir since so far you have proved barren. But that's a question that can be addressed later." He tapped one hand with the forefinger of the other. "You could always move back to Hyrst and let me manage Whitcombe. I daresay we could put a decent tenant in."

"Move back to Hyrst?" My voice rose to a squeak. "You're always saying how little room there is at Hyrst."

"You are my sister, and as head of the family I have a duty to protect and guide you. I intend to be diligent in that duty."

He shifted on his chair and drained his coffee cup, shoving cup and saucer across the table so clumsily that the cup tilted sideways. "All this after your first year of mourning is over, naturally. Although I don't believe it would be unreasonable to receive visits from prospects who are eager to show an interest, even during first mourning. Your widow's seclusion does not need to be complete. The Queen was much criticized for her utter withdrawal from the world."

He paused, clearly waiting for me to speak.

"I don't intend to move away from Whitcombe." I knew I sounded sulky. The remark about my barrenness had stung, but of course I had been complicit in letting that assumption take hold in my family.

"You could certainly afford to keep the house going." Michael passed a hand over his mouth and looked at me for a second. "The property investments and so forth are sound and well managed by Justin's solicitor, I believe. As for the farm—" He looked at Brandrick, who nodded.

"Lucius Hatherall's got that well in hand." Brandrick's

tone was dry. His imitation of Michael's educated speech did not entirely eliminate the Sussex burr from his voice, but he knew how to avoid using the dialect. "Sir Justin had an excellent grasp of the breeding of sheep for a gentleman farmer, and Hatherall knows what he's about. From what I've heard, they increased the yield and quality of the meat considerably in the last ten years. And Sir Justin owned properties in Littleberry, Broadmere, Lewes, Sandwich, even Brighton. All well improved and looked after. Even without the farm, her ladyship will suffer no loss of style or comfort."

"I have no intention of giving up the farm." I folded my arms and glared at Brandrick.

"Of course not, m'lady, not at first." Brandrick's tone was conciliatory. "But your mind will move on to other things before long. You've never had the deep interest in sheep that Sir Justin had, God rest his soul. One day you'll be ready to marry again."

Both men stared at me as if I were a breeding sheep myself, plainly assessing my qualities and future remarriage prospects. I thanked the Lord for the year and a day of full mourning. If I'd been immediately available, would they have brought a suitable mate to look me over straightaway?

I drew myself up as far as my vertebrae would stretch, annoyed at how small I felt next to the two tall men. "I'll certainly take your advice to heart, Michael. But kindly allow me some time to recover from the shock of my husband's death before we—I—make any decisions about my future."

"Very well." Michael stood, pushed back his chair, and strode to the door without saying good-bye. It was a formality he had a tendency to forget unless reminded.

"His lordship has your best interests at heart, m'lady. As do I." Brandrick also stood, and his voice was gentle. "I haven't had the chance to offer you my sincerest condolences. Please accept them now. Sir Justin was a good man."

I nodded with as good a grace as I could manage. "Thank you."

Left alone, I stared morosely at the empty coffee cups. If it hadn't been so completely typical of Michael to barge into a house of mourning to discuss what was on his mind, I would have believed this was Brandrick's doing. The man clearly thought that Dene Farm—Justin's great interest in life —should come under his own management.

"And I resent his management," I said out loud to the empty room. "I resent his management of my brother. I resent my brother's management—or attempted management—of me. And if you think, Michael," I wagged a forefinger at the empty doorway, "that you have a right to dictate what my life is to be, you have another think coming."

If only I'd been able to say that to my brother's face.

3

A WIDOW'S ARMOR

$\mathcal{B}$y the time Odelia appeared downstairs, I had conquered my annoyance at Michael. O never rose early when she was in the country. In London, she might be up at the crack of dawn to catch the best light for her paintings. At Whitcombe, she requested breakfast in bed and saw nobody but the servants until eleven.

Our first task of the day was to visit Justin's grave. Since the first viewing of one's husband's final resting place was hardly the appropriate moment to raise any grievances against my brother, I kept silent during the short walk to the Littleberry cemetery. I resolutely banished Michael from my mind as I stood staring at the six-foot-long mound of tan-colored clay, surmounted by three elegant arrangements of chrysanthemums and hothouse lilies and a large number of smaller tributes. In the mellow sunshine of October's last day, the pink-tinged lilies seemed to glow. The mingled colors of the rest of the flowers looked almost cheerful.

What, I wondered, did this horticultural exuberance have to do with Justin? How could this neatly dug rectangle of earth possibly contain his kindness and intelligence, the fond smile with which he'd greeted me every morning, the wiry, muscular body that could mount a horse or wrestle with a recalcitrant sheep as easily as a man half his age?

I couldn't cry. O and I both wore heavy veils to conceal our tears, but I, who had wept aplenty in the eleven days since my brother-in-law Ned had stood in front of me, hat in hand, to bring me the news, could find no tears to shed that morning. We spent twenty minutes remarking on the number of small bouquets that proved how well-liked Justin was, and then we turned for home.

We entered Whitcombe by the conservatory door and helped each other shed our muddy boots. Soon I would need to ring the bell for Guttridge and prepare for luncheon, but for a few minutes I allowed myself to enjoy a moment alone with my sister and Scotty. We had not taken my dog to the cemetery for fear Scotty might start digging in the loose soil of Justin's grave.

The conservatory was not particularly warm, but it offered a fine view of the distant sea, today a gray haze with a tinge of blue. The valley below us was a patchwork of greens and tans. A plume of blue smoke marked the burning of some debris by one of the farmers.

I waited until we were seated in the large wicker armchairs to broach the topic of Michael's visit.

"Michael cannot, in any way, force you to either marry or give up Whitcombe House. It's as simple as that," was O's immediate response.

"It's never as simple as that." I sighed, running a hand over Scotty's wiry, brindled coat as he nestled into the crook of my arm. "I see Michael several times a week when he's not in London—even before Justin's death our paths crossed all the time—and you know how relentless he is. I'm not sure how long I can stand up to him. The only way I could avoid him altogether would be to leave Whitcombe, and I don't want to do that."

Odelia hesitated before speaking. "Darling, forgive me for asking this—why on earth not? I mean, how can you stand it here? It's so *quiet*. And much too green."

I hugged Scotty to me and rested my head on my other hand, looking out at the magnificent view. Below us, the gentle dip of the valley was sprinkled with the white-and-brown dots of grazing sheep. Farther to the west, the land rose into softly rounded hills, punctuated by the dark greens of copses and hedgerows. In the far distance, where the headland reared into tall cliffs, the hills were a smoky blue. In front of the headland, I could see Broadmere, its fading glory wrapped in dark, encircling trees. If I crossed to the corner of the room, I'd be able to see Littleberry, a huddle of red-brown brick and tile on its low hill, its windows flashing gold in the lambent sunlight. Two small towns deserted by the sea, brooding over their former glory and prosperity, picturesque and drowsy under the wide autumnal sky.

"It's where I belong," I said at last. "I'm not like you, O. I couldn't stand living in London with all its noise and bustle. Here, I feel—"

"—safe?" Odelia snorted in derision. "Baby, darling, in your short life you have exchanged one large house looking out toward the sea for an even larger house looking out toward the sea. You've never given anywhere else a chance to worm its way into your heart."

"I spent two Seasons in London," I said indignantly. "And never came to love it."

"Because Daniel was here, and you were a very young girl in love. Of course you wanted to fly back to your mate." O shook her head, a gesture half-impatient, half-sad. "And later you allowed yourself to be steered into a marriage with Justin, and you just seemed to grow into the soil."

"I was content." I leaned back to pluck a flower from a standard fuchsia, admiring its intricate delicacy. "Justin and I were content. There's nothing wrong with that."

"Not for Justin, certainly. At his age, perhaps he had a right to be content." O stretched out a narrow foot, looking critically at her fine silk stocking. "But you're twenty-five. You should have a few years of adventure before settling for contentment."

"Justin wasn't so very old."

"He was forty-seven, even if he had a younger man's physique. You were twenty-two when you married him—twenty when he began taking an interest in you. I know it's common practice among our sort of people for older men to wed young women, but you could have had a dozen better offers. Far better than a baronet, however wealthy. Or you could have married some impoverished genius. The old Helena could have, at any rate. I always used to think *you'd* be the rebel of the family, not me."

"I don't remember being that person," I said. "And besides, in what way would I have rebelled? If Daniel had lived, we'd have married before I was twenty. We were already talking about when Daniel should approach Papa to ask for my hand."

"Daniel would have brought out the rebel in you. He'd have turned you away from Mama's herbs and potions and whisked you to Paris to soak up some Republican principles. Look how interested he was in the war between the French and the Prussians."

"Yes, he was interested in a great many things." I could hear the hard edge to my voice. "And then he was dead."

In my mind's eye, I could see the orchard on the slope below Hyrst—a place I'd avoided for two years afterward—and for a moment could smell the apple blossom, fresh and sweet. And there was Daniel, lying once more at my feet, his lips blue and cold. And I hadn't been able to save him.

"You lost interest in everything for a while." Odelia's voice was gentle. "Your studies, your little hobbies, your clothes, your friends, even Mama's herb garden. You stopped bringing home half-dead animals and sitting up all night trying to nurse them back to life. You stopped helping Mama with her patients in the workhouse and the slums. Because you no longer trusted your ability to heal anyone."

"When you realize you're useless, it's better to stop pretending you're useful, isn't it?" I rose to my feet, placing Scotty on the floor. "It's cold in here, and luncheon will be ready." I stepped inside the billiard room, preceded by my vigorously barking dog, and pulled on the bell.

"Baby." Odelia was beside me in an instant, her face close to mine. "It's as if—well, if I lost my right arm, I'd paint and draw with my left. I could never bury my gift, even if that gift had brought harm to somebody. My art is me. Even when I'm not painting or sketching, I'm doing so in my head. Right now I'm composing a sketch in my mind. I can't help it. You —you had a real talent for healing, just like Mama. For serving others. And you simply buried that talent with Daniel. I would feel as if I were only half a person." Her brow wrinkled. "You won't let Justin's death sink you into despondency as Daniel's did, will you?"

She gathered me close to her, and I gave in to the need to feel the warmth of another person. She had always been the first one to hug me and kiss me when my other sisters were distant. I leaned my head on her shoulder.

"I know it's what you're all worried about." My voice was muffled by the heavy silk of her dress. "It worries me too— but I'm not sixteen any more. I'll find my way through this. It's just that rebellion is no longer a path open to me." I sighed. "I don't have your strength. Daniel's death broke me in so many ways. If I had any rebelliousness back then, I lost it somehow."

O hugged me tighter. "Then it's time to get it back. This is your new beginning, Baby—your new chance. Don't you realize that as a widow you have control of your money and property, at least until you remarry?"

"In law, perhaps. In practice, that's not what Michael believes. He thinks he should take over everything. He and that horrible Brandrick man."

"So don't let him. I have to go back to London, darling— I'll die here. But I'll help you resist any arrangement Michael tries to impose upon you. I know a lawyer in Greenwich I can send to you if it comes to that. He won't be in the least impressed that he's standing up to the Earl of Broadmere. This family may be important in this tiny corner of the world, but it's not at all important in a city where titles are ten a penny."

Odelia released me as Guttridge stepped into the billiard room, and I smiled at my lady's maid.

"We took off our boots, Guttridge. They're rather grubby. Could you fetch slippers and neaten us both up a bit for luncheon? Lady Hastings will be getting impatient." Blanche had declined to accompany us to the cemetery.

"With pleasure, my lady. Come along, dog—you're *not* hiding under the table during luncheon again."

Guttridge was a tall woman, somewhat plain, but with a pleasing air of authority and strength. She somehow managed to pick up our outer clothing, muddy boots, *and* the dog before disappearing into the depths of the house. The diversion afforded by watching her gave me time to think.

"Don't rush to provide me with lawyers," I said eventually. "I'll have a try at standing up to Michael myself."

"Hooray!" O stretched her arms toward the ceiling in a gesture of jubilation before addressing my returning maid.

"Oh, Guttridge, how wonderfully quick you are! Now listen —don't you think you and I should put our heads together and ensure Lady Helena is outfitted properly for mourning? I've seen that dress too many times already, and I've only been here a week."

"Just what I've been telling her ladyship." Guttridge nodded in approval. "We still have a position to uphold in the county."

I followed the two of them, who were now talking rapidly about parramatta silk and crape, in silence. I was being managed once more, albeit benignly. Between the two of them, Guttridge and Odelia would ensure I looked the part of a wealthy widow—give me armor, in a sense. Something I could hide behind as I resisted Michael's attempts to control my life. Until, perhaps, I could develop a harder carapace of my own.

~

"Is there anything else you need, my lady?"

The long day had drawn to a close. Guttridge paused at the foot of my bed to survey my room and ensure she hadn't left any task undone. The day's clothing was draped over one of her long, strong arms; her capable fingers had braided my hair into two shiny plaits; and I lay alone in my bed.

Beyond the connecting door to my right, I could sense the stillness of Justin's room. I had sat in there for a while, inhaling the scents of tweed, leather, and cologne that still hung in the atmosphere. I had closed my eyes, remembering the times I had climbed into Justin's bed or he into mine as soon as our respective attendants had gone downstairs. Remembering the feel of his back, smooth and hard with muscle. His legs, brushing against mine. His arms, solid and strong.

I brought my fist down hard on the coverlet, and Guttridge opened her eyes wider.

"Are you all right, my lady?"

"I'm upset about being a widow." I grasped a handful of satin and squeezed it between my fingers. "I'm angry I was widowed because my husband chose to rescue a sheep. Why couldn't he have ridden for Farmer Hatherall instead of trying to do everything himself?"

"Was that the way of it?" Guttridge set down her burden of clothing on a chair and crossed to the bed, her expression one of mild curiosity. "I'd heard he'd slipped into the river somehow, but I didn't know he was after a sheep. Can't they swim?"

I shrugged. "I always thought so. I've seen them being driven across the river. But they found a young ram drowned downstream, marked as one of Justin's. They think he'd seen the animal in trouble and gone after it. They worked that out later, of course."

Guttridge tutted. "The farmer saw Sir Justin's horse outside his garden; I'd heard that. So he went looking for him in the fog."

"Yes. And some time afterward, when they'd gotten him out of the river, Sir Edward got involved. He'd been riding along the river path on his way to Pincham. It was he who came to tell me."

Ned had been so shaken he'd left a trail of mud to mark his passage through my house. His somber frock coat had been damp, streaked with mud and dotted with yellowed leaves, when he'd burst in upon my breakfast.

"It was a terrible shock," Guttridge said. That was a statement, not a question. I'd been having breakfast in bed, and she'd come to clear away the tray only to find me gasping and raving in my nightdress, clutching at Ned's coat like a madwoman.

"It was the meaninglessness of it all." I let go of the cover-let, which was becoming damp and creased from the pressure of my fingers. "An accident—a stupid slip—that's all it took to destroy my life. It makes me furious."

Guttridge was silent for a long moment. "If you'll forgive my saying so, my lady," she said at last, "you don't look like a woman who's destroyed. You just need to take your time to say good-bye to your old life."

"But my old life was what I wanted," I wailed. "A quiet, settled life. Neither looking backward nor creating dreams and ambitions for the future. Not major ones anyway."

Guttridge frowned. "There's no such thing as a settled life, begging your ladyship's pardon. We're always moving in some direction. You can't move back, so you must move forward."

She turned to retrieve my abandoned clothes and left the room, leaving me to reflect on the advantages and disadvantages of having a lady's maid with a philosophical bent.

"How I miss you, Justin," I whispered into the darkness a few minutes later. "But she's right, you know. I can't have you back, so I'm forced to move forward with my life. I let Daniel's death reduce me to some kind of paralysis, but you rescued me from it in the end. Perhaps this time I can find the strength to do without a rescuer."

4

THE FRENCH PHYSICIAN

I slept well and awoke refreshed. I felt more ready to face the day—and the future—than I had since the news of Justin's death had been brought to me.

That mood lasted until I entered the morning room, a pleasantly airy space on the eastern side of the house. The servants were accustomed to leaving my correspondence there. I had neglected it for the last few days, but that morning I arrived at my desk out of force of habit. I knew I would have at least two hours before I saw either of my sisters.

The pile of black-bordered letters from friends and acquaintances sent my determined mood plummeting through the floorboards. These missives were concrete proof that I was a widow—moreover, a widow with social responsibilities. I would have to answer them, every one, and with each letter and answer, a new dagger would be driven through my heart.

I set to sorting them. One pile of letters that must be answered immediately; another pile of letters of lesser importance, to which I could reply with a brief word of thanks; and a basket full of discarded envelopes.

The first pile was depressingly thick. I would have to spend the rest of the morning writing, at least until the others were dressed. Then I could relinquish one social obligation for the much more attractive one of playing hostess.

Well, one's debts to society must be paid. I sorted through my collection of pens to find the ones with the best nibs. I had just uncapped my crystal inkwell when one of the footmen entered with a calling card.

Armand Fortier, Physician and Surgeon.

The name was familiar. Justin had mentioned it once or twice. A sound man he'd consulted in preference to the other Littleberry quacks. A Frenchman who'd moved to Littleberry about a year ago, whose sister was the wife of a prominent pottery owner.

"I'm at home, I suppose. Please show him in."

Why on earth would Justin's physician think he had business with me? I knew why Justin had consulted him, but that matter had died with my husband. Was he simply here to offer his condolences?

I stood up, brushing a few specks of dust off my bombazine, and prepared to face the day's first interruption. I had little time for physicians. In my experience, they were dirty, untidy, ill-educated individuals with more arrogance than their position in life warranted. My mother had always despised them.

To my surprise, the man who walked quietly and confidently into my morning room looked as if he belonged there. I found myself extending my hand to him as if to a visiting gentleman; he took it and bowed over it, quite at his ease.

"I'm sorry to make your acquaintance under such distressing circumstances, Lady Helena." His voice was a pleasant baritone with no French accent save, perhaps, in the way he pronounced his words precisely and clearly. Englishmen often had a tendency to mumble.

"Let me offer you my sincerest condolences for the loss of your husband," he continued. "Sir Justin was an intelligent, worthy man, and I had a great deal of respect for him." Monsieur Fortier's expression held sympathy and warmth in just the right degree. "You no doubt know that he consulted me in my professional capacity."

He seated himself in the chair I indicated and declined my offer of refreshment. He was dressed for a country day's work in a plain black morning coat and riding breeches and brought with him the pleasant aromas of leather, horse, and fresh air, indicating that he'd come on horseback. His boots were worn but well-polished, and he'd clearly scraped them carefully before entering the house.

"I did know Sir Justin had consulted you." I held his gaze. The question of why Justin had consulted Monsieur Fortier was a delicate one, but I was no blushing bride.

Looking directly at Monsieur Fortier gave me a chance to appreciate the man's appearance, which was pleasing. He was much the same height as Justin had been, six feet tall. Like my late husband, he was trim and slender, although more solidly built. His shoulders, to be sure, were a deal broader than Justin's, but then he was very much younger, not yet thirty. His black hair was closely cropped, his beard neatly trimmed. His eyes were his most striking feature; an odd shade somewhere between green and amber, they were large, luminous, and thickly lashed.

"Did you come to speak with me about Sir Justin's—health?" I prompted, suddenly aware that I had been looking at him for too long.

"Not exactly." Monsieur Fortier seemed slightly uncomfortable but clearly made up his mind to proceed. "I had the melancholy task of receiving Sir Justin's body in a consulting room I keep at the Dermody pottery, for the benefit of the workers there. It was close to where they found him, and I have a suitable table. As it turned out, the inspection of the body by the inquest jury was also held there." He cleared his throat. "I'm sorry to speak to you about such matters."

"It's quite all right. In some ways, it's better to hear about what actually happened than to leave it to my imagination." Although my imagination was supplying more detail as I spoke. The water dripping down the table from Justin's clothing, the men leaning over him, the smell of the river . . .

I pushed the intrusive thoughts away and sought for something to say. "I'm glad it was you who cared for Sir Justin at such a time. After all, he had taken you into his confidence; you were not a stranger to him. Such things matter."

"I suppose they do." Monsieur Fortier didn't exactly smile, but an expression of warmth and sympathy suffused his face. "Did you hear anything about the inquest from Lord Broadmere or the mayor?"

"Very little. Sir Edward tried to spare my feelings. My brother merely informed me that the inquest had taken place and a verdict of accidental death by drowning had been rendered. He is not a communicative man."

"No, he isn't." The sympathy in Monsieur Fortier's eyes intensified. He was not, I thought, a man who could hide his emotions easily. Perhaps that was his French heritage.

"Lady Helena," Monsieur Fortier continued, "I've spent several days asking myself whether I should burden you with my doubts."

"Doubts?" I wrinkled my brow.

"I have no proof, of course. If I had proof, I would have

spoken more publicly. You see—I'm not sure Sir Justin's death was accidental."

The room seemed to tilt sideways. I was suddenly aware of movement as Fortier left his chair to crouch by my side. One hand encircled my wrist, fingers on the pulse point. The other rested gently against my shoulder, as if to prevent me from falling forward. Some detached part of my mind noted that his hands were quite beautiful, his fingers long and slender with neatly kept nails.

"Breathe calmly," he was telling me. "Slowly in through your nose—that's it—and slowly out again. Think about nothing but your breathing."

His fingers pressed a little more firmly on my wrist, and his eyes grew thoughtful. Counting my heartbeats, no doubt.

"No, I don't think you'll faint now," he said after a few seconds. "I'm sorry I gave you such a shock. I was a fool not to have led up to the subject more gently."

"I have no intention of fainting." I pulled my wrist away from his grasp. He let me go, straightening up and returning to his chair. I waited until he was seated before continuing, taking the opportunity to gather my thoughts and breathing deeply so that my voice would not tremble.

"Please explain why you think Justin—why you think my husband could have died in any other way than by accident. My brother and brother-in-law are both quite certain his death was an involuntary tragedy."

To my surprise, Fortier smiled. It was a nice smile, and I had to acknowledge he was an attractive man. It was infuriating to realize I was even capable of such thoughts at a time like this.

"You are a brave woman," Fortier said. "No tears and no hysterics. Sir Justin once told me that—how did he put it? — he admired tremendously your coolness in the face of adversity. He thought you the embodiment of that peculiarly English virtue."

"Sir Justin was quite wrong, as it happens. My ability to control my feelings is distressingly variable."

Fortier smiled again. "Sir Justin was biased, of course. He was exceedingly fond of you."

"And I was fond of him." Fortier would not have thought me so brave if he'd been able to feel the lump in my throat.

"Quite so." For a moment Fortier looked embarrassed, as if he indeed realized he'd driven me to the edge of tears. But he quickly recovered.

"It pains me to have to discuss this matter with you directly, but the alternatives were Lord Broadmere and Sir Edward. Both of them heard the vigorous rebuttal from Littleberry's other medical men when I raised my theory during the inquest. I think their minds are made up that I'm either out of my wits or have some reason of my own for suggesting foul play."

"Oh, Sir Edward is far more sensible than you're giving him credit for. Admittedly, my brother might think you out of your wits. He thinks most people are, himself excepted. So are you going to tell me upon what basis you have built your theory? Stop beating around the bush, Monsieur Fortier. My heartbeat is now steady, I'm sure the color has returned to my cheeks, and I'm determined not to scream or cry or become unwell. You're quite safe."

I curled my fingers into my palm, digging my nails in. I had made myself sound braver than I felt. This was not going to be easy—but I owed it to Justin to listen to the man's theories, even if nobody else would.

"Very well," said Fortier. "When I examined Sir Justin— given my proximity to the event, I was the first physician to do so—I remarked on some bruising around his face, neck, and upper torso. To me, those bruises were not consistent with a simple slip and fall into the river. I felt he might have struggled with someone just prior to his death or been held down in some way. After all, he was not a young man, and his physique was on the slender side. I felt he might have been held under water long enough to lose consciousness. A complete drowning would soon follow."

I dug my nails in harder, fighting nausea. "And none of the other men agreed with this notion?"

He shook his head. "When Farmer Hatherall found him, Sir Justin was caught up in a large section of willow tree that had fallen into the river. It's one of the reasons I find the accident theory so unconvincing. If Sir Justin had fallen in and couldn't climb up the bank for some reason, I don't see him panicking so thoroughly that he'd be dead before he encountered the willow. He could have used it to climb out or at least clung to it and shouted for assistance."

"Could he have suffered the bruises trying to climb out on the willow?"

"If he'd been trying to climb out, I think the bruises would more likely have been on his hands or arms. And there would have been other signs—scratches, broken nails, that kind of thing."

"It all sounds very vague and uncertain," I said.

Fortier shrugged. "Medicine is more of an art than a science. But you see, Lady Helena, I have an advantage that the other medical men don't. I've worked a great deal with the poor people of this district. I'm regrettably familiar with the bruises a person receives when subjected to violent holding or manipulation. Of course in most cases I see, the victim is a woman or child."

"So you have no proof to offer me, just some kind of feeling or instinct. Tell me, Monsieur Fortier, what good did you hope to achieve by coming to me?"

The physician looked down at his polished boots, then

back up at me. "The good that comes when the truth is brought out into the light of day." He shrugged. "I would have thought that, as Sir Justin's widow, the truth of his demise would be of the utmost importance to you."

"The *fact* of his demise is of the utmost importance to me," I countered. "It has changed my life utterly. But unless you can come up with a shred of evidence, I don't see I can do anything other than accept the verdict of the inquest."

Which didn't mean I wasn't horrified at Fortier's theory. I had the oddest sensation that I was floating—but Scott-De Quincys did not give way to vulgar hysterics, not in front of strangers in any event.

"Would you at least come down to the river to see the location where Sir Justin went in and the location of the willow tree?" Fortier continued. "This afternoon, if you can. I heard from the blacksmith that Farmer Hatherall has borrowed chains and is intending to remove the willow, as he has long planned to do. The news made up my mind about coming here."

I was trying to formulate a reply—or at the very least a sensible question—when Odelia walked in. Fortier immediately rose to his feet, and O stopped in her tracks.

"I thought you were alone," she said to me after favoring Fortier with a regal half nod. "Excuse me for interrupting you."

I also rose and spoke to Fortier. "May I introduce my sister, Lady Odelia Scott-De Quincy? O, this is Monsieur Fortier. He's a physician who treated Justin for some ailments and has come to offer his condolences."

I shot Fortier a warning glance, which he clearly understood. He made a few appropriately conventional remarks about Justin and our loss, which O answered just as conventionally. The interlude gave me a chance to recover my equilibrium by the time Fortier turned back to me.

"I must be on my way, Lady Helena. Thank you for receiving me. Lady Odelia, it was a pleasure to make your acquaintance."

He smiled at O, and I saw in her eyes that she found Fortier's smile just as appealing as I did.

"Thank you for calling, Monsieur Fortier." I held out my hand.

"I hope to see you again very soon." He accompanied this remark by a small squeeze of my fingers before he bowed over my hand in an extremely Continental fashion. Well, if he thought I would abandon my sisters to go look at the spot where my husband died, he was wrong. I was going to be busy all afternoon.

O waited until Fortier's footfalls were no longer audible before swiveling to face me. "Well!" was her first remark. "*He's* easy on the eyes. Do you know him well?"

"I've never met him before in my life." I crossed to the window seat and sat on its broad cushion, resting my forehead against a pane of glass. "Justin seemed to like him well enough. It was nice of him to call." I closed my eyes, relaxing my brow against the cold glass and feeling the tension of the last half hour dissipate. "What would you like to do this afternoon?"

"Ah. About that. You see, I had a note this morning from a dear friend. An artist, of course. She absolutely needs me to return to Town *straightaway* or her study of Lancelot will be forever ruined. Would you mind terribly?"

I opened my eyes again. "Is there really such a thing as a painting emergency?"

O looped her arms around my shoulders and rested her chin on the crown of my head. "There is when your artistic temperament is sufficiently turbulent. I'm thankful my own calling is simply that—a calling, and not a torment."

"But to leave this afternoon? What sense does that make?

Even if all the trains align in perfect harmony, you won't be in Town till very late. And Blanche will have plenty to say about bohemian manners."

"To the devil with Blanche. I've already told her, as it happens. She asked me to tell you she's suffering from nervous exhaustion and intends to sleep until dinner. And I won't reach Town today. I have a standing offer of a room for the night in Maidstone, which gets me about halfway there. Then I can leave bright and early and devote the whole morning to fixing the disaster."

"Maidstone?"

"I know, I know." O hugged me tighter. "But I owe the Maidstone friend a visit, so this will kill two birds with one Maidstone, so to speak."

I laughed, enjoying the feel of O's arms around me. One of my earliest memories was of being carried around by her, and I often wished she wasn't absent so often. But unlike me, O had made the wider world her home.

"You're itching to get away from the countryside, aren't you?" I kissed the slim hand nearest to my face, admiring its large, brilliant rings.

"Only the tiniest bit. I'd certainly like to run away from another dinner with the Marchioness of Ambition. Do you think you could persuade your lovely cook to have luncheon ready a little earlier than usual? I'm practically packed."

5

THE RIVERBANK

So it was that by one thirty I was left alone with my letters and the troubling memory of Fortier's visit. By quarter after two, I decided I simply couldn't face writing another letter. And it was November after all—how many days would there be when I could still ride out? If Blanche was determined to sleep all day, she could hardly mind if I deserted her for two hours.

The efficient Guttridge had me in my riding habit in a trice. Mank, my favorite groom, had my mare, Sandy, saddled for me and waiting in the stable courtyard. He assisted me to mount up and then led out Justin's gelding, Puck, who sidestepped and rolled his eyes at me.

"He needs a good run, m'lady," Mank said after Puck had finally allowed him to mount.

"He certainly does. Sandy's much lazier—she doesn't seem to mind at all that we haven't ridden out much lately." I leaned down to plant a kiss on my horse's neck. "Well, the proprieties must be observed, but you don't have to stick too close. Once we get down to the bottom of the hill, you can take Puck off for a gallop. Heaven knows it won't be long before we're all knee-deep in mud, so let's make the most of the dry weather."

My riding habit was brown, unsuitable for mourning, but it would have to do. I knew Guttridge had the matter of my mourning clothes well in hand. I was only going on a country hack after all—down to the river.

It was wonderful to be out in the fresh air again. Justin had been on horseback every day, and I had ridden out with him two or three times a week when the weather allowed it. We had derived so much pleasure from simply riding side by side, making desultory remarks about the weather or the state of the fields. It hurt to know I would never have him by my side again.

Yet the day was fine and bright, although distinctly autumnal, and Sandy was always a pleasure to ride. The air smelled faintly of smoke from the refuse the farmers were burning, but I could still detect the sweetness of decaying leaves, the sharp green smell of plants that had received their first taste of frost, and the pleasant mustiness of damp earth. And, of course, the taint of what the sheep left behind them —but in our part of the country, sheep were ubiquitous.

Mank and I took the horses on a wide loop to avoid the steepest route downhill, as Mank said the fallen leaves had made the path slippery. Puck was fidgety, and I didn't trust him to plod carefully downward. So when we eventually met the shining curve of the River Ealy, we were well upstream from where Justin had died.

A wide, safe path ran along the riverbank. The turf was well-trodden since this route provided a quick and easy way to ride, walk, or drive from Littleberry to the farms and villages along the valley. I saw no riders or carts that after-noon, only a few farm workers and villagers on foot, picking their way through the liberal sheep droppings or squashing it underfoot according to their tolerance for dirt.

"Puck's being a bit of a devil, m'lady, if you'll pardon the expression." Mank swore under his breath as the gelding sidestepped. "If you don't mind, it's time for that gallop. I'm thinking Mile Bottom—there aren't any ewes there for the time being, and the going's firm."

I nodded. "Give him a good run and catch up with me afterward. Sandy'll be quite happy with a trot, or even a walk."

Mank grinned and promised he'd catch me easily. He turned Puck's head toward the long field over which Whitcombe House seemed to loom close, an optical illusion caused by the slope of the land.

I urged Sandy on with a click of my tongue, reaching to open the gate with my crop. The gate was beginning to sag to the right. I'd have to have a word with Farmer Hatherall; that gate was one of ours. One of mine, I reminded myself. It was all mine.

I closed the gate with a little difficulty and continued along the riverbank, keeping a firm hand on Sandy as a group of ewes ran across our path. Sheep were ridiculous animals to my mind, always frightened but always keen to get in the way. Justin had maintained they were more intelligent than they looked, but then he would.

I noted with a strange mixture of regret and interest that out here my grief had subsided to a dull ache. In these fields, riding out as we'd so often done together, I felt Justin's absence—but at the same time I felt my wholeness, my existence as a person independent of anyone else.

"Lady Helena!"

I turned Sandy's head so I could more easily twist round and look behind me. Fortier was riding toward me on a large black animal that was almost certainly part draft horse.

"Thank you for coming to meet me," he said.

"I'm not entirely sure that was my intention, but let's take it at face value."

"That was your groom on the path with Sir Justin's horse, wasn't it? He was having a little trouble with him as they neared the spot where Sir Justin went in. The beast started to rear and buck."

"I suppose you're going to tell me Puck's behavior confirms your suspicion of foul play," I said archly. "Whereas it's far more likely that it's a matter of a horse needing exercise. Mank's on his way to gallop Puck for a bit."

"Leaving you unchaperoned."

"I'm on my own land, on a well-frequented path," I pointed out. "*Now* I suppose you're going to warn me there might be a murderer on the loose."

"If you're determined you know my mind better than I do, I won't contradict you." He smiled again, and with a pinprick of annoyance I had to stop myself from smiling back. Good grief, was I going to become one of those flirtatious widows? I pressed my lips together.

"Be that as it may, if you have something to show me, I suggest you get on with it." I sounded crosser than perhaps was quite polite. "We'll lose the light, for one thing."

Fortier nodded. "You're right. I shouldn't waste time with small talk. If I'm correct, a good man has been unlawfully killed." He turned his horse's head without waiting to see if I was following, leaving me with the conviction I'd been rather rude.

We rode downstream in silence. Fortier opened and closed gates for me, making my passage easy. We passed into the field known as Willow Bottom because of the line of huge, ancient willows that stood like stranded sentinels many feet from the riverbank. The river had once been much broader and shallower, but Justin, like many of the landowners, had had the river channel deepened and narrowed so he had more pasture for his sheep. Now the riverbank was steep, crowned with a thick growth of thorny brambles.

Fortier halted his horse and dismounted, looking up at me.

"Do you mind if we tie up the horses and walk? I want you to view the site up close. There's not much to see, truth be told, but I have a notion you'll understand my theory better on the ground."

I answered him by unhooking my right leg from the pommel, slipping the other foot out of the stirrup and sliding easily off Sandy, who was more a large pony than a horse. It took me a few moments to locate the buttonhole and fix the skirt of my habit for walking while Fortier secured the horses. The huge black horse and Sandy seemed to like each other, touching noses and nickering softly before turning their attention to the lush grass beneath their hooves.

From Whitcombe House's perch high on the hill, these fields looked small; the countryside appeared neat and contained, a patchwork bordered by hedges and drains. From high on Whitcombe Hill, you almost felt you could touch the distant hills or cross the marsh to the sea in no time. But when out in the fields, especially when on foot, I was always struck by how vast the land looked and how small I felt. The nearest hedge was a tramp of several minutes away. The drains, deep ditches filled with water or choked by bulrushes, made it almost impossible to travel in a straight line. They effectively prevented strangers from walking or riding across the fields at all, as you had to know the crossing points or risk turning in circles until darkness fell. Time was another dimension of this vastness; our land still bore traces of changes wrought over hundreds, even thousands of years by weather and by man.

The path was far more uneven than it looked from the back of a horse. I did not draw back when Fortier offered me his arm. He took me closer to the riverbank, which was rank with late-year growth and liberally sprinkled with sheep droppings in various stages of desiccation. The smells of river water and sheep dung mingled with the earthy odor that arose from the fields as the day drew to a close.

"It has rained hard, of course, since the day Sir Justin died," he said as he reached the spot he'd been looking for. "The mud was more clearly grooved and torn here that day. But you can still see marks, and look how the brambles are broken and pushed aside."

"Couldn't those marks just as easily have been made by a struggling ram? The one they found dead farther down the river?" I leaned forward to look. I felt oddly detached from the thought that this was where Justin had last been alive and, until that one fatal, final moment, safe from harm. Warm in his tweeds, looking forward to returning to Whit-combe to take coffee with me.

"If a ram had pushed through here—and why would it?—tufts of its fleece would have snagged on the thorns," Fortier pointed out. "I made inquiries about the dead animal. It had no pieces of bramble in its fleece—and you know how those thorns hook into you."

I did indeed. Brambles were a dreadful nuisance when you wore long skirts.

"And what about Sir Justin's body? Were there brambles stuck to him?"

"There were."

"This was noted at the inquest, I suppose?"

"Yes. I pointed out that even if Sir Justin needed to get close to the river for some reason, it was odd that he had chosen a spot thick with brambles and not that gap over there." He pointed upstream to a place where the bank sloped less steeply, a spot where the ewes could go to drink.

"If he'd seen the ram struggling and rushed to save it . . ." I tailed off, feeling the futility of speculation. I was sure the men at the inquest had engaged in discussions like this at length.

"There was another thing that the rain washed away. Vomit, just around here." Fortier waved a hand. "Although the young woman, Susan Hatherall, claimed that it was she who had vomited—not all that unsurprising given her condition."

"Susan? What was she doing there at such an early hour?" I felt a stab of curiosity. Farmer Hatherall's youngest daughter had been a positive fixture at Hyrst as a child, but I hadn't seen her for years. "And what do you mean, her condition?"

Fortier took a deep breath. "That's rather a delicate subject and caused something of a stir at the inquest—but I believe I must tell you since her story is bound up with yours. She appears to be with child. Lucius Hatherall tried to stop her from calling attention to herself, but I suppose it would have been remiss of her not to speak up. I gather she's unmarried."

"Oh dear. And Farmer Hatherall a churchwarden too." I shook my head, trying to absorb this new shock. "The poor man. He must be dying of shame."

"He certainly had the air of a man traveling through the lowest circles of inferno," Fortier said. "Come, you must see the willow before it's pulled out. Would you like to go back for the horses, or shall we walk?"

We decided to walk, and Fortier offered me his arm again. I had to admit to myself that I found his solid muscularity comforting. I missed the sensation of masculine closeness, I realized. Justin and I had not been one of those married couples who avoided proximity to each other after the first few months. I wondered how much more I would miss such closeness as my widowhood lengthened—and what that would mean.

"Most of the jury followed the lead of three or four men," Fortier explained as we walked. "Your brother, Lord Broadmere, of course, and the mayor. Sharrock and Finch, who both dislike me." Doctors Sharrock and Finch were the two other Littleberry physicians, both fixtures since my childhood.

"And what about the Littleberry police?"

Fortier looked sideways at me, his mouth quirked upward at the corners. "All three of them? I had the distinct impression they felt they had enough to do keeping the town clear of vagrants and drunkards and shouting at carters on market days. I did suggest we consult a police detective from one of the larger towns, but naturally my opinion didn't prevail. The great men decided it was a case of accidental death, and the police were happy to bow to their superior wisdom."

"That sounds like Littleberry. Although I imagine they listened to Ned—Sir Edward—and to the doctors rather than to my brother. Littleberry's burghers see the Scott-De Quincys as interfering incomers, you know. We've only been at Hyrst for a hundred years or so, and Littleberry's never been a town to show much respect to the nobility. They wun't be druv, as the saying goes."

"Wun't be—? Oh, they won't be driven, like the Sussex pig. Yes, I've become well acquainted with Littleberry's tradition of proud and stubborn independence in the year I've lived there. My brother-in-law, Quinn Dermody, has much to say on the subject, being one of the proudest and most stubborn of the townspeople."

We had rounded the bend in the river by now, and I could see the willow. It was a relatively young one compared to the behemoths in the field we'd just left. That is to say, it would have taken only two or three men to encompass its trunk with their arms. Two massive plow horses were grazing close to it. A team of men called back and forth as they tried to work out the best way to fix chains around its lower branches.

"Is Farmer Hatherall not here?" I asked them as we drew closer. One man straightened up from his task and tugged his forelock.

"Church business, m'lady. He said as to try and get the tree out before nightfall. I'm sorry for your loss, m'lady."

The other men chimed in with their condolences, but I soon released them to continue with their work. The day had been fine, but now the sun was sinking fast.

"So Justin was found here." I stared bleakly at the yellowed leaves and scum that had accumulated where the great tree's branches entered the water.

"Yes."

"Dear God, what a place to die." I shivered. A faint mist had begun rising from the damp earth, giving the valley bottom a ghostly air. "Monsieur Fortier, what, really, is the point of showing me all of this? To improve the quality of my nightmares?"

Fortier looked down at me, his brow furrowed. "To gain an ally in the cause of the truth," he said, his voice grave. "I'm deeply sorry if I'm causing you distress. If you feel that, as a woman, you deserve to be sheltered from unpleasantness—"

"I never said that." I shivered again.

"You're cold," said Fortier. "Let me walk you back to your horse. There's nothing else to see."

We rounded the river bend to find Mank with all three of the horses. We had walked in silence, but Fortier spoke before we were in earshot of my groom.

"Would you please consider what I've said and shown you? I know this is merely a slender thread of a theory, but if there's the faintest chance I may be right, you need to keep your eyes and ears open."

"For what?"

"Enemies. Anomalies. Trust your instincts, Lady Helena. I suppose it's too much to ask of you that you trust me."

~

Back at Whitcombe, I soaked in a fragrant bath to rid myself of the smell of horse. Fortier's words and the impressions the day had wrought on my brain spun around like leaves in a stream, bumping against boulders of doubt and denial. Should I listen to the man? And what good would it do if I did? Wasn't widowhood bad enough without the obligation of some sort of quest for justice? My husband was dead and buried, and nothing I could do would bring him back.

"Nothing at all," I murmured, turning the slippery bar of soap around between my hands to work up a lather. I'd received a note from Gerry that she and Ned were dining at Hyrst. She recommended that Blanche and I join them now that Odelia had, as she put it, "disappeared again." I'd accepted, thinking I'd like to talk to Ned. After all, he'd been at the inquest, and he was far easier to approach than Michael. I could talk things over sensibly with him.

"What did you say, my lady?" Guttridge leaned over me and sniffed delicately at my hair. "We'll have to wash it—I daresay I can get it dry enough that you won't catch your death of cold. We can't have you arriving at Hyrst smelling of smoke and horse. Were you asking me something just now?"

"I was thinking aloud," I said as Guttridge rapidly unpinned my hair and reached for the jug. "About something Monsieur Fortier said to me. I bumped into him on the river path."

"Hmph." Guttridge motioned for me to lean forward and

tipped a cascade of warm water over my head. "He's a trou-blemaker, that Frenchie. Always contradicting people and drawing attention to himself, from what I hear."

I kept my eyes tightly closed as Guttridge's long, strong fingers pushed through my hair. "And who tells you that?"

Guttridge let out her breath in a small puff of derision. "My young man is a mold maker and decorator for Mr. Dermody, so he sees the Frenchie often. Mr. Dermody lets him use a couple of rooms at the pottery for his physicking, seeing they're related by marriage."

"So I understand. I didn't know you had a young man, Guttridge. Are you planning to get married and leave me?"

"Not likely." The heady scent of roses filled the air as Guttridge shook a few drops of oil from a pale blue bottle and rubbed it into her hands. "I like to have someone to walk out with, my lady. Men are useless creatures for the most part, but they're good company when you're in the mood for an outing. Besides, it's hard to go on jaunts with other couples when you're on your own. The other girls don't like it."

I closed my eyes as Guttridge combed through my hair with her fingers. I found myself trying to encompass the idea of Guttridge on jaunts or thinking of herself as a girl. My lady's maid was forty if she was a day.

"So you don't think Monsieur Fortier is trustworthy?"

"He's a foreigner and a stranger. A good enough physician, by all accounts. They say he's always agitating about the health of the poor people, and it's known he'll take a few eggs or even a bit of pie in lieu of a fee."

"So he's a kind man." That pleased me.

"Depends on where you stand. The other doctors lose their fees when there's someone prepared to do the work for nothing at all. I don't see anything kind in depriving a man of his livelihood. I suppose *Monsewer* Fortier is living on the good graces of his brother-in-law. It's easy to be generous when somebody else is paying."

"He might have a private income," I pointed out. "He appears to be a gentleman."

"There's lots of people these days *appear* to be gentlemen when all they've got is money and a bit of education." Guttridge wrapped a robe around me as I climbed out of the bath and began vigorously rubbing my hair with a towel.

"Aren't money and education enough?" I asked. "You don't really need a pedigree going back to the Normans."

Guttridge sniffed. "New people. They'll be the ruination of this country."

I suppressed a grin. "Sir Justin's baronetcy is only three generations old, you know. They made their money in Indian cotton." I sighed. "And now the title is extinguished."

"Three generations are long enough," Guttridge proclaimed. "And Sir Justin was a real gentleman. That Fortier is always sloping off to France, did you know that? A mistress, I'll be bound, or some kind of unwholesome dealing. Smuggling or spying for the French."

"Smuggling is no longer lucrative, and we're not at war with the French anymore," I pointed out. "And my ancestors engaged in both smuggling *and* spying."

"Ah, but *they* were Scott-De Quincys," Guttridge said with an air of finality.

I couldn't help laughing at that pronouncement, and Guttridge joined in. But I soon sobered. Her words worried me.

"How often does Monsieur Fortier go to France?"

"Four times since he moved to Littleberry, the word is. With no explanation ever given. The Dermodys know what it's about right enough, but no hint escapes either of them. The servants can't fathom the mystery. The Frenchie never takes a man with him on his travels."

"I'm sure there's a perfectly normal explanation." But I could hear the uncertainty in my voice.

"People with perfectly normal business talk about their business. If I were you, my lady, I'd be careful not to be seen walking with that Frenchman out in the fields. And without a chaperone neither."

"Who told—? Oh, Mank, I suppose. Did he tell you it was he who left me alone, and not the other way around?"

"He did, but that's not the point. A lady in your position must be careful. Scandal attaches to a woman as it doesn't to a man."

I pinched the bridge of my nose. "Oh, for heaven's sake, Guttridge, don't nag. Be a good lady's maid and get me ready quickly. I'd like to spend an hour with the dowager countess before dinner."

Rebuked, Guttridge bustled off and left me alone with my thoughts, which were troubled ones. Had I been a fool to even listen to Fortier in the first place?

6

SEEKING THE TRUTH

"Have you sent for the gardener?"

My mother's inevitable question only made me hug her tighter tonight. I thought I recognized this form of greeting as a quest for reassurance in a world Mama no longer understood. Even if she never visited her herb garden, the idea of having a garden and needing to talk to the gardener must somehow form a link to the past.

My mother's troubles had begun with my father's death six years ago. Like Justin's, Papa's demise had been sudden. To be part of an adoring couple for forty-two years and then to find your husband cold and blue in his bed must have been worse than my own experiences. It had been Papa's passing and its effect on Mama that had begun to pull me out of the dreadful pit of darkness wherein I'd dwelt since Daniel's death two and a half years before. I had seen the terrible blankness on my mother's face and had no longer wished to remain curled inward around my own pain.

I had been only sixteen when Daniel died, and nothing bad had ever happened to me before. I suppose it was natural I should react to his death childishly. I had wrapped myself up in a selfish silence and withdrawn from the world where I had once been so carefree. A young woman *could* be selfish when she had no need to earn money or keep a household, and my retreat into numbness had harmed nobody but myself. Mama had tried to interest me in the world of healing again but eventually had given up and relied increasingly on Susan Hatherall, the capable—and beautiful—child she had befriended.

After Papa died, we all accepted Mama's vagueness as the result of grief. It had not seemed so very unusual that a woman in her mid-sixties should become a little forgetful. It had taken two years of increasingly bizarre and disturbing incidents—the worst being the day Mama dismissed Susan—to make Michael, who had his own grief by then, consult a London specialist about Mama's condition.

I nodded at Belming, the godsend who had been a direct result of that specialist's recommendations, as I sat down. She had risen briefly when I entered but was now back in her armchair, darning stockings.

"Now, Mama, you know the gardener will be along directly," I said, smiling into my mother's watery blue eyes. "Are you feeling well?"

Mama's gaze sought that of Belming, who seemed to sense her patient's uncertainty and paused in her darning. "Am I well?" Mama asked her. "The young lady wants to know."

"Your ladyship is quite well and has passed a happy day. We went out onto the terrace for a few minutes and enjoyed the colors of the leaves very much. Luncheon was soup followed by poached salmon, which we ate with a hearty appetite." Belming smiled reassuringly at me. "Things always become a little more cloudy toward the evening, m'lady. But it's been a good day, on the whole."

"I'm quite well." Mama nodded at me graciously, as to a visiting stranger. "Thank you for your concern."

"What's that on your table, Belming?" I indicated the large sewn book at Belming's elbow, its thick pages splayed out fanlike. "It looks like one of Mama's old sketchbooks."

"It is." Belming put down her work and reached for the book. "I found it in the lowboy. I've been sorting through drawers to see what Lady Alice and Lady Annette might like to take for their charities. Her ladyship needs so little these days."

She handed the large volume to me, and I opened the pages. Mama had once possessed a superb gift for botanical illustration, and this was indeed a treasure. The blue-purples of monkshood, the bright yellow of broom blossoms amid their glaucous spikes, the pale trumpets of nicotiana were as vibrant as the day Mama had painted them. Notes were written around some of the illustrations in Mama's firm, elegant handwriting. Here was a petal that had fallen between the pages and dried to a paper-thin wisp of pink over the years. I removed it carefully, marveling at its fragile beauty.

"Look, Mama." I angled the pages so my mother could see them. "You're such a talented artist. Do you remember the flowers?"

"No. There's no sense in it. We haven't a cloud to walk on."

Mama rose unsteadily to her feet and walked away from me. Belming shook her head.

"She won't look at them, m'lady. I've tried. She might ask for the gardener, but she won't tolerate anything that reminds her of her garden."

"What a pity."

"Perhaps you should take the book, m'lady. When Lady Alice and Lady Annette are in their organizing mood, there's no saying where things will end up. I'd like to think a bit of her ladyship will be left behind."

I smiled. "I wish Mama's talent had extended to drawing people. I would like to have seen some studies of Papa or my sisters when they were little. I only have one small daguerreotype of my father as I remember him. I never knew him without silver hair, you know."

"Will you show me the photograph one day, m'lady? Of course, I never knew him at all except from the portraits. I like the one of him with the hounds better than the one in court dress, but he was a terribly handsome man."

"He was handsome even as an older man," I laughed. "A true Scott-De Quincy in looks. I used to run my fingers through that thick hair, looking for the golden threads that remained among the silver. Yes, I'll take the book." I looked over to where Mama was hovering by a small table, repeatedly touching it as if she were trying to understand its use. "There were many other illustrations and paintings, you know. I should look for them one of these days."

By the time the dinner gong sounded and I headed downstairs, I was tired in body and mind. Mama had that effect on me. Even though Belming did all of the actual work of caring for her, I found sitting with my mother exhausting. And that made me feel guilty. Would I resent Mama if I did invite her to stay at Whitcombe? Or would I feel less guilty because I was providing for her comfort? Certainly, Whitcombe was large enough that Mama could have a bigger suite of rooms. I could make the night nurse Belming occasionally requested a permanent fixture. I did not have to watch my pennies the way Michael did. Our father had been an extravagant spender, and my brother was still trying to clear his debts.

Dinner was a subdued affair. Michael looked tired and morose while Alice and Annette were more than usually wrapped up in each other and spoke to nobody else. Gerry seemed out of sorts with Blanche, who was characteristically querulous. Lydia and her husband mostly made small talk about county society with Maryanne, who was hoping to catch a husband soon, and Thomas was not present. Julia tried to keep the flow of conversation going but looked slightly green around the gills, as if her stomach were bothering her.

The men did not remain behind in the dining room, but accompanied the ladies into the drawing room straight after dinner. Here, I thought, was my chance to talk with Ned. He was clearly bent on avoiding Michael—who had been particularly trying on the subject of the Irish question during dinner—and accepted my offer of a quiet game of Old Maid with alacrity. We retired to the gloomiest corner of Hyrst's gloomy drawing room—Michael was forever putting off Julia's pleas to redecorate, saying they couldn't afford it—and settled into a rather leisurely game.

"I've been wanting to ask you about the inquest on Justin," I said after twenty minutes, when we'd won a hand each.

Ned frowned and tugged at his heavy mustache. "An unpleasant subject, my dear." He began shuffling the pack of cards but then put the deck down and patted my hand in an avuncular fashion. "All over now, and you've been a brave little woman." He smiled, brown eyes kind under his thick, curling brows. "Best not to think too much about it, eh?"

"I can't help thinking about it," I said. "And I have to ask you—are you absolutely sure in your mind that Justin's death was an accident?"

His eyes widened. "If I hadn't been sure, I'd have spoken up. My position in the town doesn't allow me to gloss over any suspicion of wrongdoing." He frowned. "Who's been putting ideas into your head?"

There was no use in hiding it. "Monsieur Fortier."

Ned waved a large hand as if swatting at a bothersome fly. "That damned Frenchman. He's a troublemaker, my dear. A troublemaker with too much imagination. Has he been pestering you? Just say the word and I'll make it clear to him he should not."

"'Pestering' isn't the right word. He did talk to me. Do you think it's possible he's seen something the rest of you didn't see? He seems intelligent enough."

Ned looked faintly amused. "And the rest of aren't intelligent enough? My dear Helena, you must give Littleberry's leading citizens some credit for sense. We all listened to Fortier's theory, and none of us thought he'd made a sufficient case. Killing a strong man by shoving him into a river, on a well-used path, in a field which could have been overlooked from a dozen different directions—and why, for heaven's sake? Who had a motive?" He removed a large handkerchief from his pocket and wiped his nose vigorously.

"So you discounted Fortier's theory due to its farfetched nature?"

"We didn't discount it. We discussed the matter thoroughly and decided the balance of the evidence was against foul play. We even took an extra day to make inquiries around the area, to see if anyone had been spotted where they shouldn't be—or if they'd not been seen where they should be. We looked for even the slimmest evidence of someone doing something unusual and found none. In short, we took Fortier's suggestion seriously, as our responsibility as a jury demanded. And now, it seems, that arrogant pup has disregarded our verdict and taken to bothering you." Ned's cheeks, already red from the wine he'd drunk at dinner, were bright vermilion above his wiry beard.

I felt my own face flush a little. "He seemed very sure of himself," I said.

"Being sure of himself is one of his damnable flaws. Arrogance, as I said. He has a history of contradicting those in authority, especially the medical men of Littleberry. And he's often right, I grant you—he's a good physician. But not in this case."

"And you swear that if he'd raised a doubt, you wouldn't have brought in the verdict of accidental death? Supposing he supplied more evidence, even if it were circumstantial?"

Ned took up the cards again, shuffling them rhythmically as he gazed at me thoughtfully. "So you believe him?"

"I don't know what to believe, to be honest. I'm prepared to listen to him. If I don't, I'll spend the rest of my life wondering whether my failure to act proves I didn't love Justin as much as I thought I did." I cleared my throat.

"There's no question of a failure to act where there is nothing anyone can do." Ned looked at me from under his brows. "Don't clutch at straws, my dear. Now do you still want to play?"

I nodded, and from that point onward Ned seemed determined to distract me from anything connected with Justin's death. I picked out my pairs of cards automatically, thinking back over my encounters with the French physician. Was I clutching at straws? And could I trust Fortier when nobody else seemed to? Perhaps he genuinely believed a wrongheaded theory. Perhaps he was a little unbalanced. Perhaps coming to me was a blow struck in some battle against the well-established medical men of Littleberry, a chance to discredit them and gain an entry into the family of the Earl of Broadmere. Or perhaps he was telling the truth.

7

SUSAN HATHERALL

*B*lanche left the next morning. My first thought after I'd waved her off was to visit the Hatherall farm. Yet I hesitated. What would I ask them?

The truth was, I didn't want to face Susan Hatherall. My feelings about her were too complex. I remembered the stab of jealousy I'd felt when my mother brought her home for the first time—"Look at the fairy I found out in the fields!"— and proceeded to make a pet of her. I was fourteen, an awkward age. I knew by then I was not going to grow tall, graceful, and blond-haired like my parents and siblings. I still had the essentially sunny, easy nature that had made my childhood pleasant, so I made no fuss and outwardly accepted my mother's latest eccentricity. Yet I hadn't been able to bring myself to dote on the child, beauty though she was.

At six, Susan was an ethereal waif in appearance, with hair of palest blond and clear blue-gray eyes. In character, she was forward and demanding. She was used to being her father's treasured darling. Her mother had died giving birth to her, and the farmer clung to this last remnant of love like a drowning man clinging to a spar.

Susan's nature was to take, not to give, and that had irked me. She was one of those people who were never satisfied with what they had. If there were jam tarts or sweetmeats or slices of cake to share around, Susan always managed to have one more than everyone else—and she would look very carefully to ensure she received the largest. I had more than once caught her with a ribbon or sachet in her pocket that belonged to me. These were always such small items I could never really accuse her of stealing, and more often than not I'd let her take them home.

She became a regular visitor, scampering up the hill through the cemetery and slipping through the iron bars of Hyrst's grand gate to appear in Mama's herb room with a wide grin. My dislike of the child had perturbed me; after all, she was just a little girl and the daughter of one of our churchwardens. Guilt that I was breaching the aristocratic duty of kindness and care toward the lower orders added to my inclination not to question my mother's decisions, so I kept silent.

I hadn't seen Susan since she was thirteen. Eighteen months after Papa died, Mama had driven her from the house one horrible day. My calm, competent mother had been in a screaming rage, shouting incoherently at Susan and quite literally foaming at the mouth. We had never known why. I had avoided Susan since—out of guilt? Awkwardness? Or relief?

I couldn't deny it was relief that washed over me when my plans for the day were disrupted by Odelia, returning to Whitcombe as abruptly as she'd departed.

"Maidstone was a disaster," was her reply when I expressed my astonishment at seeing her so soon. "Sometimes I think the bohemian set are the most dreadful, selfish people in existence. It quite pulled me up short. I felt weighed down by guilt that I had left you all alone at a time like this. I knew none of the others would be much comfort to you, and yet there I was, deserting you for the sake of somebody else's art. So I'm back to do penance. I'm going to send for my dressmaker and ensure you're fitted out properly for mourning." She bent down to caress Scotty, whose high-pitched bark had made it difficult to hear each other speak. "Goodness, little dog, you'd think I'd been away for a twelvemonth. Won't you just love to see your mistress in pretty new clothes?"

I smiled at her. "That would be a tremendous help—your dressmaker's such a good one. And now that Blanche has gone, we can be comfortable together. Blanche gave me quite a headache this morning, lecturing me on the correct way to grieve with many little tales of how the 'dear Queen' sets the example to all British widows."

"Of course Blanche knows far more about the dear Queen than us ordinary mortals." Odelia raised a sardonic eyebrow. "You'd think *she* was invited to those house parties rather than her son. I don't suppose Dederick tells her much about the goings-on of the Prince of Wales's set, and I certainly don't see him supplying tidbits about the Queen."

"And if Blanche were really so keen to follow the Queen's example, she'd be in black all the time. As it is, I expect she'll be out of full mourning for Justin on the very day the four-month period expires."

"Well, black doesn't suit her. It does me." Odelia looked smug.

"She says I should have my carriages repainted and reupholstered in black and put the footmen in black livery."

"Will you?"

"Probably not." I gathered Scotty up in my arms and

dismissed Blanche from my mind. "What would you like to do today?"

"What were *you* going to do before I decided to impose myself upon you?"

"Spend an hour or two on my wretched letters. I still haven't finished replying to all the messages of condolence, which is scandalously rude of me. And then I was thinking of riding down to Dene Farm to call on the Hatheralls."

"Oh, don't." Odelia made a face.

"Why not? Farmer Hatherall is my tenant now after all."

"And if he has something to discuss regarding his tenancy, the proper thing to do is for him to write for an appointment. Which reminds me—aren't you going to appoint an agent to oversee the farm? Or are you going to take up Michael's suggestion of letting him and Brandrick manage your farmland? It's not all that big a holding after all. You're fortunate not to have the responsibility of a huge estate. I suppose Justin's other properties are managed by his solicitors in Hastings."

"They are." Putting Scotty down, I shuffled through the papers on my desk. "They sent me a report, something to do with the assessment of death duties. I'm not sure what to do about Dene Farm, to be honest. Justin always managed the farmland himself."

"The curse of the gentleman farmer," O groaned. "You need an agent, and a good one, so you can travel around a bit. I always thought it was rather a shame you and Justin never traveled."

"We were perfectly content at Whitcombe," I said.

"He for sheep alone, she for God in him?"

"Justin was not my god, and I'll thank you not to misquote Milton at me. To return to the point, why shouldn't I visit the Hatheralls? I haven't seen Susan for years."

"That horrid child. Why would you want to see her?"

"Did you think she was horrid?" I felt oddly pleased. By the time Susan had attached herself to Hyrst, Odelia had long since decamped to London to be with her artist friends, but then, as now, she would visit Hyrst whenever the spirit moved her. I'd always thought she doted on Susan like the rest of them.

"She was a little sneak. Always hiding around corners listening, and I swear she crept into people's rooms." O sighed. "She was a beauty though. I've got a sketch of her somewhere. I was thinking about doing a picture of fairy children, and she was perfect. If I'd liked her more, I'd have asked her to sit for me, but I thought her head was quite swollen enough. Why do people pay so much attention to beautiful children? There's no especial merit in being born good-looking."

"I just thought it was time I saw her again."

I felt reluctant to tell O that Susan was pregnant.

"Well, don't. You simply don't need to assume any responsibilities at this time in your life. It's a good thing I decided to come back, Baby. I shall amuse and divert you—in ways appropriate to your newly widowed state, of course. Guttridge and I shall manage the business of your new wardrobe down to its last detail. And I promise not to leave for at least a week."

~

In the end, Odelia stayed for almost two weeks—and if her purpose was to amuse and divert me, she certainly succeeded. In truth, I enjoyed having her to myself at Whitcombe. Her single-minded pursuit of art and her reluctance to appear downstairs until most of the morning was gone meant I had sufficient time to myself to catch up with my correspondence and spend time with Mrs. Eason, going over housekeeping matters. In the afternoons, she was a most congenial companion on walks, during which I would have plenty of time to enjoy the view or take Scotty for a stroll while Odelia made sketches of what she called "valuable background material." O was a good horsewoman, so we rode out frequently to enjoy the fine early November weather. She had her dressmaker make us new, very smart riding habits in a fine black wool she'd ordered from London.

The weather deteriorated two days before O left and probably hastened her departure. I always found London rain the most bleak and depressing kind of weather, but O declared there was nothing worse than staring out of rain-streaked windows into thick mist as the clouds brushed the top of Whitcombe Hill.

The day after O left, the rain dried up, although the sky was still a solid mass of sulky gray cloud. I felt very much at a loose end, and by three o'clock in the afternoon I'd made up my mind to pay Farmer Hatherall that long-delayed visit. If he were out in the fields, I could talk to Susan and see how she was. It was my duty now that Justin was not here.

Matters were made easier—or possibly more pressing—by the fact that Farmer Hatherall had touched his hat to me in church the previous Sunday and spoken a few polite words of condolence as he passed by my pew. I reminded myself I had no reason to dislike him. He was known to be an intelligent, upstanding man, a teetotaler, and was called "Mr. Hatherall" by the lower classes in deference to his position as churchwarden. Justin had thought highly of him and had often counted as a blessing that he had such a hardworking, honest tenant.

I took the long way around for Sandy's sake and once more agreed with Mank that he should take half an hour to gallop Puck while I was at Dene Farm. His return would give me a good excuse to leave.

I passed the spot Fortier had shown me with just a slight quickening of my heartbeat. Ned was right, wasn't he? I shouldn't clutch at straws. I merely shook my head over the devastation to the riverbank caused by the removal of the great willow that now lay a hundred yards back from the path, thick gouges in the turf evidence of the effort it had taken to drag it there. In the spring, I would have to ensure the riverbank was properly repaired.

Dene Farm was a large square house built of solid red brick. It had the tiled upper half so characteristic of our part of Sussex, decorated with two rows of round-cut tiles. The front door was surrounded by wooden fretwork, freshly painted white. The house had a well-kept look of prosperity and cleanliness, almost gentility with its carefully trimmed hedges, rose garden, and neat fenced kitchen garden to one side. Behind the house, I could hear the clucking of chickens.

The servant who answered the door knew me, as most people did. She greeted me cheerfully. Behind her, I saw the tall form of Farmer Hatherall loom into the narrow hallway.

"I'm sorry to descend on you like this." I checked the state of my boots, wiping them well before walking into the house. The mingled scents of soap and stew greeted me from the open door of the kitchen. I could hear the sound of someone vigorously operating a butter churn.

"It's no trouble, m'lady." Farmer Hatherall was in shirt-sleeves but quickly removed his jacket from a hook in the hallway and donned it before ushering me into his parlor. "There's not so much to do with the ewes not spread around the fields. It's hard to believe I didn't have Sir Justin to oversee the breeding with me this year, but we managed."

"I'm sure you did." I sat down in a well-stuffed armchair. The parlor was a pleasant room, decorated with large samplers and a bright painting of flowers. A plain wooden cross hung from a nail near the door.

"I'm sorry I didn't come earlier to talk to you about the farm," I said.

"Lord Broadmere and his man of business have already done that." He spoke well, with a slight burr but with precision in his speech.

"Yes, I suppose they have." I felt a twinge of annoyance, but of course I wouldn't show it.

"That Mr. Brandrick knows almost as much as Sir Justin did about the care and breeding of sheep. Of course, they've more land than we have, but more of it's rough grazing, and their ewes don't get as fat as ours. The grass in the river bottoms makes the meat sweet."

"I've heard Sir Justin say that a thousand times." I smiled. What had started as a hobby of Justin's on the slopes of Whitcombe Hill, which belonged to the house and not the farm, had long before our marriage become a consuming passion for both men. The sheep, in fact, were nearly all Justin's, and "tenant" was not really the right word for Farmer Hatherall. A complicated arrangement existed whereby he shared in the profits of the meat sales in a carefully calculated proportion, taking into account their respective acreages and the number of sheep he either owned or managed for Justin. They had been so successful that Justin had been trying to buy some more land so he could increase the herd.

"You'll take some tea, m'lady? Ruby!" He shouted into the hallway, and the servant appeared to tell him the kettle was already halfway to the boil.

"I'm grateful for your visit," he said as he reseated himself. "It shows you care about how we go on now that Sir Justin's gone."

"And how do you go on?" I asked. "Is Susan well? And Maggie?"

"Aye, Maggie's well." A smile creased the farmer's face. He was quite pleasing to look at, a bit like a German burgher, tall and well-built, with wavy light brown hair and intelligent eyes. A heavy fringe of whiskers that met under his chin disguised the fact that his face was a little too long to be really handsome.

"She married a dairy farmer, didn't she?"

"That's right. Out at Pincham. He owns his bit of land."

I could hear a faint bitterness in the farmer's voice. Justin had often told me Farmer Hatherall had the tiniest chip on his shoulder about being a tenant farmer rather than a landowner despite his high standing in the community. There was nothing for him to be ashamed of—Dene Farm was an excellent concern, and working alongside Justin had ensured the Hatheralls were better off than most tenant farmers in the vicinity. He could easily have made a good second marriage, but Justin said he seemed to find most of the suitable women beneath him.

"Do they have children?"

"Aye, three little girls." A light came into his eyes as he said the words.

"And Susan? I haven't seen her for so long."

I held my breath, looking into the farmer's face. He stared back into mine, seemingly reading my expression, and sighed.

"You've heard, then."

"Yes. From Monsieur Fortier, the French physician. He explained that Susan became ill and that she'd told the inquest why. I'm sorry. Is there anything I can do to help?"

He shook his head. "I can take care of her, thank you, m'lady. I'll not cast her out. Maggie will take the babe and rear it as her own. Of course, the whole town will hear in the end, and probably every village for a league around, but we must make the best of it."

"When will the child be born?"

"Sometime around the Annunciation."

That was the end of March, and a most unfortunate allusion to the Virgin Birth. Susan must be four months along. I made an appropriate noise of sympathy for the father of a wayward girl. A kind father, moreover, who would not ban his daughter from his house and force her into the workhouse as so many would.

"I'd like to see Susan before I leave," I told him. "I haven't set eyes on her for years. She doesn't come to church."

His face darkened. "Susan walks to Pincham of a Sunday morning to join her sister at the church there. That started after—well, after she was no longer welcome at Hyrst. We were worried the dowager countess would take against her again."

"Ah." Of course, my mother had attended services until about two years ago. "You should have let us know. We would have ensured that Lady Broadmere didn't attend the same service as Susan." I felt a little ashamed that none of us had thought of that particular difficulty.

"It's been a good way for Susan to stay close to her sister, m'lady. She still needed a bit of mothering, you see. I think that's what she was looking for at Hyrst, even though I told her it was presumptuous to think such a thing where the gentry were concerned. Her mother died giving birth to her, as I'm sure you know. Before that, two stillborn sons and one who only lived six months. It's not surprising my children should cling to one another a little, even now that Maggie's a wife and mother. It's a shame her husband won't have Susan to stay with them, but a man is lord in his own household."

We fell silent as Ruby brought in the tea, pouring for us both and sparing me the social convention of presiding over the teapot. I drank the tea with pleasure—it was strong but good, and riding always made me thirsty. After a few minutes of small talk, I drew a deep breath.

"This may seem strange," I began, "but I have a strong desire to know more about the circumstances of my husband's death. I've been told so very little, you see."

I had rehearsed this speech in my mind on the way to the farm. Reluctant as I was to let Fortier's interfering ways perturb me, I felt I owed it to Justin to at least settle the doubt the Frenchman had raised in my mind.

"I know my brother and brother-in-law—Lord Broadmere and Sir Edward Freestone, that is—wish to protect my feelings," I went on. "But the less I know, the more I listen to speculation. For example, I've heard that a question was raised at the inquest of my husband's death not being entirely accidental. That it was suggested—well, not to put too fine a point on it, that he was pushed into the river or even held under the water. Could such a thing possibly be true?"

The farmer's honest brow wrinkled in concern, his face suffusing with indignant color. "How could you have come to hear such a terrible thing?"

He leaned forward, and for a moment I thought he was going to pat my knee. "It's quite right that a lady such as yourself should be protected from nasty, wicked gossip like that. With your delicate upbringing and all."

Hang my delicate upbringing, I thought. I hoped he wouldn't refuse to talk altogether on the pretext of sparing my feelings. I essayed a tremulous smile.

"Were there—*very* nasty details? Being kept in the dark is quite giving me nightmares. Please tell me everything you can. You may wish to spare me, but I beseech you not to. Help put my mind at rest."

His face, on which thunder was gathering, suddenly cleared.

"You want to know these things so you can be reassured Sir Justin's death was an accident?"

I put my cup and saucer down carefully, delivering my words in a loud whisper. "I simply want to feel my husband is at peace."

"He is in Christ's rest, I could swear to that." The expression on the man's face was strange; envious, perhaps, or sad or beseeching. I couldn't read it. After a moment, he spoke again.

"You know I found Sir Justin's body?"

"Sir Edward told me that."

"It was the horse that alerted me." He nodded in the direction of the front of the house. "Sir Justin's horse, Puck. I was just on my way out of the house—Sir Justin had said he'd knock on my door, but he was late—and I saw the blessed horse, a-wandering and stretching his neck over my side gate, trying to get at the bit of greens I still had growing in a half barrel. So of course I started to wonder, and my first thought was to go to River Bottom. We were due to start separating out the skinny ewes, to graze them for a bit in Fat Quarter before putting the ram to them, and I knew Sir Justin's habits. He always rode round by the river path, making sure all was well."

I nodded. Justin spent hours in the fields on Puck, gazing at his much-loved sheep and setting small matters to rights.

Farmer Hatherall gazed out of the window for a moment. "I ran to get the horse quick before it ate my greens, but I didn't feel overly alarmed. I knew it to have a mischievous streak, that animal. So I took it with me and walked along the path. There was a bit of mist in River Bottom, as there sometimes is just after sunrise, but it was going to be a fine day."

"How long did you search for him?" I knew what he meant about the mist. Autumn mornings could sometimes present a view from Whitcombe House that looked like a bowl of smoke as the mist rose from damp fields.

"Twenty minutes, maybe more. I tied Puck to a gate and walked the path. I couldn't understand why I didn't see Sir Justin—until I saw him, that is."

"In the water." It gave me a strange feeling to say such a thing.

"Aye." He nodded, sympathy on his face. "I almost missed him. Those brown tweeds of his sort of blended in, y'see, and he was all meshed up in the branches of that willow. I'd been waiting on Ted up at Twin Oasts to loan me his plow team and chains to get that blamed thing out. We'd been trying ever since the storm that felled it in September, but it was too big to manage without a proper team."

"And Sir Justin was dead when you found him?" Of course he had been, but I wanted to hear the story.

"Most certainly dead, God rest him." The farmer shook his head regretfully. "I was more or less certain when I saw him, but I jumped right in to make sure. Didn't even think to take off my coat or shoes."

"That was good of you."

"Foolish of me, more like. I could have drowned too. But I didn't think, m'lady. I was in the water up to my chest before I knew what I was about."

"So you could stand?"

"Aye, that bit's not too deep, as it turned out. Not that it was easy to get to where Sir Justin was, but I managed. They do say fright and excitement give a man strength he doesn't usually have. I was that intent on getting him free of the willow and seeing if there was any hope. I got his face above water, and I—do you really want to hear this, m'lady?"

"I do." I didn't, but I'd promised myself I wouldn't shirk my duty.

"Well, I could see in a moment that life was well extinct, as the coroner said." He hesitated, then plunged on. "His eyes and mouth were open."

The tea I'd drunk sloshed uneasily in my stomach. I could have cheerfully slaughtered Fortier and his theories at that moment. I nodded all the same.

"I understand. Thank you for trying to get him out."

"I thought I'd be able to get him onto the bank at least. But I soon realized I didn't have a hope working on my own. The men who were supposed to be helping with the sheep were walking from Pincham and wouldn't be there for a while. Sir Justin wasn't a heavy man, but he was wearing tweeds, and they were sodden. I pushed and pulled and cursed for a while—got myself wet from head to toe and my hands all scratched up—and then I had the sense to start yelling for help, and Susan heard me."

"She couldn't be of much assistance, surely?"

"No more she could be, m'lady, and the fool girl's first thought was to run up the path to see if the Pincham men were coming. All that did was make her sick, what with the baby and all. I was up to my calves in mud by that time and shivering with the cold, and I never yelled at her so hard in my life. Then she did the sensible thing and ran to the bridge, knowing Dan Smallie and his sons were living in the old ferry keeper's cottage. Of course there were drays and suchlike already on the road, so we soon had all the help we needed."

"I'm glad you were saved." I gave him a half smile, my mind on Fortier's theory. "How do you think Sir Justin got into the river in the first place?"

"Blessed if I know." He frowned, looking out of his window once more. From this low down on the hillside, you couldn't see much of the river, just a line of darker green where the brambles grew along its banks. From Whitcombe, high above, the river was a limpid greenish-brown ribbon of water, spangled with the reflections of the sky as its surface rippled gently.

"I've seen him nearly go in once or twice before," he said eventually. "There's bits where the bank slumps, see." He held up a hand at an angle to indicate a slope. "The sheep go down there to drink or find different grass or do whatever gets into their daft heads. I've told him before, just leave 'em be and most times they find their way up again. They've got four legs, after all, and know how to use 'em." He snorted briefly.

"But that day a ram went in."

"Aye, from Huck Bottom."

"That's on the other side of the river, isn't it?"

He nodded. "We'd moved some younger rams there the day before since we were moving the ewes away from Willow Half. Seems one fool animal decided a field full of ewes was worth risking his life for. Found he couldn't swim as well as he wanted to."

"And Sir Justin decided the ram was worth risking *his* life for."

He shrugged. "There's no way of telling. Perhaps he slipped and fell, not seeing his way in the mist."

"So you don't believe in the notion of an assailant?"

His mouth turned down in derision. "Sir Justin had no enemies, as I'm sure your ladyship knows. No quarrel with anyone that I know of. If it weren't uncharitable, I'd have a thing or two to say about those who spread wicked lies—"

He stopped short, listened for a moment, then called out. "I can hear you there, Susan."

Curiosity twisted me around in my chair as the door

opened. It was indeed Susan, but the years had erased the fairy child of my memories.

Not that she wasn't still pretty. There was something winsomely elfin about her face with its high cheekbones and regular features. She had taken trouble with her appearance, arranging her hair, which had darkened to a honey blond, in small curls around her face and tying it with a bright blue ribbon. She wore earbobs and a ribbon around her neck, from which hung a medallion I remembered Mama giving her.

But her skin was poor, her hands red and chapped, the yellow hair dull and dry-looking, dark shadows under her eyes. She stood a little hunched forward with an air of hangdog resentment that spoiled the efforts she'd made to look attractive. Of course, I told myself, her lot in life was a hard one; and she'd seen enough of the life of her social superiors to understand the distinction. Without Mama's interference, she might have made a happy marriage to some farmer by now. Instead, she had probably inherited her father's inability to be content with his lot, compounding her innate thirst to receive more than her fair share.

"Ruby said her ladyship was asking to see me, Father." She dropped an awkward curtsey in my direction, no doubt remembering the days when she would address me with a cheeky insouciance born of her protected position at Hyrst. The apron she wore over her blue dress was tied a little high, clearly to disguise the pregnancy that was beginning to mold a curve into her still-slender figure.

"I was." I rose to my feet and held out my hand. "It's good to see you again, Susan."

I felt cold, limp fingers press mine for an instant, and then her hand dropped back to her side. "Likewise, I'm sure, m'lady."

"Her ladyship was asking about the morning I found Sir

Justin," her father said. "I told her how you found me in the river trying to rescue him and how you ran in the wrong direction and were sick."

His voice was oddly hearty, considering the subject matter. Was he trying to show her he could talk about her condition openly? It was as if he sought her approval.

"Aye, I was sick all right." Susan glanced downward and then at me. "I suppose you know why. M'lady," she added reluctantly.

"I do. And if I can help in any way, please let me know."

Her only answer was a small shrug that said, *What help can you be?* But these were my people, on my land; the offer had to be made.

"Did Ruby see or hear anything?" it occurred to me to ask. "She was up and about by that time, wasn't she?"

It was Susan who answered. "Ruby had the range and fires to attend to, the bread to knock down and set to prove, the cleaning up after breakfast, and a dozen other things beside. It's likely the Last Judgment could have happened without her noticing."

"And you saw nothing else?"

"I heard Father shouting, and then I did a great deal of running about." She sounded sulky now. "When I'd found help and seen that Father was still alive, I went back to the house and helped Ruby put the bath in front of the fire and start heating water. I washed the cups and jug we'd used for breakfast and made some more cocoa so that Father and the other men could have something warm inside them. I went to Father's bedroom and found him some dry clothes and set those to warm by the fire as well."

Farmer Hatherall was nodding approval. "All just as you should do, my maid—my girl." He turned to me with a smile that, again, seemed too hearty. "Susan knows her place is inside the house, m'lady. Womenfolk must see to the small concerns and leave matters of life and death to the men."

I couldn't help looking at Susan, swelling like the fruit on a summer tree, and think that women had everything to do with life and death.

It was getting dark. I could see Mank outside, a dim vertical shape flanked by the larger bulks of the horses, so I said my good-byes and left. Farmer Hatherall politely followed me out of the front door and assisted me to mount Sandy.

"You'll forgive Susan if her manners sometimes need mending, won't you, m'lady? She's not really herself at the moment."

I thought she had been very much herself, but I smiled and nodded. I rode home thinking about the young woman, partly as a way to evade the picture of Justin's wide-open mouth and eyes that the farmer had painted, but partly for her sake. In a small place like Littleberry, a bastard child would be hard to live down, even if decently adopted by Susan's sister. Perhaps it fell to me to find a solid, practical way to set Susan on a better path than the one she now trod.

8

FAMILY LIFE

"You're supposed to be in mourning."

Michael's handsome face was marred by the ferocious scowl he assumed whenever he decided his role as head of the family was being challenged. He strode up and down in front of the ornate marble fireplace that was the best feature of Hyrst's drawing room. Julia and I sat at opposite sides of the fire—the day was cold—giving each other looks whenever Michael couldn't see us.

"I *am* in mourning." I indicated the dull black silk of my new mourning dress, which was every bit as fine as O had promised it would be.

"You know perfectly well what I mean," Michael snarled. "The moment Odelia leaves, you're paying calls on the Hatheralls. Of all people."

"I'm doing nothing wrong, Michael. I can't stay cooped up in the house all day. I need fresh air, and the horses need exercise. Why didn't you tell me you and Brandrick had already paid a visit to Farmer Hatherall? May I remind you that he's *my* tenant?"

Michael looked shifty. "Brandrick thought it best to

ensure we had matters in hand at the farm. In case you didn't want to."

"Really?" I arched my brows at him. "I suppose it slipped your mind to consult me?"

"It's no good, Michael." Julia's tone had the exact note of decidedness that always worked with her husband. "You can't bully a widow who has full control of her late husband's property, you know. Neither in law nor, apparently, in fact. You owe Helena an apology."

Michael turned to his wife with the odd mixture of bafflement and respect that so often characterized his demeanor toward her.

"I'm not bullying Helena."

"You should listen to yourself, my dear." Julia lifted her chin. She was a tall woman with a regal bearing, handsome rather than pretty, perfectly suited to the role of countess that she had assumed without fuss or bother when Michael was still grieving the death of his first wife. At twenty-five, she was two years older than her young husband and was one of the few people capable of standing up to him when he was in one of his rages. "You may not think you're being a bully, but you're thundering like Jove himself over nothing at all—a mere visit to a tenant. Don't forget Mockford is about to bring the children down. You know how they cower when you raise your voice."

The wind seemed to go out of Michael's sails all at once. He abandoned his commanding position by the fire to drop into a Louis Quatorze chair that had seen better days. It creaked ominously.

"Don't worry, Michael, darling." Julia's tone was light. "Helena isn't challenging your role as head of the family. She appreciates your desire to help her—don't you, Hel?" She lifted her eyebrows at me.

"I do." I held out a conciliatory hand to my brother.

"Come on, Michael, be friends. I do appreciate what help you can give with the estate—I'm not terribly interested in sheep farming—but I'm not such a ninny as to want you to simply walk in and take over. I may be the smallest person in the family and far from a fighter, but I have *some* pride."

To my surprise, Michael took my fingers into his and gave them the briefest of shakes before dropping my hand as if it burned him. For Michael, that was effusive affection.

The arrival of the children interrupted our moment of sibling closeness. It was always odd to see Michael abandon his dignity and sink to his knees on the carpet, the better to embrace his offspring. It was as if the fact that children *would* be affectionate—given the chance—had the power to break through his aversion to touching and being touched. James, his oldest son and heir, came to stand by his father's side with his arm around his neck in an almost protective stance. The little ones, three-year-old Quentin and toddling Annabelle Alice, giggled and hugged their father.

Annabelle Alice soon deserted Michael for her mother, demanding to be lifted onto Julia's lap. The two boys stayed by their father's side, Quentin chattering about the toy guardsman he had brought down with him. They were a study in contrasts. James resembled his late mother, Cecilia, who had not survived his birth. He was tall and thin for his age, with Michael's coloring but so delicate and pale in the face that his eyes looked huge. Quentin was clearly Julia's child, solid and robust, with his mother's wavy black hair and gray eyes. It was already evident that he was going to be stronger than his older brother.

Michael had married Cecilia just six months after our father's death. Papa had disapproved of the match, saying, quite rightly as it turned out, that Cecilia's health wasn't strong enough for children. I'd had no part in my family's maneuvering to ensure my grief-stricken brother made a more suitable match as soon as possible, but I liked his second wife more than I'd liked the first.

Julia, who had married Michael primarily to escape spinsterhood, had the misfortune to fall desperately in love with him by the end of their first year of marriage. She bore the situation with a good-natured sense of humor that endeared her to me. She put up so cheerfully with Michael's faults that their marriage did indeed seem to be turning out rather well. The lively, affectionate children she had borne him seemed to enliven young James, who unfortunately had his mother's dreamy, rather melancholy disposition.

I moved to sit closer to Julia, the better to play peekaboo with Annabelle Alice. She was an irresistibly mischievous child with strawberry blond curls and eyes of clear gray, like the sea on a misty day. I had always told Justin I was content with our childless existence, but in the presence of Annabelle Alice I had my doubts about how deep that contentment ran. When she climbed into my lap or said, "Auntie, WOOK!" to capture my attention, a strange little flutter of covetousness pierced my heart.

Of course, motherhood had its drawbacks. "She's going to be a real handful when she gets out of the nursery," I said, wincing as Annabelle Alice clouted her mother on the nose. The little girl laughed riotously as Julia's eyes glazed over with tears from the shock of the blow.

Julia turned her daughter around so she couldn't make a second attempt, blinked, and breathed hard for a moment. "I wonder if we can afford a second nursemaid? Especially since," she lowered her voice, "there's going to be another."

"Oh, Julia. Another child already?" I kept my voice low to match hers. "Does Michael know?"

"He hasn't said anything, but I imagine he's guessed. You know Michael. We won't tell the rest of the family just yet. Although if I keep turning green at the sight of food, they'll all know before long. I've been feeling like I'm on a boat on the Channel for about a month and a half." She sighed. "I wish Mama-in-Law were still able to concoct her potions. I felt the same way with Quentin—I'm sure it's a boy this time too, as I didn't feel nearly so rotten with this little lady—and she gave me the most marvelous remedy. Made of common weeds, she said."

"She used to wander around the fields early in the morning and come back with armfuls of thistles and dock leaves." I smiled, but sadness suffused the memory. "I used to go with her, before Daniel." I frowned as a memory worked its way up to the surface. "Thistles—that was it—something to do with thistles if you feel sick. Clearing the liver." I remembered Mama's vibrant voice, deadened by the early morning mist, and the satisfied look on her face as she held up a spiky, gangly plant.

"I don't know if it's my liver that needs clearing, but I'd certainly like to stop feeling this way." Julia bent forward quickly to stop Annabelle Alice from ruining her dress as she slid to the ground, intent on something she'd seen across the room. Monkford, the nursemaid, quickly followed her.

"Perhaps I can take a look through Mama's journals and see if I can find the recipe," I said. "I can remember enough about the basic methods of preparation, I think. Mama kept extremely precise notes about dosages and was always cautious. If you'd trust me, that is." I felt a strange mixture of excitement and dread at the notion of venturing once more along a path I'd long thought to have abandoned.

"Where does she keep her journals?" Julia asked. "I've never seen them."

"They're in her herb room, I think."

"Ah." Julia nodded. "Well, I have a guilty conscience about neglecting that room. You'll have to forgive me in advance of entering. When Michael and I were first married, I was keen to tidy it up, but Mama-in-Law wouldn't let anyone touch it. And as she forgot about it, so did we. Just the other day Michael mentioned he'd like it cleared out. He wants a larger estate office for Brandrick."

"Of course he does," I answered dryly.

"What are you saying about me?" Michael paused in the act of explaining the rules of cricket to his eldest son. Quentin roared around the room waving his toy above his head. Julia was right, they probably already needed a second nursemaid.

"I'm saying you want your Mama's herb room cleared out, dearest. Helena wants to find her journals."

"The whole lot should be thrown out." Michael caught Quentin around the waist and regarded him sternly. "Quentin, it's time to be quiet." He returned his attention to us. "You'd oblige me tremendously by giving me an extra room, you know."

Julia looked at me, and I shrugged. "Well, when asked so nicely, what can I do but oblige my brother? Leave it to me, Michael. Julia's got enough to do."

After all, I thought as I climbed into the brougham to return to Whitcombe, it had been eight years now since Daniel died. Perhaps I'd been wrong to blame myself for being unable to save him. Maybe it was time I took an interest in Mama's work again.

9

A NASCENT VOCATION

J spent Thursday receiving a visit from some old friends of Justin's who came to console me. In the afternoon, I had a most satisfactory interview with Justin's Hastings solicitor, who managed his various properties. It seemed I had enough income to keep Whitcombe House going in whatever style I wished.

Of course with Justin gone, I would not be giving dinner parties or having people to stay other than family, so my expenses would be much reduced. But I had no intention of giving up Whitcombe as Michael had suggested. The truth was that I *liked* my grand baroque house, perched high on its hill overlooking Littleberry, Broadmere, and the marsh between. I was sure I could find a use for all that space.

On Friday, I betook myself to Mama's herb room at Hyrst to see if I could find her journals. I brought Guttridge with me since Guttridge was showing signs of boredom, and that would not do at all. A good lady's maid must be kept happy.

"What a mess." Guttridge stood in the doorway of the herb room and gaped at the cobweb-strewn jumble, lit only by the light filtering through the filthy windows.

"I'd forgotten how bad it was. It's like the Miss Havisham scene in *Great Expectations*."

"I always thought the dowager countess was the most organized of women." Guttridge picked up a cushion lying in the middle of the floor. It had almost certainly come from the drawing room.

"She was. The changes began so gradually we didn't notice them at first. She just seemed a little forgetful. She'd have to make an effort to recall the names of plants, and then she began to forget ordinary, everyday words. But she'd suffered a terrible shock with my father's death, and we all thought she'd eventually recover."

"I had an aunt went that way. She'd go wandering in her nightdress all over Croydon."

"Yes, we had one or two excursions in nightclothes. Everything became disordered somehow. I remember once when the dowager came in from the garden with a huge armful of foxgloves, torn out by their roots and shedding dirt all over the hall carpet. She dropped them on the dining room table, turned around, and went out for a walk. This room gradually became more and more chaotic—everything in the wrong place."

Indeed, the herb room was a page on which the disintegration of Mama's mind was clearly written. It was a jumbled mess of glass beakers, withered plants, torn and strewn pieces of paper, paintbrushes and other painting paraphernalia, and books. Dust was everywhere. The wizened herbs that hung in bunches from hooks in the ceiling were festooned with thick, ropey cobwebs, so smothered in dust that no spider would now want to dwell there. I could hear the rustle of mice in the wainscoting. Michael would do well to bring in a cat or two from the barns on his estate.

"This won't do at all." I used the cushion Guttridge had picked up to clear the dust from a portion of the large marble-topped table that took pride of place in the middle of the room.

"My lady, your dress." Guttridge sounded faintly agonized.

I looked down, noting the smears of dust on my black skirts, and headed to one of the cupboards. Finding an apron on a hook on the inside of the door—at least something was where it was supposed to be—I put it on. Guttridge darted forward and undid the cuffs of my day dress, rolling up the sleeves.

"Why didn't his lordship have this cleaned up long ago?" she asked. "I thought Lady Alice and Lady Annette ran this house better."

"Lord Broadmere did order the servants to tidy up after the dowager countess at first. But she started shouting at them. There were several huge rows when she accused one housemaid or another of stealing from her or hiding her things where she couldn't find them. The staff got terribly upset about it. In the end, Lord and Lady Broadmere decided to leave well alone. Even Lady Alice and Lady Annette agreed it was best left till after Mama was no more."

"Or so far gone, as she is now . . ." Guttridge let the thought trail away into the dusty air.

"Precisely. The time has come."

I adjusted the ties on my apron, a familiar one of Mama's. It gave me an oddly comfortable feeling to be wearing it, as if I were falling back into an old habit. Cold and dusty and disordered as the room was, I felt at home in it. The herb garden outside its long windows had been kept in trim by Hyrst's gardeners. The ginkgo tree Mama had planted, sheltered from the cold by the herb garden's walls, was a cheerful bright yellow with glowing pale orange fruit. I almost felt I could smell the room's long-lost sharp odors of herbs, fruits, and vinegar. I could see Mama as she was, her tall, willowy form bent over her task, her thick blond hair escaping from the net into which she bundled it to keep it out of her way.

I sighed and looked around for the journals. There were many of them, scattered all over the room. Some were on shelves, some in cupboards, and some just lay abandoned on the floor.

I opened them at random as I gathered them up and placed them on the large table. They were part journal, part records of Mama's increasingly confident experiments in herbalism. Some pages were simple lists, others densely written over. Sometimes Mama had annotated them by writing sideways in the margins or even writing over the top of her earlier notes with a different colored ink. There were many drawings of plants and flowers, some simple sketches and others small masterpieces of fine detail.

"That's it," I pronounced after pouncing on the last journal, which was hidden under a pile of rags in one corner of the room. "Guttridge, can you find someone to pack these up and have them taken to Whitcombe House? There are far too many for us to carry."

"I'll have them well dusted first, m'lady." Guttridge's tone was phlegmatic, but her pleasantly plain face was pinched into the expression Nanny always got when we played in the mud as small children. "If you'll forgive me reminding you, we should return to Whitcombe. Mrs. Eason wants to go over next week's menus this afternoon, and luncheon will be ready soon. I'll just go fetch a clothes brush."

~

I was not so confident of my skills, rusty as they were, that I felt I could proceed without at least consulting someone. After considerable thought, I decided Fortier was the obvious candidate. I could use the opportunity to tell him I'd talked to the Hatheralls and ruled out his theory of a mystery assailant.

I sent a note to him at his sister's house, and he duly attended me the next day. He found me surrounded by Mama's notebooks, which were now wiped free of dust.

"I see a light in your eyes that wasn't there before," were his first words after the formalities of greeting were over. "Did you summon me here because you've made progress with your investigations?"

There was a light in his eyes too, and for a moment it flustered me. He looked hopeful, less arrogant, less assured. But I had to dash his hopes then and there.

"I talked with the Hatheralls and found nothing that would confirm your suspicions. Sir Edward has also assured me he's quite certain the jury's verdict was correct. I see no reason not to trust his judgment."

"Ah." To my surprise, Fortier shrugged, the most Gallic gesture I'd yet seen him make. A rueful smile spread across his face. "I don't blame you for not believing me. Nobody else does. I told you when we first met, I struggled with the whole notion of revealing my doubts to you. Alas, it's in my nature to expose what's in my heart and mind. I dislike dissembling. I have at least remained true to myself in this, and perhaps some good will come of it in the end. The delightful good of making your acquaintance is already an unexpected gift." He bent to pat Scotty, who had come to inspect the new arrival. "And yours too, Monsieur."

Now his smile was decidedly charming, and I wasn't sure what to think. Should I allow myself to be bedazzled by this mysterious French physician? Or did he have some ulterior motive behind his flowery words? Being English, I hid behind conventionalities.

"That's very kind of you. In fact, I asked you here for some medical advice." I indicated my mother's notebooks.

"Susan Hatherall, as you know, is *enceinte*, and—well, I know somebody else who is in the same situation without the inconvenient lack of a wedding ring. Susan doesn't look entirely well, and my—my friend has confessed to suffering dreadfully from nausea."

"It's not uncommon for a woman to feel unwell in the first three months or so. Would you like me to prescribe something? It's a little unorthodox to do so without seeing the patient, but I could suggest a very mild remedy if discretion is required. And in Susan's case, discretion is very much required."

"Well," I began and then realized I was starting to feel very foolish and presumptuous. What was it Guttridge had said about depriving medical men of their fees? I cleared my throat. "The thing is, my mother was an herbalist."

"I know. She's still much praised by the poor people of Littleberry."

"And for a while, I assisted her."

"That was laudable of you."

"It was a long time ago. I stopped—I stopped before my marriage. But now it has occurred to me that Mama's journals might contain an efficacious remedy for these women. It might be possible for me to prepare a simple tisane or tincture." I hesitated. "I may need a little guidance at first."

Fortier passed a hand in front of his mouth, and I suspected he was hiding a smile. "Well, Lady Helena, the first order of business would be to ascertain what may be wrong with the women in question. You can't simply begin physicking people to see what happens, especially those who are with child. Some natural remedies are dangerous."

"I do realize that." I sounded as cross as I felt. "I'm sufficiently aware of my inadequacies."

Fortier was bending over the table on which I had piled Mama's journals. The only open volume was the book of watercolors Belming had found. He turned the pages toward him with a flick of one long, finely shaped finger.

"This, for example, is a natural abortifacient—by which I mean it could bring about a miscarriage." He pointed to the page on which Mama had drawn the various parts of a tansy plant.

"I happen to understand the word 'abortifacient,'" I said rather sulkily. "I had absolutely no intention of experimenting on anybody. At this stage, I wish mainly to gain a little knowledge without doing any harm."

He grinned. "So now we ascertain the reason for the light in your eyes. It was not investigatory zeal, but the spark of a nascent vocation."

"You know, I'm sufficiently accustomed to my family treating me like a child, but I'd rather not hear it from you."

His eyes widened, and he placed a hand on his heart.

"I beg your forgiveness, Lady Helena. I did not intend any offense. I'm sincerely glad to see you taking an interest in the world around you after your sad loss. If you need my help or advice, you only have to ask."

"Hmph. Well, to begin with, I remember my mother telling me that thistles are good for some types of nausea. Does this mean anything to you?"

He frowned. "If you mean milk thistle, that's a very good example of a little knowledge being a dangerous thing. Milk thistle is an excellent remedy for the nausea consequent upon over-imbibing. I would not, however, recommend giving it to a woman in a delicate condition."

"Oh." Well, I had been right to feel foolish and presumptuous. Why did I even think I could follow in Mama's footsteps?

"Now I've made you feel foolish." Fortier's tone was gentle.

It annoyed me that he'd apparently read my thoughts. I

drew myself up to my full height, a good four inches shorter than I'd like it to be.

"You've made me feel I was right to consult you."

His eyes crinkled. "Well, at least you're brave enough to admit you're wrong. There are several innocuous remedies you could give to your friend. A preparation of ginger root or perhaps some raspberry leaf tea; peppermint or anise; even a little lemon juice . . . I will write you a list of ingredients with which you may experiment at will. And if you find anything in your mother's notebooks that you think could be useful, do ask me about it. My expertise, such as it is, is at your entire disposal."

"Thank you. I will swallow my pride for the sake of not poisoning my friends and accept that in this instance I may need a man's help."

"Nothing to do with me being a man." He glanced over the journals again. "The dowager countess, for example, was clearly an excellent herbalist. It's more a matter of opportunity for study. I became interested in the medical arts at the age of fifteen and was afforded every opportunity to study by my father, who paid for some of the best tuition in Europe. He sent me to Paris when I was sixteen. While I was still a smooth-cheeked lad, I received a most interesting education in treating battle wounds, epidemics, and weaknesses of all kinds resulting from starvation. You've heard of the Siege of Paris, I take it?"

"Of course I have." The conflict between the French and the Prussians had been a favorite topic of conversation in '71, and Littleberry had taken in a few dozen refugees. It was the same year Mama had befriended Susan Hatherall, and I remembered it well.

Fortier smiled. "I was there, and it's how I got my own grounding in herb lore. Beldames who understood the properties of plants were in great demand in a city where nothing could be obtained from outside. I learned a great many things from women in all walks of life, both medicinal and culinary. Have you ever eaten flower fritters?"

I shook my head, laughing. "I can't say I have."

"They're better than you'd think. I have fond memories of a certain Madame Durand. She was seventy-five and appallingly vulgar, but she managed to coax more food and medicinal plants out of her little plot than I would have believed possible. What's more, she hid it so well from view that nothing was ever requisitioned by the army. Her fritter recipe was used in some of the finest restaurants in Paris— alongside cat, rat, dog, and exotic animals from the Paris Zoo. On Sundays, she would give me a dish of the sweetest radishes I have ever tasted, with a fresh bread roll and a pat of butter. I was a growing lad still, and my mouth would begin to water when I saw her house. She taught me a great deal."

"So you've been practicing medicine for—how many years?" I began to realize there was more to Monsieur Fortier than what I saw on the surface.

He smiled. "Eleven, if you count my baptism of fire in Paris as a beginning—and I do. The day I opened the flesh of a man's neck to retrieve a bullet was the day I passed from student to doctor, in my estimation. He lived too."

I shook my head ruefully. "I'm ashamed of my own ignorance."

Fortier took my hand in his for a brief moment, squeezing it gently before letting go. "Don't be. There are so many intelligent, beautiful, and resourceful women in this English countryside forced to waste their intelligence, beauty, and resourcefulness on entertaining their husband's friends and running their households."

And with how many of those intelligent, beautiful, and resourceful women was Fortier acquainted? I wondered. I was sure the heat that mounted to my cheeks was annoyance at my own susceptibility to the man's charms.

"I'm sorry I've disappointed you as an investigator," was all I could find to say.

"You have not disappointed me in any respect."

He turned away with a brief, sidelong glance as he said this, as if he too were a little embarrassed. He turned the thick pages of Mama's sketchbook, at first in a casual manner but then with more interest. For two minutes or so, the only sound in the room was the soft sigh of the paper.

"How odd." Fortier spoke at last. "Every plant in this book is poisonous. Did the dowager countess have an especial interest in poisons?"

I peered around Fortier at the book, which was open in the middle. The glorious purple-blue of a monkshood flower was reproduced on a large scale on one side, the spotted pink of a foxglove blossom on the other, with assorted drawings of the whole plant and its various parts carefully arranged on the page. A neat list of each plant's medicinal uses formed a column beside each flower drawing.

"She was certainly fascinated by what she called the 'powerful plants,'" I said. "In the years before her illness began, she treated some serious conditions with great success." I frowned. "I remember something else. When she started to become vague in her memory, she wrote to an herbalist she knew in London and had her more dangerous extracts sent to him. She said she was afraid of causing harm by mistake and that she trusted nobody else with such fearful substances."

Fortier nodded, his eyes on the pages in front of him. "A sound and far-thinking decision."

"She also taught us not to touch the plants in her herb garden unless absolutely necessary," I added. "Before her illness, my mother had a tremendously well-ordered mind. I think Michael—Lord Broadmere—gets his mania for logic from her, but she never rode roughshod over people the way he does. She cared for everyone. I don't think there was a single person for miles around she didn't know something about. She had a tremendous sense of fairness and a need to know that things were done right. That, also, is reflected in Michael."

Fortier closed the book and turned to me. "I think I would have liked her. I—"

But whatever he was going to say was interrupted by the advent of a footman with a message from Mrs. Eason. Scotty, who had been asleep by the fire while we talked, gave a short bark of welcome. He went to inspect the man's silver-buckled shoes, the white plume of his tail wagging hopefully. Footmen, he knew, often carried food.

I surreptitiously consulted the clock. As I thought, twenty minutes had passed. That would be Guttridge's doing. Fortier and I had been talking in Whitcombe's large library with the doors wide open, but my lady's maid regarded it as part of her job to ensure I was interrupted after twenty minutes of any conversation alone with a man under the age of sixty. I had been married and did not strictly need a chaperone, but gossiping tongues could still wag if I wasn't careful.

Fortier understood the conventions as well as I did despite his complete lack of any tendency to stand on ceremony. He seemed perfectly comfortable at Whitcombe, unlike most professional men who tended to find the house's baroque grandeur intimidating. He made his good-byes in a pleasant, easy manner and departed, leaving me to reflect that he had taken his disappointment over my investigations, or lack thereof, very well. I hoped we were done with any and all accusations of foul play.

10

THE SORT THAT CAN'T BE TRUSTED

*F*ortier's list proved useful. Mrs. Eason readily produced dried ginger root, a serviceable lemon, and some honey from Whitcombe's large pantry. I set to work with a pleasing sense of purpose. My presence in the kitchen occasioned some gawping and awkwardness until Mrs. Foster, our cook, sent maids and boot boys scurrying with a few well-chosen words.

"I might have to set up my own herb room," I told my nephew Thomas when he came to tea. "With a paraffin stove and a shiny copper kettle like Mama's." I wrinkled my brow. "Come to that, I could use Mama's."

"You could use any and all of the contents of the herb room," Thomas suggested. "I'm sure Uncle Michael wouldn't care."

"Oh, he'd be glad to get rid of it all. Julia's already given me carte blanche to clear out the room."

"Then why not d-do it?" Thomas brooded over the sandwiches with a distinctly hungry air, selecting four to place on his small plate. "It's good for you to have something to d-do."

"I feel I have plenty to do, but I appreciate the thought." I cut myself a slice of Victoria sponge.

"Do you f-feel all right?" Thomas asked. "The whole grief thing, I mean. I'm sorry if I'm putting it clumsily."

"You're striking exactly the right note. Well, I still feel grief, of course. I still turn around in my chair sometimes to ask Justin a question. I still find it odd to see only one table setting when I'm dining alone. I find myself crying sometimes because I've thought of Justin and he isn't there."

Thomas nodded. "Like a h-hole in the middle of your life."

"Precisely. But it's not the first hole that's been torn in my heart. I learned long ago that death is part of life and that I can survive loss, however much it hurts."

"A very philosophical s-stance, Auntie." Thomas looked down at his empty plate.

"Darling boy, do take one of everything if you're hungry. Have seconds and thirds and fourths. You don't have to be polite for me. But don't give anything more to Scotty." I eyed my dog, who was lying at Thomas's feet, trying to look unconcerned. "Unlike you, he'll get fat."

Thomas grinned and duly crammed a large slice of sponge, a teacake, and a small tower of sandwiches onto his plate. I nibbled sedately at my cake, watching him dispose of the food in short order.

"That's better." He put down the plate and picked up his teacup with a sigh of satisfaction. "Although I might have some more of those teacakes. So succoring a sick friend is taking you out of yourself?"

"It is." I hadn't told him about Julia's condition, so I had to deflect his questions. "I must do something after all. You see this?"

I picked up the journal that had been lying on the table next to my chair and showed it to Thomas.

"It's a notebook."

"Very observant. It is in fact the very earliest notebook of Mama's that I have in my possession. I removed them from Hyrst a few days ago, and Guttridge has sorted them in chronological order. This one dates from when your mother was a small child and my own birth was many years away. It's odd, isn't it, that we seem to have come into the world in groups, several years apart? Your mother must have been born a year or two after my parents married."

"Sixteen or seventeen months after, I believe. Safely within the confines of wedlock."

"I should think so, and don't be vulgar. Well, after Gerry there's a seven-year gap before the twins. Then four children in quick succession—the twins, of course, but also Blanche and Odelia. Then ten years before Michael and I were born."

"It's entirely possible there were children in between." Thomas looked interested. "Miscarriages, s-stillbirths, and so on." He stopped, blushing. "Am I allowed to mention such things to a lady?"

I rolled my eyes. "I'm country bred, Thomas dear, not one of those fainting London women. I can stand to hear the word 'miscarriage.'"

"Good. Or there were children who died, perhaps."

"Surely not. We would have known about them because our parents would have visited their graves."

"No living children, then. I doubt G-Grandmama would have told you if she'd had miscarriages. L-Ladies don't discuss such things, even in the country." He wrinkled his nose at me.

"That's true," I conceded. "Mama was never one to complain or make a fuss. Poor thing, now all her bad memories are locked away in her head, and she can never tell anyone."

"I hope she doesn't have too many. She and Grandpapa doted on each other, didn't they?"

"In the way of old married couples—with little outward show." I looked at the journal again, smiling. "Here Mama's mostly writing about her early fascination with herbs. It all started when she began talking to the gardeners at Hyrst. One of them explained you could make a soothing salve with the petals of the calendulas he was setting out. She talks about going to the bookseller in Littleberry and ordering a book about salves. Perhaps her hands were dry."

"Of such a small beginning is a passion born."

"A purpose," I mused. "A life lived with purpose. Mama used to say I was her last hope for drumming the notion of a purpose in life into her girls."

"She succeeded with some of the others though. Look at the twins, always doing something useful. And Auntie O lives for her art, spurning all offers of marriage. Of which I'm sure she's had many."

"Your mother and Blanche were conventional enough to make good marriages." I smiled. "Even if your father's in the wine trade, his family is so eminently old and respectable—and Blanche outshone us all."

Thomas shrugged. "You made a g-good marriage too."

"I can't help feeling I let Mama down somehow. I let my grief over Daniel overwhelm me and rob me of all ambition, all energy. I became an empty girl who thought of nothing. Even when the worst of my sadness had passed, I idled my days away and drifted into marriage."

"Did Grandmama intend you for a b-bluestocking, then?"

"She wanted me to be a healer, like her. I must have been a disappointment. And now my husband has gone and with him my purpose in life. I feel useless, Thomas. I suspect Mama felt the same way as a young bride, but she was a countess and obliged to play a role in the county. I don't even have that."

Thomas's mouth twisted. "At least you're free to decide what you want to do next. You don't have to clerk for your father."

"Is it really so bad?"

"I'm an embarrassment to the old m-man." Thomas's handsome face flushed with color again. "I suppose it's nice of him to employ me, but I'm no use. I c-can't dash around like he does, jumping in and out of carts to inspect the merchandise. I can't even open a bottle easily. I have someone else do it to spare Father the embarrassment of watching his crippled son struggle. I don't write well. I suspect I wasn't born to write with my left hand, and I smear the ink over the ledgers. I've tried hard, Auntie Helena, for four years. I've had enough."

I looked at my nephew closely. "You have something else in mind, don't you?"

"I want to go into the ch-church." Thomas looked defiant. "It makes sense. As a v-vicar, I could do some good in a small way in some remote parish. I shan't need much to live on unless I marry. And I'm not the b-best of marriage prospects."

"Aren't you?" I murmured, looking at his beautiful face. Privately, I thought my handsome, intelligent, kind nephew would make an excellent catch—but he was right, perhaps not among the county gentry whose lives revolved around hunting, shooting, and other active pursuits. A nice church mouse might be just the thing.

But there was one question that had to be asked. "Is this a vocation? I've heard that loving God is something of a prerequisite for a priest. Even in the most worldly corners of the Church of England."

Thomas frowned. "I'll admit I might have some making

up with God to do. I've been pretty angry with Him. The rector says faith's a slippery business at the best of times and that if I can find my way back to God, I'll stick right enough."

"That's clever of the rector. So what do you need to do?"

"That's the difficult part. I'll need to go to university if I want to be ordained. I can p-prep for the entrance exams under my own steam—I can afford to pay a Latin tutor—but Papa will have to cough up my university fees."

"And why shouldn't he?" I asked. "Your father's a reasonable man."

Thomas used his good arm to push himself to his feet and lurched toward the window. He stared at the sudden December squall of icy rain that was spattering the panes of glass.

"It's going to look like petty jealousy, isn't it?" He sounded despondent. "Because Petey's being made ready for school. I don't want P-Papa to think I'm behaving like a girl who wants the same dress as her sister."

The analogy made me smile, but I didn't want to laugh at Thomas. I rose and went to stand beside him. "If Ned refuses to pay, tell him I will. His pride won't let him accept that. And if by some remote chance it does, I *will* pay. After all, I've no son and plenty of money. Justin would have said the same thing."

"I didn't come here to ask for money."

"Of course you didn't. But speaking as one useless person to another, I think we should help each other find our vocations. You give me hope for my own future."

I felt the weight of Thomas's good arm around my shoulders, a solid comfort.

"Very well, Auntie," he said with mock meekness, giving me a quick peck on the cheek. "You've always been on my side. To t-tell the truth, I've already started working with the Latin tutor."

"So your mind is made up."

"All but the difficult part of telling my parents. I tell you what—if I promise to take steps to change my life, will you promise to work on finding your vocation and not just let this family push you into another marriage? This is your chance—perhaps your only chance—to make your own decisions. You were a good wife to Uncle Justin, but fate—or God —has decreed you'll have some t-time to yourself. Use it wisely."

~

Evensong was my favorite church service, and St. Michael's in Littleberry had an excellent choir. I decided by the second week of December that I could decently put in an appearance, suitably veiled. I took Guttridge with me, both of us well wrapped up against the damp cold.

To my surprise, on the way out a familiar voice accosted me.

"It's good to see you here, Lady Helena." Monsieur Fortier was smartly and soberly dressed, a picture of respectability in his silk hat and spats.

"It's astonishing to see *you* here. I thought you were a Catholic, being French."

"My father began attending a Protestant church five years after we came to England. To the horror of our relatives."

"But I've never seen you at evensong before."

"Have you not?" His lips twitched. "Well, we sit somewhat farther back." His eyes sought the Scott-De Quincy family pew. Although not boxed off as happened in so many churches, it was nonetheless reserved for us alone. We had sat directly under the pulpit for the last hundred years, watched over by the banner that proclaimed the church's loyalty to the Crown.

"Are you a Republican, Monsieur Fortier?"

"I'm not a monarchist, certainly. France is better off without the weight of a useless, expensive top tier of society."

"Like us?" Fortier no doubt couldn't see my expression behind my heavy veil, but I was sure he could hear the ice in my voice.

"England has at least espoused some measure of reform. I don't mean to insult you, Lady Helena. What I meant to say was that most Frenchmen are now sufficiently accustomed to the way things are."

I decided to let the matter drop. It wasn't good manners to stand in the transept of one's church arguing politics with a Frenchman. Guttridge stood behind me and slightly to one side, ostensibly not listening but of course a party to every word.

"How is your patient?" Fortier asked.

"My—? Oh, my patient. She's feeling rather better."

"And Susan Hatherall?"

"I haven't seen her lately."

Farmer Hatherall had greeted me as I'd slipped into the family pew. In his Sunday clothes, he looked as distinguished as any man in Littleberry, with nothing of the farmer about him. Why some widow hadn't snapped him up was a mystery to me.

A young woman who'd been talking to her friends now swept past us. She bobbed a little curtsey as she passed me, but her eyes were on Fortier, who smiled and lifted his hat. The young woman headed for the door, swaying her hips in a manner that indicated her mind was perhaps not entirely on the evening's service. Behind me, I heard Guttridge's "hmph" of derision.

"I was thinking of setting up my own workroom," I said to Fortier, keeping a tight rein on my desire to ask him who the young woman was. "I can bring my mother's equipment and so on over from Hyrst."

"A very commendable hobby, Lady Helena."

That stung. "It's not intended as a hobby. I wish to learn some skills that will be useful to the people around me."

His thick black eyebrows rose. "I apologize again. I seem to have developed a skill for saying the wrong thing this evening. And as always, I will be delighted to help you in any way I can."

He bowed and turned in the direction of a dark-haired woman I thought was his sister. She was accompanied by a tall man—no doubt her husband, the pottery owner Quinn Dermody.

"Hmph," Guttridge said again as we climbed into our carriage.

"Who was the girl?"

"Nobody. A shopkeeper's daughter. Engaged to be married, and her making eyes at the Frenchman."

"He's a good-looking man." I felt a rush of relief at the news that the young woman was engaged, followed by guilt that I felt relief.

"He's a rum 'un. And you heard what he said about useless and expensive. His sort would murder us in our beds, the servants along with the masters."

I put a steadying hand on the carriage's window frame and leaned backward as the horses made their careful way down the steep street. "He doesn't look like a revolutionary."

"Don't you be taken in, my lady. His sort can't be trusted."

~

Despite Fortier's disparaging use of the word "hobby," I rose early the next morning in an optimistic mood. I'd read some more of Mama's first journal before falling asleep, and her fascination with her new interest was catching.

When she'd written that journal, she'd been younger than I was now. Born late into the family, I had no recollection of Mama as a young woman. My memories of her began with the woman of almost fifty, the countess, the mother of seven children, the grandmother.

Those memories were strong when I awoke. Perhaps I'd been dreaming of her. I remembered walking along Littleberry's narrow, cobbled streets, seeing people greet Mama with respect and even effusiveness, making way for us as we proceeded. When she entered a room, those already in it would become more alert, as if something had changed in the air. The servants at Hyrst picked up the pace of their work as she passed by. Energy, power, sheer force of will— that was the Mama I remembered, a persona fully formed.

Reading the story of her formative years felt like a wonderful privilege. This journal was the first of many. Through them, I could recapture the vibrant, beautiful creature who had been the Countess of Broadmere. I could keep that memory alive against the reality of the sad, vague, often angry woman who rarely ventured outside her suite of rooms at Hyrst.

I practically leapt out of bed and sang as I lathered up my favorite rose-and-geranium soap. Lists, of course there must be lists. I would visit Hyrst with my own notebook in hand and make a long list of all the equipment I could use for my workroom. I'd talk to the gardener about taking cuttings and divisions of the plants in Mama's herb garden. The weather was so mild down here by the coast that some of that work could be done even now. I'd speak to my own head gardener about the best site for my herb garden. I'd make a list of the steps that would have to be taken come the spring.

I had just finished the best-tasting breakfast I'd eaten for some time when the footman announced the arrival of my sisters Alice and Annette.

"Ally! Netty! What are you doing here?"

My twin siblings rarely graced Whitcombe House with their presence. Excellent organizers, they were much in demand on committees and charity boards in Littleberry and Broadmere. Even when they were at home, I almost never saw them. They were so absorbed by their own concerns that they took most of their meals by themselves. They seemed to have no need whatsoever for friends. They showed little inclination even for the company of their siblings. They were whole, complete, in a way few married couples ever were.

Today they wore identical mourning of practical bombazine. A rather old-fashioned fringe of elongated jet beads made a faint tinkling sound as they moved. I thought it might be their second mourning for Papa made over, as the twins were notoriously thrifty. Their earnest, heart-shaped faces were dominated by their large, round, blue-gray eyes, whose otherworldly quality was magnified by the mirror effect of seeing them side by side.

"We have some news you won't like."

The twin who'd spoken kissed me on one cheek, and the other one saluted me in identical fashion on the other side. Their lips were cold and dry. Having greeted me, they seated themselves on the sofa in my morning room with the air of two judges about to render a verdict. Scotty settled at their feet like a small heraldic lion on a crusader's tombstone.

"We don't like listening to gossip," the other twin said and added helpfully, "Do we, Ally?"

"You know we don't like gossip, Baby, dear," said Alice. "But we thought it was *very important* we impart this particular piece of news to you. It concerns a person you have permitted to enter Whitcombe on more than one occasion. We feel you must be warned."

"After all, your position—"

"—is a delicate one," Alice continued smoothly, picking up Annette's interjection as if it hadn't happened.

"—is a *prominent* one in this county," Annette said as if Alice hadn't spoken. "In a year or two, God willing, you will cast off your widow's weeds and be once more the happy beloved of some fortunate man."

"Not ever relinquishing your sorrow for dear Justin, of course." Alice leaned forward, her hands clasped in her lap.

"Not ever," echoed Annette.

"So you must be *careful*—"

"—of the company you keep—"

"—and *not* allow such persons to accost you at church."

"Accost—?" I was puzzled, and then my mind cleared. Oh, how quickly the gossips of Littleberry worked. "Do you mean Monsieur Fortier?"

"The very same. The *Frenchman*." Alice clutched at her sister with one hand, peering solemnly into my face.

"Precisely. The physician," Annette said at the same time.

I shook my head, smiling. "I've spent perhaps two hours with him, all told, in my entire life. He was Justin's physician, not mine. And now that we're acquainted, it's hardly surprising he'd take a moment to greet me at church. Many people do."

Alice's eyes narrowed. "The devil is full of subtlety and mischief."

I stared at her. "That's ridiculous. Unless you've come to tell me he's done something alarming, I'll put your lapse of charity down to concern for me. I have no intention of cultivating Monsieur Fortier's acquaintance beyond a mere casual contact."

"But he *has* done something alarming." Alice sounded triumphant. "He has brought disgrace down on the head of a most respectable man, one closely connected to you—"

"—in short, your tenant at Dene Farm."

"Disgrace? Farmer Hatherall?" My first thought was that it must have something to do with the day of Justin's death. Had Fortier accused the farmer of some kind of misconduct? Of lying? More importantly, had he done so without even telling me first?

"Disgrace." Alice once more took the lead. "You will find it shocking, Baby, dear, to learn that Susan Hatherall is with child, and no father in sight. It was Mrs. Bearcroft of the Moral Improvement Society who found it out. She had a quiet word with Farmer Hatherall, and he quite broke down, poor man, right in the church vestry."

"When was that?"

"Yesterday, after evensong."

Soon after I had left, then. I supposed Mrs. Bearcroft had been lurking, waiting for the right moment to do her mischief.

"You wouldn't think these stolid men of the earth could suffer from nervous prostration, would you?" Annette raised her eyes to the ceiling. "But it took the combined efforts of the rector, the verger, and of course Mrs. Bearcroft to calm him down."

"He was perfectly distraught, from what we heard," said Alice. "Of course, he must have known the truth would come out. It's very hard to hide such a catastrophe in a small town like Littleberry."

Given that the gossips and busybodies in Littleberry probably outnumbered the more generously minded towns-people, it certainly was. At that moment, I felt sorry for Susan.

"But what does Monsieur Fortier have to do with all this?" Had Fortier tried to help the farmer and somehow made things worse?

"Why, he's the father of the child, of course," said Alice. "The young woman confessed the whole thing."

For a moment, I was struck utterly dumb. I stared at my sisters, who sat back on their sofa with an air of satisfaction at having imparted the news to me. When I found my voice, it came out as a hoarse squeak.

"*Susan* said that?"

Scotty yipped at the sound of my voice and deserted my sisters to run to me. I didn't normally treat him as a lapdog, but now I picked him up, seeking the comfort of his warm body and wiry coat.

Annette laced her fingers together. "Not at first. Mrs. Bearcroft insisted the rector accompany her straight to Dene Farm while the verger and a curate stayed with Farmer Hatherall. They found the young woman at her darning and immediately confirmed the truth of her condition."

"She was silent for a long time," Alice said. "But Mrs. Bearcroft cannot be withstood."

I bet she can't, was my thought. But I kept my own counsel and waited to see what would come next. I scratched Scotty behind the ears, noting mechanically that he needed a bath.

"Susan confessed she had fallen victim to the Frenchman's charms." Annette sighed. "We live in a broken world of sin and sorrow, don't we? Ally and I are inclined to forgive the young woman."

"We certainly are," said Alice. "We're sure the French physician is a most persuasive and insinuating man—"

"—and a poor, simple farmer's daughter was no match for his wiles."

"She will have to go to the workhouse," Alice said lugubriously.

"No!" I stood up, putting Scotty down on the carpet. My sisters' expressions changed to surprise.

"Her father is willing to keep her until the baby is born, and her sister, Maggie, will take the child as her own," I said.

I realized my fists were clenched and I was trembling slightly. Did I even believe the story about Fortier? I didn't think I did—I knew I didn't want to—but then I remembered the girl in the church.

"You knew about it!" cried Alice and Annette at exactly the same time.

"And what if I did?" I held my head up high. "The Hatheralls are my tenants. What, pray, does Monsieur Fortier say in answer to these accusations? Has he been informed?"

Was he still there when those accusations were made, I wondered? Were they delivered in front of his sister and brother-in-law?

My sisters ignored my question. They looked at each other the way they often did, seeming to communicate without words. Annette gave a minute shake of her head and turned back to me.

"The unpleasant discovery that you knew of Susan Hatherall's condition causes us much grief, Baby."

"We are concerned your friendship with the Frenchman is even deeper than we feared. We will have to talk with Michael about this."

"Don't be silly," I said, exasperated, although I knew Michael would soon be informed and would no doubt have something to say on the subject. "Michael will be about as useful as the Tsar of Russia. The first order of business is to give Monsieur Fortier the opportunity to make a public refutation of Susan's claims. If Farmer Hatherall can no longer cope with his daughter's disgrace, I'm quite happy to give her a bed in the servants' quarters here while we work out what to do next. I won't have her go to the workhouse."

Again I had the sense that my sisters were communicating with each other by thought alone. They both rose to their feet. As they were taller than me, I felt very much outnumbered, but I stood my ground.

"If you like, I'll go with you to talk with Monsieur Fortier," I said. "We can go to the Dermody house—it's possible he hasn't started his day's work yet. Just give me a few minutes to get ready."

"But he won't be there. Quite apart from the fact that a newly bereaved widow cannot possibly—"

"Why won't he be there?" I interrupted.

"He's not in Littleberry."

"Then we can go to the Dermody house and inquire when he'll be back. I don't see why I shouldn't be able to do that, mourning or no mourning. At least we can find out whether he even knows about the accusation, the poor man. Perhaps we should also call on Mrs. Bearcroft and ensure malicious gossip doesn't spread until the facts have been ascertained. And talk to Farmer Hatherall to see if *he* thinks Fortier is the father of Susan's child. At least then when Monsieur Fortier returns, we won't have been guilty of failing to find out the truth—"

"But he isn't going to return." Alice held up a hand to stem the flow of my words.

"What do you mean?" I was completely at a loss.

"Of *course* someone went to the Dermody house to find him, to give him a chance to respond." Alice sounded exasperated. "But his sister said he was gone to Eastbourne, and would they come back in the morning."

"And then this morning she said he was gone altogether. To Dieppe on the *Ousil*, and she could not say when or even if he would return. She would not reveal the nature of his business."

"And that confirms his guilt entirely." Alice began talking the second Annette stopped to draw breath. "All the town is talking about it. And your name has been mentioned, more than once, because the Frenchman has been seen talking to you, and *everyone* knows he visited Whitcombe."

I clenched my jaw but said nothing. I had grown up in the knowledge that everything our family did was of interest in Littleberry, but such close scrutiny was very trying. And I was furious with Fortier. How dare he disappear just at the moment when he needed to prove—or at least proclaim—his innocence? If he *was* innocent.

Well, there was certainly one way to find out.

11

A GENEROUS OFFER

"This isn't a formal call," I said as soon as Ruby, the Hatheralls' servant, opened their front door, releasing a strong smell of baking. "Is the farmer home?"

"No, m'lady." Ruby was cheerful and friendly, as always, but her eyes were wary. She knew what my business was.

"Good. I'd like to speak with Miss Hatherall." I looked down at my boots. "I'm too muddy for the parlor. Would you do me the favor of letting me into the back garden?"

Ruby's eyes widened slightly, but she led me to the side of the house and unlatched a gate hidden between two tall hedges.

"If you'll just wait a moment, m'lady, I'll fetch her directly."

I glanced up at the hill behind the farmhouse before I slipped inside the garden. Up there was Guttridge, waiting for me in the cemetery. I had ostensibly gone out to visit Justin's grave. I had indeed laid the wreath my gardener had prepared that morning on the mound of clay, now settled a little but still nastily raw-looking. By my instructions, the grave was kept in good order daily, with fresh flowers or greenery depending on what was growing in the green-houses or conservatory. Today it was a wreath of shining green bay leaves decorated with sprigs of bright-berried holly and pure white hellebores.

I had left the cemetery via the lower lychgate and under-taken the slippery descent down to the lane that led from Littleberry to Dene Farm, using an old walking stick of Justin's that I'd thought to bring with me for balance. I leaned on that stick now, enjoying its solidity under my fingers. Its chased silver cap was worn by years of the pressure of Justin's hand, its ebony shaft nicked and dented by much use.

I could hear the two women arguing inside the house, Ruby's voice soothing and persuasive. I didn't have to wait long until Susan emerged, brushing flour off her apron. She approached me with the air of a convicted prisoner facing the executioner. Her hair was speckled with white here and there, as if she'd been pounding the dough so hard that flour had flown into the air. Her skin was pasty, and a rash of pimples had broken out on her forehead. Her eyes, shadowed before, now looked heavy and almost bruised.

"I brought you something." I held out a glass jar containing a creamy substance. "It's to soothe your hands— forgive me, but they look very dry and sore. I had my maid buy it from the apothecary in Littleberry to see what it should look like—I've a mind to make some of my own. In the meantime, I'd like you to have it."

She unscrewed the lid and sniffed suspiciously at the ointment. "Looks like something old Lady Broadmere would make."

"You rub it in like this." Ignoring the disrespectful refer-ence to my mother, I took the jar out of her grasp and dipped my finger into the pleasant-smelling substance. Taking her wrist, I gently rubbed a little of the cream into the back of her hand with a circular motion.

After a few seconds, she withdrew her hand, but gently. "Why are you being so nice to me?" she asked. "I thought . . ."

"That I was coming to scold you for telling lies about Monsieur Fortier? I'm not, but you must set the record straight. It's so unfair to him. And I would like to make you an offer of employment."

"Employment?" Now she sounded completely incredulous.

"At Whitcombe, in my workroom. Or at least the workroom I plan to set up. I've a mind to learn the herbalist's art after all."

"Learn it again." Her voice was flat. "You used to know quite a lot."

"Yes, I did. But I've forgotten it. I think I made a deliberate effort to forget it all back then."

"When you went all strange after your cousin died. I remember." She hesitated for a few moments, then burst out: "I was glad."

"Glad?"

"Because her ladyship wanted me by her all the time after you stopped helping. And I wanted to be with her ladyship. I would do *anything* for her ladyship." Her hands clutched at her skirts as if she were trying to communicate the earnestness of her statement.

"Why don't you go and see her, then? She'll have forgotten her . . . outburst . . . a long time ago."

Susan shook her head slowly. "No, I won't go to Hyrst. But I don't understand why you want me, of all people."

"I need someone who's used to rough work and doesn't mind getting her hands dirty, but also knows about indoor tasks—cooking and the like. I know you don't do much farm work, but your hands say you work hard. And then there's the years you spent with my mother. Haven't you ever been tempted to practice the skills you learned from her? I'm sure some of it must have remained with you."

She looked sulky. "Father said I shouldn't. He said she didn't do me any good, filling my head with recipes for potions when I should be learning to be a good plain cook. He said that being his housekeeper was the right place for me, not up in the big house. He wouldn't like me going to Whitcombe."

"He'd let you if I asked him."

"But *why?*" She almost shouted, as if she were frustrated at me.

"Because I think you must be desperately unhappy. I think you accused Monsieur Fortier of fathering your child because you're protecting someone else—a married man, perhaps. I'm not going to ask you who it is."

She stuck her tongue into her cheek, considering my words. "Do you like him? The Frenchie?"

"I . . . neither like nor dislike him, Susan. My late husband liked him and trusted him, and he's not here to speak for himself. I suppose I feel I must be as fair as possible to him and to his family by giving him the benefit of the doubt. Why did you name him in particular?"

She hesitated, licking dry lips as she clearly considered where the greater risk lay—in telling the truth or not. By now, I was quite convinced she had been lying about Fortier. My initial affirmation had been in the nature of an arrow shot into the air to see how Susan reacted; but the fact that she had not vehemently insisted Fortier was indeed her child's father had confirmed my instinct.

At last, Susan drew a deep breath. "He's a foreigner and a bachelor. That means he can move elsewhere if there's scandal. A little will rub off on his family to be sure, but that Mr. Dermody don't care two groats for anyone else's opinion. Nobody will stand against him once his temper's up. And that Frenchman, he's got all sorts of tales around him already —one more won't hurt him all that much. I couldn't believe my luck when I heard he'd gone away. Maybe he'll stay gone."

"It's wrong, Susan. Wrong to accuse a man of something he hasn't done, especially something as serious as getting a woman in the family way." I could hear the anger in my voice. The calculation Susan had just expounded to me reminded me strongly of why I had disliked her as a child. She had always been fond of using other people for her own benefit.

"Wrong?" Susan grinned. "There's a deal wrong in the world, m'lady. Sometimes you have to choose the lesser of two evils, as Father says."

I didn't like that either, but I was determined to stick with my initial purpose. "If you came to Whitcombe, I'd let you have two half days as well as Sundays so you can see your child."

To my astonishment, Susan's face turned blotchy as tears rose in her eyes and spilled down her pale cheeks. "I don't *want* to see it," she shouted. "I wouldn't have Maggie take it, only she says she and Bert are talking about emigrating to Canada and I'll never have to see it again. It's a monster, and I hate it. If your ma still knew the top of her head from the sole of her foot, I'd ask her for a potion to get rid of it. I'd like to throw it in the river and watch it drown."

I raised my hands in a defensive gesture, as if to ward off Susan's words, feeling the horror of them slide down my spine.

"Don't say such terrible things."

"I'll say what I want. It's ruined everything." She sniffed loudly and wiped her nose on a corner of her apron.

"You're more fortunate than most women in your position," I said, and I could hear the hardness in my voice. "Your father won't banish you from his sight, and your sister will take the child. For heaven's sake, Susan, what more could you want?"

My question hung in the air for a long moment, accompanied by the clucking of hens from the run on one side of the farm's spacious garden. Susan was indeed more fortunate than most. I had never realized how pleasant Dene Farm really was.

"I want *more*," Susan said at length, the hunger in her voice evoking a strong memory of the little girl who always wanted a bigger piece of cake than anyone else's.

"Well, you won't get it by falsely accusing Monsieur Fortier." Realizing how harsh I sounded, I modulated my tone. "Susan, I'm offering you a chance to improve your lot. Working at Whitcombe will teach you far more than you'll learn here at the farm. I know it seems strange that I want to help you, but I feel my family's responsible for your discontent with life. If you work hard, I'll make sure you're given opportunities to suit your abilities. I and my family have a vast acquaintance in the county, in London, even abroad. We can find a place for you where nobody will know about the baby, where you can start again as a woman with valuable skills."

I could feel myself embroidering a wonderful future for Susan in my mind. Despite my personal dislike of her, I could help her, just as I could help Thomas. I had the means to do so. By helping others at the same time as I pursued my own vocation, I knew I could, in the end, erase the feeling of uselessness that so often assailed me since Justin's death.

And perhaps, just perhaps, she might change her mind about the child once she'd given birth to it. I could encourage her to think kindly of the poor little mite. I would welcome it into Whitcombe House and ensure all of my people welcomed it too. I hated to think any child could be rejected by its mother in this way. It, too, was one of my people, and I determined then and there to help it as much as I was able.

"But there's a condition," I said as Susan nodded her head, unspeaking, in response to my words. "You must let me bring Mrs. Bearcroft and have her hear you retract your accusation. This must be done as soon as possible."

"As long as you make sure the old—Mrs. Bearcroft doesn't ask me whose it is again. I'm not telling, not if you had me torn asunder."

"It's a bargain." I pulled Justin's stick out of the clay underfoot; it made a soft sucking noise. "I'll allow you to keep your secret."

"Because it's not fair, is it, m'lady? Every Sunday in church we pray to God not to lead us into temptation, and every day there's the temptation that He's been and gone and led us into. And the less people deserve the temptation, the worse He makes it."

"I don't think it's necessarily God who does the leading, Susan."

"Oh, it is, m'lady." She sounded oddly confident. "But I'll tell Father of your kindness, and of your conditions, and tell him not to fret over me anymore because I won't be in his sight. He won't like it, but I know how to set his mind at rest."

I didn't like the sly little grin with which she delivered these last words, but it was getting cold as the sun sank to the horizon, and poor Guttridge would be shivering alone in the cemetery. I took my leave of Susan with a heavy heart.

1 2

THE DERMODYS

I still felt subdued as I walked to Hyrst two days later with Guttridge. She and I didn't have much to say to each other as we passed the three cottages in Hyrst Lane and entered the tree-lined drive that signaled the approach to the house. I was preoccupied with thoughts of Susan and, if I had to be quite honest with myself, of Fortier —where *was* the dratted man? Guttridge had seemed downcast for the last day or two, possibly as a result of spending an hour and a half alone in a cemetery.

"Maybe we should have taken the carriage after all." Having raised my widow's veil, I could feel the damp touch of mist on my cheek, almost rain but never quite making up its mind to form into drops of water. "Or I should have come with a footman—but footmen never like to walk, and they're such bad company."

"It's quite all right, my lady." Guttridge clutched a bag containing my notebook and pencils. "I like a walk on a day like this." She sniffed the air. "Almost Christmas and we've hardly had any frost. Besides, I don't like being stuck at

Whitcombe all day by myself, as your ladyship knows well. Hyrst will be a nice change of scene."

"You're wishing I were paying calls and giving dinners like before, aren't you?" I looked sideways at Guttridge, who had the grace to look shamefaced.

"I shouldn't have said that, my lady. It's not my place to complain when you're still grieving Sir Justin."

"It's all right." I swallowed hard. "You probably know more about my grief than anyone, being my collector of damp handkerchiefs. But grief is for my private side, and mourning—the splendid, public isolation of it—*is* rather dull, especially at Christmastide. There seems so little point in changing when you just exchange one black dress for another, and Mrs. Foster must be getting so tired of making meals for one person."

"You could invite your family for dinner," Guttridge suggested. "A nice quiet gathering just before Christmas would be a fine thing."

"It would." My spirits, momentarily depressed by the thought of the damp handkerchiefs, rose again. "Thank you, Guttridge. I'll speak with Mrs. Foster and cheer her up with the prospect of a grand meal."

We walked past the large stable block, our boots making little noise on the damp gravel. The enormous beeches lining the drive were nearly bare of leaves by now, just a few stragglers clinging on here and there. Their branches reached out to one another across the wide drive like long-lost lovers yearning for an embrace. The effect, made stronger by the low, misty clouds, was like walking through a very high, airy tunnel. The dense growth of rhododendrons that surrounded the stables intensified that feeling of seclusion. Rustling noises to our right indicated the presence of Scotty, looking for rabbits and voles and nasty things to roll in.

To the left, the land dropped away sharply to the marsh.

With no leaves on the trees, we could see the Downs as vague blue-gray shapes in the distant mist. On a clear day, one could spot the white cliffs where the great ridge of land met the sea, but today our view was marshland criss-crossed with drainage ditches, a grayish smudge indicating the sea beyond. Where the valley that lay below Whitcombe was a bright, fertile green, the marsh was a patchwork of duns and yellows. The fields were interspersed with strips of tan-colored clay where little grew and with patches of water much loved by birds in the summer. I could see the whitish dots of Michael's sheep. A movement in the middle distance betrayed the road to Dover, frequented by drays and coaches. As we walked, the mist gave way for a moment to a breath of the sea, a freshness that struck our cheeks with the promise of cold weather to come.

The housekeeper's son responded to Guttridge's pull at the large iron bell that hung at Hyrst's gate. Within twenty minutes—time for me to say a brief hello to Mama and Belming and learn that his lordship was not at home—I'd sent word to Julia that I'd join her for luncheon, borrowed an under-housemaid, and taken possession of Mama's herb room.

Two hours later Julia put her head around the door to find me in a hot and dusty condition. Guttridge perched on a windowsill, my notebook in her hand, while the under-housemaid stolidly wielded a dustpan and brush. Julia raised her eyebrows at Guttridge, who looked as if she'd like to shrug her shoulders if her training permitted it.

"Her ladyship insisted on this division of labor," she informed the countess.

"Her ladyship is perfectly capable of moving a few pieces of equipment around," I elaborated with a grin. "It's quicker if I decide and Guttridge writes. And Tilda is doing a marvelous job cleaning up in my wake. You're quite happy, aren't you, Guttridge?"

Guttridge responded by raking me from top to toe with her eyes. Her look clearly proclaimed that the work she was spared now would descend on her later. It was certainly true that there was now a great deal of dust and dirt on my person, clothes, and hair, and mourning clothes took a huge amount of brushing out if they were to appear spotless. I pulled a thick, sticky strand of cobweb from my apron, looked at my dress where the dust had missed the apron entirely, and pantomimed an overly dramatic expression of contrition for Guttridge's benefit. I had the pleasure of seeing her purse her lips in a failing attempt to hide a laugh.

"In any case," I continued, "if I don't handle this stuff, I'll have no idea whether it's going to be useful or not. Most of it will be once it's been cleaned of all the dried substances and —ugh—spiders." I shook something nasty-looking and hopefully very dead out of a bottle.

"Michael will be delighted someone has finally cleared out this room," Julia remarked. "He's always complaining there isn't enough space to keep us in a style befitting an earl's family."

"Yes, I know," I said with feeling. "Papa always said the lack of room at Hyrst was an advantage. It provided him with an excuse not to hold huge house parties. Although he attended enough of them, usually without Mama." I turned away to sneeze violently, having made the mistake of sniffing the contents of one of the bottles. "Talking of Mama, do you think we could have luncheon in her rooms? Is she well enough?"

"There's only the three of us, and Belming, of course, so if Mama-in-Law gets confused, nobody will mind." Julia seized a rag from the pile of clean ones on the table and used it to remove something from my hair. "And it's her favorites—

cock-a-leekie soup with treacle tart to follow. Now do come along, Helena. Let Guttridge and Tilda get something to eat. You've been slave-driving them long enough."

A short while later, thoroughly brushed down by Guttridge and pronounced fit for company, I found myself alone with Julia as we waited for Mama.

"'Tweedledum and Tweedledee came to see me this morning," said Julia, using Odelia's nicknames for the twins. "Apparently, you've managed to get the Hatherall girl to take back her claim that Monsieur Fortier is the father of her child."

"Yes. I had to get Mrs. Bearcroft to promise not to question the girl. She settled for giving Susan a forty-minute lecture on depravity and the evils of compounding sin with deceit. I truly wanted to kick her by the time she was done."

"Mrs. Bearcroft or Susan?" Julia grinned.

"Both. Susan deserved the lecture, but I certainly didn't deserve to sit and listen to Mrs. B."

"Dreadful woman. Still, you've done the French physician a favor, if only he knew it. Perhaps he'll come back now." She tilted her head to one side. "Would you like that? Odelia thinks you would. I had a letter from her this morning."

"O shouldn't even think of such a thing with me so recently bereaved."

Julia waved a hand. "O thinks of such things all the time. She ought to think of getting married herself. Then perhaps she wouldn't always be imagining silly romances between parties who are quite unsuited to one another. Michael thinks her bohemian life among the artists overheats her brain."

"Michael just wants O to bury herself in the countryside and leave the London house all to him. Which is silly because he doesn't like the disruption of going to Town for the Season anyway. And for heaven's sake, Julia, don't listen to O.

Monsieur Fortier is a pleasant, intelligent man, but we have little in common. And I'm not interested in any man." I sighed. "I do actually miss my husband, you know."

"I know you do." Julia kissed my cheek, then fished a clean handkerchief out of a hidden pocket and wiped a smudge from beneath my ear. "Goodness, Guttridge is going to have to scrub you down later."

"I received a note from Mrs. Dermody this morning." I made a face as Julia showed me the black mark on her hand-kerchief. "Thanking me for defending her brother. She hesi-tates over the presumption of coming to see me at Whitcombe but says she's at home tomorrow if I should care to call and receive her thanks in person."

"And shall you care to call?"

"I might. It would make such a nice change from receiving visits of condolence at home."

"And somebody of that class might be uncomfortable at Whitcombe."

"Of what class? I have no idea what the Dermodys might be like. They own one of the best houses in Littleberry, very near Ned and Gerry, in fact."

"My dear, in Littleberry everybody's near everybody else."

"You know what I mean. They appear to be wealthy and respectable people."

"The two don't always go together. Is this Fortier fellow a gentleman?"

I frowned. "I think so. He certainly behaves as if he's our social equal—calls me Lady Helena and not m'lady, that sort of thing. His manners are impeccable." I thought back. "In fact, I'd say he's as well-bred as anyone we know. Better than some."

"It's so hard to tell with the French." Julia sighed. "All those years of turmoil. Republic, empire, monarchy, republic, empire—where are we now?"

"Republic, silly. The Prussians turned out the last emperor, and he exiled himself to England. He lived and died in Chislehurst; his widow's still there as far as I know."

"Perhaps your Monsieur Fortier is exiled royalty."

"Wouldn't he tell everyone if he were? And he's not *my* Monsieur Fortier, I told you. In any case, he's gone—for good, people say."

"That's something worth visiting the Dermodys for. You could ask Mrs. Dermody if he's really gone."

"I suppose I could."

Lunch with Julia and Mama was a lighthearted, relaxed affair. For once, Mama forgot to fret about the gardener. I avoided any topic that had to do with herbs. References to that part of Mama's life seemed to distress her, no doubt because she was unable to perform tasks she'd once accomplished with ease.

By the time I got back to the herb room, Guttridge had taken over. She'd commandeered two footmen and given them precise instructions for the packing of all the glass and metal equipment "on the assumption that you'd want it all, my lady." She'd made a small display of items about which she was doubtful and set Tilda to cleaning the floors and cupboards. She'd notified Brandrick that the room was nearly cleared and that work could begin on it as soon as he wished. To cap her efforts, she'd produced a set of much-improved lists for my perusal.

Presented with this evidence that I was superfluous to requirements, I spent a half hour sorting through the assorted odd and ends. As Guttridge had suspected, most of them were only fit for the rag-and-bone man.

Bidding good-bye to the helpful Tilda with the gift of a

few coins, Guttridge and I walked back to Whitcombe through a drizzle that did nothing for the state of my dress. By the time I was cleaned up, the rain had started in earnest, and I had nothing to do but read Mama's journals.

My mother had rapidly progressed from her first, faltering steps to a fast-growing knowledge of the properties of plants common to our area. This was when she'd started the herb garden. The journal was full of lists of plants she'd ordered, plants she had yet to find, and plants she'd located in the fields around Littleberry.

Gerry made the occasional appearance in the journals; my father, never. I wondered what he'd done while Mama surrounded herself with books and plants—but an earl does have a certain number of local and parliamentary responsibilities. I presumed Papa and Mama had done what, in my experience, happily married people did: develop their own interests and come together at the end of the day to discuss them. The kindly Papa of my memories had always shown the amused tolerance toward Mama's activities that I supposed was a man's way of exhibiting approval.

The following morning was rainy and blustery. I had the winter carriage brought round nevertheless and set off for Littleberry. I had ventured forth from Whitcombe so little since Justin's death that I found myself excited at the prospect of an outing, especially since I would see a new house and new people.

We descended Whitcombe Hill slowly, as the road was muddy and perilous. Once on Littleberry's cobblestones, we were soon ringing our way through the massive medieval gate up into the High Street. The steady fall of cold rain kept most people indoors, but we still had to maneuver carefully past pedestrians with umbrellas and the occasional cart as we picked our way along the crooked, narrow thoroughfare. The air smelled of fish, tar, and manure, all the aromas of

Littleberry's industries mingling with the reek of damp clothing, wood smoke, and mud.

By the time we were climbing the hill again, heading for the Dermody house, the great clock in St. Michael's church was booming out the eleventh hour. We left the noise and smells of the High Street behind and found ourselves in a more genteel corner of our tiny town. Here was the calm dignity of solid red-brick houses and large peaceful gardens behind high walls. The secret lives of Littleberry's better citizens were kept more secret still by shutters, drapes, and heavy front doors.

The Dermody house was set in a corner near the churchyard. It benefited from a convenient sort of half-courtyard where a carriage could pull in off the cobbles. I watched through the rain-marked window as the footman jumped down, shedding copious amounts of water from his hat and caped raincoat, and pulled on the bell outside the house's main entrance.

Naturally I was admitted with alacrity. Merchants' wives are generally at home to the aristocracy. It wasn't more than a minute before Mrs. Gabrielle Dermody arrived to greet me.

She was older than her brother by perhaps five years. She wasn't exactly beautiful, but like many Frenchwomen she had that sense of style that is often better than beauty. Thick, wavy black hair swept up into a smooth, elegant chignon surmounted by an enameled comb of extremely good quality. Her gown's relatively simple skirt was compensated for by its finely embroidered bodice.

"You are very welcome in my house, Lady Helena," she said as she took my hand. Unlike Fortier, she had a slight accent, but she spoke as one who has lived in England for many years. "I am most grateful for what you did for Armand." Luminous brown eyes, less unusual than her brother's but nonetheless striking, held mine with an expression that was friendly yet slightly wary.

She glanced round as a maid opened the parlor door. "Will you take a cup of hot chocolate with me to ward off the morning's chill? My cook makes the best hot chocolate this side of the Channel."

I assented with pleasure and sat in the seat Mrs. Dermody indicated as the maid closed the door. A fire burned in the grate, but it was not too warm. This was fortunate since I had not removed my hat or manteau as a sign that my visit would be brief.

We made small talk until the chocolate arrived. The mildness of the season and whether we thought we would ever have frost or snow made excellent topics of conversation. I was able to admire the size of the garden I could see through the many-paned French windows. It looked well kept, and the parlor was paneled in softly gleaming pale oak. A small room compared to any at Whitcombe House, it nonetheless had an air of elegance and spaciousness thanks to the tall windows with their window seats and the careful choice of furnishings. It was artistic and harmonious, a real change from the usual crowded rooms with their heavy furniture and overabundance of ornament. Justin would have liked it. The fire spat and crackled behind the fireguard, making the blue Delft tiles of its surround flicker with oranges and reds.

"This is delicious." My compliment was genuine. The chocolate was delicately flavored with cinnamon and allspice, and pleasantly sweet.

"I'm glad you like it." She smiled in a friendly manner. "Armand says I have too much of a sweet tooth. He will not touch a drink with sugar or cream in it."

"Is he—I mean, have you heard from him?"

Now she definitely looked wary, but her demeanor remained friendly. "He sent word that he reached France safely. I'm afraid our method of correspondence is somewhat circuitous, and the distances are great. I did write to him about the ridiculous accusation against him, but I doubt he's received my letter yet. Now I must write to reassure him all is well. Poor Armand—after this, he may decide to return to London rather than live in Littleberry."

"You think he'll come back to England, then?" That, if I admitted the truth to myself, was what I'd been waiting to ask.

She shrugged, looking very like her brother in that moment. "There is room in our house for him whenever he wishes to be here, but I do not order Armand's life."

"Did he move to Littleberry to be with you?" I asked and then felt flustered. "I'm sorry—I don't mean to pry." But I wished very much that Mrs. Dermody would tell me what Fortier was doing in France.

"He thought the coast would be a better place to live." I had the distinct impression she was giving me a partial truth, being careful not to say too much. "He had perhaps not reckoned with the drawbacks of a gossipy small town."

"I hope he has better fortune in France, then."

"Oh, small towns are the same everywhere."

I saw her catch her underlip between her teeth and realized she had given me at least one clue. Fortier was not in Paris.

"I'm glad to have been instrumental in clearing up one piece of gossip." I decided not to press her on Fortier's whereabouts, however curious I might be.

"It was kind of you." She sighed. "Armand is an attractive man, but he's held himself aloof from the young ladies of the town, and that has given rise to a certain amount of antipathy. Added to the fact that you English are always quick to think the worst of a Frenchman."

She smiled to dilute the comment, and I smiled back to

show I had taken no offense. It was time to lead the conversation onto safer ground.

"I can't deny we usually seem to end up on opposite sides of a conflict. And yet we've been friendly neighbors and trading partners for the best part of this century, haven't we? Sir Justin and I attended the Universal Exposition in Paris as part of our wedding trip, along with my sister and brother-in-law. It was a splendid exhibition."

"Considering our political difficulties. Would you like a little more?" Mrs. Dermody lifted the chocolate pot.

"Yes, please. Sir Justin and I thought the head of the statue of Liberty Enlightening the World quite magnificent, if a little stern. I hope they succeed in taking it to America."

I could see Mrs. Dermody felt a little more at ease, so I essayed a more personal question.

"Did you move from London to live here?"

She smiled. "I did. I attended an artists' *salon*, and there I met an Englishman of Irish extraction who would become my husband. And by marrying a pottery owner, I changed as an artist, finding a passion for the art of ceramics."

"Did you paint those?" I had been wondering about the two large vases that sat either side of the fireplace. "They're astonishingly beautiful." I was starting to realize that here indeed was a woman with a vocation.

"Thank you. Yes, they're my work." She smiled as she watched me rise to my feet so I could get a better look at the relief decorations of fuchsias and lilies of the valley, enhanced here and there with gold leaf. "I sell a few pieces from time to time to the Liberty shop in London. But I mostly do these things for my own amusement."

"Does your brother also work for his own amusement?" The graceful interior of the home and Gabrielle Dermody's appearance were beginning to convince me that Fortier could indeed be a gentleman.

"Oh, I wouldn't say amusement comes into it. Armand is quite serious about his life and his work."

Another slippery answer. Mrs. Dermody was clearly not going to divulge any interesting details about Fortier to *me*.

I was already standing, so it was undoubtedly time to go. I sought for something to say.

"If you do manage to correspond with your brother, please tell him that I, for one, am trying not to be prejudiced against him. That I am a little ashamed of having, for a short time, believed the worst."

"And yet you pursued the truth of the matter."

"It seemed only fair."

"Ah, the English sense of fair play. I admit my brother is unlikely to make it easy for you—or for anyone—to know him unless there is some trust between you in the first place."

"I will undertake to communicate my newfound trust in Monsieur Fortier to my family."

"Thank you. Your family's good or bad opinion makes a great deal of difference in Littleberry despite the town's much-vaunted independence from feudalism."

"Then you have my word I will mention his innocence in the right places."

"The word of a lady?" She looked hard at me for a moment, her eyes serious but with the faintest curve of amusement on her lips.

"Every word I speak is that of a lady." I returned her stare with interest. Scott-De Quincys are not easily intimidated by anyone outside the family.

"Very well." The curve of her lips became more pronounced. "And you have my word I will not hold anything you previously thought about my brother against you."

We shook hands cordially. I realized I rather liked this

woman. Like her brother, she was a mixture of reserve and open passion where her feelings were engaged.

I crossed to the parlor door as Mrs. Dermody rang the bell to summon her servant. The door opened immediately, but the maid wasn't behind it. I recognized Quinn Dermody from church; close up, he was clearly the sort they called the Black Irish, as lean and swarthy as any Spaniard. He loomed over me with an expression that wasn't entirely welcoming.

"Lady Helena Whitcombe, my dear," said Mrs. Dermody by way of introduction.

"I was just leaving," I said as Mr. Dermody bowed over my hand. He didn't look particularly pleased to see me. The merchants of Littleberry, even wealthy ones like the Dermodys, generally had little to do with the landed gentry who held the estates in the surrounding countryside. Their belief that we held entirely too much power in relation to our usefulness no doubt intensified each time my brother-in-law was elected mayor.

Mr. Dermody raised one thick black eyebrow, but a glance at my mourning clothes seemed to chasten him. "I'm sorry for the loss of Sir Justin," he said formally. "He was a good man."

"I thought so." I nodded. "Thank you."

"But I must say I'm a little surprised to see you here." Clearly, he was not a man who minced his words. "County paying calls on town? And so soon after your husband's death. It's a mystery, to be sure."

"I suggested that Lady Helena call on me." Mrs. Dermody's eyes held a warning. "I thought it better this way. I wanted to thank her for helping Armand."

"And the Hatheralls. I hear you've offered Susan work."

I supposed I should not be astonished at the way news flew around Littleberry, but I always was.

"I thought it the right thing to do."

"Noblesse oblige?" He seemed to consider the phrase, which he had pronounced in good French, for a moment before continuing. "Do you always look after your people so well?"

"I try to. I don't think there's anything wrong with feeling an obligation toward those who make their living on my land. I also find myself under an obligation to Monsieur Fortier for attending my husband before his death and participating in the unpleasant tasks made necessary by the nature of his demise." I tried to stare him down, difficult since he was a foot taller than me. "Do you find that overly feudal?"

"Quinn." There was a note of reproach in Gabrielle Dermody's voice. "Lady Helena is trying to help."

Mr. Dermody's glare softened a little. "Well, I suppose Lady Helena can't help the habits ingrained in her by centuries of—"

He stopped as his wife made a small sound like a squeak of protest and began again. "That is, it's kind of you, but Armand doesn't need the protection of the aristocracy. His own innocence in this matter should be protection enough."

"I'd better go," I said to Mrs. Dermody, ignoring the insult her husband had just directed against me. If I was, as Mr. Dermody clearly thought, a representative of an outmoded and interfering class, at least I had that class's ability to hide its feelings. "It was delightful to meet both of you."

And with that, I proceeded out of the front door, which was held open for me by the Dermodys' maid. The rain had almost ceased, just a few drops scattering out of a sky that was a vivid mixture of ragged cloud and cerulean blue. Overhead, Littleberry's ever-present seagulls screamed and swooped.

"Take me home," I said to the coachman. "I've had quite enough visiting for one morning."

13

LADIES MUST HAVE THEIR OCCUPATIONS

"The man should take a whip to his daughter." Michael glared at his wife across the expanse of my drawing room.

"No, he shouldn't." Julia linked her arm through mine. "Helena's quite right that we should all leave the girl be. After all, she may have been forced. And of course we'll make sure that everyone knows Monsieur Fortier's innocent of any wrongdoing. A word here and there should discourage gossip. These people aren't worth losing your temper over."

"I never lose my temper." Michael pushed back the skirt of a rather old-fashioned frock coat he always insisted on wearing on ordinary days and rested a fist on his hip. "But it galls me that Hatherall should raise that girl to—to gad about and do what she oughtn't, and tell lies into the bargain. Lies against a—well, I suppose Fortier's a gentleman, even if he *is* a Frenchman. Hatherall may be a churchwarden, but he's nothing but a tenant farmer after all."

"Darling, you're a relic from an earlier age." Julia went to kiss her husband on his cheek, ignoring his flinch and stare of annoyance. "These are the days of the train and the telegraph. Hatherall's the coming type of man; he was more of a business partner to Justin than a tenant."

"Coming? Helena should send him packing." Michael ground his teeth.

"It's sweet seeing you so indignant on Monsieur Fortier's behalf."

"I am *not*—"

"Now then, you mustn't shout at me in my condition." Julia sent a wink in my direction.

"It's public knowledge, then?" Catching Julia's mischievous mood, I also went to kiss Michael. "Congratulations, Michael."

"Hmph." But Michael looked almost pleased.

"Since you're not going to shout, I have some worse news for you." I took a deep breath. "I'm going to employ Susan Hatherall as a sort of assistant in my workroom."

It was quite amusing watching Michael controlling the impulse to begin shouting again. He would, of course, take Julia's warning quite literally. My sister-in-law was extraordinarily adept at keeping the Earl of Broadmere where she wanted him.

"Is there *any* logical reason for this peculiar decision?" he said at last.

"Yes. Susan needs a fresh start, and I need an assistant. Having her here will prevent the nastier elements of Littleberry from making her life a misery. And perhaps getting her away from Dene Farm will allow her father to make a fresh beginning also."

"He'll have to resign as churchwarden," Julia said, a note of sympathy in her voice.

"I expect he will. Churchwardens are supposed to set a good example after all. I suppose his days as churchwarden were numbered the moment Susan's pregnancy became known." I looked at my brother. "But, Michael, could you please talk to the rector? Let them at least allow him to resign quietly? I don't see it's the poor man's fault at all."

"I'll see what I can do," Michael muttered.

"That's all I ask. Now do come and see my workroom. Guttridge has gone above and beyond her role as my lady's maid and is positively organizing my life. She and Mrs. Eason have found a carpenter to build extra cupboards. The scullery maids have scrubbed all the glass jars and things until they're gleaming. They're going to take the wallpaper off the walls and put distemper on. Guttridge says it's more practical if I'm going to be dragging bits of plants indoors and making a mess. We can just repaint it when it gets too dirty."

Julia's cheeks dimpled. "Sounds like the nursery at Hyrst."

"And they've already taken Mama's big marble-topped table," Michael remarked. "Brandrick's going to like the new estate office."

"Yes, *my* new table is being repaired and polished up." I ignored Michael's remark about Brandrick. Making the dreadful man happy was of little consequence to me.

"They had to take it apart," Julia said. "As they did when Mama-in-Law first commandeered it, according to Inchkin. He said it was the pastry cook's table, and the cook up and left in a rage, and when your father heard about it he laughed so hard he was sick."

"I hadn't heard that story." I laughed. We had arrived at my new workroom, and I opened the door with a feeling of pride, even though there was nothing yet to see.

"But that's Justin's study." Michael looked deeply offended.

"He doesn't need it, Michael," I said, ignoring the catch in my throat. "He barely used it anyway. He preferred the smoking room off the library for his writing and business conversations. That's where all his papers are." Which meant

I could put off the heartrending task of going through my late husband's personal papers for a very long time.

"It's a lovely big room." Julia eyed the brighter spots on the wallpaper where pictures had been removed. "It'll look splendid when it's painted."

"Yes, and it overlooks the location where I'm planning to put my herb garden." I stood aside to allow two of the menservants to pass. "Guttridge and I thought we'd look through the attics to see if there's any furniture and so on I could use. There's so much up there."

"It really is going to be like the nursery at Hyrst." Julia had a wide grin on her face. "Give the children the old furniture so they can play."

"Helena's not a child, Julia." Michael stood in the middle of the room, his arms folded, looking out through the window to where the distinctive tower of Littleberry's church could be seen in the distance. "She wants to be useful, like Mama."

"Well for heaven's sake, my brother's defending me," I murmured. "So you're not going to try to force me to move out and rent Whitcombe to strangers?"

"Brandrick said I am being too hasty." Michael looked down his nose at me.

"*Brandrick* defended me?" I went to the window. "Is the sun going to set in the east today, do you think?"

～

"The news that I'm going to employ Susan went over better than I thought," I said to Guttridge once we were alone again. "Lord Broadmere's color barely reached vermilion."

"Mrs. Eason's ready to take the girl in hand. She'll stop the other maids from bullying her. You're very kind to do this, my lady."

"Do you disapprove?"

"It's not my place to approve or disapprove. I don't know the girl anyway." We had hired Guttridge to be my lady's maid after my marriage; before that, I had shared a maid with my twin sisters. So she had never known much about my life at Hyrst.

"I hope the farmer doesn't mind losing his daughter," I mused.

Guttridge tutted. "He can easily get another woman in to help Ruby with the house. Sooner or later you lose your daughters to marriage. A son can stay and work on the farm, but girls are more trouble than they're worth sometimes."

"What a devastatingly practical mind you have, Guttridge. Am *I* more trouble than I'm worth?"

"A *lady* is a different matter, my lady. Ladies provide employment and make themselves useful in society—leastways, some do. They're useful to their husbands once they're married and ornamental when they're young."

"And they breed the next generation of the country's generals, archbishops, and judges?" I rolled my eyes at Guttridge. "If they do breed, that is."

"I've always thought it a great shame your union wasn't blessed with children," Guttridge said impassively.

"Yes, well, it wasn't. Now this Savonnerie carpet should go, shouldn't it? I'll spill things on it."

Guttridge folded her arms and contemplated my future workroom, lips pursed. "There's some old Indian rugs in the attic, in a pretty sort of blue. If we used gray distemper on the walls and maybe painted the cupboards and things dark blue, the whole would look quite nice."

"It would." I was pleased Guttridge was taking such an interest in my workroom. It was amusing to have someone to plan with. "Guttridge, do *you* think I'm entering my second childhood? Lady Broadmere seems to think so."

Guttridge looked arch. "Ladies must have their occupations, my lady. I hear the dowager countess was a great deal of help in the county with her remedies." She waved an arm, indicating a corner of the room. "A couple of Morris chairs would look well in that corner. You can write to Morris & Company to order them."

"You're enjoying this. And there I was thinking that all you ever wanted to do was look after my clothes."

The shrug Guttridge was unable to hide was expressive. "There's not much to do with you in mourning, my lady. I won't be sorry when we're able to entertain again."

"Entertain! That's what I wanted to talk to Mrs. Eason about. We should settle on a day for our family dinner."

"How about the twentieth? Mrs. Eason was saying she was hoping we'd have a Christmas tree this year, even with Sir Justin gone. She can get one brought in the Saturday before. She's already had Mary dust those fancy glass ornaments Sir Justin liked."

"Christmas." A strange, yearning feeling settled in the pit of my stomach. This would be my first Christmas without Justin.

"Of course we must have a tree," I said, dismissing my sadness. "I'll speak to Mrs. Eason about it. The twentieth it is, then. We'll have a tea and a puppet show for the children and then a late dinner after they're all in bed. Mourning or not, I'm going to enjoy Christmas, just as Sir Justin would want me to do."

14

FORTIER RETURNS

"*V*ery nice, Baby. You *have* been busy."

Blanche and I were standing in the middle of my workroom, now almost ready. Mama's bottles and jars, gleaming softly in the gaslight I'd had installed, were lined up on the cupboard shelves. Her paraffin stove stood near the fire, the large copper kettle on top cleaner and brighter than I'd ever seen it.

"Are you actually *making* anything?" Blanche surveyed a line of beakers and retorts, all perfectly clean.

"We're almost ready to start making things," I said. "Of course it's winter, and I don't have many herbs yet. I've been preparing some ingredients for later use." I bent to open the door of a low tin cupboard that sat on the other side of the fireplace from the paraffin stove. "See? This little cupboard is for drying things, don't you remember?"

Blanche sniffed. "As if you think I ever concerned myself with Mama's hobby. Needlework would have been much more dignified."

"Mama was probably just as bad at embroidery as I am." I pulled out a shelf from the drying cupboard. "Smell these." I sniffed appreciatively at the slices of ginger root and orange peel. "I found a recipe of Mama's for sore throats, the one I always liked because it had lots of honey in it. I thought she made it that way because it tasted nice, but according to her journals the antiseptic properties of honey—"

"Are you really spending all that time and energy just to doctor your household's sore throats? Littleberry has an apothecary, does it not? And any cottage dweller can brew up a tisane from her garden."

Blanche's brow contracted under her mass of flaxen hair as she gazed at the drying ingredients. A small diamond tiara perched atop her coiffure sent back the light in dazzling little flashes. I had been pleased when, during the family dinner, she'd expressed an interest in seeing my workroom, but I should have known her purpose was to criticize, not to encourage. Her next words confirmed her motive.

"It must be nice to have so much money that you can fritter it away on a hobby."

I sighed. The money other people had—and spent—was one of Blanche's favorite topics. With my large house and comfortable income and with my husband no longer present to protect me, she was becoming ever more acidic in her remarks. As she stayed at Whitcombe nearly every time she came to see the family and considered the room known as Early July—Whitcombe's twenty-four bedrooms were named after the months, a quirk of Justin's father's—to be almost hers by right, she was biting the hand that fed. But to point that out would have been ungracious. I kept my voice even as I replied.

"The equipment was nearly all Mama's, and much of the furniture comes from the attics. And it's not a hobby."

"It's hardly a profession, so what do you call it? Or are you intending to earn money? How vulgar."

"I have no intention of charging for my services."

"I should hope not. Our sort never earns money."

"Justin earned money from his sheep," I pointed out.

"That's money from land; that's how a gentleman lives, even if Justin spent more time than he should on his blessed sheep. But in a man, such enthusiasm can safely be counted as an eccentricity. A lady who allows her interests to impinge upon her duties as a wife, mother, and hostess is in danger of being thought a bluestocking. A bluestocking, may I remind you, is the most odious kind of woman in existence." She touched my cheek with a satin-gloved hand. "Soon, Baby, you will be a wife and a hostess again. Providence may even vouchsafe you the gift of motherhood—who knows? So you're either wasting your time and money or, worse, you're creating something that will cause strife between you and your future husband."

"Why do you imagine I'm going to marry again? *You* didn't."

Blanche struck an attitude of noble abnegation. "I devote myself to Rawdon's interests. A mother must sacrifice her own comfort and happiness to promote that of her children, particularly when she has a son in Rawdon's position."

"Rawdon" was how Blanche usually referred to her son, Dederick, who had been Viscount Rawdon before his father's death. Deddy, as he preferred *not* to be called, was now the Marquess of Hastings. Blanche had married up—and she never let us forget it.

"Why don't you call O a bluestocking?" I suppressed a grin. The reason Blanche never lectured Odelia on the evils of pursuing a vocation was because she was afraid of Odelia's extremely sharp tongue.

"I'll be glad when Rawdon marries," Blanche continued, ignoring my question. "He must marry *very well*. He's promised to give me a larger dress allowance if I help him find a suitable bride." She turned toward the door. "It's *so* trying to have to depend on one's own son for the finer things in life. The late marquess had *no idea* how much a widowed marchioness needs to live well."

I made a face at Blanche's back as we walked back to the drawing room. The late marquess was thoroughly familiar with Blanche's tastes, which were extremely expensive. He had restricted her widow's jointure and other allowances to an amount that wouldn't drain the estate before Deddy grew old enough to be sensible about money. Which he hadn't; Blanche had pushed her son to the very top of society by maneuvering him into the glittering crowd that surrounded the Prince of Wales. Not only did Deddy have to maintain an establishment in keeping with such an exalted position, he had learned to play cards for exorbitantly high stakes and ride excessively costly horseflesh.

"So you've seen the witch's lair, Aunt Blanche?" My niece Maryanne laughingly hooked her arm under Blanche's as we entered the room. My siblings and assorted spouses and children were sitting in groups, digesting what I was glad to say had been rather a good dinner. The room smelled of perfume, coffee, and the sweetmeats the servants had placed around the room in china dishes.

"Who are you calling a witch?" I wrinkled my nose at Maryanne, whom I'd always liked. Thomas, who sat with his sister Lydia working out a hand of Patience, winked at me as I passed. His father hadn't said yes to university, but faced with my offer of paying the fees if he refused, his pride wouldn't let him say no either.

I went to sit next to Gerry, who was working on a piece of crewel embroidery. "This dress makes me look rather witch-like, I think," I told her. "Blanche was just telling me I was in danger of becoming a bluestocking." I accepted a cup of coffee from the footman, adding cream and sugar before I settled back onto the sofa.

Gerry's pale blue eyes focused on me for a moment. "I don't think there's any risk of that," she said. "I can't see you not marrying again. You were always such an affectionate little thing, and you like men."

I was taken aback. "I suppose I do," I said after a few moments' thought. "But why shouldn't I marry and have some intellectual or practical pursuit as well? Mama did, and it caused no problems."

"Do you really think that?" Gerry returned her gaze to her work, carefully inserting her needle into the wing of an embroidered parrot.

"What do you mean?" But Ned had come to join us, coffee cup in hand. He settled himself into an armchair with a grunt of satisfaction.

"You're looking very well, my dear. That dinner was delicious—do let your cook know how much I enjoyed it." He leaned forward a little and dropped his voice. "I wanted to thank you—for Thomas."

"Thank me? I thought you'd be annoyed at me for forcing your hand."

He took a sip of coffee and licked a drop from his mustache, prompting a small explosive sound from Gerry. "I've been waiting for years for the boy to stand up to me and tell me how much he hated being in the business."

"You don't really mean you're going to pay for university, do you? With Petey's school fees as well?" Gerry sounded exasperated. "Do you really think he's going to amount to much as a vicar?"

"There's nothing wrong with his brain." Ned's voice was a low growl. "If he applies himself, he'll be able to get a small living somewhere just on the strength of the Scott-De Quincy connection. It's about time the lad showed some ambition."

"Well, at least the church is a suitable place for a gentleman's son. And there's no title to inherit, which is a blessing." She smiled at her husband. Ned was just an ordinary knight, not a baronet, and Gerry, to her credit, didn't mind that one bit.

"Thank heaven for marrying a wine merchant, eh, my love?" Ned smiled fondly back and then turned to me. "It's good to see you host a dinner again, dear girl. You're far too young and lovely to retreat into solitude. It's a dashed shame about Justin."

I was about to make an appropriate reply when a disturbance in the room caught my eye. Even among family, my role as hostess demanded that I investigate any unusual incident immediately. I rose with an apologetic smile and walked over to where one of the footmen was hovering by the door.

"What is it, Robert?"

"There's a . . . gentleman . . . arrived asking for you, m'lady." Robert looked perplexed.

"At this time of night?" It was almost eleven o'clock. "Who is it?"

"Fortier," said a voice from behind Robert. The man himself hove into view. His usually tidy appearance was marred by the stains of travel, including, I rather thought, an unsuccessful attempt to remove a streak of vomit from his sleeve. I deduced he had just made the Channel crossing—at such a time of year!—and that as one would expect, it had not been easy. He swayed a little.

"Robert, please show Monsieur Fortier into the library and bring him"—I surveyed Fortier closely, noting his pallor and the shadows under his eyes—"a large brandy. A very large brandy. Sir Justin's *best* brandy, you understand. And a sandwich or two. And coffee. Make sure he's warm and comfortable and take his coat to Mrs. Eason for cleaning." I nodded at Fortier. "I'll give you a few minutes to find your feet, and then I'll join you."

I watched my visitor retreat and then turned to my brother-in-law, who had drawn close, an alert look in his brown eyes. Behind him were the faces of my family, expressing various degrees of surprise or annoyance depending on their personalities.

"You'll come with me, won't you, Ned? I believe Monsieur Fortier would benefit from your presence."

When Ned and I entered the library a few minutes later, we found Fortier sitting as close as he could to the fire, his feet only inches from the crackling embers. Without the stained traveling coat, he looked a little more like himself, and he had taken two bites from the beef sandwich Mrs. Foster had sent up. The warm fragrance of good brandy rose from the goblet he held in his hand.

Ned had also furnished himself with brandy and carried a small glass of cordial for me. Fortier rose as we entered and hurried to pull forward a chair so Ned could sit between us. We made a cozy group, the three of us, huddled close to the flickering flames.

Ned wasn't mayor of Littleberry for nothing. Instead of pressing Fortier with questions, he sat silent, nursing his brandy and waiting for the younger man to recover his equilibrium. I was silent too, mostly because I didn't know what to say. I watched the color return to Fortier's cheeks under his faint tan and the tremor in his hands become still.

At last Fortier spoke. "The first thing I absolutely must do is to assure the two of you of my complete and utter innocence with respect to Susan Hatherall. I haven't led a blameless life, but seducing farm girls is not one of my sins."

"She's retracted her accusation already, thanks to Lady

Helena." The laughter lines gathered at the corners of Ned's eyes, but he didn't smile.

"She has? *Dieu merci.*" The relief in Fortier's voice spoke volumes.

"Your sister wrote to you. I expect you missed the letter," I said.

"Has she named her seducer?" Fortier asked.

"No. She may never do so, and I'm not going to try to make her. If the father of the child were an honest man, he'd have come forward by now, wouldn't he? And you should know she's living here now. I've employed her as a sort of assistant."

Fortier's eyes widened, but all he said was, "And what does her father think of that?"

I shrugged. "He's telling people she's not in her right mind. I suppose that makes it easier for him to bear the disgrace, but it's not true. She's not the most agreeable company I could have, but she does her work well. She remembers quite a lot of what my mother taught her. I just wish her health were better. This child seems to be draining the energy from her."

"I hesitate to ask, but would you like my medical opinion?"

"She may not wish to see you," I said. "She seems to hate the child. I think she'd welcome losing it."

Ned shook his head. "As far as I can see, Helena, you're the only person in Littleberry who'd welcome the birth of this baby. And you'd be wrong. Children born on the wrong side of the blanket have a terrible start, and life for the lower classes is hard enough as it is."

"Then I'll do what I can to make it easier." I swallowed the last sip of my cordial and put the glass down with a bang. "Whether Susan wants me to or not."

Truth be told, I was looking forward to the birth of a baby

at Whitcombe, for reasons I did not care to explore. This wasn't the first time I'd found myself prickly and defensive on the subject of Susan's baby.

"You could come by tomorrow to see my new workroom," I said to Fortier, anxious to change the subject. "Susan will be there. It's perfectly respectable."

I delivered that last sentence rather loudly, and not to Fortier but to Ned, who had made a noise in his throat.

"I will do my best to safeguard both our reputations," Fortier said gravely, his eyes on my brother-in-law. "I can't afford any more gossip attaching to my own name. And you, Lady Helena, should not suffer for being kind."

"Oh, don't worry about me," I said cheerfully to both men. "I'm a Scott-De Quincy. As my sister the Marchioness of Hastings is fond of saying, our sort make our own rules."

I had the satisfaction of making Ned swallow his brandy the wrong way, but the spluttering that ensued was mingled with laughter.

"It's hopeless," he said to Fortier. "They're all the same— but that's why I married one. And it's about time I took my lady wife home."

Fortier glanced at the grandfather clock that had been sonorously counting off the seconds of our conversation and swallowed the last of his brandy. He looked straight at me, his eyes lit gold by the candlelight.

"Forgive me, Lady Helena, for intruding on your dinner party. My anxiety to clear my name is my only excuse. I've only just realized how very late it is and how very wrong of me it is to arrive at such an hour."

"You're forgiven." I tried to look stern. "It's a good thing my family's here though. Kindly refrain from visiting me in the evening in future."

He broke into a short laugh, in which he was joined by Ned—who seemed to like him now.

"You're quite right," Fortier said after clearing his throat. "To be honest, after the journey I've had I'd lost all sense of time. I seem to have been traveling in the dark for days."

"Bad crossing?" Ned inquired mildly.

"The worst. Dante got it wrong—the deepest circle of Hades is surely located in the English Channel." He shuddered. "The boat from the ship to the shore was the worst part. I thought they'd never get it in. Most of the passengers stayed on the ship to wait the night out, but I was foolish enough to accept the captain's invitation to try for the shore." He smiled suddenly, which did something odd to my knees. "I'm glad I did now."

Ned stood up. "Well, then, Fortier, may I offer you a place in our carriage? It's just me and Lady Freestone—my children are staying at Whitcombe for the night. After all, we're near neighbors."

"That would be delightful." Fortier also stood, looking much better than he had upon his arrival, even though he'd barely touched his food. "I hope my sister will forgive my homecoming at such a late and unexpected hour. Lady Helena, I will come to see your workroom by appointment, in my professional capacity, in the most proper and respectable manner possible. Would late in the morning be inconvenient?"

"I am generally at home at half past eleven," I said gravely.

I remained in the library for a few moments after the two men had left together, Ned taking Fortier by the elbow as if to make absolutely sure he could not return to me. Yes, he liked Fortier, I decided, but like the rest of my family he was wary of him. And despite my resolution to trust him, I knew Ned was right. Fortier was plainly not going to tell us what he'd been doing in France.

15

A GRUESOME DISCOVERY

I'd been right to worry about Susan. When Fortier called at precisely eleven thirty the next day, I was pacing the floor of my workroom in the throes of acute anxiety.

"She's delirious." I grabbed Fortier by the arm, heedless of his polite greeting. "She had a fever this morning, and Mrs. Eason told her to stay in bed. Now she's absolutely burning up. The whole household's in a panic in case it's something contagious." I gestured at the large bag Fortier was carrying. "Are those your medical supplies?"

"Yes. Have you given her anything?"

He was following me closely as I led the way through the house, and I turned around so suddenly that he almost fell into me.

"No." My pent-up frustration with myself burst forth. "I feel like a fraud. All I've managed to do so far is to produce a reasonable throat linctus from one of my mother's recipes. And quite a good ginger brew for the countess—you may as well know she's the friend I spoke of since her delicate condition is starting to become apparent. Perhaps my family's right and I'm just a dilettante. I don't even know where to begin to help Susan."

"You've only just started your studies." Now he was leading the way, as we'd plainly arrived at the staircase leading to the servants' bedrooms. "If you wish to learn, simply observe. This is a good opportunity."

"Mrs. Eason has been sponging her down to reduce the fever. She's the only one who'll go near her."

"I can give you the name of a woman who'll take care of her."

Fortier knocked on the door I indicated, and we both entered in response to Mrs. Eason's summons. We found my housekeeper seated by Susan's bedside, a bowl on another chair by her side. The plain but not unpleasant room was heated by a fire burning in the small grate. Mrs. Eason had removed the crocheted bedcover, and Susan was covered only by a sheet and a thin blanket.

"I'm glad to see you, sir," my housekeeper said. "I fear for both mother and child."

Fortier nodded and bent to his patient. He spent a few minutes examining her and asked questions, which Mrs. Eason answered readily. He folded down the covers and produced a stethoscope with a flexible rubber tube.

"I am certain the child still lives," he said after about two minutes. He gently pulled down one of Susan's lower eyelids, then the other. "I don't think this is a contagious fever. Do you see the yellowish tinge to her skin? And here, on the inside of the eyelid and the white of her eye. I think it's her liver. I wonder . . ." He turned Susan's hands over to study the palms and pulled up the cover from the end of her bed to look at the soles of her feet.

"What are you looking for?" I asked.

"Signs of the pox." He looked directly at me. "The black-guard who got her with child may have infected her. I will have the nurse look more closely for certain indications, but it can be very hard to tell if the early symptoms are missed." He felt around Susan's throat, his eyes thoughtful.

"Lady Helena," he said at last, "if you would like to help her, there are some tisanes you can brew to clarify the liver. They will likely be every bit as effective as anything you can get from the apothecary, although you may need to send to him for some of the ingredients. Others you may have— coriander seed, lemon leaf, lemons, ginger, licorice root."

"We have those, sir." Mrs. Eason smiled. "If her ladyship doesn't already keep them in her workroom."

"We can go through the list together," I said, feeling a rush of relief at the thought I could actually help someone.

"I'll write down some instructions for you and give you something for her fever." Fortier returned his stethoscope to his bag. "The nurse will administer the tisanes. I'd rather you don't come into intimate contact with her until I'm quite sure there is no rash or chancre. Now let's look at that workroom of yours." He grinned. "According to my sister, your eccentricities are being much discussed in Littleberry."

It took us a few minutes to ensure a message was dispatched to the nurse. By the time we'd finished, Guttridge had joined us, hovering in the background like a guardian angel as Fortier inspected the workroom. He praised some arrangements and made a few practical suggestions. He then asked for a sheet of paper and wrote down a list of ingredients.

"None of these will harm Susan or the baby, so you can experiment with proportions at your leisure and taste the tisane yourself. Try to come up with a light tisane, sweetened with just a little honey, and see the nurse gets Susan to sip it as often as possible. When it begins working, her urine will be of a light color and plenteous."

I nodded, pleased that Fortier was taking my willingness to help so seriously.

"And this is powdered willow bark." He produced a white packet. "The proportions for preparation and the dosage are written on the paper. Don't give her any more than it says here."

"I'll make that while you prepare the other potion," said Guttridge, coming forward and holding out her hand.

"When do you think she will emerge from her delirium?" I asked.

Fortier shook his head. "The acute phase of the fever may last for a while yet. I don't think she's in any mortal danger, but you must be prepared—a fever is always risky. She could lose the child or her own life."

"I see." We all knew the danger of any kind of fever or infection. Papa's death had followed just days after he'd begun to recover from a bout of pleurisy. The general consensus of the medical men had been that the infection had weakened his heart.

Fortier smiled reassuringly. "She's young. She may take days to recover though. I'll come back and see her often, but good and careful nursing is what she really needs. Her father should be told."

"I'll write a note to Sir Edward immediately." I picked up my pen and dipped the nib in the inkpot. "He sent word to me this morning that he's planning to go see the farmer at lunchtime."

"In the course of his mayoral duties?" Fortier looked surprised.

"He's a good mayor because he really cares about people. It bothers him that Farmer Hatherall is so very upset about Susan. Sir Edward heard from the rector that he broke down again, during a meeting between the two of them this time. The rector's done what he can to comfort the poor man, but apparently he's quite inconsolable—all the more now that he's lost his position as churchwarden. Ned said he must feel as if the world's coming to an end. He—Ned, I mean—feels that Farmer Hatherall needs to hear from a man in a position of authority that it's not. Ned's heard more stories of disgrace and recovery than he can count."

"I can understand his sense of disgrace." Fortier watched as I crossed to the bellpull. "The common people are good at closing ranks and keeping quiet about any kind of trouble, and the gentry can send a girl abroad for a while to avoid a scandal. It's those who are desperate to be respectable, climb the ladder, as you might say, who panic and fear they'll never be able to hold their heads up again."

"Please have this sent to Sir Edward's offices immediately." I handed the folded piece of paper to the footman who'd answered the bell. "Sir Edward will know just how to speak to him," I said to both Fortier and Guttridge. Despite Guttridge's well-trained silence, Fortier's words had earned a nod of approval from her, and I could see the light of interest in her eyes.

"Good." Fortier picked up his bag. "I'll come back this afternoon to see how Susan does. If she should happen to be much worse, I'll ride past Dene Farm on my way back to Littleberry and let the farmer know. Perhaps this illness will make him feel more charitably toward his daughter."

"You're very good, considering the trouble she's caused you."

He shrugged. "I've learned one can survive much, and I am not one of the seekers of respectability I referred to. Lady Helena," he bowed briefly over my hand, "I look forward to seeing you this afternoon."

Guttridge waited until Fortier had left before speaking. "Perceptive, isn't he? I don't know many gentlemen who understand the lower orders so well."

"Do I detect a little warming toward Monsieur Fortier, Guttridge?"

"Oh no, my lady." Guttridge held up the beaker she was using, ensuring that the powder was properly dissolved. "He's still an interfering Frenchman. But fair in his opinions, I'll say that for him."

~

I heard the result of Ned's visit firsthand, as it happened. Guttridge disappeared upstairs to deliver the febrifuge and lay out my evening dress, and I decided to work on some of the recipes Fortier had given me. We had enough ingredients for me to begin, and I sent to the apothecary for the rest. The ginger root I'd had drying in the tin cupboard was sufficiently desiccated to use, and by the time the hall boy returned with the licorice root and lemon leaf, I had carefully ground some of the other ingredients in Mama's brass spice grinder, put them in jars, and labeled them. At the same time, I put some larger pieces of spice into a pot of water to boil slowly on the paraffin stove. I wasn't sure whether whole spices or ground would be most efficacious.

I had my luncheon delivered to the workroom on a tray and picked at it while I worked. I rather enjoyed the informality of this arrangement. I worked slowly, of course, due to my inexperience and the fact that I didn't have Susan to help me, but by two o'clock I felt I'd made real progress. I was able to deliver a large pot of fairly pleasant-tasting tisane to the hired nurse who'd come to replace Mrs. Eason.

Susan was no better—if anything, I thought she looked worse. This was all the motivation I needed to work harder. The spice grinder had to be dismantled, carefully washed, and dried before each new ingredient was ground. I realized I probably needed some kind of scullery next to my workroom, as going down to the stillroom disrupted the servants' work.

I'd been furiously scribbling in my notebook, noting down the proportions I'd used and sketching a plan for a scullery in one corner, when I realized someone else was in the room.

"My dear."

I looked up to see Ned smiling at me.

"I've said hello twice." He still wore his coat. From the mud on his shoes, I surmised he'd walked to Whitcombe rather than bother with a carriage.

"I'm so sorry, Ned. How rude of me."

I gave him a quick kiss on the cheek, enjoying the mingled scents of cologne and the outdoors that clung around him.

"Susan is still very poorly, and I'm trying to follow Monsieur Fortier's recipes for tisanes that will help her. I'm expecting Fortier at any moment, in fact. Did you get a chance to see Farmer Hatherall?"

"I did." He unbuttoned his coat but didn't shed it. "I'm glad I got your note—it arrived just as I was leaving. I thought I'd call on you before I did anything else. It's on my way since I have to go to the workhouse about a matter of more room needed for burials. Then I'm due to talk to one of the brickyard owners, then I have to go to the police station to chat about a case of theft. A mayor's life isn't all ceremony, you know." He eyed the cold chicken and buttered bread left on my tray, and his stomach gave an audible growl. "Is that . . ."

"Of course you can have it. I'll ring for more, if you like."

"Not at all, my dear. This will keep body and soul together for the moment, and they always give me cake at the workhouse." He took large bites and talked with his mouth full. "I'm sure most people think I attend banquets every day, wearing my golden chain. If only they knew."

It took Ned about three minutes to dispose of what was left on my tray. "Now then," he said, wiping his mouth with his handkerchief, "to our business. I told Hatherall his daughter was ill, as you asked, but he says he won't come to see her. He was very difficult to talk to, if I'm being honest. More angry than upset, and he's directing some of that anger at you. Says Susan should have stayed at home with him and not flaunt her belly in a big house where there's impressionable young men and women. I suspect that if you weren't the lady of the manor, he'd drag Susan home."

"I didn't mean to cause a rift between them," I said, surprised. "Susan said she'd talked with her father and he'd agreed to the change."

"He might have done, at that. He didn't say what he thought as directly as I've relayed it to you—I'm translating the gist of it. He's a clever man, that one. Talked around and around his true thoughts like a Member of Parliament, and if I asked him a question, I never got a straight answer. Made me think of Shakespeare: 'Meet it is I set it down that one may smile, and smile, and be a villain.' He's wasted as a farmer."

I frowned. "He seemed simple and direct enough to me."

"I always thought he was. But it was as if he'd discarded the persona of the humble churchwarden and honest tenant farmer and clothed himself in a more prickly skin. We went into his study—have you seen it?"

"I've never been anywhere but the parlor."

"Crammed with books on self-improvement, with Samuel Smiles's *Self Help* given pride of place. A copy of Debrett's too, well-thumbed."

I raised my eyebrows. "I wonder if he encouraged Susan to go to Hyrst as a little girl, then. But how can he be both angry at me and so eager to get on? Usually, people either want to toady up to us or they reject us utterly and let the world know we should all be put to the guillotine like the French *aristos*." I shivered.

"Perhaps it's ambition that's at the root of his behavior," Ned suggested. "Resenting you for not helping him hide Susan's disgrace?"

I sighed. "Justin thought so highly of him. He would have known the key to the conundrum. He spent countless hours with Hatherall and must know—must have known the man better than anyone else except his daughter."

Ned was buttoning up his coat again. "I wonder—do we ever really know other people? Even those you see daily can have hidden lives. Not that I think Hatherall is running a house of ill repute on the sly or anything like that. I mean his inner life. Are you going to spend the rest of the day making potions?" He planted a farewell kiss, tickly with beard and mustache, on my cheek.

I rolled my shoulder blades against the cut of my bodice to ease my back as much as I could. "Only until Monsieur Fortier has been and gone. I'd really like a walk or even a ride. I've been working hard today."

Fortier turned up about twenty minutes after Ned had left and by my instructions was shown straight upstairs to the servants' bedrooms. By the time I made my way upstairs, he was packing his bag.

"I don't have any encouraging news," he said when he saw me. "She's in an utter stupor. Did Sir Edward speak with her father?"

"Yes. He didn't want to visit her here."

Fortier frowned. "That's unfortunate. I wish he would. I suppose I will ride by the farm, then."

"Can you wait a few minutes?" I glanced out of the window, where the sun was already quite low. It was the shortest day of the year. "I'm quite desperate to get outdoors. It'll only take me five minutes to get into my riding habit. I've already sent word to Mank that he should have the horses ready. I can see you're on horseback." Fortier was indeed dressed in his everyday riding clothes, looking for all the world as if he'd never left Littleberry.

"Of course I'll wait. Do you mean you wish to call on Farmer Hatherall as well?"

"Not exactly *call*. Ned said his behavior was rather odd. Riding down to the farm will kill two birds with one stone. I'll get some fresh air, and I'll lend your visit a little more weight by my presence. I agree with you—he should come to see his daughter."

Fifteen minutes later I was in the stable yard, Mank assisting me into the saddle while Fortier swung himself up onto his huge black horse. The air was tinged with frost yet damp with approaching nightfall, the sun slanting low and bathing everything in golden light. I breathed deep; after the work of the day, the ride would set me up marvelously well for dinner and a good night's sleep. If only I didn't have a sick servant to worry about, I might be able to enjoy such a day despite the grief of Justin's absence.

We picked our way carefully downhill, but once we reached the river path we urged our horses into a fast trot. Given that our ride would be short, Mank didn't ask to gallop Puck, so the gelding was inclined to frisk about. Sandy's gait was smooth and steady, her ears pricked well forward.

We passed Ruby on the way and slowed to speak to her.

She carried a small basket, which she uncovered to show four jars covered in squares of bright fabric.

"For the rector," she said. "The master asked me to take three jars over as a sign he don't hold nothing against him for losing his place as churchwarden. How's Miss Susan?"

"She has a nasty fever," I said. "Didn't Mr. Hatherall say anything about her?"

Ruby shook her head. "I'm sorry to hear that. No, he just said to take the raspberry jam to the rector and wish him well, then stop at my sister Sally's for the night. The fourth jar's for her."

I looked at Fortier and shook my head sadly. What kind of father wouldn't come to see his sick child? But I didn't want to labor the point with Ruby, who was clearly in a cheerful mood at the prospect of spending time with her sister.

"So your master's in?" Fortier asked her.

"He was when I left." Ruby's carefree smile brightened her face again as she moved off.

Dene Farm was soon visible, its red brick lit invitingly by the golden rays of the fast-declining sun. A wisp of smoke drifted up from its tall chimney stack. Even so near Christmas there were one or two roses on the vine that clambered over the porch, their petals withered but still bright. Behind the farmhouse, the slope of Whitcombe Hill was bright green and fresh-looking, dotted with the silently munching shapes of ewes.

We dismounted, leaving the horses with Mank. Fortier rang the heavy bell by the front door.

"He may forget he has to answer his own bell," said Fortier after we'd waited in silence for two minutes.

"Or he could be out in the fields taking one last look at the sheep. It's the sort of thing Justin always did."

Fortier reached for the door handle, which turned easily.

"Unless he's hiding somewhere, hoping we'll go away." He grinned briefly. "Come along."

Used as I was to the ceremonial of being admitted by servants, it was strange to simply step over someone's threshold. Fortier seemed quite at home. No doubt he was accustomed to visiting the houses of sick people who didn't have servants and probably often let himself in.

"If he's anywhere, I imagine he'll be in the kitchen. I saw no lights upstairs." Fortier moved easily through the darkened hallway toward a door at the rear, under which a strip of glowing light showed clearly. It took him a moment to locate the handle, almost invisible in the gloom.

"Hatherall?" he called as he stepped inside the room. "Hath—"

He backed out so quickly he trod on my toes.

"Fils de putain!"

He whirled around and steadied me as I danced on one foot.

"You can't go in there."

"Why not? Ow." I put the throbbing foot gingerly back on the ground. *"What* did you just say? It sounded very vulgar."

"It was, and I apologize for swearing in front of a lady. Hatherall's hanged himself."

"What?"

I sniffed the air, which was redolent of something stronger than cooking.

"What's that smell?"

Fortier sighed. "He voided his bowels at the point of death. Hanged men generally do."

"Oh, heavens." I put a hand to my nose. "So you're quite sure he's dead?" The reality of what lay beyond the door was beginning to impinge on my senses, and I felt cold and dizzy.

"Very sure. The room is well lit." He gave me a little push in the direction of the front door. "Can you go find your groom and tell him to ride for help? Or you could undertake the ride if you don't mind going alone—head for the bridge. I need assistance getting him down and another witness that I found him hanging."

"Oh no." I faced him squarely; he was in shadow, the light from the kitchen outlining him and gleaming on his dark hair. "*I'm* going to witness this death and make sure nobody can make any more wild accusations against you. They won't question my word."

"But it's unsightly. It's unfit for a lady's eyes."

"I'll be the judge of that." I pushed past Fortier before he thought to stop me—and before I had a chance to change my mind.

It was indeed unsightly—ghastly might be a better word —but I was forewarned. After the initial, heart-pounding shock of seeing him I was able to look at the swollen black tongue and protruding bloodshot eyes with surprising detachment. The farmer had hanged himself from a stout hook driven well into a beam near the fireplace, its original purpose amply suggested by the huge smoked ham placed carefully on the table. The ceiling was not terribly high; he'd used a very short length of fairly thin rope, and his feet dangled perhaps a mere twelve inches off the floor. This meant the gruesome face wasn't so very far above me, and the distasteful aspects Fortier warned me about were all too near my nose. I removed myself to the other side of the room, feeling sick.

"What do you think he was standing on?" I asked faintly.

"That." Fortier indicated a stool lying on its side by the dresser. "He probably kicked it all the way over there as he flailed about." His face was solemn. "He may even have been trying to find his footing. He wouldn't be the first suicide to have regrets."

"How awful." I looked around the room, recovering

myself now that I wasn't looking directly at Hatherall. "Shouldn't we look for a—a note or something? Aren't suicides supposed to leave a note?"

"In novels." Fortier raised his eyebrows and slipped his hand under my elbow. "Come now, Lady Helena. Let's prove my complete innocence by finding your groom and sending him to raise the alarm. I suppose I'd better leave him up there after all; he's very definitely dead."

IN THE DOVES' NEST

"*I*n the circumstances, I'm truly not expecting anyone to worry about providing for my comforts," I said.

I watched as Fortier replaced the glass chimney on the lamp he'd just lit. He'd brought me into the Hatheralls' parlor, cold and cheerless now. Cold indeed—it was, after all, December, and the sun had sunk below the horizon. I shivered.

"You need a fire." Fortier moved swiftly toward the fireplace. It had been laid with fresh kindling atop a few crumpled pieces of paper, with larger logs ready on the hearth. But before he could light the fire, a disturbance at the front door heralded the return of Mank, and he had someone with him.

"Never mind that." I flapped a hand at Fortier. "I'm warmly dressed, and I daresay I can start a fire myself if need be. Let's see who's come."

Providentially, the new arrival turned out to be one of the borough constables. He removed his regulation helmet with a respectful "m'lady" and eyed Fortier, whom he evidently knew, with a wary stare before making his way to the kitchen. Fortier followed. When they returned a few minutes later, the constable looking somewhat green in the face, we embarked upon a brief conference during which I made it crystal clear that Fortier and I had found Hatherall's body together.

During this time, poor Mank had ridden back in the direction of Littleberry. He soon returned to report that he had reached the nearest public house this time and that several Littleberry men were on their way to lend assistance. He looked chilled to the bone and swayed slightly as he spoke to us.

"You'd oblige me by taking the horses back to Whit-combe." I spoke as crisply as possible to disguise my concern for my groom. "Monsieur Fortier's horse, too, if you can manage it. Do you mind if we stable your animal for the night?" I turned to the Frenchman. "It's not good for them to stay out in the cold much longer."

"I don't mind at all." Fortier blew into his hands to warm them. "It's very good of you, Lady Helena."

"Nonsense. Mank, see you get something hot to eat while the stablehands look to the horses. I'd appreciate it if you could return for me later on foot. We can take the short cut up the hill and not bother with the carriage."

"You're not staying, m'lady?" The constable, whose name escaped me, looked as disapproving as he could manage.

I stiffened my back and gave the man a good, hard stare. "I will remain until Mr. Hatherall is removed from the premises. He is my tenant."

I watched the constable's face as his thought processes clearly staged a battle between arguing with the aristocracy and allowing a woman to remain in the house. The arrival of a large group of men put an end to the discussion, and—

since I was clearly not welcome anywhere near the scene of the tragedy—I retreated back into the parlor, leaving the door half-open. The sounds of the constable trying to gain control of the situation while Fortier insisted a search be made for a suicide note and the men all expressed varying degrees of dismay reverberated down the hallway as I stared around the room.

It really was cold. Well, lighting a fire wouldn't be too difficult, particularly since Fortier had left a box of Flaming Fusees on the hearth. I was preparing to strike a match when something caught my eye.

It was my own name, written in dark blue ink on one of the crumpled pieces of paper on which the kindling lay. No doubt Ruby, or perhaps the farmer himself, had used the contents of the wastepaper basket for the fire; I had seen my own servants do as much.

I put the match carefully back in the box and removed the kindling that lay atop the paper waste. It didn't seem right to read someone else's private papers, but that person was dead, and it was, after all, my name. I flattened out the paper, which was of reasonably good quality, and carried it to the pool of light shed by the lamp.

After a moment's consideration, I realized that what I had was two different drafts. On one side of the paper there were notes concerning spring lambing, marred by a huge blot where the writer's pen had clearly failed. I guessed that the farmer had thriftily put the spoiled paper aside for future use; he had always struck me as a careful kind of man.

I turned the paper over, and the words "Lady Helena" jumped out at me. So it *was* about me. Seeing my own name in what I presumed was Hatherall's writing gave me an odd feeling, but as I read on I could see nothing startling in the few lines of neat, slanting script.

My own dear daughter I cannot approve I cannot see why
you understand fully understand why you forsake our own
doves' nest where you have been so happy. You are not Poor
Susan [the next part was illegible, being heavily scratched
out] you are not outcast and never will be. Lady Helena will
have her whims and fancies as she is entitled to do being a
lady and as it has always been thus with the family. The great
house is not your place [another illegible passage] but your
loving father waits ever for you in hope [here the writing
ended, without punctuation.]

I returned to the fireplace, removing the rest of the kindling
and inspecting the other pieces of paper carefully. There was
nothing of any interest on them; nevertheless, I smoothed
them out and tucked them into the pocket of my riding habit,
reluctant to dispose of them until Fortier had seen them.

A noise in the hallway brought me to the half-open door.
Four men were carrying in what looked like an old door. It
seemed plain to me that their purpose was to transport
Hatherall to wherever they had decided to take him. Was this
how Justin had been taken to Fortier's rooms at the pottery?
I stepped into the hallway as soon as the men had passed
my door.

At a shout from one of them, the kitchen door opened. I
had a glimpse of a still, heavy form lying on the kitchen table
before Fortier emerged and shut the door behind him.

"You're freezing," was what he said as soon as his eyes
focused on me. I realized he was right. I hadn't noticed till
that moment that my teeth were chattering.

"I'm a-all right," I forced out through a stiff jaw. "H-have
they found any kind of note?"

"No, and we've had a fairly thorough look through all the
rooms except the one you were in. Why didn't you light the
fire? You could have called me to help you."

"I don't *need* help lighting a fire." It stung me that Fortier could think I was so helpless. "I found something. I don't think it's significant."

I was sorry to quench the flame of excitement that had leapt, momentarily, into Fortier's eyes, but the next second he had hold of my hands and was pulling me into the parlor again. The reason for his action was made amply clear by the noise and movement in the hallway as the men—complaining somewhat since the passage was not wide and they had difficulty maneuvering the door with its burden—carried the farmer out of the house.

"*Now* may I take you home?" Fortier asked. "The moment your groom arrives at least. I suppose the proprieties must be observed."

"They must. Look at this."

My hands were stiff with cold, but I managed to unfold the sheets of paper and hand them to Fortier. "Only the top one. The rest don't seem to mean anything."

Fortier was silent for a few moments, reading. He held the paper up to the light, clearly trying to see if he could make out the obliterated words, but I knew he'd have no more luck than me.

"'Doves' nest' is somewhat poetic for a farmer," Fortier said eventually. "Almost lover-like. But the rest—kind and fatherly, as we'd all certainly believed."

Naturally, I seized on the most damning remark. "Lover-like? You're not suggesting—Fortier, that's disgusting. I refuse to believe it."

"Hadn't it occurred to you?" Fortier's tone was dry.

"Of course it hadn't. He's—he *was*—our churchwarden, for heaven's sake. Look at what's he's written—was trying to write—that he forgives his daughter and would welcome her home." I wrinkled my brow for a moment as my own words stirred some memory, but the fleeting thought was immediately gone. "Those are the words of a good man, Fortier. And besides," I added more practically, "even if your revolting theory were true, Susan would never admit to it."

17

A SHOCKING ACCUSATION

*O*ur conversation had ended there, interrupted by Mank's arrival. Twenty minutes later Fortier and I were walking slowly up Whitcombe Hill in the dark, Mank plodding ahead of us with a lantern. The night was the coldest we'd yet had. I could feel the slippery crunch of frosty grass under my feet and was glad for Justin's old walking stick, which Mank had thought to bring back for me. There was no moon, but above us the thickly clustered stars served as a backdrop for the brighter constellations. Yelping cries in the dark line of trees to our left indicated the presence of foxes. Occasionally a short, sleepy bleat could be heard from the night-bound sheep.

Neither of us spoke much. We were both in a subdued mood and, in my case at least, very hungry.

In the end, it was I who broke the silence. "You'll stay and eat some supper, I hope? It's the least I can do."

Fortier shook his head. "I wanted to see you home and look in on Susan, but after that I must get back to the body. They're waiting for me at the pottery."

"I'll have sandwiches and coffee sent down for all of you."

And I would abandon formality and eat by the fire, then soak in a hot bath for a long time. At least the physical exertion of walking up the hill had brought some life back into my cold limbs.

"That's kind. I've sent for Sir Edward."

"Poor Ned. I expect he was looking forward to a quiet evening after such a busy day."

I saw the gleam of teeth as Fortier smiled. "I expect he was. So was I."

"Poor you too, then."

"I'm used to it. I really will be most grateful for the food and coffee."

We walked on in silence for a few moments. The hill was steep, and Fortier offered me his arm to keep me from slipping.

"You won't say anything to Susan until she's on the mend, will you?" he asked me. "If she survives . . . and perhaps it's better if she doesn't."

I dragged my sluggish senses away from the contemplation of the feel of Fortier's arm under the broadcloth of his jacket and focused my mind on what he'd just said.

"That's a horrible thing to say. Is it because of what you think?" I let go of Fortier's arm momentarily but grabbed it again as my left foot slipped. I felt, rather than saw, Fortier staring at me.

"I don't necessarily think it—call it a cynical notion if you will. I can hardly build a theory of incest on two words, so let's leave it aside. But don't you realize what Hatherall has done, whatever his motive? As a suicide, his estate is forfeit. His children will inherit nothing. Susan is destitute—a candidate for the workhouse—her only hope now is the charity of others."

The truth of his words struck me like a physical blow. "Susan and her baby have a home at Whitcombe House as long as they need one," I retorted. "As if I'd let one of our people go to the workhouse."

But he was right; that was charity—the start of a lifelong dependence on the whims of others unless Susan could find a husband. Or unless my plan of providing her with training for the future succeeded.

Fortier's words also had deeper implications, I realized. "This is going to be terrible for her, isn't it?" I asked. "They won't want to bury her father in the cemetery either. And him a churchwarden . . . Dear God, Fortier, I wish you hadn't raised the possibility of . . . that. But if I refuse to believe it, and I do, why would a respectable man like Farmer Hatherall take his own life? Why commit such a crime against God, his family, himself—and with no explanation?"

I felt Fortier shrug. "There are other plausible theories, of course. Despair over his daughter's disgrace. Some knowledge, perhaps, of the father's identity that made him afraid. Fear of the child's paternity being betrayed by a physical resemblance. Or, at the most fundamental level, simple fear of the future."

"What do you mean?"

"Think about it. An ambitious man loses his patron; Hatherall must have been anxious about his future now that Sir Justin is gone. A man who lays great store by his respectability loses his standing in the community; he would never have been churchwarden again, that's for sure. Your people may lose their money or their health or their possessions or their sanity, but they never lose what makes them fundamentally themselves—the name that ties them fast to a position in society. But for a working man, status is a fragile thing. It's tied up with what you do—what you are seen to do every day. The workhouse or, less drastically, a slide into a life where you lose your comforts and must spend your old age struggling against poverty is a frightening abyss beneath your feet."

We had mostly spoken in near-whispers, mindful of Mank's presence, but Fortier's voice strengthened on the last few sentences. I could have sworn I heard Mank grunt assent to those last words.

"He should have trusted me more," I said loudly—for Mank's benefit as much as for anything else. "I could have helped him. I'd never let any of my people suffer poverty in their old age."

"Yes, I've no doubt you would want to help. But you may remarry."

I bit my lip. I was not going to discuss my prospects with Fortier—I didn't know him well enough for that. And I certainly wasn't going to talk about them with Mank listening. But it seemed to me that his words hung in the frosty air like a threat, and I understood what he meant.

We reached the top of the hill, and the tall windows of Whitcombe House came into view, hidden till now by the slope of the land. I had a sudden picture of my house holding its breath, waiting to see what I would do next. For the day I put my hand into a man's—out of love, out of loneliness, or simply to please my family—the property that had once been Justin's and was now mine, and the lives of those who had worked for us, would pass into the keeping of my new husband. For a second, I understood what Fortier meant by fear of the future.

~

Fortier turned back when we reached Whitcombe. My first act when I walked into the warmth and brightness of my home was to order food and hot drinks to be sent down to the men working at Dene Farm and the pottery. I surmised from the subdued, wary faces of my servants that the news of Farmer Hatherall's suicide, brought back no doubt by Mank with the horses, had been the evening's main topic of discussion.

My second act was to open a missive from Gerry that was waiting for me on the silver tray in the hallway. She stated she'd persuaded Ned to go to bed early as he'd looked unwell and refused to awaken him—and she'd sent a note to Fortier to say as much. And did I really think Ned should turn out on such a cold night, suicide or not? And *what* was I doing dabbling in such unpleasant events, getting in the way of the men? "Really, Baby, I think Michael may have a point—you can't be trusted on your own." From which I deduced that the news of the suicide had flown to Littleberry just as quickly as it had climbed the hill to Whitcombe.

I trudged wearily up the servants' stair to look in on Susan. I was relieved when the nurse informed me she'd drunk a reasonable amount of the tisane. But she was sunk in a deep slumber, her skin hot and dry, and clearly far from out of danger.

Only with these necessities completed did I allow myself to collapse into an armchair by the fire in the small library. I barely had the energy to touch the food brought to me. Guttridge had to rouse me from the doze into which I'd fallen to get me up to bed.

Susan was my first thought the next morning, and I visited her room before dressing. She was still sleeping, but her color was better. I reiterated my instructions to keep all news of her father's suicide away from her and returned to my room wondering if Fortier would come by to see his patient and collect his horse.

An hour later I was dressed and seated at my desk in the morning room, trying to apply my mind to my correspondence. I should write a letter to Justin's—now my—lawyer about Dene Farm. The tenancy had lapsed with Farmer Hatherall's death; should I look for a new tenant farmer? What about the blessed sheep, Justin's pride and joy? I knew Justin and Farmer Hatherall had employed shepherds, but I had a feeling that was casual labor. Somebody would have to look after the animals. Was I really going to have to give in to Michael and appoint the odious Brandrick? Much as I disliked him, I could think of nobody more knowledgeable or capable.

"What's the most responsible action?" I asked myself out loud. "Does a well-regulated landowner take a personal interest in all matters pertaining to her land, even when she has neither competence nor inclination?" For in truth, my interest in my fields and streams, pathways and copses was mostly the enjoyment I took in riding around them.

I dipped the nib of my pen in the inkwell, watching a shiny black drop fall back into the liquid. "Or does she let her annoying, interfering, but quite possibly correct brother take over and have his nasty steward run her estate?" Another drop of ink fell. "Does not knowing the answer make her an empty-headed female not capable of looking after her land?"

A prickling behind my eyes heralded the fall of a drop that wasn't ink, a salty warmth sliding down my cheek and tickling the sensitive skin of my chin. "Drat you, Justin, why did you have to die?"

I raised my head and wiped quickly at my face as I heard movement outside the door. When Ned entered, I felt a small surge of relief. Here was somebody I could consult.

"Ned, I need to—what's wrong?"

Most incongruously, my brother-in-law was wearing his mayoral robe of fur-trimmed scarlet, his heavy chain of office glinting against his starched lace jabot. He clutched his tricorne hat in one hand and a piece of paper in the other. His face was almost as gray as the tips of his whiskers.

I stared for a moment and then realized I'd been so preoccupied with the problem of Dene Farm that I'd forgotten *why* there was a problem. Of course—Ned must be terribly cut up about Hatherall's suicide. And Gerry had said he wasn't well.

"Oh dear." I jumped up and grabbed Ned by the arm, leading him toward an armchair. "Ned, darling, please sit down. You needn't worry about me; I'm quite all right. This is all too much for you."

"This? This?" Ned looked confused, and a qualm assailed me. Was he more ill than I'd thought?

"The whole business with Farmer Hatherall. The poor man—what despair he must have been in. Fortier gave me a perfectly reasonable explanation—several, actually—but I can't help feeling he knew who fathered Susan's child."

Fortier's horrible theory of incest rose in my mind again. I dismissed it firmly and continued, sticking to my own, far more likely version of events. "But unless Susan tells, and I don't see how we can force her, that secret's died with him."

"That's just the point." Ned coughed to clear his throat and stuck a finger inside his stock, easing the fit of the cloth around his neck. "It hasn't died with him." He waved the paper he was holding in front of my eyes. "I slept like a stone last night—I suppose Gerry told you I've been a bit under the weather. I was late for an important function this morning, so I grabbed my letters as I left and took them with me. Just as well, really, that I opened this in the retiring room and not in front of your sister."

"Who's it from?" I felt only a mild curiosity.

"Hatherall." Ned grunted, spreading the letter out with his fingers. "He calls it a confession."

"A confession?"

"I'll read it to you in a moment, but first I'd better tell you the gist. You won't like it."

"I'll like it even less if you spin out the suspense. Spit it out."

"In short, he names Justin as the father of his daughter's child."

I sat frozen for a few moments while I felt the blood rush to my face in a tide of red. Finally, I spoke.

"No. That's not possible."

"The confession of a dying man, he says. One who will no longer damn his eternal soul by withholding the truth." One corner of Ned's mouth twitched up. "Although, if you'll forgive me for saying so, he's damned his soul rather more effectively by committing *felo de se*."

I opened my mouth to mention Fortier's theory that Susan's father was her child's father and then shut it again. Two words might be enough to raise a suspicion in Fortier's mind, but they weren't proof of anything. Until that proof was established, it would be entirely wrong of me to defend Justin by making an even worse accusation.

"It's not possible." I fell back on my previous words. "It's not true. I don't know what game Hatherall was playing, but that's a complete untruth."

"We could always ask Susan," Ned said. "How is she, by the way?"

"A little better. And no, I'm not going to harangue her about something I know to be untrue. The poor child's going to awaken to the knowledge that her father has died in the worst way possible—that any inheritance she might have hoped for is gone—no, I'm not going to ask her. If the truth was so bad that she and her father have both lied to shield whoever it was, then perhaps it had best lie dormant."

I got up and walked halfway across the room, then realized I had to lean on the back of an armchair because my legs were shaking.

"My dear." Ned's voice was very gentle, very kind. "All

men might succumb to a moment of weakness. It doesn't mean Justin loved you any the less."

"NO!" The word emerged as a strangled shout. "There isn't a word of truth in it, Ned. Not a word. I will swear to that on oath. I know—knew—my husband, and I can tell you categorically he didn't father Susan's child."

A cough behind us made me whirl around. I saw Fortier standing in the doorway.

"Forgive me, Lady Helena," he said, bowing slightly. "I plead urgent business for my abrupt entrance, but I believe I may have been overtaken by events. I—well, I overheard a few seconds of your conversation." He looked at Ned. "I think you need to give Lady Helena the benefit of the doubt."

I felt myself flush again, to the roots of my hair. "You may as well know the rest, then. Mr. Hatherall sent Sir Edward what he called a confession. Containing a lie that Justin—" I choked on my words. I felt Ned's arm around my waist, reassuring.

"Steady on, old thing. If you say it's not true, it's not true. But it's dashed odd. What did the man hope to achieve?"

"Scandal." Fortier drew in his breath suddenly as if a thought had occurred to him. As I turned, I saw a look pass between him and Ned.

"I can't suppress it," Ned said.

"I know." Fortier sounded almost miserable.

"Suppress what?" I asked.

"I'm sorry, Helena." Ned folded the letter and put it into the pocket of his robes, forgetting his promise to read it to me. "This letter will have to be read out at the inquest."

"No." If I had flushed before, I was sure I was pale now. I felt as if all the blood had vanished from my body.

"Is there no doubt at all the letter is from Hatherall?" Fortier asked.

"It was handed to my housekeeper in person by Hatherall's servant yesterday evening. I'm sure I can get her to confirm his handwriting." Ned ran a hand through his thinning hair. "Gerry put it with some other letters I'd received while I was out, but by the time I got home last night I felt unwell. I didn't put up any resistance to my wife's insistence that I go straight to bed. It pains me to think I might have had time to prevent him carrying out his terrible plan."

"You wouldn't have," I said. "Monsieur Fortier and I saw Ruby leaving Dene Farm last night. From the timing, I imagine Farmer Hatherall hanged himself almost the second she'd shut the door."

"It was a very determined attempt." Fortier nodded his agreement. "Most suicides dither—if they cut their wrists, for example, you will see several smaller cuts have been made before the successful one. People intending to throw themselves from bridges or jump from high places often hesitate so long that they're noticed by someone. The mind revolts at the enormity of ending one's own life."

"He must have had the rope handy," I said, remembering the still, heavy body. "How long does it—take?"

"Five minutes at the most." Fortier looked sideways at me. "Probably a lot less. He must have planned the thing carefully —measured the drop, cut the rope to length, tied the noose with care so that it wouldn't slip. And then he spoke quite naturally with Ruby. She told me he'd joked with her about her eagerness to spend some time with her sister and held forth on the qualities of her raspberry jam. It was my conversation with her that sent me here in such a hurry—well, to the town hall first, but they told me the mayor had already left."

"In full fancy dress." Ned looked down at his costume ruefully. "I thought I'd better speak to you, Helena, before I spoke to anyone else. But now I'll have to submit this to the coroner without delay. I'm sorry, my dear. I really must go. Would you like me to send Gerry to you?"

Ignoring the fact that the floor seemed to be swaying very slightly under my feet, I went to my brother-in-law and gave him a kiss on the cheek. "I'll be all right. I'm going to ask Monsieur Fortier to look at Susan Hatherall before he leaves." Then a thought struck me, and the swaying feeling intensified. "They won't interrogate her again, will they? About the baby? After all we did to make Mrs. Bearcroft leave her alone?"

"You can't rule out that she may be called as a witness," said Fortier. "There may now be only two people left on this earth who know the identity of her baby's father—the man himself and Susan. I don't know if such an inquiry would be deemed relevant to the inquest or whether they will simply dismiss Hatherall's letter as the ravings of a madman. After all, since he committed suicide there will be a presumption of insanity."

"He must have been insane," I said. "Because Justin had nothing to do with Susan Hatherall's child."

To my surprise, Ned enveloped me in a brief hug, the fur lapels of his mayor's robe tickling my cheek. "You're a brave little woman."

I didn't feel so brave once Ned had left. I turned to face Fortier.

"I'm not sure if he believes me."

"From his point of view, you said what any staunchly faithful wife would say. This is a damnable mess, Lady Helena. If Hatherall was trying to protect someone, he's been fiendishly clever about it. He accuses a dead man with a dying confession—which is almost certainly inadmissible as evidence in the general way of things, but the coroner won't ignore it. It will be read and discussed, and Sir Justin's good name will be stained—and this time there is no possibility of the accusation being retracted."

I bit my lip. "Are you going to say anything about the possibility of—of what you said? Drag Susan into that accusation? Supposing her father forced her, Fortier? After all, whatever it is, the secret must be a terrible one for Hatherall to go to such lengths. He was a churchwarden, for heaven's sake. A religious man. He must have seen suicide as one of the worst possible sins he could commit, yet he did the deed as coolly and efficiently as if he were putting a sick sheep out of its misery. He left his youngest child destitute—and I've no doubt at all that Maggie will be besmirched by this. You know how people talk. All this tragedy and disgrace—and for what?"

"There's something very rotten at the heart of all this," said Fortier. "I'm more convinced than ever Sir Justin's death is connected to something he knew or discovered." Seeing my face, he added, "I'm sorry, Lady Helena. I know you don't believe me—don't *want* to believe me—but I must speak what's in my mind."

I looked hard at Fortier for a few moments, the implications of his words blossoming in my thoughts.

"Wait," I said. "Connected—are you now implying the Hatheralls had something to do with Justin's death? This is getting worse and worse."

"Lucius Hatherall at least." Fortier looked grave. "Think about it, Lady Helena. We have only his word that he found Justin drowned in the river and jumped in to see if he were really dead."

I put my hand to my mouth. "If he had pushed Justin into the water—held him under—he would be soaking wet. The story about jumping straight into the river when he saw

Justin by the willow would be necessary to provide an explanation for the state of his clothing."

"Exactly. I've always thought it strange Hatherall didn't at least remove his jacket before jumping in."

I frowned. "Well, seen in the light of a devoted tenant desperate to save his employer, I suppose such an impulsive act would be understandable. You'll have to forgive me, Monsieur Fortier, but it's hard for me to see this particular question from a man's point of view. We women are so tightly laced and buttoned into our clothes that if I saw a drowning child, for example, I might well jump in without taking several minutes to unbutton my boots."

"And drown as well." There was the faintest twinkle in Fortier's eyes. "But you would at least shed any outer clothing—a cape, manteau, paletot, or any of the other ingenious variations on what in a man is simply a coat?"

"A heavy piece of clothing, yes. Most garments designed purely to add a layer of warmth when outdoors are comparatively easy to take off."

"A man's jacket is easily removed. Hatherall would only have to undo some buttons and slip his arms out of the sleeves."

"And yet you didn't raise this point before?"

"I did ask the question at the inquest, but as you said, the picture was that of one man devoted to another, and Hatherall's account of his actions was extremely convincing. This suicide paints everything in a very different light. It reveals Hatherall to be a master dissembler. Just think—knowing he intended to kill himself directly, he was yet able to talk naturally to his servant and never give her any qualm that something was wrong."

"And one of his last acts was to assassinate the character of the man to whom we all assumed he was devoted." I drew in a sudden breath.

"What?" Fortier's eyes were alert.

"I've just remembered something Ned said yesterday. Good heavens, was it only yesterday? When he came to see me after talking with Hatherall. He talked about him having a hidden life; said he avoided Ned's questions with the skill of a politician. And yet all Ned was trying to do was comfort him about Susan's baby, make him see that disgrace doesn't last forever. Ned quoted Shakespeare; that a man could smile and smile and be a villain."

"The mayor's a clever man." Fortier smiled, and I couldn't help smiling in response. In talking, we had somehow drifted toward the morning room's large window and seated ourselves at opposite ends of its long, broad window seat with Scotty between us. The sharp, frosty night had given way to a damp, cloudy morning. The hills that marked where the land rose to cliffs towering above the unseen sea were a deep blue-purple, brushed on their summits by feathery fingers of cloud. A dark bank of oncoming rain lowered almost to the sea, leaving just a narrow strip where the light broke through.

I looked away from the view and down at my hands. There was a discussion I was going to have to have with Fortier, and I wasn't looking forward to it. There were things no lady should ever have to discuss with a man who wasn't her husband. Even between Justin and me, such matters were rarely subjected to the brutality of words. But as it happened, Fortier spared me the pain of broaching the subject.

"Hatherall made one big mistake, didn't he? Perhaps he did indeed silence Sir Justin for the sake of whatever secret he and Susan were—are—hiding. And then he tried to kill him a second time, so to speak, by accusing him of wrong-doing—and again, by so doing he could protect himself and his daughter." He lowered his voice, and his words were gently spoken. "But he made an accusation that more than one person knows to be impossible."

We'd left the door open, naturally, for the sake of propriety. But now I rose swiftly to my feet, putting out a hand to indicate to Fortier that he should remain seated. I crossed to the door of the morning room and shut it as quietly as I knew how. Of course, my servants would know; I was surprised we hadn't been interrupted so far. But I would not allow any eavesdropping, not for this, not even at the risk of my reputation. The window seat was too far from the door to allow any servant to listen at the keyhole.

I seated myself again, feeling rather short of breath. The morning room was spacious, but closing the door gave me a feeling of unaccustomed intimacy. I gave myself a second or two to recover my equilibrium, passing a hand over Scotty's brindled coat before I spoke.

"Was that your professional opinion? That there was no hope?"

Fortier's remarkable green-gold eyes were fixed on mine, his expression sympathetic. "Very little. There are no true remedies for impotence. Only the quacks claim to be able to restore manhood to those unable to, well, to please their wives."

"Justin *was* able to please me," I said quickly. Now that I was forced to talk about this matter, I was determined to be frank. It was ridiculous to act like a blushing bride. I didn't want anyone, let alone Fortier, to see Justin as any less than a full man. "He was as . . . as attentive, and, ah . . . accomplished as I could wish. There are more things in life than . . . that, as I'm sure you know."

Good grief, I *was* blushing. Fortier cleared his throat.

"I beg your pardon, Lady Helena. That was most unfortunate phrasing. He did tell me your marriage was consummated."

"Yes. The, ah, problem wasn't so bad at first."

Silence fell between us for a few moments as we both contemplated the failure of an essential part of my marriage. But it *hadn't* been a failure in any way that mattered. We had known great joy in our marriage bed, Justin and I.

"Does anybody else know?" Fortier asked at last.

"Nobody."

Unless the servants knew, of course. Servants always knew more than you hoped they would, and one could only pray they wouldn't gossip. But I had told nobody in my family.

"They all supposed it was my fault," I said, knowing Fortier would understand what I meant.

"And you never spoke up to defend yourself against the assumption you were barren."

"Of course I didn't." A small spark of anger was flaring inside me—at what, I didn't know. At Fortier, perhaps, for knowing more about the most secret part of my life than I would want him to, physician or no. "I would do anything to protect Justin from scorn."

"You may have to speak up now." Fortier was looking at his boots.

"Speak up?" Then I realized what he meant, and now the heat that spread up my neck to my cheeks had more to do with fury than embarrassment.

"Nobody would ask me to speak on this matter. Nobody. How can you even think of such a thing?"

Fortier looked outwardly unmoved, but two spots of color appeared on his tanned cheeks. He leaned forward and jabbed a finger into the palm of the other hand.

"That letter of Hatherall's will be read at the inquest, if only to support a verdict of insanity. It may be possible to avoid having it read publicly, but it will be read. And I don't see how I can be involved in this and not come forward to testify that what Hatherall says cannot be true."

"You can't do that."

"You'd prefer that people think your husband was a seducer?"

"Stop." I put my hands over my eyes as if I could hide the picture Fortier had put in my mind. "Stop it. I won't hear this. I wish you'd go."

I felt strong hands around my arms, and Fortier pulled my hands away from my eyes—gently but with inexorable force. Scotty growled softly.

"The most destructive trait of the aristocracy, in my opinion, is its tendency to wish to keep everything it doesn't like hidden in a corner. I happen to believe in a more enlightened, scientific society where we can look our problems in the face." He gave my arms a gentle shake, then let go. "I would far rather you be the one to defend Sir Justin, you know. People already suspect my motives for just about everything I do. What will they imagine if I speak up in the name of truth?"

"They'll call you an interfering foreigner—as you are." I knew I was being horribly rude and probably quite unjust, but I was past caring.

"As I am." Fortier stood up. "And you, Lady Helena Whitcombe, are living in a dream world. You think your position in life and yes, even your money, make it possible for you to do as you want. I'm here to tell you that position and money are no protection against trouble, and hiding your head in the sand won't make the trouble go away. And now if you'll excuse me, it's time I went to see Susan."

18

SHAME AND SORROW

I maintained what I hoped was a dignified silence while Fortier made his bow and strode out of the room. By the time the sound of his footsteps was no longer audible, my legs were shaking so much that I sat back down on the window seat with a thump. That startled Scotty, who came to curl up against me with a sigh. I leaned my head against the panes of glass and stared out at the valley, where rain had begun to fall, willing my heart to stop pounding.

I felt raw and exposed, as if Fortier had ripped off my skin. I supposed I had known all along, since the first day I met him, that he was privy to Justin's secret; but Justin had gone beyond shame or sorrow, or so I thought. I hadn't considered I could feel shame or sorrow *for* him as if he still lived somewhere inside me, so it astonished me how deeply upset I was by the thought he could be publicly unmanned. That this would be the lasting impression people had of him rather than the picture he had presented in life, vigorous and strong. I would a thousand times prefer that people thought of me as barren.

And I had called Fortier an interfering foreigner, no doubt wounding him in *his* most vulnerable spot. I'd done what all of Littleberry did, making him the outsider who had no right to stick his French nose into our English business. I had broken the rules of courtesy and hospitality by which my sort of people lived, just because a man insisted on telling the truth.

But why *did* he have to tell the truth?

I watched the cloud descend upon Whitcombe Hill, a smothering mist that hid the valley from view, reflecting that I was far less fortunate than the other women in my family. Gerry had her kind, influential, responsible husband to lean on. Blanche could retreat behind the wall of self-serving ambition that seemed to make her impervious to other people's opinions. Annette and Alice had each other, and O had her art and cared little for anything else. I had few allies, and I'd just insulted one of those few.

"Stop feeling sorry for yourself." I pushed myself upright, facing the reflection of my face that had begun to emerge out of the dimming fog behind the windowpane. "You're a Scott-De Quincy. Don't sit around moping when you can find something useful to do."

I kissed Scotty on his silver-gray head, rose, and went to stand in the middle of the room. What had I been doing when Ned arrived? With a sinking feeling, I realized I was still faced with the correspondence concerning Dene Farm. Well, I couldn't postpone that. My lawyer needed to hear from me before the rumor of Farmer Hatherall's suicide reached him. I sat at my desk and pulled a sheet of paper toward me.

Half an hour later that task was done and the footman dispatched with the letter. But what about the blasted sheep? I paced the morning room for a further thirty minutes and then rang for Guttridge.

"Please tell Mrs. Foster I won't be in for luncheon after all," I told her as she fastened the bodice of my walking dress. "I'm going to Hyrst, and I expect to eat with my brother."

"You'll be taking the carriage, won't you, my lady? It's turned into a right murky old day out there."

I spared a fleeting thought for Fortier, who must have departed into the mist and drizzle on horseback. He would probably be soaked by the time he got home. Served him right. He should have come to say good-bye at least. And then it occurred to me that Fortier was no doubt as angry with me as I was with him.

"All the fault of that dratted letter," I fumed under my breath as I climbed the stairs to the servants' quarters to visit Susan before I left. "I should have snatched the thing from Ned's hand and thrown it into the fire. Why do men have to be so honorable?"

Susan was still weak and sleepy but most definitely on the mend. The nurse told me the French physician had given a good report of her, recommending broth to start with and vegetable soup once she began to show some signs of appetite.

I did my best to be cheerful and encouraging, even though I had a constant feeling of dread in case the young woman asked after her father. Every moment I spent with Susan unsettled me more. How long should I wait until I told her? Should I delay the news until she was strong enough to walk around? Should I ask her—no, I would ask her nothing. She had made it clear she didn't want to talk, and perhaps she had called her child a monster because she had been forced. I would protect her from further distress if I could.

It was a relief to drive away from Whitcombe in the dead-ening mist, cocooned in a swaying carriage where I could brood in peace. I hadn't asked Guttridge to come with me; I didn't need a chaperone to visit my brother.

I had guessed correctly that Michael would be at home on a Thursday three days before Christmas. Julia had gone to Littleberry to visit Gerry. I hoped Ned had held his tongue and they were all blissfully ignorant of Farmer Hatherall's so-called confession. My first Christmas without Justin would be difficult enough.

"I was going to have luncheon with Brandrick," was Michael's irritable reply when I suggested we might eat together. I sighed.

"But you have the opportunity of eating tête-à-tête with your sister, Michael. Rather than with a servant."

"Brandrick is not my servant; he's my land agent. And I like eating luncheon with him."

"I suppose he needs to hear what I want to ask you anyway."

To my surprise, luncheon with Michael and Brandrick was less tedious than I thought it would be. Conversation naturally turned purely on business matters, but Michael, I discovered, could be more interesting on business matters than I would have believed when prompted with the right questions. Brandrick certainly knew how to manage him.

"I came here for a reason," I declared once I'd eaten the last bite of lamb rump. One of Michael's animals, I presumed, and it compared well with the Whitcombe meat. They had clearly been working on their breeding.

"Of course you came here for a reason." Michael drained his glass. "You wouldn't just arrive with no purpose."

I glanced at Brandrick, who looked down at his plate. "Honestly, Michael, that remark was purely meant to introduce my request. Don't take everything so literally. You've heard, of course, that I've lost my tenant farmer."

"He killed himself." Michael wiped his mouth with his napkin. "You'll need some help with your sheep over Christmas."

"Exactly." Well, at least I was spared having to ask nicely for the help I had previously refused. "Would it be possible to arrange that for me? I don't know who the farmer would have hired."

"I've already sent word to a couple of our shepherds out on the marsh," Brandrick said. "I've found a family who'll put one of them up. The other will stay at the Wild Boar—his sister's the barmaid there, and they've got an attic room. They'll keep an eye on the flock until you can make a permanent arrangement."

"Thank you," I said weakly.

"Brandrick's not interfering." Michael rang the silver bell lying near his plate—he did not insist on a footman being present during a casual luncheon, as his staff was not large. "I asked him to do it. So *I'm* interfering."

"I suppose I'm glad you are." I patted Michael briefly on the hand. "As long as you understand it's a temporary arrangement."

"You won't find a better one than I'm offering you." Michael glared at me and moved his hand away. "Why can't I find you a husband straightaway as well? Julia says I have to give you time to mourn, but I married Julia exactly eight months after Cecilia died. Why are you different?"

"Well, for one thing it's only been two months since Justin died," I said.

"Two months and two days." Unable to read a calendar, Michael was somehow able to keep an exact count of days in his head.

"And you had a baby son who needed a mother."

"Perhaps we could find you a widower with a child." Michael's face grew thoughtful. "If you can't have one yourself, that would be logical."

I practically flew out of my chair in my haste to prevent the two men from seeing the sudden tears that rose to my eyes at Michael's remark. I stalked to the window and glared out at the mist, biting my lip furiously until I had my voice more or less under control.

"Allowing you to take temporary control of my land and livestock does not give you the right to assume control over the rest of my life, Michael. Don't try my temper any further."

Behind me, I heard Brandrick cough, possibly to remind Michael that he shouldn't be hearing this conversation. I welcomed the reminder myself as it stiffened my back and stemmed the flow of tears. I surreptitiously wiped the moisture from my eyes and turned back to my brother.

"I'm going to see Mama. My patience with men is running out."

⁓

"She's not in good humor, m'lady." Belming greeted me at the door leading to Mama's rooms.

"That's all right, Belming. I still want to see her. What's wrong?"

"The time of year, I reckon, m'lady. The mist and the damp and the long, dark nights."

I could hear a keening noise from the bedroom, so I headed in that direction.

"You mustn't worry if she gets cross with you," Belming said behind me. "She's been shouting and yelling something awful of an evening this last week. Cursing too. You'd think a lady wouldn't know all those words."

"Oh, we know them." I grinned at Belming. "We're just taught to pretend we've never heard a curse word in our lives. Papa had the most colorful vocabulary and sometimes forgot we were listening, so we all learned early."

My mother was sitting on her bed in a state of considerable disarray. Her long, thick white hair had escaped some of its pins and was tumbling down on the left side only, giving her a lopsided look. Bare feet stuck out from under her nightdress. One of her slippers was on the top of her wardrobe, the other on the windowsill.

"You stay out of my parlor," she growled as we approached. "I don't ever want to see you in my garden again, do you hear? It's not right. It's not right."

"There, Lady Broadmere, cheer up now, do." Belming didn't seem in the least bit put out. "Look who's come to see you."

My mother turned to me, blue eyes brimming with tears. "Who? Who?"

"It's Helena, Mama." I put my arms around her and kissed her cheek, feeling the tremble in her frail, bent back. "I'm your youngest daughter, remember? May I help with your hair?"

Without waiting for an answer, I began to ease hairpins out of the snarled mess. Belming nodded approvingly and went to fetch Mama's hairbrush.

"You're good with her, m'lady. The countess is too, but you have the real healing touch. You'd have done well in the nursing profession if you weren't a lady." She tutted as Mama screeched, "Go! Go!" at her. "Now then, Lady Broadmere, I'm just bringing her ladyship the brush. You be nice now and let her put your hair to rights."

"I'm not a child." Mama's lips set in a thin line. "I'll kill you tomorrow."

"Mama!" I expostulated, taking the brush from Belming. "You can't talk about killing people. It's not nice."

"Why not? Sometimes you have to kill people, when they're really nasty. She's a nasty wheelbarrow."

"Heavens, poor Belming," I murmured as I finished untangling Mama's hair and set to work with the hairbrush. "Mmm, your hair smells of lavender—did Belming wash it? It feels nice and clean."

"That's one of the reasons we're angry." Belming began folding the things Mama had pulled out of her chest of drawers. "We don't like having our hair washed."

"Ah. I notice you don't praise my sisters' skill with Mama." I parted Mama's hair and began to braid it.

Belming sniffed. "Lady Alice and Lady Annette are too—well, you'd think Lady Broadmere was a child at school. I suppose the way they are comes of being busy all the time."

"And having so many opportunities to tell other people what to do." I grinned. "And Lady Geraldine tends to ignore Mama. Lady Odelia never seems to know quite what to do with her and spends as little time as possible with her."

I reached out a hand for the ribbon Belming was offering me and incorporated it into the last inch or two of the braid. I finished by wrapping it tightly around the hair and tying it in a firm bow. Mama had fallen silent, staring at the window, where the mist was darkening into the early nightfall of late December.

"There." I finished the second braid. "Mama, you look quite beautiful now. Oh—what's wrong?" For my mother was crying silently, large tears finding their course through the deep vertical wrinkles on her cheeks like a river through a valley.

"Dear Mama, don't cry." I wrapped my arms around her again and rested my head on her shoulder. "What's so wrong today?"

"The garden," my mother moaned. "It's full of—of creatures that sit, sit on my head, sit on my heart."

I looked at Belming. "Has she been down to the garden lately?"

"No, m'lady. She won't go. She says the things that grow there burn her. Or sometimes she says we must set fire to it all. Or she talks about a deep river that runs through it, that she's afraid of falling into. I think she mistakes the path for a river."

"There's nothing in the garden that'll hurt you, Mama. We can't even see it today. It's foggy."

"Where?"

"Outside. Look, you can't see anything out there."

Mama rose and shuffled to her bedroom window. It had been fitted with bars on the outside for Mama's protection, but the fog was becoming so dense even the bars couldn't be seen. Mama scraped gently at the glass with the nail of her forefinger, looking pleased.

"Nothing can get in."

"No, nothing." Behind us, I heard Belming shut the door quietly, the only sound remaining the tick of the clock on the wall. "When the fog's like that, you could believe the rest of the world doesn't exist, couldn't you?"

"They will all go away and leave us in peace." Mama's voice was a mere whisper.

If only that were true. I leaned against the window frame, watching the two faces of Mama, reality and reflection, as she stared out into the darkening day. Here, in this room, all problems seemed to be reduced to their purest essence: whether to sit or remain standing, what Cook would make for dinner, whether to sleep or be awake, whether a sight or sound or word was upsetting or conducive to happiness.

I knew the world was a terrifying place to Mama and did not often envy the flight from reality she'd embarked upon after Papa's death. Today was an exception.

"I wish I could stay here forever." I smiled at my mother. "Just you and me and the rest of the world far away from us. Especially the men."

"They sit on my heart."

"Yes, Mama. They do. And I'm so tired of them. I wish I could tell you about today."

"What about today."

It didn't sound like a question, but I needed someone to talk to. If Mama's mental powers hadn't been failing, I would have confided in her about Justin—but in the end I had told absolutely nobody. Now I felt my heart might burst without the relief of words.

"I walked into our marriage with my eyes open, Mama. Justin told me before we married that he wasn't as virile as he'd like to be. He warned me I might be better off with a younger man."

"I remember him."

"Do you? Justin?"

"The other one."

I sighed. "And we thought there still might be some hope, at first. We thought it still might be possible to have a child. One would have been enough."

"Enough is as good as a feast."

My eyes widened suddenly, and I felt as if a flame had licked its way down my insides.

"Supposing . . . supposing I kept silent about Justin's inability to father a child? Mama, supposing I let the world think that what Farmer Hatherall claimed is true? I would be almost morally obliged to bring up Susan's baby, wouldn't I? People would understand that."

"If I burned it with fire, nobody would know." Mama breathed on the glass and then turned away to shuffle across the room.

"Fortier's right," I said to her retreating back. "We do prefer to keep things hidden. If I wish to preserve a dignified silence on the subject of my late husband's health, I have a right to do so. I don't see how they can compel me to speak, and they'll just assume Fortier is making trouble as usual. I think I've found a solution that's right for Susan and her baby."

And for me.

19

AFTER THE INQUEST

"The inquest has taken place."

Fortier stood rather stiffly in the doorway to the drawing room. When I motioned for him to sit down, he chose one of the least comfortable chairs—at a distance from me.

He'd been visiting Susan every two days since Christmas. Her recovery now seemed certain, and she hadn't lost the child. Yet there was something about the pallor of her face and the dark circles under her eyes that looked horribly unhealthy.

Part of this, of course, would be due to the shock of her father's death. She had wept very much when I'd told her, moaning like an animal in pain as she lay on her narrow bed. When her sobs turned to a racking cough that seemed to shake her very core, I'd pleaded with her to calm herself in case she harmed her child.

"Damn the child." She'd pushed me away so hard I nearly fell backward. "It's to blame for everything. We were happy, Father and I, and we were prosperous. Then the devil made mock of us."

I'd seen Mrs. Eason, who had stayed with me while I delivered the news to Susan, make the two-fingered sign against evil behind her back. "The devil needs us to do his work for him," she'd said as we'd descended the stairs. "Don't let the girl take advantage of you, m'lady."

I'd said nothing to anybody about the interest in Susan's child that was beginning to grow in my heart. There was Maggie, Susan's sister, after all. But I could do far more for any child than Maggie could, and maybe she wouldn't want another child in the house. There would be time yet for me to step in and offer to help.

And I had been waiting to hear the result of the inquest. The coroner had not sent for me, and I had heard nothing from Ned.

"So . . . did they read out the letter?" I asked now, trying to keep my tone even and not start an argument with Fortier again.

There had been a distinct coolness between Fortier and me in the last few days. Now he looked like a horse with a burr under its saddle—highly irritable and inclined to bite. He scowled thunderously, his thick black brows drawing down over his eyes so that they met in the middle.

"They did not. The mayor managed matters in that splendid way you English have. He approached one or two of the most important men on the jury—not including the earl —to show them the letter, in order to persuade them that what was contained therein had no real bearing on the farmer's death. That it would be sufficient for those men to testify they had seen the letter, that it contained allegations that were clearly untrue and would harm a lady, and that these allegations should not be aired in public. It appears that chivalry and consideration for the fair sex are sufficient to smother evidence in this benighted corner of the country."

"Oh," was all I could find to say. Naturally, I was relieved to know the lie about Justin was known only to a handful of men, no doubt selected by Ned for their discretion. I wasn't sure I wanted to know who those men were. I might have to look them in the face across the dinner table.

"Oh." The level of sarcasm in Fortier's echo was enough to sting me into further speech.

"What good would it have done?" I asked. "Ned's right—Hatherall's note was a vindictive lie designed to cause scandal."

"But it was evidence." There was open derision on Fortier's handsome face now.

"What was the verdict?" I refused to go any deeper into a discussion that had already caused strife between us.

"*Felo de se*. And the Crown did not waive its right to forfeiture—mainly, if I understood the arguments, because of Hatherall's attempt to use his own death to cause the scandal they refrained from discussing. If you weren't mixed up in the business, the Crown might have been more lenient. So you could say you've been the cause—unintentional, of course—of Susan Hatherall's destitution."

Seen any way you like, that was a very uncomfortable proposition, but I had my answer ready. "I am prepared to look after Susan and her child exactly as if the baby *were* Justin's. I feel I'm under a moral obligation to do so."

"I would agree with that." One corner of Fortier's mouth quirked up, but it wasn't a smile.

"You're angry with me."

"I'm angry with the whole damnable system that allows one set of people to bend the rules into any shape they want. It's an offense against justice." Fortier almost spat out the last words, but then his face softened a little. "Even when the ultimate purpose is to protect a lady; although, God knows, Lady Helena, I would be the last person to want to drag you into this mess."

I felt my own anger abate a little. "I thought you were going to," I confessed. "I've been waiting for some kind of summons—on tenterhooks because I didn't know what I might have to do. I'm still not sure what I would have said if I'd been asked the direct question as to whether or not I thought Susan and Justin could have—" I swallowed. "I think I would have said yes. I would be disloyal to my husband either way, and I'd rather have taken the course that preserved his dignity. People would understand a man making a mistake."

"So you're happy not to have been asked."

"Of *course* I am." I could hear a rising note of hysteria in my voice. "I'm sorry, Monsieur Fortier. You, no doubt, are accustomed to witnessing death. I am not. I've lost my husband, whom I loved dearly. I've been present at the discovery of the gruesome death of my tenant—not, you'll admit, a routine experience for a woman in my position, even if I did insist on seeing him. I've been worried I might have a third and fourth death on my hands with both Susan and her baby in danger. Can you blame me for wanting a little peace and quiet?"

Fortier regarded me gravely with those unearthly eyes. "Thank you for explaining your position more clearly, Lady Helena. I'm sorry to have troubled you. I'll leave you alone now."

"Wait." He had risen to his feet, but my exclamation made him sink back into his chair. "You haven't fully explained the verdict to me. Is he to be buried at the crossroads?"

"With a stake through his heart?" This time he did smile. "That hasn't been done for half a century. But he will be interred at midnight tonight in a far corner of the cemetery —albeit with a full service. For a churchwarden, that's a bad end."

"I'll have to tell Susan that, I suppose. How awful for her.

Is nobody he knew to be present at the service? His family should be represented."

"His only family are women. His son-in-law has been asked and has refused. I believe the other churchwardens will be there."

I felt my shoulders slump at the sadness of it all. "I'm going to have to see what I can do to provide both sisters with a little money."

"Noblesse oblige?"

"I do wish people would stop throwing that phrase at the aristocracy." I folded my arms. "Yes, we do feel that we're under an obligation to care for those who rightly belong under our care, as feudal as it sounds. And I have the additional burden of having inadvertently caused Maggie and Susan to lose their inheritance. I will do what I can."

"A life of dependence for Susan, then."

"No." I felt my temper rise again. "I'll train her for a useful occupation and give her enough money to make a start in life —with or without the child. Is that so terrible? The work-houses are full of people who have nobody to care for them. Surely, some help from a landowner is better than that. Like it or not, Monsieur Fortier, we have a system that works."

"American slave owners said the same thing." Fortier's tone was challenging.

"We are not American. We are British, and that makes all the difference in the world."

"If you say so, Lady Helena."

❧

Left alone at last, I tried to seek repose—and could not. I prided myself on not being one of those tiresome women who were always complaining about their nerves, but for once I sympathized with them. My nerves had been strewn on the floor and thoroughly stamped upon and were bent on getting their revenge.

I found fault with Guttridge over a button she'd not sewn on with quite her usual care. I scolded a footman with more than my usual degree of acidity for winking at a maid. I did not enjoy my dinner, which was mutton stew, and sent a scalding note to Mrs. Foster about avoiding mutton stew in the future—unfair, since I had arranged the week's menus with her.

Instead of retiring at my usual early hour, I had the fire in the small library replenished and betook myself thereto with a goblet of Justin's best brandy and some of Mama's journals. I read steadily while the rocking ship set into a glass panel in the grandfather clock marked off the seconds, minutes, and hours with its sonorous tick.

I had been reading the early journals slowly, as they contained a great deal of information I wished to absorb. My own progress was extremely slow thanks to Susan's illness, her father's suicide, and the Christmas season in general; but, I reassured myself, time spent on study was never wasted. I often went back over Mama's notes in order to understand them better.

As Mama's knowledge grew and the descriptions of her work became ever more confident and expansive, details of her personal life began to creep in—with, I was startled to realize, a note of unhappiness. She mentioned Gerry from time to time; she was clearly as enamored of my oldest sister as one would wish a mother to be of an only child. Gerry appeared to give her no great trouble; for a small child, she was quite well-behaved, responsible, and unimaginative. Exactly as she was now, in fact. The most daring thing Gerry had ever done was to marry a man who, as well as benefiting from a private income, as did all of our acquaintances, was a wine merchant and therefore, technically, in trade.

Mama almost never mentioned Papa, and there were hints of long hours and perhaps even days spent alone. Had Papa been neglecting her at this time, and why? Was there some kind of estrangement between them, or was it simply the usual course of an established marriage? Papa would undoubtedly have been a busy man. This journal dated from shortly after the Queen's accession to the throne. My father, then in his early thirties, had recently inherited the earldom and would no doubt have been active in the House of Lords as well as in the county. Unlike Michael, who disliked his parliamentary obligations, Papa had relished his role in the country's government and had spent much time in London.

I lingered over a wonderfully detailed, partially colored sketch of a foxglove, one of the best drawings Mama had produced by that time. She'd drawn a bumblebee pushing its fat, furry body into the tube of the flower, its white tail and twin loads of yellow pollen vividly rendered against the purple shading she'd used on the flower. Beside the sketch, she had written some botanical terms and a note: "These are the bees' favorites. I believe they are mine too."

So long ago. I closed the journal, seeing in my mind's eye a sunny June day and a solitary, perhaps lonely, young woman sitting sketching and writing, her blue eyes lost in thought, concentrating. Perhaps there was a small child playing near her, a child I'd never known. By the time I was born, Gerry was married and a mother.

I started a little at the first stroke of the clock's bell, then counted. Eleven o'clock. Heavens, poor Guttridge must be waiting up for me—probably dozing in an armchair in the servants' hall. But the day nagged at my mind, and I knew I was never going to sleep. In one hour, Lucius Hatherall would be buried, along with—if I were fortunate enough—the last things he'd wanted to say to the world.

I shifted restlessly in my chair, unable to get comfortable.

Ned had said Hatherall's study was crammed with books full of information and advice about how a man could advance himself in life. All that study was vanished now. If I lost interest in herbalism, all of Mama's knowledge would likewise be scattered to the winds, her journals a mere family curiosity to gather dust in an attic at Whitcombe until my heirs—heavens, who would they be?—or their heirs, or someone generations from now, disposed of them. Why did one write journals anyway? For posterity? Posterity was a highly uncertain concept.

I shivered, realizing that the fire had burned down to a fine layer of glowing embers atop a bed of ashes. Going to the window and pulling aside the velvet drapes, I could see the mist had lifted, but I couldn't make out more—the night was quite dark. A gloomy prospect for a funeral. With no family in attendance . . .

"Blast it." I rose to my feet. The house was still and silent. There would almost certainly be a footman or a boy in attendance in the Great Hall, but this side of the house was reasonably private.

It didn't take me long to reach the small mud room off the conservatory. There was the old manteau I refused to throw away and used whenever I wished to step into the garden in cold weather. It was dark green, the velvet collar a little moth-eaten. Underneath its peg stood my low galoshes. I slipped off my slippers and slid my feet into the rubber boots, cold even through my winter stockings.

I used the candle I had carried with me to locate the small oil lamps Justin had always insisted on keeping in the cupboard along with the matches. Justin often liked to walk around the outside of the house before retiring or visit the stables, and I sometimes accompanied him, hand in hand, our lamps swinging with the rhythm of our steps. So I knew where the bolts on the conservatory doors were located, and they were kept well oiled.

Stepping out into the night brought back a sharp memory of doing so with Justin, but the night seemed far more menacing now that I was on my own. Still, I had grown up in the country, where nights were always dark, and knew Whitcombe Lane like the back of my hand. Five minutes' brisk walk brought me to the turnpike road, and I headed downhill, watching my footing carefully. Thanks to the mist, it wasn't icy, but mud could be as dangerous as ice.

The path to the cemetery led through the workhouse burying ground, a large field where the unmarked resting places of the poor were shown, for a time, by the six-foot strips of mounded clay. I couldn't see them, of course. Only the low iron railing that bordered the burying ground could be seen in the circle of lamplight that guided my feet. I said a quick prayer for the poor wretches whose graves would remain anonymous for eternity and then turned my thoughts to the man who would be buried that night.

There were lights not too far off. I extinguished my own lamp and used the others as a guide, treading with extreme caution so as not to turn an ankle or trip over a flint sticking out of the packed clay of the path. It was hard to judge distances or anything else in the darkness, and I had to stay out of the light.

Not that I was committing any kind of crime or offense in coming to the cemetery. But ladies did not go about unaccompanied at night. Ladies did not attend funerals. Ladies did not suffer from a compulsion to see their tenant safely into the ground, to represent, in a sense, the relationship that had tied him to Whitcombe land for two decades. Ladies did not appease their restlessness by nighttime wanderings.

The burial site was at the far side of the cemetery, near the dense barrier of oak, hawthorn, and beech that had been set there long before St. Michael's churchyard ran out of burying space and the town of Littleberry purchased the acreage to the west of the workhouse. I picked my way along the foot of the trees, cursing as I encountered roots and hollows in the overgrown grass.

I was close enough now that I could see the men's faces. Three lanterns. Two men in working clothes resting on their shovels; they were waiting, no doubt, to fill the grave. A lantern turned the white of a surplice yellow—that was the priest, but not the rector. He was speaking in a low voice, as if fearful of waking the more respectable dead whose resting places clustered near the twin chapels and the path that ran between them. The small book in his hand would be the Book of Common Prayer; I wondered briefly how many passages in the burial service one had to avoid for a suicide. All those words about deliverance, bliss, eternal glory; would Lucius Hatherall have any of those?

The priest had raised his voice a little, and now I could hear him. "Thou knowest, Lord, the secrets of our hearts; shut not thy merciful ears to our prayer; but spare us, Lord most holy, O God most mighty, O holy and merciful Savior, thou most worthy judge eternal, suffer us not, at our last hour, for any pains of death, to fall from thee."

I shivered. Now that I was standing still, the cold of the night seemed to be seeping into my very bones. I looked hard at the other men; there were five, I thought, but it was hard to see. They were all dressed in sober black, their faces half in shadow. Two bowler hats—that would probably be the other churchwardens. The flat cap of a countryman. I wondered if that could possibly be Maggie's husband after all, and hoped so very much.

Two gentlemen in tall silk hats; and suddenly I recognized Ned's abundant beard. Dear, kind Ned. Not many of the people of Littleberry had the mayor in attendance at their interment, and his presence was bound to ensure that the townspeople would speak of Farmer Hatherall a little less unkindly. I fervently hoped the night air would not worsen Ned's indisposition.

Was the other man Fortier? I could barely see him, but somehow I was certain it was the French physician. I moved a step closer—and put my foot straight into a rabbit hole. I pitched forward but mercifully was able to grab hold of a slender tree trunk to arrest my fall. I couldn't stop myself from gasping and saw the faces of the two gentlemen turn toward me. Yes, the second one was Fortier.

I moved as carefully as I could back into the shelter of the hawthorn, wriggling my foot out of the hole. I was lucky I hadn't broken my ankle, I realized. What kind of lunatic was I to creep through the dark to attend the burial of such a man as Hatherall? My reasons for doing so now seemed as nonsensical to me as they would to anyone else. Suddenly, I couldn't wait for the ceremony to be over so I could make my way home and have Guttridge undress me and put me to bed.

Now they were all speaking in unison—that was the Lord's Prayer. And then the priest raised his voice once more.

"The grace of our Lord Jesus Christ, and the love of God and the fellowship of the Holy Ghost, be with us all evermore."

I heard them all say, "Amen," and then the light of the lanterns went in three separate directions. One stayed by the grave as the two men with shovels began vigorously throwing earth on top of the coffin. By the hollow sound of the wood, it was a very plain one. Another light departed in the direction of the chapels, and with it the white surplice of the priest and a solid knot of black-clad men.

The third light came straight toward me. I couldn't run—

what would be the point? I couldn't see where I was running, and they could see me.

It was Ned and Fortier, of course. They were moving casually, no doubt in order not to alert the others, but they moved with purpose and were soon close enough to see who I was.

"I told you I saw somebody." Ned spoke in an undertone. "Helena, for heaven's sake. What kind of insane behavior is this?"

"I couldn't sleep," I said defensively. "I just—I don't know. I didn't want him to be buried with none of us there. If you'd just *told* me you intended to be present—"

"Are you all right, Lady Helena?" Fortier sounded concerned. "You must be frozen."

I realized my teeth were chattering. "I'm a little chilled, but no harm done. I stepped into a rabbit hole—no, it's quite all right; it's not sprained or anything." Fortier, who was carrying the lantern, had lowered it to the level of my feet.

"Home. Now." Ned had swiftly unbuttoned his overcoat while Fortier and I had been talking and now dropped it over my shoulders. "If we stand here talking, some of the others might realize there's something up. Fortier, lead the way."

Our progress toward the cemetery entrance was complicated somewhat by the need to avoid running into the other group of men, who were saying good night to one another. The priest had shed his surplice and was climbing into a four-wheeled dogcart driven by a man swathed in a scarf that must have been ten feet long. He offered to take the other men home; the two churchwardens readily assented, while the third man explained that he was going down the hill to the King's Head. It *was* Maggie's husband, I was sure of it now.

"Don't you have a carriage?" I asked Ned when the cart had gone.

"I didn't think it necessary to make my driver wait, my dear. Fortier and I walked up from Littleberry together, and we'll walk back. It's a good night for a walk."

"But now you're going to insist on seeing me home, aren't you?" I asked. "Won't you at least stay the night at Whitcombe?"

"And make it obvious to everyone you've been out of the house?" Ned huffed into his beard. "We'll see you in as quietly as you left. Through the conservatory, I'll be bound."

"How do you know?"

"That was how Justin and I got in." I saw Ned grin. "Once not long after you were married—d'you remember that badger hunt old Fortescue got up? And then there was the time you were laid up with influenza." He coughed. "On both occasions we'd had rather a lot to drink and thought we'd better not disturb anyone."

"Hmph. So you're bent on keeping the secret of my derring-do?"

I saw Fortier smile, and for a moment felt the coolness between us melt a little. He and Ned seemed to like each other, I'd noticed.

"Up to a point."

Ned's answer to my question made me look at him in surprise.

"Look, Helena, old girl." Ned squeezed my arm, which was looped under his, more firmly against his side. "I love you dearly—almost like another daughter—and I'm most dreadfully sorry about Justin. But this," he waved a hand around to encompass the night, the cemetery, even Fortier, "has to stop. People will talk. People are talking already. You're dashed lucky you didn't break a leg out there and die of exposure."

I ground my teeth for a moment or two before replying.

"So what exactly are you going to do?"

"Nothing much. Just mention to Michael, in a general sort of way, that you might benefit from a more constant companion. A *female* companion." He looked sideways at Fortier.

"A jailer?"

"A friend. You need a friend."

AN INVITATION

*W*hen Odelia arrived four days later, I strongly suspected Ned was behind her visit. She denied it outright.

"Town's unbearable at times," was all she said. "One's friends have the most perverse way of deciding to leave just when one needs them. So I thought I'd come to see the most restful person I know."

"Restful? Me?" If only O knew how very *un*-restful my life had been lately.

"Oh, believe me, compared to everyone I know you're a haven of peace and quiet."

"Why didn't you come and see in the New Year with us if you're so tired of London?" I asked. "You seem to like it one minute and hate it the next."

"Oh, I was quite busy over the New Year. Parties and things. You know artists."

"I don't know artists at all. I know nothing about your life in London."

"Maybe it's about time you did. How's the delectable Frenchman?"

"Fortier? Annoying. And I'd hardly call him delectable."

"No? I'd like to paint him." O narrowed her eyes as if Fortier were in the room and she were studying him for a portrait. "He has nice, clean lines. He'd look good as a medieval knight."

"Like that dreadful engraving of the late Prince Consort? A medieval knight with side-whiskers?" I tossed my head. "If you like him so much, you have my permission to invite him to Scott House, where you can paint him at your leisure."

"I don't like him in *that* way. I hear he's been at Whitcombe quite often of late."

"I've had a sick servant. Susan Hatherall—you remember her, of course. Her father died."

"By his own hand. I know. And you're determined to make it up to her. Although why you should bother at all with that horrid girl is beyond me. And you and the Frenchman actually found Farmer Hatherall hanging in his kitchen—positively gruesome. Although, if you're as hard-hearted about it as Gerry says, could you give me some details? Not for me. I have a friend who's rather daring with what he paints—and we've all heard that Claude Monet painted his wife on her deathbed." She made a face. "I don't like this new vogue for half-finished paintings, do you?"

"Has the whole family been talking about me?" I refused to be drawn into a discussion about painting, about which I knew very little.

"They have, rather. The impression is that you're going a little off the rails." O studied the bright jewels in her rings critically. "Nervous exhaustion, perhaps. Maybe you've had too much excitement—for a restful person. Come to think of it, why don't you come up to Town with me—stay for a while?"

The invitation was so uncharacteristic, and delivered with so much studied casualness, that I stopped short and stared at O, suspicion growing in my breast. "You've *never* invited me to stay at Scott House. The only time I see the inside of the place is when Julia is there with Michael, and that doesn't happen often. Have the family put you up to this?" I was beginning to imagine the flurry of letters that might have been passing to and fro behind my back.

"Put me up to what?" O did her best to look innocent, but she had entirely the wrong sort of face for the endeavor.

"Getting me away from Sussex. Did Michael summon you down here, then, if it wasn't Ned? Oh, he did." O was definitely avoiding my eyes. "What's your side of the bargain? I can't imagine Michael can afford to increase your allowance."

O looked decidedly shifty. "I owe Michael a favor," she said, "and I can't help how he called it in. He won't give me the details, but apparently he—and others—feel a trip to Town would be a nice change for you. The company of . . . well, of different people."

I could definitely detect Ned somewhere behind this. "Won't Michael need to stay at Scott House himself when the parliamentary session opens?"

"Oh, that's not until February. And most of the time he stays at his club. He says it's cheaper."

A thought struck me. "I hope Michael's not thinking of sending a string of potential husbands along. Is that what you meant by 'different people'?" I studied my sister's face. "O, you can't be serious. I've been a widow for just over two months."

O held up her hands in a placatory gesture. "Obviously, there won't be any actual wooing involved. But apparently several London acquaintances have written to Michael that they'd like to communicate their condolences in person."

"Vultures." I stamped my foot. "Men who espy a fortune. Hags of mothers and sisters who'd like nothing better than to winkle their way into my confidence with a view to making an introduction at an opportune moment."

"What a dim view you take of London society. All you have to do is say no." O smiled, a little secretively. "As I do."

"Haven't you ever wanted to marry?"

My sister shrugged. "All the ones I like are taken. Baby, *do* come to London. Please do. It'll be tremendous fun, and it'll arrange things nicely between me and Michael into the bargain. It's positively an act of charity."

"But what about my workroom?" I asked. "My herbalism studies?"

"Surely, you're not going to turn a hobby into a reason for never leaving Littleberry. That's what Mama always did, and you know how it infuriated Papa."

"I don't know anything of the kind. And there's Susan; she's not well—"

O rolled her eyes. "For heaven's sake. Whitcombe will run itself perfectly well without you. Your Mrs. Eason's quite the treasure. Susan will survive your absence, and she can complete any little tasks for the workroom that can't wait until your return. And I'll get you a reader's ticket for the Museum Library—how about that? You can positively *wallow* in musty old books about herbs. You can become the most complete bluestocking, and then no man of sense will want to marry you anyway."

I heard Blanche's voice in that last sentence—well, it was inevitable that she'd have written her opinions of me to O.

"I don't know." I was beginning to waver a little. My nerves *were* a bit frayed after all.

"And winter in Littleberry is so *dull* unless you can dine at other people's homes several times a week." O slipped her arm through mine. "Not at all suited to a widow's seclusion. In Town, you can bend the rules a little. You're not known the way you are here, with everybody gossiping about your every move. And it's easier to get about when the weather's bad. Here it'll rain and blow sou'westers endlessly, as it always does, and you'll hardly be able to ride at all."

She was right about that. With Justin, winters had been different—friends to dine with and long, delightful evenings together by a bright fire.

"I suppose Guttridge would like a change of scene."

"There you are, then. And from her vowels, I'd say she was London-born; although she speaks well, I'll give her that."

"But what about Dene Farm? I need to find a tenant."

"Talk to Michael."

"I'll think about it, O. And that's all you're getting from me for the moment."

∼

"How is Mama?" Michael's harsh voice came from directly behind me and made me jump. As I often did, I'd dropped in on Mama before proceeding to my business at Hyrst, which was Michael.

"Difficult, and I wish you wouldn't creep up behind me like that."

"I don't creep. You wander around with your head in the clouds."

I led the way into Hyrst's library, which was far shabbier and mustier than either of Whitcombe's but just as welcoming. I had warm memories of sitting on Papa's knee in his great leather armchair while Mama bustled in and out issuing brisk instructions to the servants. She would pause a moment to drop a kiss on my head and then on Michael's— in my memories he was always sitting on the rug, paying no attention to anything except what was going on in his own head. If he wasn't screaming, that is.

I smiled at my memories as I crossed the room. How fond my parents had been of one another. I remembered Papa saying, "Your Mama is a wonder, isn't she, Baby? No woman can match her."

"Many have tried," said the Mama of that particular memory. Papa had laughed, but the expression on Mama's face had not been jocular.

I dropped into Papa's chair, noting with displeasure that there was a crack in the leather over the curve of the chair's broad arm.

"If I seemed preoccupied," I said pointedly to Michael, "it was due to concern for Mama. If you visited her more often, you'd understand why. The long nights seem to be having a bad effect on her this winter. She's been crying a great deal and telling Belming she doesn't want to stay in this house anymore."

I was gratified to see Michael look surprised. "Where does she want to go?"

"That's just the thing—if you ask her that, she starts talking about her bedroom in the house where she grew up and insisting she could go there. It's no use telling her the house passed into new ownership thirty years ago. It's as if she longs for the time when she was a girl, before she married—before any of us existed. And she's being difficult about food."

"Why? It's always the same five dishes." Michael looked wistful—he, too, would be content eating the same dishes in a predictable rotation. "If she wants to change them, Belming only has to tell Inchkin or Cook."

"It's not that. She keeps insisting the food's been poisoned. Belming has to go through a whole rigmarole of tasting each dish and saying how delicious it is. Like with a little child."

"I would go to her rooms more often if she didn't behave

like that." Michael looked uneasy. He saw eating as a necessity rather than an enjoyment and was a little squeamish about food. He settled himself more firmly into his armchair and fixed me with a stare, clearly dismissing the subject of Mama from his mind.

"Have you come to discuss going to London? I suppose Odelia's had time to talk to you." He looked hopeful.

"She couldn't wait. Whatever it is she owes you or you've promised to do for her must be significant."

I would almost have preferred it if Michael had looked smug, which was what most men would have done. But his handsome countenance remained impassive, only altering as he looked toward the open doorway.

"Ah, Brandrick. Anticipating my wishes, as always. Lady Helena is going up to London for a few weeks—"

"—I didn't say that," I interrupted.

"—is going up to London for a few weeks, if she has any sense at all." Michael's voice drowned out my words. "It is my strongest recommendation as the head of the family—"

"—if you try to bully me, Michael, I'll simply leave."

"But people are talking about you." Michael used the slow speech one might adopt when talking to a backward child.

"What people?"

"People who count. Your behavior has become most eccentric. Insisting on staying after you and the French physician found Hatherall hanging by the neck—"

"Do we have to discuss this in front of Brandrick?" I asked coolly. "The man was my tenant. I felt a sense of obligation."

"Do you think you have an obligation to keep his daughter too?"

"In a sense, yes."

"Ask Brandrick what people in Littleberry have been saying about that."

"Well?" I fixed Brandrick with a cold stare, which seemed to bother him not one whit.

"The common people have what you might call a talent for invention, m'lady." His tone was pleasant and even. "They don't like the Hatherall girl being singled out for special treatment when she should, as a matter of customary practice, be sent to the workhouse. They're drawing the worst kind of conclusions."

I didn't want to ask what those conclusions were. "I have not singled her out for special treatment," I said to Michael rather than to Brandrick. "Don't forget she has a long-standing connection with this family."

"Connection!" Michael barked. "She wormed her way into Mama's affections for a few years. She's a slut."

I was shocked by Michael's use of the word. "Her father was a good and respectable man who served Justin and the town of Littleberry well for nigh on twenty years. I'm sorry, Michael, but my decision in this matter is final. Susan stays. Why should we care what Littleberry thinks?"

Brandrick coughed. "The opinion of the townspeople carries more weight than it used to, m'lady. The middle classes have far more wealth and power than they did fifty years ago—and a stricter view of morality. Your actions could be misinterpreted."

I was starting to feel I was losing the argument. Those of us who lived in the great houses of the county were the objects of intense interest—and occasionally a species of malice that would spring up even among those who professed to admire and like us. I was aware that there were many in the country calling for our hereditary powers to be reduced and our wealth to be more heavily taxed. It was time to sacrifice a pawn or two in this conversational game of chess.

"If I agree to go to London for a while," I said as calmly as

I could, "I would like your undertaking that Susan will not be sent away in my absence."

Michael leaned back in his chair, and I saw Brandrick's gaze sharpen. A minute glance passed between them.

"And what of Dene Farm, m'lady?" Brandrick asked. "There's the matter of the tenancy to be settled."

I sighed. "I have the distinct feeling that a proposed solution is looming on the horizon."

"It's always the same solution." Michael's jaw tightened as he watched me run a finger over the crack in Papa's chair. Other people's fidgeting always irritated him. "Logically, it would be in your best interest to run your farmland alongside mine."

"We could put the flocks and grazing land together, m'lady," Brandrick said. "Expand a little, if you're willing to make the investment. The whole thing could be run more efficiently on a larger scale. We could move Farmer Geddings out of that house on the marsh—it's got terrible rising damp, and I think it should be torn down and a new one built. That way you'd have a really solid man looking after the Whitcombe end of things, and we could get a much better rent for a better house at Marsh Farm. If you like, m'lady, I'll bring round my accounts ledger and explain how it could be done."

"How much?" I looked at Michael, noting that the fingers of his right hand had curved inward and were scratching vigorously at his palm. Michael always did that when he wanted something very badly. Hyrst depended on sheep farming a great deal more than Whitcombe did, and I knew Papa's debts were a great worry to my brother.

"We wouldn't ask more than you could easily afford. Brandrick has a plan to send the meat to Smithfield as well as selling locally. If we succeed, we'll both be better off."

Faced with the prospect of helping Michael and his family, I felt myself relenting. After all, what good was wealth if I couldn't use it for those I loved? And I *did* love Michael, for all his faults.

"I would be willing to listen to your plans," I conceded. "Of course if I do marry again, my new husband might not like having the management of my land in someone else's hands."

"Safe, family hands." Michael scratched harder at his palm. "Your new husband should be content with the money. And if you have any sense, you'll marry someone of substance, and Whitcombe can be let when you leave for your new life."

"Hmmm. So if I go to London—and let you manage Dene Farm—and allow whatever silly gossip may have arisen to die down, I would like Susan Hatherall to remain at Whitcombe at least until she's had her child. Then we'll see what's to be done."

"What you do in your house is your affair." Michael had visibly relaxed, folding his arms and looking almost expansive. "Although if you'll take a brother's advice, I hope you'll see less of that Frenchman."

"I have no intention of seeing anything much of Monsieur Fortier in the future." I refrained from telling Michael that we'd argued over the business of the letter. "I'll leave instructions that he should be called in if Susan becomes ill. Otherwise, all she'll need is the care of a competent midwife when her time comes. I'm sure Mrs. Eason can see to that."

"An unmarried servant with child, kept on and not dismissed without a character." Brandrick shook his head. "It'll still be talked about."

"You can smooth it over, can't you, Michael?" I asked my brother. "After all, you're the earl. Call it charity on my part. Or eccentricity. You can take your pick." I looked hard at

Brandrick. He, in turn, looked at Michael and gave a quick lift of his eyebrows.

"The bargain's sealed, then," I said. "We'll talk about the investment you want me to make later."

How much would Susan Hatherall cost me? I wondered as I settled into my carriage for the short ride back to Whitcombe. On the other hand, I saw no actual harm in Brandrick's scheme for the farm. I had to do something with those blessed sheep, and investing money in an expansion would no doubt have been Justin's preference over abandoning his enterprise.

"Well?" O asked when I found her in the morning room.

"I suppose you and Michael win. In fact, I think I've conceded rather a lot. I forgot to make it clear to Michael that I won't have him throwing suitors at me, for one thing."

O rose and came to kiss me. "That's what I mean about you being restful, Baby. You're so good-natured."

"Meaning I let my family twist me around their little fingers." I sat down in my favorite chair with a sigh. "I suppose I'd better tell Guttridge to start packing for London."

21

THE RETURN

o my surprise, once I'd settled into the elegant but dilapidated house the Scott-De Quincys had somehow managed to hang on to since the reign of William and Mary, I started to enjoy myself. Scott House boasted only a housekeeper, a maid, and a manservant they called a footman but who filled a variety of roles. A plain cook, another maid, and a second man lived out, and we breakfasted on hot rolls delivered to the door each morning. Even the gardeners found employment elsewhere for the winter. The house, nestled inside walled gardens that hid it completely from the din of London's streets, had a strangely cozy feel to it, as if O and I were almost alone. The coziness was intensified by my insistence on paying for extra coal so that the rooms could be properly heated; no wonder Michael didn't stay there much.

I didn't see all that much of O for a large part of the morning and early afternoon. While the light was good, she worked in her studio—two large rooms at the top of the house that had once been a nursery and schoolroom. At two o'clock, she would join me for a late luncheon, after which we would take the air in London's parks with Scotty.

We rode in a closed carriage since I was recently widowed, but O always seemed to find acquaintances to stop and talk to. We had a number of places where we liked to walk, and at times we entered the public buildings. I liked the new Natural History Museum and the Victoria and Albert Museum best, but O was fondest of the National Gallery. I had to admit it greatly entertained me to see how many working-class families derived entertainment—sometimes of a vulgar nature—from the pictures. Being in this great metropolis where few knew who I was freed me to watch other people for a change.

The silver salver in Scott House's front hall quickly began to overflow with cards, often bearing notes of condolence. In the end I had black-bordered cards printed to the effect that I was at home two days each week between two and three o'clock. We received visits from bohemian oddities as well as society notables. I was glad to note that some of O's friends were highly intelligent and exceedingly amusing.

Some visitors I easily identified as sent along by Michael to inspect me with a view to marriage. One gentleman in particular was quite persistent. He was fairly good-looking apart from the fact that one eye was oddly sunken, and I spent my time wondering whether he could see out of it. He had fought the Ashanti under General Wolseley and carried a folded engraving of that illustrious personage, cut from *The Illustrated London News*, in his pocket-book. He clearly thought everyone was as fascinated by the subject of African warfare as he was, and it took a considerable degree of rudeness on O's part to drive him away. I was grateful; I had begun to dread spending yet another hour watching the flicker of the black iris in his sunken eye and the peculiar way the eyelid wrinkled when he smiled.

I put my reader's ticket for the library at the British Museum to good use. My theoretical knowledge of the uses of plants grew fast, and my journal filled with notes of remedies I wanted to try once I got home to Whitcombe. I visited several interesting shops in London and sent packets of seeds, exotic ingredients such as cinchona bark from India, and a few books back to await my return, enclosing instructions to Susan on how I wanted them stored or arranged.

"Does that girl ever write back to you?" O asked one evening when I had finished writing to Susan.

"A few words here and there. Mrs. Eason is a better correspondent. She says Susan is plagued by pain in her left hip and lower back. And that she occasionally has recurrences of fever and has lost weight. Mrs. Eason's not sure if she's just pining for her father or really ill."

"She's malingering, you mark my words." O closed her eyes in pleasure as she sipped her coffee, which she took strong and black.

"I don't think so. She doesn't have enough work, of course, when I'm not there."

O sniffed. "Couldn't Mrs. Eason find her some work to do in the house?"

"And impinge upon some other servant's province? You should know better."

"You know, one of the things I love about living in Scott House is the minimal presence of a bunch of silly servants with their notions of hierarchy and their continual bickering." O stretched and leaned back in her chair. I sipped my own coffee, well sweetened and laced with cream.

"I'm sure my servants don't bicker. I hardly notice them—well, except Guttridge, of course."

"Hmph. You really don't need a woman to wash you and dress you like a doll. It's easy to hook a corset and button a bodice all by yourself—look at me, I do it every day. It keeps me supple." O, whose hair was a darker shade of blond than the others but who was a true Scott-De Quincy in every other way, tall and slender, proved her point by folding her long body in half until her forehead touched her knees.

"Guttridge is essential to my well-being. And I can hardly run Whitcombe without servants. I might have to hire an extra gardener when my herb garden is finished."

O rolled her eyes. "Michael's right, that whole business of trying to step into Mama's shoes is ridiculously expensive. Quite a dreadful waste."

"When did he say that?"

"Oh, he said something to Annette." O stretched, an easy thing to do in her "artistic" dress, which was daringly loose. Beside her on the sofa, Scotty whined in his sleep and moved his paws as if chasing a dream rabbit. "But I do understand, Baby. You're trying to recover the sense of purpose you had as Justin's wife. Not that I think there's much purpose in being a wife, but to most women it's the be-all and end-all of their existence."

"Perhaps you should be glad, then, that I've departed from the path of most women. After all, why should you be surprised? When I was younger, I fully intended to make healing my vocation."

"But you're trying too hard too soon. It's too early to make big decisions about your life. You must give yourself time to grieve, Baby. That's why deepest mourning should be carried out with the mirrors covered, you know. You're not supposed to be looking at yourself and considering who you are. You're supposed to be thinking of Justin."

"I *do* think of Justin. I think about him all the time. But I feel so different now that he's gone. He's left me with resources I never dreamed of having to myself." I shifted round in my seat. "Look at it this way, O. You've done what you wanted to do—what you've felt called to do—but you've always had to do it in the context of dependence on others. The allowance from Michael, living in the house he owns—"

"Well, I do make *some* money from selling my paintings." O lifted her head in a proud gesture.

"You do? I'm glad. But put yourself in my position. Suddenly, I realize I never have to depend on anyone else again. And at the same time, I realize I've healed from the shock of Daniel's death. The scab, for want of a better word, that formed over my heart after he died has dropped off. Justin did that. Feeling that raw place where I'm grieving for Justin has made me see how much he did to put me back together."

"The dear man." O sighed.

"Yes, the very dearest. And now I'm me again—the me from before Daniel died—but I'm no longer a girl, dependent on Mama and Papa. I'm a woman with . . . well, with power."

O made a small noise but then fell silent, as if she were considering what I'd said. In my own mind, all I could see was that day in the orchard, feel the moment when for the first time in my young life I had felt utterly powerless. Daniel and I, together, had seemed so strong. We had been so happy, engaged in the tentative and wonderful transition from cousins to lovers. We'd rejoiced in the gift of young, strong bodies, indulging in a childlike game of tag simply because the weather was bright and breezy and we'd been too long inside. I could still hear myself screaming for help, see my beautiful cousin with his shock of rust-colored hair drop like a stone, his lips blue. For months after that day, I had heard my screams inside my head.

"I brought one or two of Mama's journals with me," I said at last, to drive my memories out of my mind. "I'm at the point when Mama found she was with child again—of course, she didn't yet know it was twins. She seems happy."

Indeed, at this point in her writings Mama mentioned

Papa frequently. She had even gotten him involved in a new venture, that of beekeeping. Since I'd never known hives to exist at Hyrst, I supposed this particular experiment had failed.

"Five years and more before I was born," Odelia mused. "Heavens. Fifteen years at least before you made an appearance. Why does the past interest you so much, Baby?"

"I suppose I'm trying to reach Mama," I said. "And perhaps myself—the younger myself, that is."

O came to me then, draping a long arm around my shoulders. "I rather like the self you are now. The woman of power." She was laughing, but not cruelly, as she kissed me on the top of my head. "Just don't change too fast, will you?"

~

O's words were very much on my mind as our carriage bounced along the road from Hastings on our way home. Guttridge and I had been obliged to hire a carriage instead of following our plan of taking the train to Littleberry. It appeared the sudden cold snap that had settled over Sussex was interfering with the mechanism of the steam train.

It had grown cold indeed. The frost rimed the bare twigs of the hedgerows with white, making the rose hips and the few hawthorn berries the birds hadn't yet eaten stand out starkly red. Holly berries there were too, the leaves shining deep green where the low rays of the sun had struck them and melted the frost a little.

It was so cold I'd insisted Guttridge borrow one of my fur muffs and sit next to me rather than opposite. That way we could huddle together under three woolen rugs with Scotty for additional warmth and make the most of the foot-warmers provided for us in Hastings. I was grateful for Guttridge's solidity so close to me, her faint fragrance of wool and soap pleasantly human on a day where the cold had robbed the land of its usual smells of dirt, sheep, and green growing things.

"Ah, it's good to be out of those woods." Guttridge moved slightly so she was in the sunlight that now shone through the dirty glass of the carriage window.

"Yes, I always like this part of the journey. I don't mind not coming by train at all, except for the temperature. Who'd ever think I'd pine for the ladies' waiting room at Hastings and its smoky fire?"

Guttridge laughed. "I've walked along this road of a summer. I'll say this for the countryside, the views are very fine."

"This ridge was part of England's southernmost cliffs once, did you know that? The sea came right up to the foot of them. Broadmere was a port—a very prosperous one."

"The Littleberry people say the sea's always waiting to take its own back." Guttridge stared out to where the sea showed as a sparkling dark blue strip with a line of azure on the horizon. "They talk of a huge storm, hundreds of years ago, that washed Old Broadmere under the waves. They say if England's in peril, you can hear the bells of the old church ringing, far out in the water."

I snorted softly at the old tale, settling back into the faded velvet of the carriage seat. Brought up within two miles of the sea, I had, since my earliest memories, sought the sight of it on every return from a journey. How could I ever ally myself with any man who dwelt inland? I couldn't possibly live far from the coast.

"Ah, there's Whitcombe." Guttridge's words brought me out of my reverie, and I looked out of the other side of the carriage. My home was an airy confection of red brick and sandstone, serene and shining in the sharp morning light. From a distance, perched on the top of its hill, it looked like a dolls' house waiting for a giant child to swing open the front and grasp the little people within.

Now Littleberry appeared to our right, its brownish-red houses huddled around the great church whose distinctive tower could be recognized from as far away as the Downs. We would have to descend the hill and wind our slow way through its narrow streets to find the other turnpike road, up, up again until we reached Whitcombe Lane at the road's highest point. This part of the journey always made me feel oddly impatient. I had seen my home but must needs delay the welcome moment of stepping over the threshold because of the natural obstacles of hill, valley, and river that turned our part of Sussex into a maze to puzzle strangers.

"Ugh." Guttridge and I held our noses at the same moment. The belching fumes of kilns had given way to the worst of Littleberry's odors, the salty stench of the fishing boats that lined the spreading river, beached on the mud till the tide returned to float them off again. Farther along, the fish smell would compete with the tar of the boat builders and the stink of the weekly market, the dung of the sheep and cattle driven into Littleberry as the halfway point of their journey from green field to butcher's hook.

We rattled over the new bridge that, mercifully, had replaced the river ferry, over the railroad, and into the street of humble dwellings that ran along the lower edge of the town. There, inevitably, we were delayed.

"Hmph." Guttridge managed to push down the window on her side enough to stick her head out. "There's a horse in the way."

I took her place at the window, shivering as the frigid air from outside hit me. Two huge drays, one laden with barrels and the other with what looked like the entire contents of a house, blocked the road. Their drivers were engaged in a furious altercation with each other and with a person hanging out of the upper window of one of the houses. The cause of the blockage was clearly the large black horse tied by its reins to a fence; it had, in the contrary way of horses, decided to move itself out into the road so that it narrowed the thoroughfare substantially.

"It's a gentleman's horse," said Guttridge.

"It's Monsieur Fortier's horse." I had recognized it instantly. "I don't think anybody else in Littleberry rides such a huge animal."

I was proved right by the appearance of the horse's owner, who clapped his silk hat onto his head as he hurriedly shook the hand of the householder. He was carrying his medical bag, from which I deduced he'd been called out to a patient.

My insides gave a funny little squirm as I watched Fortier untie his horse and lead it round in our direction, apologizing to the drivers as he did so. He was dressed for riding, as I'd so often seen him, in breeches, tall boots, and a cutaway coat. He looked somehow more *real* than any of my hopeful male visitors in London.

He walked his horse toward us, talking to the animal and swapping jocular remarks with a knife-grinder heading in the opposite direction. Then he saw me with my head sticking out of the carriage window, and recognition lit up his face. More than recognition—joy, if I was any judge. But in a moment his face had assumed the friendly expression of a gentleman greeting an acquaintance.

"Good morning, Lady Helena." He lifted his hat, then let go of the horse's bridle for a moment and put down his bag so he could shrug himself into the overcoat he carried over one arm. "I'm afraid Lucifer has lived up to his name and decided to make life difficult for us all. I apologize on his behalf. And on mine—I should have taken the extra time to lead him round to the back."

It was the first time I'd heard the horse's name. I grinned as it took advantage of its master's inattention to turn its huge nose in my direction, snuffling at me as it recognized my scent. Behind me, Scotty began barking furiously, and I heard Guttridge shush him.

"Lucifer, is it? Beelzebub might be better." I patted the horse's bony face, laying my cheek briefly against its velvet-soft nose.

"Oh, I don't know." Fortier pushed at Lucifer's neck to stop him from nibbling at my hat. "He's quite the angel most of the time, and I need a strong beast with all the riding I do. How was London?"

"More interesting than I thought it would be. I've had so many things sent back for my workroom. You wait till you see them."

A small cough sounded behind me, and I remembered all the trouble my so-called eccentricities had gotten me into. "Of course, you're only likely to come to Whitcombe if Susan's ill again. And I understand she's tolerable."

I thought Fortier's face fell a fraction at the clear implication he was not to approach me again other than in a professional capacity, but he nodded. "It's unlikely she'll need me," he said. "But if she does, I am at your entire disposal."

"Thank you." I looked down at the plain black wool of my traveling coat and felt a sudden surge of despair at the gulf that lay between me and Fortier. In other circumstances, we could have been friends. But I had my family to consider.

While we'd been talking, the drays had managed to extricate themselves from the odd angles they'd assumed when trying to get around Lucifer, and the carriage driver was looking at me in anticipation. Fortier saw my quick glance upward.

"I'd better let you get home before you and Miss Guttridge freeze." He tugged gently on Lucifer's bridle to urge the horse farther away from the carriage and tipped his hat to me politely.

"I wish you good day, Lady Helena. My compliments to your family."

There was nothing I could do but nod and withdraw my head into the carriage. As I pushed the window up, I watched Fortier mount his horse with the considerable display of athleticism necessary in the case of such a large animal and thought incongruously of the aristocrat with the sunken eye. If I were to marry again, it would have to be a man accustomed to the vigorous life of the countryside.

"You're doing well to keep the French gentleman at arm's length, my lady, if you don't mind me saying so." Guttridge's tone was approving. "It's best that way."

I bit back a retort that I *did* mind her saying so. Guttridge had my best interests at heart. They all did. There was no reason I should see Fortier now unless our paths crossed accidentally. If he were right and Farmer Hatherall had played some part in Justin's death, well—Hatherall was dead. All I could do now was grieve, and as O said, I needed time to do that. In the quiet and seclusion of a widow's first mourning, I would find myself—and yet there was something about the last half hour that had taken the sparkling edge off the bright winter's day and cast a shadow over my homecoming.

22

A SENSE OF PURPOSE

I walked up the front steps at Whitcombe House with the usual feeling of gratitude that I could breathe the fresh air of the coast again, even if it was too cold to smell the sea. London air was stale and flat, that of Littleberry too often malodorous; but as always before entering Whitcombe, I turned around and breathed deep, relishing the wide prospect below me, the shadowed hills beyond the valley, the blue-tinged presence of the Channel to the south.

"It seems very large and very empty," I said to Guttridge after we'd greeted the other servants, who had assembled to welcome us. My voice echoed in the Great Hall, where the winter sunlight struck gleams from white-and-gray marble and a roaring fire did its best to counteract the day's chill.

"It's a grand place." Guttridge looked around with an air of satisfaction. "Scott House is well enough, my lady, and it was a fine thing to visit my old auntie in Bromley, but I'm glad to be back home with my friends."

"And your young man?" I asked slyly.

"Him too." Guttridge grinned.

"Let's go upstairs and shake off the dust." I headed toward

the wide staircase, sparing a second's glance for the first baronet, Justin's grandfather, who surveyed us with his usual sideways glance from over the fireplace, his hand forever thrust into the breast of his richly brocaded coat. Scotty's claws clicked as he ran upstairs, barking a welcome to the house. Yes, it was good to be home.

"I'm eager to see my workroom," I said as we walked up the dark mahogany stairs. "To see how Susan's progressed with the materials I sent home."

Stepping through the door into Whitcombe had fired me with a sense of excitement and purpose I'd not had since the Hatheralls had accused Justin of fathering Susan's child. Now perhaps I could settle down in peace to learn the herbalist's art. And in just a few weeks, there would be a baby in the house. Would it really be so hard to persuade Susan to accept my charity and keep the child at Whitcombe? The house would not seem so big and empty with a child in it. And it seemed fitting somehow; had my mother not cared for Susan when she herself was a motherless child?

It didn't take long, with Guttridge's help, to remove my traveling clothes and don one of my plainest dresses, over which I could easily slip an apron. Guttridge stayed upstairs, as the trunks would soon be brought up. After a brief conference with Mrs. Eason about meals and maids—we had lost a kitchen maid to homesickness—I ran lightly down the staircase and sought out Susan in my workroom.

She was not a prepossessing sight. The fine, abundant hair that had once shone like moonlight in summer now lay limp and dead-looking against her scalp. Her eyes, dull and resentful, were ringed with dark shadows. Her belly was a taut growth on a body that had become awkwardly angular.

"How are you feeling?" I asked as she dipped a curtsey, more for something to say than anything else. She was clearly feeling dreadful. "You seem to be doing very well with the room." That, at least, felt warm and welcoming. A fire of apple wood burned in the grate, and the air bore the scents of spices and alcohols. "Is Mrs. Eason looking after you?"

"Yes, m'lady, she looks after me fine. She's always on at me to eat something or the other. And she's had that Mrs. Kenny—that's the midwife—to me three times. Says she's thinking of calling in the French physician, but I don't want him near me."

"One of the other physicians, perhaps? I would understand your not wanting to see Monsieur Fortier." I couldn't resist an allusion to the trouble Susan had caused. "You do look a little thin."

"It's the child, m'lady. It's sucking the life out of me." She looked downward at where her dress bulged out in a tight curve, an almost malicious hatred on her face. "I daresay I'll feel better after it's born."

"I suppose you will. Although I wish you'd think of your baby as a little boy or girl rather than an 'it.'" I tried to look her in the eyes, but she turned her head to one side. "Do you still suffer from fever?"

I thought of laying a hand on her forehead, which looked red and dry, but she took a step backward as if she anticipated the impulse and wished to forestall it. And in fact, I didn't want to touch her. There was something about her that made my thumbs prickle and sent a chill down my spine.

"I get fevers, m'lady. Not too bad though, not like that one time. I don't bother Mrs. Eason too much about them." She gestured at two bundles of dried leaves that hung from the ceiling. "Mrs. Kenny brought me these raspberry leaves, and I make a tea. Seems to help, and I like it."

For a moment, she sounded like the bold Susan of her younger days, and I smiled despite my misgivings. She did at least seem to be interested in the herbs. I could see several of the jars now had ingredients in them and were labeled in large, round, neat handwriting. If Susan found the work congenial, I had more chance of convincing her to stay at Whitcombe with her baby. Even the worst theory of how the child came to be conceived wouldn't make him—or her—any less of a person deserving of love and care.

"I thank you, m'lady, for getting them to bring my bits of things from the farm." Susan pushed a hand under her cap to scratch at her scalp. "I'm never going in there again."

"You didn't ask for much, from what Mrs. Eason tells me. You didn't want your father's books? I heard you only asked for his Bible and a book of poems."

"His learning didn't do him much good." Susan sniffed. "The Bible and Mr. Wordsworth are all I need to remember how we were once happy."

"I expect the new tenant's in now." I tried to sound cheerful. "Come, Susan, show me all you've done while I've been away. I have a few more things in my trunk—we can look at those together once Guttridge has unpacked."

Susan did seem a little brighter once we began discussing impartial topics such as the difficulties of powdering licorice and the properties of the cinchona bark I'd found, and the next two or three hours passed pleasantly. From time to time, she would grunt or touch her side as if the baby were moving, and I had to discipline myself not to stare at her round belly. It was wrong of me to covet her child, and I knew it. He was not mine; he was certainly not Justin's; and it would be better for all concerned if he moved to Canada with Maggie and her husband.

And yet . . . more than any of Michael and Julia's children, whom I had loved to hold as babies, this possible future member of my household exercised a hold on me that I couldn't deny.

23

SHADOWS OF PAST AND PRESENT

J saw much of Julia over the following five days while I was making up for lost time with Mama. This gave me ample opportunity to scrutinize my feelings about babies in general. Julia was almost six months along by this point and glowing with vitality. The contrast with Susan was stark, and my concerns about the younger woman's health grew.

"I've tried one or two very simple remedies that Mama specifically said were good for women in a delicate condition," I told Julia as we sat in the window of Mama's sitting room, watching a turbulent sky through windowpanes smeared with salt-laden rain. Where, on a clear day, we could have seen the sea, there was only a bank of mist on the horizon.

"Do they help?" Julia stretched as lazily as she could within the limitations of her close-fitting bodice. Behind us, Mama uttered a stream of almost unintelligible words. She was becoming increasingly agitated; I'd arrived to find her accusing Belming of ripping the dress she was wearing— which was quite intact—to shreds. Worse, she'd fallen into the habit of removing her clothing at odd times. She'd exposed her flesh to me that day in so startling a manner that I wasn't surprised Michael now refused to visit her.

"The remedies might help if Susan would take them. But she tries them once and then goes back to her raspberry leaf tea. I've also made a list of some calming remedies I might try on Mama."

"The oil of lavender was a good idea." Julia sniffed the air appreciatively. "Although poor Belming's hands must smell of lavender from morning till night."

"I don't mind, m'lady." Belming spoke quietly from the corner where she'd been silently engaged in some darning. "Her ladyship seems to like the feel of having it rubbed into her neck and shoulders, and we're sleeping a little better. Though we do wander something terrible some nights."

"We're going to have to get a night nurse," Julia said to me in an undertone. "Look at Belming—she's got such dark shadows under her eyes. Supposing she gave notice? I can't imagine what I'd do."

I nodded. "I'll pay for an extra nurse. And before you tell me that Michael won't accept my help, he jolly well will. She's my mother too."

Julia grinned. "I agree, although we're not as badly off as Michael sometimes makes out. He's doing a good job of settling the late earl's debts, and giving him free rein with Justin's—your—land and flocks is bound to help us. James is perfectly happy with old Mr. Munns teaching him his reading, writing, and arithmetic, and Michael agrees with me that he's too sensitive for Eton just yet, future earl or no. So we'll save on fees."

"Thank heaven for Michael's abhorrence of Eton," I said. "I can't say I much like the practice of sending small boys off to school either."

There was a disturbance in the room as tea arrived. Julia

and I moved to the settee to sit with Mama. As soon as the maid set the sugar bowl down, Mama grabbed it and deposited about twelve lumps into one of the cups.

"I expect you'd like some tea, Mama." I removed all but two of the sugar lumps from the cup, half filled it with tea, and put in plenty of milk.

"I don't care what you think." Mama glared at me. "Your opinion is of no consequence."

"It never is. That's the worst of being the youngest girl." I stirred the tea until I was sure it was sufficiently cool, then handed Mama the cup without a saucer. Mama held the cup balanced oddly on her palm—watching her drink tea had become a worrying process, but in fact she never spilled it.

"Annabelle Alice is quite desperate for this child to be a girl." Julia handed Mama a tiny cucumber sandwich without a plate—that too was a lesson learned. "She says she's trying to be a good girl so God will answer her prayers on this particular subject. I'll admit, even though I'm sure it's a boy, I'm on her side—I love the idea of another little girl running around the place. Imagine the mischief two Annabelle Alices would get into."

"She never stops talking," Mama said, putting down her cup on the very edge of the table. "Thinking she can bring me round. Worming her way into my confidence. She's a nasty, dirty beast."

"I presume you're not talking about Annabelle Alice, Mama-in-Law. Would you like another sandwich?" Julia leaned forward with a dainty morsel poised between her fingers.

"I'm not eating that." Mama batted Julia's hand away so that the sandwich flew apart. Naturally, both pieces of bread landed butter side down on the rug. "It's poison."

"Of course it's not, Mama." I peeled the pieces of bread off the carpet and rubbed ineffectually at the greasy spots with my napkin. "It's a cucumber sandwich. You just ate one."

"We think a lot of things are poison lately." Belming nodded her thanks for the cup of tea and plate of sandwiches I'd brought her. "Especially things to drink. Some days it's hard to get a drop of liquid into her ladyship at all." She shook her head. "It's not good for a body to go thirsty. Barley water, now *that* her ladyship will drink, if she takes anything at all. But no cocoa, and it used to be such a favorite."

"I shouldn't imagine cocoa's good to drink if you're thirsty." I spoke absentmindedly, my mind on the notion of supplying some tisanes Mama might like. Would that be a pointless gesture? "Mama and Papa drank cocoa every day together before retiring to bed, but they would also have a glass of water."

"Your Mama and Papa were so close." Julia smiled. "Such an adoring couple."

"Murderous bastard."

I felt my eyebrows shoot up and saw the same expression on Julia's face.

"Good heavens, m'lady." Belming's voice was controlled and deferential, but there was definitely a hint of emotion. "We can't talk like that. Such language doesn't befit a dowager countess."

"Does Mama often say things like that?" I inquired.

"At times." Belming slipped the darning mushroom from the stocking she'd just finished and stowed it in her workbasket. She folded the mended stocking carefully and placed it on top of the pile. "Sometimes we think there's a man with a knife behind the curtain."

"Poor Mama." I went to kiss the pure white hair that met the freckled skin of my mother's brow, breathing in the scent of lavender. I remembered the sensation of Mama's arms, strong and capable back then, encircling my shoulders. "You're quite safe here, you know. We all love you."

"I'm afraid." For a moment I saw my mother—my real mother, not this poor, confused woman—look out of Mama's eyes.

"Afraid of what?"

The expression in my mother's eyes shifted again, becoming childishly cunning. "I shan't tell you. You have to ask the gardener."

"Would you like to come and see the children?" Julia pushed herself out of her chair, not without a little difficulty.

"I would. Do try to be calm, dear Mama. I'll visit you again tomorrow."

I suspected Julia's request was an excuse to give us a change of scene. I was proved right when, instead of heading for the nursery floor, Julia led me to her boudoir. This small, pretty room had once been Mama's and then of course Cecilia's, but Julia had sensibly asserted a new bride's privileges and transformed its faded Regency tints into a medley of gold tones that suited her warm coloring.

"Goodness, that's better." Julia stretched herself out on the chaise longue that took up most of one wall. "I hope you don't mind deserting your mother, Hel."

"Not at all. And I'm serious about the night nurse. Would you tell Belming to make inquiries? She'd be the best person to choose her own subordinate."

"I will, with many thanks." Julia leaned back, careful not to disturb her coiffure. "Perhaps it's my condition, but I'm beginning to find the dowager rather exhausting."

"It's not just your condition. Poor Mama. I've been reading her journals from the early 1840s, you know, and it gives me pangs of sadness to compare the happy woman of those years with the poor, miserable wretch she is now."

"Was she happy then?" Julia wriggled her shoulders. "Dash it, now I can't get comfortable."

"Wait." I darted forward and fiddled with the cushions. "It might help if you got this book out of the way."

"*That's* what I've been meaning to tell you. I put it there to remind me. This is yours—O sent it with some other things Michael wanted from Scott House. She said she'd borrowed it from Whitcombe to copy the trees, if that makes any sense."

I tucked the green-and-gold volume under my arm and continued adjusting Julia's cushions until she relaxed. A memory flickered again, a feather tickling the edges of my mind, but I failed to grasp it.

"Yes, she seemed perfectly happy," I said, reverting to our conversation about Mama. "She'd had three children, the twins and Blanche, at an interval of just sixteen months. Gerry was nearly eight, and from the look of the entries in the journal, Mama spent an awful lot of time curing the poor of Littleberry."

"Curing them?"

"Well, not always. Some of the entries are quite funny— like when she gave a tincture of hops and valerian to Mrs. Pike for anxiety. The old lady spat it out onto the floor and said she'd rather worry. I hope Mrs. Pike wasn't punished for her rudeness by the workhouse authorities. Mama spent a great deal of time there."

"I wish I'd known her then."

"She had become extremely knowledgeable. She wrote three pages on how she'd used foxglove leaf to help a Mr. Beamish—I think he must be the East Street butcher's grand-father—with his heart ailment. She started off very cautiously and increased the dose until he began to show signs of improvement. And then there's another two pages on the preparation of a liniment for rheumatism and neuralgia, made with belladonna and aconite. I don't know if I'd ever dare use such dangerous plants. Mama used to tell me never to touch the aconite in her garden unless she was there to supervise."

"That's monkshood, isn't it?"

"That's right. I must show you the sketch she made of the flowers—it's beautiful. She wrote 'EXTREME CAUTION—MORE POWERFUL THAN PRUSSIC ACID' underneath."

Julia laughed. "I wish you could see your face," she said. "Positively lighting up while you're talking about poisons."

"Healing plants," I said. "Knowledge I don't suppose I'll ever obtain. I wasted so many years, Julia."

My sister-in-law shifted her body so she could stretch out an arm toward me. I took her hand, feeling the heat that seemed to radiate from within her, and knew it for a healthy warmth, the incubation of a strong life.

"You're young," she said. "Your mother didn't become knowledgeable in a day either. Stop worrying about the past —or the future—and concentrate on what you're learning now. Which, from the sound of it, is already quite a lot."

By the time I left Hyrst, it was growing dark. The weather had turned warmer—perhaps March was coming in like a lamb instead of a lion this year—and a pearly gray mist permeated the air. It was impossible to see more than a few feet ahead, even though my driver had lit an extra lantern. The gravel of the drive muffled the sound of the horses' hooves as we headed away from the house, past the stable block on the left and the unseen bluff on the right. The air was scented with the musty fragrance of last year's moldering leaves and an indefinable green smell that spoke of the coming spring, of the bright spikes of snowdrop and the circular ruffs of winter aconite, the blue monkshood's innocent namesake. Yes, I reflected, Julia was right—I did know something about plants, and I was learning more every day. Perhaps I could make up for lost time.

We proceeded steadily onward under the great trees that occasionally showed stark and black as the mist shifted, reaching the lane and then the turnpike road without encountering man, beast, or carriage.

The world was quiet and somber on this first day of March, seemingly peaceful. It was an odd peace, mingled as it was with the tension inherent in being blinded and deafened by the smothering mist. In such a fog, anything could appear. The stagecoach, perhaps, to crash into us. Seventy years ago, my fears might have included highwaymen.

"Ridiculous," I scolded myself. Making a deliberate attempt to relax, I rocked with the rocking of the carriage. I promised myself a pleasant evening spent alternately reading Mama's journals and gazing into the fire in the small library. Perhaps the next morning would be fine and the going firm, and I could take Sandy out for a hack around fields awakening to the spring.

I ran my hand over the book that lay on my lap. I had recognized it at last, as a wedding present I had rather liked. Justin had laughed at it as a saccharine compilation of poetry and engravings of bucolic scenes, but we had read a few of the poems curled up together one evening in the small library. If it hadn't been dark, I'd have leafed through the pages in an attempt to recapture that happy time of my life.

The mist seemed a little lighter as we approached Whitcombe House, and the close shadows of the lane gave way to the wide-open sky of the hilltop. The hedges and neatly clipped shrubs around the house loomed as twiggy black shapes, here and there haloed in the darkest of greens. I shivered a little as I felt for the carriage steps with my feet, the driver's hand hard and impersonal under my palm.

The door opened at my approach, as I'd expected. But I hadn't expected the look on Mrs. Eason's face, drawn and gray with deep vertical lines in her cheeks.

"It's the girl, m'lady."

As she spoke, I thought I heard the sound of a distant wail.

"The—Susan?" I heard a sound again as I stepped into the Great Hall. We both looked upward, although the wide staircase led only to the family bedrooms, which I knew to be vacant.

"Yes, m'lady. She's ailing again, but very bad this time."

"Is it the fever?" I shucked off my manteau and looked around for Guttridge, who by rights should have been standing by waiting to help me with my outer clothing. She wasn't there, so I deposited coat and book into the arms of a hovering footman without even noticing which one it was.

"She's a little feverish." Mrs. Eason followed as I turned in the direction of a service staircase reached through a green baize door to the rear of the house. "But it's her belly that pains her. It came on quite suddenly about an hour ago."

"Have you sent for the midwife?" I was hurrying now. How far along was Susan? Quite close to her time, I thought. But surely the unflappable Mrs. Eason wouldn't be so worried if these were the pains of normal childbirth.

"Of course, m'lady." I could hear the clicking of heels as Mrs. Eason, older and stouter than I, struggled to keep up with me. I racked my brain for any remedies that might ease Susan's pain, but only gentle potions for stomachache came to mind.

The scream that assaulted my ears told me this was no stomachache. It was the cry of a woman in agony, a desperate, wordless entreaty for the end of torment, and it sent a wave of despair crashing through my own body. Even as I increased my pace, taking the stairs two at a time despite my heavy skirts, I felt the weight of my own inadequacy. I had been playing at healing, concocting imaginary dishes out of grass, leaves, and mud. Faced with real pain, I doubted I had any ability to relieve it.

I stopped abruptly, swinging round to face Mrs. Eason. She was several steps below me, panting hard.

"Send for Dr. Fortier," I said, noting inwardly that I had called him "Doctor" for the first time.

"The French physician? Shouldn't we try one of the proper English ones?" Mrs. Eason sucked in a deep gasp of air, having clearly exhausted her supply of oxygen by arguing. "Although none of them are accoucheurs, not to my knowledge. The old sawbones who attended the difficult childbirths was in Broadmere, and he died last year."

"I trust Fortier," I said shortly and spun back around to continue my progress. It was a clear signal to Mrs. Eason not to further the discussion, and I was glad to hear her footsteps heading downward.

I could feel perspiration on my upper lip and forehead as I reached the attic bedrooms. I turned the door handle, noting that my hand was not entirely steady.

I wasn't surprised to find Guttridge bending over the narrow bed. For a second, the sight reassured me. Then Susan let out another cry that sounded as if she were being ripped apart from within, and this time it wasn't muffled by an intervening door. The sheets and blankets that had covered her hung from the end of the bed, pooling on the floor as Susan alternately curled inward around her belly and flexed outward, bending backward in agony.

"My God," was all I could find to say. A wave of panic sent pins and needles into my fingertips.

I bent over Susan in my turn, laying my palm on her brow

in a futile attempt to calm her. She was sweating heavily, not dry with fever like before. She didn't seem to notice I'd entered the room. Her eyes were screwed shut, her teeth clamped together in a rictus of pain. To my consternation, I noticed there was blood on her teeth.

"She bit her tongue." Guttridge dipped a washcloth in the basin by her feet and swabbed Susan's face with it. "She'll take some water from time to time—I can't think what else to give her."

Guttridge's plain, slightly heavy face was calm yet watchful, with the eyes of an officer on the field of battle. I wanted to hug her for being there with Susan—and with me.

I watched the writhing body for a few seconds. The thin nightgown Susan wore was sweat-soaked and indecently revealing. Her heavy breasts and belly looked as though they barely belonged with the wasted limbs and bony face. She had lost flesh from arms and legs, face, neck, shoulders— everywhere except for what was needed to sustain the baby's life. She was an ugly sight.

"There's barely any blood." Guttridge indicated the bottom of the bed, where a few smears of crimson and some nasty-looking brownish clots did nothing to improve the appearance of the sheets. "I don't understand why she's in so much pain. I don't think it's normal."

I shook my head. "Neither do I. I feel so ignorant." But I knelt before the bed, taking the washcloth from Guttridge's unresisting hand. Dipping it into the basin, I squeezed out the water, folded it, and laid it across Susan's forehead. It was a futile gesture in the face of the agony expressed in the young woman's every movement and posture.

"Would laudanum help, do you think, my lady?" Guttridge asked. "For the pain."

"Laudanum? I don't keep it in the house."

"I can probably get some chlorodyne from Mrs. Foster."

Guttridge's brow furrowed. "She swears by Freeman's for her neuralgia."

"The dowager countess thinks all these patent opiates and cocaines are bad for you," I said absentmindedly—and then wondered how I could state Mama's opinion so clearly. A memory surfaced of a long-ago day at Hyrst, Mama talking with determined cheerfulness while I stared blankly at the view below us, unable to comprehend a world without Daniel in it.

"We'll wait until the midwife—or better still, Monsieur Fortier—arrives," I decided. "Neither of us knows enough about what we're doing."

For the next twenty minutes or so, the two of us did the best we could to alleviate Susan's pain. We helped her change position whenever she seemed to need to do so, and I discovered that rubbing her lower back helped a little. If we touched her belly, hard and round under her damp gown, Susan's cries redoubled. I found myself constantly moving my hands over her back, soothing and hushing her as if she were herself an infant.

"The physician will be here soon," I assured her when her eyelids fluttered open and she looked directly at me. "And the midwife. You'll feel better once the child is born."

"Feel better?" I was surprised by the sudden strength in Susan's voice. "I'll feel better if it dies. I hope I die too, and quickly, because I swear I'm splitting in two." She panted for a few moments. "My belly feels like it's ready to burst."

A thought struck me, and I looked up at Guttridge. "Perhaps we should send for the rector." I tried to form the words without Susan hearing, but the panting stopped and the word, "NO," burst out of her.

"There'll be no blessings for me and this child, whatever happens." She grimaced. "My father was right; it's the devil's work. Better to let us both die and our memory fade from the earth."

"Please don't say that," I whispered. I desperately wanted this baby to live. And, I suddenly realized, I felt almost as horrified at the thought of Susan dying. Not just for her own sake—however I had felt about her, I had never wished her any harm, poor Susan—but, I realized suddenly, for Justin's. Susan was the last link with the truth that seemed to lay tantalizingly just out of reach.

I thought again of Fortier's theory that Farmer Hatherall had fathered his own child's child and heard him say that he could not justify basing such a theory on two words. What were those words? "Doves' nest." The words Lucius Hatherall had used to describe Dene Farm to his daughter.

And then the memory that had been prowling around the edges of my consciousness opened the door, walked in, and made itself at home. Poor Susan. A poem of that name, by Mr. Wordsworth, was in the book O had borrowed. Justin and I had read and discussed it not long after our marriage.

"Dash it all, he makes it sound like the girl's father is her lover." I heard Justin's voice, light and yet a little cynical, a mature foil to my inexperienced ideas. "'A nest like a dove's' indeed. Brain-rotting stuff, if you ask me, and degenerate to boot."

"I like Wordsworth," I heard myself say. The memory of Justin's warm breath on my cheek as he laughed once more, the rise and fall of his chest, came so vividly to me that my own breath almost stopped in my throat.

One of the books Susan had asked for was a volume of Wordsworth's poems. There it was, on the small shelf above her bed. A fine binding of soft calf leather and gilt, unusually fine for a man of Hatherall's station in life. Perhaps he had bought it from a sale when the library of a great house was broken up—Justin had acquired a few books that way.

A theory built on two words—but a theory that had just gained credence in my mind. I leaned closer to the writhing figure on the bed.

"Are you sure you don't have something to confess to the rector, Susan? I see no better time to unburden yourself. You see—I think I know what it might be." I took a deep breath. "Did your father force you? Did he sire your child? Is that why he killed himself?"

A small, strangled sound made me look up at Guttridge, and I saw horror in her face. I instantly felt terrible about interrogating such a sick woman, and then my own guilt was obliterated by the screech Susan gave. Not of pain, but of laughter. It turned into a howl of agony, and for a few moments Guttridge and I busied ourselves trying to relieve Susan's distress.

"I'm sorry," I gasped as soon as Susan stilled for a moment. "I just thought—if your father raped you, Susan, you're in no way to blame."

"I won't—" Susan panted for a few moments and then began again. "I *won't* have you saying such things about Father." She narrowed her eyes at me. "Is that what you're all going to think if I die?"

I opened my mouth to apologize again, to say I was in the wrong, that I had been cruel and unkind. But Susan's next utterance stopped the words in my throat.

"You listen here, Lady La-Di-Da. There's one thing I won't have, and that's you passing judgment on Father when you don't know the half of it. If what went on between Father and me was anyone's doing, it was mine. I wanted it, and he was lonely, and your old Ma knew a trick or two." A sly grin flitted across her face, followed by a grimace as a fresh pain took her. "I nicked a bottle or two from her when she started to go dotty. After she threw me out, mind, but I knew how to get into Hyrst without being seen. It was a pity she sent it all away in the end, all those useful bottles. A woman's powerful when she knows what's in those bottles."

"But why?" I shook my head, uncomprehending. "Why not another man? Why did it have to be your father?"

She shrugged. "I wanted him to spend what he'd saved on *me*, not on his damned sheep. Who cared if he had a bit of land of his own? It'd still be a farm, and me working on a farm and married off to some clodhopper farmer like Maggie was. I wanted better than that. I wanted to go somewhere else—somewhere far off, where nobody knew us. To find someone to teach me to be a lady and catch me a decent husband. The sin of pride, Father said, and perhaps he was right. Because God—or the devil—punished us right enough."

The last words came out in a series of pants, forced out as if by a supreme effort. "So that's why your father killed himself—" I began, only to have my words drowned out by a scream of such volume that I put my hands over my ears. Susan twisted like an eel, the tendons of her neck standing out as she arched backward. A bloom of dark red blood appeared on the back of her nightgown.

Guttridge grasped my arm. "Someone's coming." She was right—with immense relief I heard a commotion somewhere in the corridor, running footsteps. Help had come at last.

My relief was all the greater when I saw Fortier, the midwife at his elbow. I pushed my aching body upright, heedless of how ungainly I must look. I moved toward Fortier while the midwife dodged around me, rolling up her sleeves and hissing through her teeth with concern.

"It's her belly." I realized as the words emerged how stupid I sounded. Of course it was her belly—she was with child. "I mean, is this what it's always like?" I could hear the tremor in my voice. "I don't think it's supposed to be like this. And she's said the most awful things." I pronounced the last words in a whisper, my eyes on the midwife. "I'll tell you later."

I turned toward Susan again as the girl let out another scream. I was standing so near to Fortier that turning brought the whole of the back portion of me into contact with him. For a brief moment, I felt his arms around me, holding me close. Then the sensation of warmth and reassurance was gone as he stepped back and to the side a little. I turned, following his movement, and looked up into his eyes.

"You don't need to stay." His voice was soft, almost caressing. "Mrs. Kenny and I will look after the poor girl." He nodded at Guttridge, who was trying to help the midwife untangle Susan's nightdress from the sheets. "Your maid too; she should go. To look after you."

"I thank you, *Monsewer*, but I'd rather stay." Guttridge's reply was immediate and abrupt. "Unless you need me, my lady."

"I also intend to stay." I unbuttoned the cuffs of my black silk dress and rolled up my sleeves in imitation of the midwife. I was foolishly overdressed for the circumstances, I knew that—but I didn't care. "I'm not leaving her, whatever happens."

This time Fortier's grip on my arms was stronger and more insistent. "My dear," he hissed in a hoarse whisper close to my ear, "this is going to be more unpleasant than you can imagine. Messy, with much blood. And I don't think we'll save the child—maybe not the mother either." He glanced over at the bed. "This is no place for a woman of gentle breeding."

"To damnation with my gentle breeding." I wriggled out of his grasp, my cheeks flaming at the endearment I couldn't deny I'd heard. "Susan—and her child—are my responsibility, and I believe we still have things to say to each other. Will you please stop fussing about me and attend to them?"

I was fairly sure I heard Fortier utter an oath in French under his breath as he moved toward Mrs. Kenny. She was passing a hand over the top of Susan's belly, muttering to herself, while Guttridge grasped Susan's shoulders and tried to keep her still.

At Fortier's approach, the midwife said something to him I couldn't hear and then stepped back and looked at me.

"I need a clean sheet."

She spoke as if I'd been a servant, but I didn't care. What bothered me most at that moment was that I had absolutely no idea where a clean sheet might be located in my own house. I truly deserved the sobriquet "Baby." I looked help-lessly at Guttridge.

"You hold her, my lady." Guttridge relinquished her post. "I think Mrs. Eason went to fetch clean sheets and water, but I can just get a sheet from the servants' linen cupboard for now."

"Two sheets." Mrs. Kenny had started to pull the soiled fabric from under Susan, exposing the worn ticking of the mattress.

The linen cupboard must have been nearby as Guttridge was back in a moment. The midwife snapped the first sheet open and insinuated it under Susan's body with considerable skill. I let go of Susan's shoulders for a moment to help her. She then draped the second sheet over Susan's legs, which she raised into a bent position before disappearing under the linen. Fortier took the midwife's erstwhile place and ran his hands over Susan's taut belly, his head on one side, for all the world as if he were listening with his fingers.

Susan yelped and twisted as Fortier's hands moved. Mrs. Kenny emerged from under the sheet to give Fortier what I could best describe as a speaking look. Fortier turned to rummage in the large leather bag he had brought into the room, withdrawing a stethoscope. He hooked the shining metal ends into his ears and spent a few moments pressing the tube of the instrument to Susan's belly.

I could see he was being as gentle as possible and thought Susan was making an effort to lie still. Her eyes were half-closed, her teeth clamped together, her face a sickly pale color. When he moved the instrument higher, she screamed again and raised her hand as if she would snatch the tube away.

Fortier gently grasped the hand to keep it from wrenching at the stethoscope and then turned it over to view the palm. With a gesture at Mrs. Kenny, who was waiting to speak to him, he let go of Susan's hand and cupped his fingers around her chin.

"Open your mouth, please, Mademoiselle. I would like to see your tongue."

Susan's eyes opened a little wider, and she breathed out a puff of derision. But she stuck her tongue out as far as she could. Behind me, I heard Guttridge make a small sound of comprehension.

"She's poxed, then, as well. Gawd Almighty, the little whore."

I turned to look at my lady's maid, startled as much by her language as by the realization that she understood a lot more than I did. The Frenchman simply looked at Guttridge with a tinge of wry amusement overlying his professional gravity. The expression was gone in a second, and he motioned the three of us to the door.

We stepped out into the cream-painted corridor. Fortier began to speak, fast and low so that Susan couldn't hear.

"The child is almost certainly dead," were his opening words. "She is bleeding inside. That's what is causing her so much pain."

"She's having contractions—very short ones," added Mrs. Kenny. "And close together, although she's not nearly ready to give birth." She pushed back the scant black curls that had escaped her topknot and attempted to pin them into place. "If she goes on like this for much longer . . ."

"She will die too." Fortier nodded. "I propose a caesarean delivery to save her." He shrugged slightly. "She may die anyway, you understand. Blood loss, shock, infection—her weakened state of health."

"Guttridge said . . ." I didn't know where to begin.

"She has a syphilitic infection." Fortier's voice was flat and expressionless. "It can be very hard to diagnose, but her pallor has made the rash on her tongue and hands more evident."

"And the soles of her feet." Mrs. Kenny shook her head. "It's not often I hope the babe's dead, but in this case—" She sighed heavily. "If you save her, she'll die a worse death later."

"And nevertheless, I must try. At the very least she won't suffer the agony she's in now."

He was speaking to all of us, but his eyes were fixed on me, making me feel self-conscious. Now his gaze shifted to the midwife. "I have chloroform with me. That, too, has its dangers—in the circumstances it may stop the young woman's heart—but I have studied the dosage well, and I only need a few minutes to do the work. I have morphine, heroin, cocaine—I can relieve her pain once the child is delivered in whatever way seems best."

Mrs. Kenny nodded. "Just tell me what help you need."

"And what are Guttridge and I to do?" I asked.

Fortier pinched the bridge of his nose. "I hesitate to place either of you ladies in danger," was his eventual reply. "Especially you, Lady Helena."

I lowered my gaze to avoid the tenderness I saw in his eyes. He took a deep breath and continued. "We don't yet know the causative organism of syphilis, and there will be much blood and—other fluids. At least let me see your hands and arms so that I may be reassured you have no cuts or abrasions where infection may enter."

We obediently held out our hands, mine looking small next to Guttridge's. Fortier inspected them carefully, turning them with his fingertips. I couldn't help looking up into his face; he was absorbed in his task, his luminous eyes hidden behind their lowered lids.

A noise at the end of the corridor coincided with a yell of pain from Susan, and our small group scattered in all directions. Mrs. Kenny hastened back to her patient while Guttridge, seeing Mrs. Eason approach with three housemaids in tow, all laden with various articles, darted toward them. I followed Fortier back into the room and touched his arm.

"The rector," I said softly. "We have to send for him, even though she says she doesn't want him. She seduced her own father, Fortier. You were right after all."

Fortier's eyes widened. "She told you that?"

"Yes, and she says Farmer Hatherall wasn't to blame."

One thick black eyebrow rose in an expression that was decidedly ironic. "It takes two, Lady Helena."

"She used some concoction of my mother's, she said."

A noise behind me made me turn to find Guttridge staggering under the weight of a pile of assorted linen. Obeying her jerk of the head, I stepped out of her way so she could deposit her load on the dresser. Behind her, Mrs. Eason stood guard over three huge pitchers of steaming water and a stack of enameled basins. More linen was in her hands. The housemaids were retreating down the corridor, talking in hushed voices.

Guttridge, having freed her hands, took something from Mrs. Eason and shook it out. It turned out to be a voluminous apron. She quickly tied it around my person, pleating it to make it shorter. She then pulled sleeve protectors, of the kind used by maids when cleaning, over my arms. To finish, she wound a length of cotton around my hair. Accustomed as I was to being dressed by Guttridge, it didn't occur to me to object.

"Mrs. Eason," I said with as much dignity as I could muster as Guttridge tucked in the last fold of cotton with a nod of satisfaction, "kindly send for the rector or one of his curates. Monsieur Fortier believes Susan's life is in danger, and that of the child."

"Certainly, m'lady. Are you sure you'll be all right? Do you really want to do this?" She looked beyond me at Guttridge, who was rapidly donning a costume similar to the one in which she'd swathed me.

"I do." And I did. The long years of numbness after Daniel's death were gone. The shock of my more recent bereavement had evaporated, and even Susan's terrible confession fell into insignificance in the face of the task before us. I felt the strength and curiosity and determination to help of my childhood return to me, rendering me oddly alive—and I could swear I saw a similar spark in Guttridge's eyes. She was afraid, as was I—I could see the faint tremor in her hands, or perhaps that was merely excitement. It was clear that neither of us was about to turn tail and run.

24

A TINY MOMENT OF HEROISM

*T*ime seemed to behave oddly from then on. It moved both much too fast and much too slow. It stretched and expanded, then snapped back into a sudden rush of sensations.

The one constant was Fortier, most decidedly in charge of the proceedings. At some point, he shed his coat and rolled his shirtsleeves as high as they would go, revealing surprisingly muscular arms stippled with a fine down of black hair. He made us wash our hands and arms with a bar of shiny red soap he said was his own preparation. Mrs. Kenny washed Susan's belly and nether regions while I held a sheet to shield her modesty and Guttridge did her best to comfort her.

Susan did not seem receptive to any sort of comfort. The nature of her cries had changed; they were weaker yet just as angry. Strangely, her rage seemed to be directed at me. Whenever I looked toward her, I saw her eyes, once a luminous blue with gray centers but now muddy-looking, fixed on me with—what? Scorn? Hatred?

Fortier made some sort of preparatory arrangements using the windowsill and washstand while with part of my mind I tried to follow what he was doing. He concluded his preparations at about the same time Mrs. Kenny finished washing Susan. He moved around the bed until he could lean over Susan and speak directly to her.

"I will put a piece of gauze over your face, and you will sleep. This is so I can make a cut in your belly and remove the child. Do you understand? It's the only chance of saving your life."

Susan grimaced, and I saw the hard mound of her belly change shape as a contraction took her. When it had finished, she spoke.

"Seen Father do it to ewes when the lamb's stuck." She looked at me again, the same indefinable expression in her eyes. "I know a lot more about birthing than my lady there."

"I'll learn," I said shortly.

"Why do you have to be here?" Susan asked. "You're not beholden to me. You're not family."

"I wish to help." I knew I sounded defensive. "I care for you and your child."

"*Care for?*" Susan ran her tongue over her lips. "After what I've told you?"

"Yes." I paused for a moment, searching for the right words. "I can't change the past. You're part of my household, you're in pain, and I will care for you. Now and afterward. I won't abandon you." I spoke perhaps more out of the *noblesse oblige* everyone always flung at my head than from any other feeling, but I meant what I said.

"Well, if that doesn't take the bloody biscuit." Susan stared up at the ceiling and gave a muted bellow through gritted teeth as the pain took her again. Panting, she regarded Fortier, who was approaching with a dropper bottle in one hand, a gauze cloth wrapped around a curved frame in the other.

"I suppose I'm sorry about your husband, when all's said and done." She twisted her head away from the gauze so she could speak to me. "Father said he had a noble spirit, your man."

"He did," I whispered.

"That wasn't Father's fault either," she said, and I looked at Fortier in puzzlement. What did she mean?

Fortier straightened up and very carefully set bottle and framed gauze on a chair. He looked over at Mrs. Kenny. "Would you leave us for two minutes?" he asked her, and as she complied—a little puzzled, naturally—he bent down to Susan again.

"One does not accidentally hold a man under water until he dies," he said very quietly.

I felt my hands go cold and numb. Guttridge, whom Fortier had not asked to leave, stood still as a stone, only her eyes moving.

"Father was very sorry he did it; truly, he was." Susan, too, spoke in an undertone. "He was terrified; that's what he told me. Afterward, he realized Sir Justin would probably have done his best to make it right—given us the chance to go away or something like that. He said he was doubly damned for killing a good man. But he had to—he had to. And what I'd given Sir Justin in the cocoa made it easier. He sicked most of it up, but it weakened him."

"What did you give him?" Fortier asked, as if this were an everyday conversation and he was displaying polite interest.

"Foxglove. Another of old Ma Broadmere's potions, but I got the dose wrong. So Father had to help me because Sir Justin said I put something in his drink."

I had been looking from one to the other in a daze, but now I found the strength to speak.

"You tried to kill Justin? *Why?*"

"Did he know, or suspect, about you and your father?" Fortier asked.

Susan, who had been squirming into a variety of positions, stilled for a moment.

"Not a bit of it. I just wanted to get my own back. All my chances of happiness were gone, so why shouldn't *she* suffer?" She grinned at me, traces of browned blood visible among the mucus that coated her teeth. "All of you should suffer. All you damned Scott-De-La-Di-Da-Quincys, lording it over us from up high on your hills. It would've been you next."

"You nasty, dirty little piece." It was Guttridge who spoke —I was too shocked to utter a sound. "If you wasn't dying already, I'd kill you with me own 'ands." Her normally correct accent was disintegrating into pure Cockney. "What's 'er ladyship ever done to you? There's a special place in hell for you, I'll be bound."

"Maybe." Susan's expression turned malicious. "Your precious ladyship. Little she cares about either of us—never saw her for years after Ma Broadmere threw me out."

"I do care." My voice sounded weak and faint. "I just don't understand."

I barely had time to finish speaking before Susan screamed again, bringing Mrs. Kenny back into the room. The midwife's expression was anguished as she looked at Fortier.

"You can't put this off any longer, sir."

Fortier nodded, picking up gauze and bottle again. "Stand well away, ladies. I don't want to render you unconscious by mistake."

We all retreated as far as we could and watched as Fortier unstoppered the bottle. He held the gauze over Susan's mouth and nose and with great care counted the drops he let fall onto the cloth. A sweetish smell perfumed the air, and we watched Susan's eyelids flutter closed, her jaw relaxed at last.

Fortier called us back and stationed Guttridge near Susan's head with instructions to watch her breathing and color with great care. She was to alert him if anything looked wrong. The midwife, with astonishing speed, inserted a thick pad of sheeting under Susan, straightened her inert body, and, at a word from Fortier, bared her belly while swathing a clean sheet over the anatomy below.

"Perhaps you shouldn't look," Fortier said to me and Guttridge as he lifted a small knife. "I don't want either of you fainting."

We looked. And we continued looking as Fortier did what seemed like horrible violence—although with great delicacy and precision—to the young woman's body. He worked at an incredibly swift pace, his movements deft and assured.

"Is there always so much blood?" The question was forced out of me by a particularly nasty gush of watery red mixed with dark purple clots.

"It's not all blood." Fortier turned his head into his shoulder in an effort to wipe away the sweat that ran down the sides of his face. I instinctively grabbed at the nearest piece of clean linen—my apron—and awkwardly pulled one end up so I could wipe down his face as if he were a lathered horse.

"It's fluid from the womb as well," he continued as he emerged from my ministrations. "But far too much blood, you're right about that. It's difficult to tell how much she's lost."

As he said this, his hands disappeared inside the opening he'd made in Susan's flesh. He rummaged around for a few seconds, reminding me of someone who'd dropped a pocket watch into a carpetbag full of clothing and was trying to find it.

My fascination with what Fortier was doing had prevented me from feeling light-headed. Up to that moment, that is. When Fortier pulled a slender, grayish object from Susan's belly, there was a second or two when I thought I might faint.

It was the baby, of course. Even I could see it was dead. This, then, was the child I had secretly held in my heart as being—not Justin's, that was impossible—but perhaps, one day, mine.

It was the ugliest thing I had ever seen.

"Did you injure it?" It took some effort to force the question through my lips. Mrs. Kenny reached quickly for the child—a boy—and wrapped it, swiftly but with commendable gentleness, in a piece of linen. But not so swiftly as to prevent me seeing the horrible red patches that disfigured its limbs, nor the raw mess on its tiny face, as if it had been hit.

"That's how they look, at times, when there's pox." The midwife caught her bottom lip under her prominent, chipped front teeth and shook her head in seeming sadness. "It only gets worse as they grow. The doctor did as good a job as any I've seen." She took a fresh piece of linen, wrapping the infant in a double layer. "I didn't know you were an accoucheur, sir," she said to Fortier.

"I'm not." Fortier had his arms deep inside Susan and now barked an order at me. "A basin, quickly. Hold it beneath my arms."

I complied as fast as I could, and he continued talking to Mrs. Kenny. "I've never done this before. But I've seen it done and studied the principles thoroughly. I've had some experience in field medicine."

I did my best to hold the basin steady while Fortier

scooped what looked for all the world like a large piece of offal into it.

"Is that the afterbirth?" I wrinkled my nose at the smell and the nasty clots of blood Fortier was shaking off his hands.

"It is. Give the basin to Mrs. Kenny—she needs to examine it. And you, provide yourself with plenty of cloth. I need you to wipe up the blood as I sew." He spoke as if I were a male colleague.

"I'll do that, if her ladyship would take my place." Guttridge stepped forward. "Somebody needs to hold the baby." She jerked her head at the midwife, who was clearly looking for a suitable place to lay down the child.

The midwife looked at me, her eyes wide. I held out my hands and received the tiny parcel into them, holding it close to my bosom. I saw Guttridge's eyes, intent on her task, flick momentarily to me with a look of infinite sadness. My lady's maid, the fastidious ruler of my wardrobe and the arbiter of what was and wasn't suitable to my station in life, had not made a sound of protest or revulsion during the whole messy business. She had stuck to whatever job was assigned to her with the steadfastness and dependability of a soldier.

Fortier and Guttridge worked swiftly, but I no longer observed their actions. The tiny thing in my arms seemed to deserve all of my attention and respect. I found my lips forming silent prayers, asking God for mercy on the little soul that had departed this earth today. And for mercy upon the mother that bore him in sin and shame.

I was still praying when a knock sounded on the door and Mrs. Eason announced the arrival of the rector.

~

"You *attended the birth* of that woman's child?"

Michael spat out each word as if it sullied his lips. He had burst into the morning room, where I was sitting hollow-eyed with lack of sleep and too much emotion, without any kind of greeting. He had entered so fast that a picture on the wall beside the door slid sideways and now rested at an odd angle. He was followed, of course, by the odious Brandrick.

"Not in front of Brandrick, please." I rubbed my forehead with the fingers of one hand, grateful that I'd let Guttridge cajole me into taking a cup of café au lait, a boiled egg, and some toast. After the night's proceedings, I hadn't wanted to eat at all, but in the end I'd seen the sense of it. Guttridge had run a bath for me at six o'clock in the morning, and that had also revived my appetite.

Guttridge had presumably also found time to bathe. She was as neat and clean as you'd wish of a lady's maid. She sat in a corner of the morning room meticulously repairing a summer shawl as if she'd never gotten her arms red to the elbows with Susan's blood during the mopping-up operations. She shifted now to watch me as I rose to my feet and confronted the two men.

"Mr. Brandrick, I appreciate the great care you take of my brother, but there are some topics that are truly private—whether Lord Broadmere thinks they are or not," I finished with a glare at Michael, who was clearly getting ready to contradict me. "Indulge me in this, please. Guttridge will ensure you are served coffee in the library."

Guttridge put down her work and rose to her feet with the merest twitch of her eyebrows. Straightening the picture as she reached the door, she held it open.

"Do come with me, Mr. Brandrick." Her tone was that of one senior servant to another, polite and conciliatory. "I'll make sure a footman attends you directly."

She stepped back as another figure loomed in the doorway. To my relief, it was Ned, who, like Michael, was still dressed in his topcoat.

"Fortier's given me all the details, and I've spoken to the rector." Ned kissed my cheek and held my hands for a few moments, ducking his head to look into my eyes. "Terrible business. Are you sure you're all right?"

"I'm fine. Guttridge, when you've settled Mr. Brandrick, please return here—and I don't suppose I need to ask for coffee for Sir Edward and Lord Broadmere."

"You don't, my lady." Guttridge squared her shoulders and gave Brandrick a hard look. With one last glance at Michael, the steward accepted the inevitable and followed Guttridge out of the room.

Ned shucked off his topcoat and took a seat opposite me after handing me into mine. Michael snorted but also sat, as usual making the chair creak by dropping his full weight onto it instead of lowering himself down.

It was Ned who spoke first. "I'll say one thing for Fortier, he didn't look at all smug when he told me his theory about Justin's death had been correct. I suppose the young woman's affirmation would stand up in a court of law under the dying declaration rule. Not that I'm envisaging court proceedings, but I might have to talk to the coroner about the possibility of a revised verdict." He sighed heavily. "The rector thinks we can bury the girl—with her child—by her father. In view of her confession and repentance, he's prepared to conduct the burial by daylight this time, but with as little fuss as possible." He looked up at the ceiling. "Have you made arrangements for the—the removal?"

"She's being laid out, and yes, Mrs. Eason has made appropriate arrangements. Susan's sister, Maggie, is with her. I sent my carriage to their farm before dawn when it became evident that Susan was dying. She was able to speak to her before it happened."

During this exchange, Michael had risen from his chair and stalked around the room fiddling with things. He straightened ornaments that were perfectly well positioned, pretended to find dust on the back of a chair where there was none, and generally endangered my possessions and peace of mind. Now he could contain himself, if that's what he thought he was doing, no longer.

"Did they tell you what Helena *did*?" he thundered at Ned. "Attending the sickbed of a servant, well, that's perfectly appropriate for the lady of the house. But remaining to *watch* —and perform *menial services*—as the girl was butchered? Holding that monstrosity of a dead—*thing*—and praying over it? Entirely beyond the pale."

"I will do as I please in my own house," I snapped. I was most definitely too tired to put up with Michael. "And Fortier didn't butcher Susan. He even sent for Dr. Sharrock after he'd performed the operation to see if there was anything else that could be done. They all agreed—Mrs. Kenny included—that he'd done the best for Susan in the circumstances. He spared her an agonizing death, you know. She was in terrible pain before he delivered the baby. She died of what she would have died of anyway—too much blood lost from a constitution already weakened by disease."

Ned leaned forward to pat my hand. "That is the verdict of all present, my dear. Nobody except Michael is trying to throw any blame on Fortier. The young woman was able to enter death peacefully. The rector said she was sufficiently conscious to understand what he was saying and make responses to his words of preparation for death. Not always satisfactory ones, I understand, but it appears that when her sister arrived she persuaded the girl to repeat a prayer of penitence and the Lord's Prayer."

I nodded. "She died at seven thirty. She was more or less

conscious until six. Nothing anyone could do would stop her losing blood."

"All right," Michael growled from somewhere near the window. "I take back what I said about butchering. But why did you have to be there, Helena? Women die in childbirth all the time." The ferocious look on his handsome face softened a little. "My first wife died because she bore me a son, and there's not one second of that day I will ever forget. But I at least had the decency to let the physicians do their work alone until—until they summoned me."

"What exactly is it you're objecting to?" I rose to my feet and went to stand close to Michael, who was staring out at the dull gray morning. I didn't touch him, but some instinct told me he would welcome my closeness. He almost never mentioned Cecilia.

I made sure my next question was delivered in a controlled, reasonable tone. "Are you worried my eccentricities may damage my chances on the marriage market? Because, my dear brother, the sort of man who would object to my personal involvement in an attempt to save a life would not be the kind of man I'd contemplate marrying anyway, even if he were royalty. Justin would have understood perfectly."

"You wouldn't have done such a thing had Justin been alive. You behaved like a proper wife and lady then." He pushed his fingers through his thick blond hair. "And now we have to live with the knowledge that Justin was murdered. By that slut and her father."

"It's the Hatheralls you're really angry at," I said softly. "And you're angry at them for my sake, aren't you?"

I wished I could wrap my arms around Michael and hug him hard. Most of the time I forgot that this difficult, charmless man was my little brother, a mere twenty-three years of age. His title and his place at the head of our family often made him seem invulnerable, the head of the pride of lions. But he wasn't.

"Look, Michael," I continued. "I can't even begin to understand the two of them. Yes, they've hurt me, horribly. They took my darling husband from me. They tried to besmirch his name. They caused such trouble for Monsieur Fortier. Yes, I know you don't like him—you don't have to make that face—but he was entirely innocent of fathering that child. And they committed the most dreadful sins. I thought the rector was going to faint when he realized one of his churchwardens managed to encompass murder, incest, *and* suicide in the space of a year. But they're dead, Michael, darling. And I'm glad I didn't just run away from helping Susan because there was mess and blood and disease and I'm a lady. I'm glad I had the strength not to turn my back on her because of the hurt she'd caused me. Allow me a tiny moment of heroism in my pointless, selfish life, won't you?"

I could see Ned was about to speak, to say something nice to me no doubt, but I shook my head at him before returning my gaze to Michael. To my surprise, I encountered the direct glare of his very beautiful blue eyes. It was almost unheard-of for Michael to look anyone directly in the eye, with the exception of his children.

"I'm sorry I shouted at you, Helena." His tone was emotionless.

"I forgive you. Friends?"

I held out a hand. Michael grasped the very tips of my fingers and looked at my hand as if it had suddenly material-ized out of nowhere. Then he gave an enormous sigh and, taking a firmer grip, raised my hand to his lips and actually kissed it. The merest peck, but enough to make my heart sing.

"Friends." Michael dropped my hand as if it had burned him.

"Well, well." Ned, beaming, came to lay a hand on my shoulder and give Michael a nod of approval. "As terrible as all this has been, it's all over. Helena, my dear, you've stood up marvelously well to another terrible shock, and I admire you for it. And I believe I hear the sound of your excellent coffee being borne in our direction, so let's all sit down and enjoy our return to normality."

25

LADYLIKE PURSUITS

*N*ormality, of course, was a state of affairs to be grateful for. It was also rather dull. By the time the best part of a week had elapsed, both Guttridge and I were out of sorts.

"It's no good, my lady. I can't get this curl to come out right. You must have slept on it wrong." Guttridge crossed her arms, regarding my reflection in the mirror with a discontented air.

"It's perfectly fine." I tugged at the offending curl, which immediately sprang back into its somewhat eccentric position.

"I'll heat the curling iron." With an air of exaggerated patience, Guttridge pulled the heavy tongs out of the cupboard where they were stored and positioned them over the embers of my dressing room fire. I flicked at the discarded curl papers for a moment and then looked up, meeting Guttridge's eyes in the mirror.

"I suppose it's normal to feel like this after all the excitement we went through," I admitted.

"Hmmm." Guttridge stared with vacant eyes at my hair,

which she'd arranged pompadour-style on the top of my head. It was a few moments before she spoke again.

"It was—exciting, though, wasn't it, my lady? When the doctor was working, my heart was beating so fast I thought it'd jump out of my bodice."

"You should have seen it from where I was standing," I said, hearing the wonder in my own voice. "He was cutting in *layers*, Guttridge, down and down. I kept thinking he must have finished and wondering where on earth the baby was—"

I let my hands, with which I had been gesticulating in an attempt to convey Fortier's technique, drop into my lap. "It would have been exciting if Susan had lived." I bit my lip. "Oh, Guttridge. Even with everything she did, watching her die was awful."

"I know, my lady." Guttridge's expression managed to be sympathetic and bracing at the same time. "But the French physician stopped that terrible pain and let her die easy. I can't bear to think about how it might have been otherwise." She hesitated for a moment. "I don't suppose he'll have reason to visit the house now."

"No he won't, and I'm not going to seek him out else-where, if that's what you're worrying about. Haven't I been endeavoring to lead an exemplary life the last few days? The kind of which they'd all approve, all those men who presume to have opinions on how I should spend my days."

"I suppose you could call planting an herb garden normal." Guttridge looked doubtful.

"Arranging a garden is the perfect ladylike pursuit. And March is the perfect month for doing it. And all I'm doing is standing around supervising the gardeners anyway." I grinned.

"You haven't spent much time in that workroom of yours."

"Too much to do outdoors," I said defensively. "And it

feels so empty in there. I'll have to find a new assistant. I liked having someone to work beside."

"Hmmm."

I often wondered what Guttridge really meant when she made that sound.

"Susan wasn't a good companion, but she was there," I continued. "My life can be lonely at times."

"With only the servants for company."

"Quite."

I swung round to face my lady's maid, who met my glare with steady eyes.

"I'll forgive you your impudence, Guttridge." I put as much frost into my voice as I could summon up, but Guttridge was impervious. "You're right, of course. I live a privileged life, and I shouldn't complain. But venal as she turned out to be, Susan did her work methodically and with a certain appreciation as to its value. Even Lady Odelia admits she was useful. She heard of Susan's death from someone in the family, of course."

"I imagine the whole of Littleberry knows by now." Guttridge retrieved the curling iron from the fire and pulled a long, strong hair from her own head to test it. Finding it didn't burn, she began the delicate task of curling my front hair while I froze into position.

"I hope the nastier bits of the tale haven't spread," Guttridge said as she removed the iron. "The pox and the— well, the goings-on between the two of them." She shuddered as she crossed to return the iron to the hearth. "If anyone does hear, you can rest assured it won't be through me, my lady. I'll keep that secret till my dying day. The murder's bad enough."

"The rector might have told his curates, of course. And you know how they gossip." I nodded my approval as Guttridge carefully tweaked the curls with her fingers, then stepped back to observe the finished article. I liked my hair—it was abundant and glossy, and although its wavy smoothness was more suited to the styles of Mama's youth, it held a curl well when the occasion called for a few ringlets.

"I do appreciate your discretion, of course, Guttridge. And I trust you completely." I rose and stepped into the skirt Guttridge was holding out for me. "May I tell you something in confidence?"

"Of course, my lady."

"This may sound peculiar, but I feel better now that I know Sir Justin's death wasn't just some random and pointless accident. I couldn't help imagining it, you see—Sir Justin slipping down a bank because he was trying to rescue some idiot sheep—and it all seemed so futile, as if Sir Justin didn't matter. As if—oh dear, I do find this hard to explain. What is life worth if we're to be winked out of existence for nothing? One moment alive and looking forward to the future, the next a corpse—and all for the slip of a foot."

Or you could be an apparently healthy young man, running around in an orchard on a sunny spring day, playing games with his cousin, and the next moment a dead man with blue lips. The senselessness of Daniel's death had filled my mind for months afterward. It had rubbed my life clean of all meaning, as if a careless hand had wiped the words of it from a slate. I had fought hard not to allow Justin's death to take me down the same road.

"I refuse to believe our lives are in any way futile." Having buttoned my bodice, Guttridge made a twirling gesture with her finger to indicate I should turn around, then nodded in satisfaction at my appearance. "We all have our place and our part to play. It's not for us to question the Almighty if He decides to end our time on this earth by a slip or trip. It's quick, at any rate. Better than getting so old and feeble there's nowhere for you but the workhouse."

"Good heavens, Guttridge," I murmured. "It's a good thing I have you here to put me right about everything."

"Happy to oblige, my lady." Guttridge's expression didn't alter. "Now will you be needing me for anything in particular this morning?"

"Probably not. I have letters to write, then there's the herb garden. After that, I'll probably read Mama's journals until it's time to visit her. I'm having luncheon with the dowager and Lady Broadmere."

Guttridge nodded in approval. "The journals will cheer you up, my lady."

"No doubt. I must write to Lady Odelia and tell her how prominently she figures in the latest one. I had no idea she was such a naughty child."

~

"I'm sorry, Helena. I know you wanted to have luncheon in Mama-in-Law's rooms, but I did warn you how much worse she is at the moment. You'll have to make do with me."

Julia rubbed carefully at the damp spot on her dark red velvet dress. Like the other women in the family—myself excluded, of course—she was now out of mourning. My sisters had decided that four months with no half mourning was sufficient. Blanche, despite her injunctions to me to observe the deepest mourning possible after the example of "the dear Queen," had been particularly insistent that she could not afford six months of mourning and one month of half mourning. Besides, she'd claimed, purple was death to her complexion.

I settled myself in my seat at the small table laid for two in Hyrst's library. "It is rather shocking to see one's own mother spitting and drooling her food out of her mouth like a small child," I said. "Poor Belming. She's an absolute saint."

"Your offer to pay for a night nurse has been a godsend." Julia took her own seat. "And I've made sure one of the under-housemaids—Mary, that little one with the wen on her face—reports to Belming twice a day now that there's so much more cleaning and laundry to do. I won't risk Belming giving notice, and your Mama's getting far too difficult for one woman to manage. I'm going to be much less useful myself once this little one arrives."

She smoothed a hand over the curve that had become more apparent once she was seated. I suppressed the tiny pang of envy that shot through me.

"Now what were you telling me about Odelia and your mother's journals?" Julia nodded at the footman to begin serving the luncheon.

"Ah yes. I wrote to O this morning." I smiled my thanks at the footman who was pouring barley water into my glass. "I'm almost jealous. O seems to have engaged Mama's attention more than any of her children, except possibly Gerry when she was very small. 'Wayward, mischievous, highly intelligent, and consummately charming' is how Mama describes her. She often notes how like Papa O was. And still is—she's so much warmer than the others, isn't she? Papa was like that. People were drawn to him."

"If only Michael had a little of *that* particular trait." Julia raised an eyebrow. "People are drawn to you too, Helena. You have an innate seriousness that never takes itself seriously, if you see what I mean, and you care about people. You've always been the most wonderful hostess, and you're never a difficult guest. Talking of which, I hope you don't mind barley water and scrambled eggs—you must feel you're back in the nursery. I can't seem to get enough of either."

"I adore barley water and scrambled eggs." I took a bite of the creamy yellow food, which in my case was augmented by a serving of kedgeree. Julia, I noted, took her eggs plain.

"See what I mean? Always a smile and never a complaint."
Julia attacked her own eggs with evident appetite.

"I bicker all the time with Michael," I pointed out.

"Yes, but Michael is Michael. He may be named after a
saint, but I'm sure all the saints bite their lips to avoid
cursing when he gets up to his aggravating tricks."

I laughed at that, and Julia smiled broadly. Dismissing the
footman, she waited until the door shut behind him to
continue the conversation.

"So you're reading the journals to cheer you up? You do
seem a little brighter lately."

"Life seems more precious somehow after what
happened." I paused to drink some of the barley water. "Naturally, I'm reading Mama's journals mainly for their instruc-
tive value. Yet there's something irresistible about witnessing
the time before I was born. After all, half my family's history
happened before Michael and I made an appearance. And
this particular volume contains so much family life." I knew I
sounded a little wistful, and Julia clearly understood my tone
of voice.

"Yes, your sisters got so much more out of your mother
and father, so to speak. So you've got to where O was a tiny
child? That means the twins and Blanche were still in the
schoolroom. Gerry must have been a young lady making
her debut."

"Mama mentions the preparations for Gerry's first
Season. It seems the late '40s were an especially happy time,
with Papa home for long stretches. Not in Town and not at
those house parties he clearly liked so much."

"And your parents were in a state of domestic bliss?"

"So it would seem. Mama is far more concerned than
before with entertaining. There are pages of notes about
exciting ways to use herbs and spices in food. There's a
recipe for pear cake with rosemary syrup that I passed

straight on to my own cook; you'll have to come and sample it."

"With pleasure." Julia grinned—she and I shared a love of trying out new cake recipes.

"There are some hints Mama was facing opposition from the physicians of Littleberry over her doctoring," I continued. "I wonder if that also contributed to her newfound interest in domestic affairs."

Julia shrugged. "Knowing the dowager, I would have thought opposition would have made her more determined. At the very least, such antagonism would have been a sign she was becoming successful, wouldn't it?"

"It must have been something fairly serious," I laid my knife and fork carefully down on my now-empty plate and contemplated the scratched but gleaming silver with its family crest, "for people to have stood up to a countess."

Julia snorted. "I know from bitter experience that the style and dignity of 'countess' doesn't stop men from looking down on you as a little woman."

~

I had several occasions to remember Julia's words about being viewed as a little woman in the month that followed our luncheon. In the time left after dealing with correspondence, visits, household matters, supervising the confection of my herb garden, and taking exercise on Sandy, I worked doggedly at my herbal studies but often found myself sighing over the slow progress of my skills and knowledge. I had done nothing about hiring a new assistant, so I only had time for a limited number of tasks every day. It was surprising how much time each task took even with the new stillroom I'd had installed next to my workroom.

As March sobbed and gusted its way toward April, I occasionally found myself in a low mood. I fought it, of course. But left to my own feeble efforts amid the isolation of my widowhood, I felt small—which I was quite literally. I compared myself to Mama as she had been and found myself wanting.

My sister Blanche was particularly good at making me feel insignificant, so given my mood it was perhaps not the best of circumstances that she came to stay. She was at Whitcombe for the greater part of March and into April for one of her regular rounds of "seeing the family." I chafed under Blanche's critical gaze; her blue eyes were paler and colder than my other siblings', and even Michael's stony expression couldn't beat Blanche for the degree of calculation with which she considered the world around her.

My favorite tactic for diverting Blanche from her outspoken contemplation of other people's faults was to talk about her son.

"Have you heard from Dederick this week?" I asked now as we sat at tea together. "Heavens, it must be two years since I've seen him."

Waiting for her to finish eating and reply, I suppressed a sigh as I glanced out of the window. It was a perfectly splendid early April day, and I was itching to ride out on Sandy. My occasional glumness had in part been due to the necessity of selling Puck. Justin's horse, used to being ridden hard all day and every day, had become quite ungovernable despite Mank's best efforts. But we had other horses in our stables, and Mank, I think, was rather relieved to ride out with me on a serviceable but dull gelding and not have to spend every outing galloping Puck in an attempt to tire him. Mank was getting on a bit, and exercising an overly fidgety horse was tiring for an older man.

"He's quite well as far as I know." Blanche closed her eyes in bliss as she popped another tiny cream-filled choux bun into her mouth. "I must say, Baby, your cook's quite marvelous. My son is in Town, I believe—at least the last note I had from him was on his club's paper. He seems to be keeping himself busy. Of course, His Royal Highness's whims and wants absolutely *rule* Rawdon's life." She sighed, eyeing the cake stand in a clear struggle between her greed and her figure—she was tall but rather stout.

"Still," she added, giving up the fight and selecting a cream-filled brandy snap, "he will certainly meet the right sort of woman moving in such exalted circles. At least he doesn't seem interested in other people's wives, which is such a complication for the dear Prince." This cryptic statement was accompanied by a sly smile that clearly stated Blanche knew much more about royal goings-on than I did.

"Heavens." I put down my teacup. "I should jolly well hope Deddy's not interested in other people's wives. Aren't you a bit shocked he should be in such fast company? He's only twenty-two."

"What can one do?" Blanche's strong white teeth crunched into the sweet confection. "He's been his own master for four years, don't forget. Once my darling Francis passed away, I couldn't control Rawdon at all, even when he was up at Oxford. I certainly can't control him now. He has far more money than I do, for one thing."

I pressed my upper teeth into my tongue so I wouldn't sigh or yawn. Blanche's lack of money was her favorite subject, and I could see what was coming.

"You wouldn't understand, Baby." Blanche's eyes took on the particularly calculating look that preceded an appeal for funds. At least that meant she was planning to go home soon. "You're really quite wealthy, aren't you? Such a fortunate girl." She tilted her head to one side in what was supposed to be a winsome expression of sisterly love but instead resembled a tiger contemplating its prey.

"I suppose I am wealthy," I replied as briefly as possible. "The sheep are certainly doing well under the new farmer Michael put in."

"My dear Baby, I don't need details of how you *get* your money. How vulgar sheep are." Blanche's smile slipped a little, but she went gamely on. "And of course you are so fortunate to own so many properties."

I couldn't argue with that, so I nodded.

"You don't have to cut corners, I can see," Blanche went on, looking around the room. "Your Mrs. Eason plainly has repairs done as soon as needed. I have rarely seen a better kept house, and, my dear, I have been a guest in the houses of the very greatest in the land. Whereas I, in such straitened circumstances, have to be positively calculating. My conversations with my housekeeper are about how we can hide what we can't afford to renew."

"Why don't you move to a less expensive house?"

"The very idea. Don't be ridiculous, Baby."

This time I sighed out loud. "I don't think it's ridiculous to suggest you cut your coat according to your cloth."

"Then you clearly have no notion of the style in which a marchioness should live." Blanche softened the retort with another fetching smile. I could feel the weight of a forth-coming demand settle between us. "Clothes, for example. Coming out of mourning is so *complicated* when one is forced to make do and mend."

I felt a momentary sense of relief. Given Blanche's complaints about the state of her house, I'd been worried she was about to present me with a bill for a new roof.

"I can see how that must be," I murmured, instantly ready for complete and utter capitulation in the matter of clothes. "I'll tell you what, why don't you let me help since, in a sense, I've put you into this situation? Why don't you ask your dressmaker to send me the bill for, say, three new outfits?"

I knew Blanche would stretch the point to include boots, hats, slippers, and probably a new fur-trimmed cape. Still, it would be a while before I was able to vary my own wardrobe, and I wasn't entertaining much, so my expenses were very low. And I could easily afford it.

"Oh, I couldn't possibly." But the gleam in Blanche's eyes told me that yes, she could.

"Of course you could." I smiled as brilliantly as I knew how. "After all, you represent our family at the highest levels of society." She was almost never invited to anything really grand, but it didn't do to let on I knew that. "It's the least I can do after forcing you into mourning for four months."

"Well, it *has* been challenging." Blanche contrived to look grave. "I suppose I should accept for your sake, Baby. And for dear, dear Justin's."

"That's the spirit." I'd given in very quickly, of course, but at least Blanche would stop hinting now. I was quite sure she decided in advance of her visits on the monetary limit of her demands.

Once the kill had been made, there was only one more ritual to observe. I waited for her to launch into it.

"It must be nice to be so powerful." Here it was. Blanche was about to find a way to make me feel entirely powerless, lest I should come to believe I could exert any influence over her in return for my generosity. Having demanded and received that generosity, she must now regain the upper hand. No wonder I struggled with feelings of worthlessness.

"Of course, Whitcombe House is going to be rather left out of everything in the county now that there's no man in it." Blanche looked pointedly at the teapot until I remembered to pour her another cup. "Rawdon may not spend an awful lot of time with his Mama, but he does give a certain cachet to my little establishment. I still receive *floods* of visitors, my dear. I find this house terribly quiet by comparison."

"I have just as many visitors as I want, thank you, Blanche. And don't forget I'm still in deep mourning."

I didn't mention that several of my regular visitors, hearing of Blanche's presence, would delay their next visit until she was gone. Blanche's little assertions of superiority and gripes about money tended to put people off.

"I feel sorry for you, Baby, stuck here alone in this huge house. And I'm sure the nasty business of a servant dying in your attic, awash in blood from what I've heard, is quite the social setback. You must be *very careful* to ensure there's no more scandal of any kind attached to your name." Blanche dabbed at her plump lips with her napkin before depositing the linen at the side of her plate. "Above all, no more visits from that nasty French physician. He's caused you quite enough trouble."

I felt the warmth rising to my face. "Monsieur Fortier is a perfectly respectable medical man. His sister is married to one of the town's leading merchants."

"A pottery owner."

"A wealthy pottery owner. Money has to come from somewhere."

"Well, for that sort of person it does." Blanche, seeing me about to reply, rolled smoothly on. "In any case, he is a physician and thus belongs to the lower orders of society—not our kind at all."

I pursed my lips, knowing I couldn't really argue with that assertion either. Discussion of who was or wasn't our sort of person had pervaded my life ever since I could remember. I had had the importance of social distinctions drummed thoroughly into me before I was old enough to argue. And despite my conviction that Fortier was a gentleman by birth, I had no proof to offer.

"I have no reason to summon Monsieur Fortier here in any case," was my somewhat feeble reply.

"Mind you keep it that way." Blanche, having performed the task of worming a present out of me, was rewarding herself with a little righteous wrath. "I shall speak to Michael about ensuring you get a few invitations of the *right* sort in a month or two. You must be assiduous about entertaining in your turn and *not* doing anything more out of the ordinary."

"But my mourning—"

"It's true that you haven't exactly kept to the seclusion that's proper for a new widow." Blanche had clearly decided to brook no argument. "But we can work with that. A woman with an active nature is attractive to a certain sort of country gentleman. You may ride out with your groom or walk with your lady's maid as much as you like. It'll keep your figure trim." Blanche, no sylph herself, eyed my slightly plump form. "And that herb garden and workshop of yours are acceptable, I suppose. The garden will be quite pretty, and many country ladies are known for their gardens. As long as you keep things in proportion—a ladylike hobby, a few salves and potions for the poor and so on. By the time your year and a day is over, the events of the past few months will be almost forgotten, and you'll simply be charmingly eccentric. Just like Mama."

"But Mama did so much more than produce a few salves and potions, didn't she? At least that's how I remember it."

An expression of annoyance—or something stronger—passed over Blanche's face. "When *I* was at home, Mama behaved with a fair amount of decorum. Of course I married at sixteen, my dear, *straight* out of my first Season." Blanche permitted herself a triumphant smirk. "I'll admit Mama became rather strident once you and Michael were born, but one can attribute that to her change of life, I imagine." She sighed wistfully. "I didn't pay much attention. Those were such happy days for me. Imagine, at just seventeen I became the mother of such a darling little boy, and my beloved Francis *doted* on us both."

I would reach Blanche's Season and marriage in the journals before too long, I thought. "Strident?" I asked. "In my memories, Mama managed to combine an active and useful life as a healer with her role as countess rather well. She always seemed to manage everything splendidly."

"Do you think so?" Blanche gave me a rather odd look out of the corners of her eyes. "Well, you were always rather wrapped up in your own little world, Baby. And everyone petted you so."

I frowned at that and opened my mouth to make further inquiries, but Blanche did not give me the opportunity to pursue the matter. She put down her teacup, patted her hair, and said brightly, "Now—*who* do you think came to visit me in Tunbridge Wells and asked *especially* after you?"

And by the time I had endured a detailed account of the interest shown in me by a certain extremely eligible widower —whom I knew to be silver-haired and gouty—I had entirely forgotten to ask Blanche more about Mama.

~

"Well, that's a mercy."

Hearing the voice behind me, I turned to see Guttridge descending the front steps of Whitcombe House. Her ostensible excuse for using the front entrance was the manteau she held draped over one arm, but I suspected she was giving herself the satisfaction of watching the carriage carrying Blanche and her lady's maid rattle around the corner of the house. Having seen the family, Blanche had accepted an invitation to stay at Hawthorn Hall in Broadmere. That house had seen better days but had the advantage of being at the center of a social circle considered, by itself, to be the most select in Sussex. Its denizens and visitors showered Blanche with deference and reacted to every word about the Prince of Wales's set and her son's role in it with breathless admiration.

"Are you quite warm enough, my lady?"

"Perfectly so, thank you, Guttridge."

We fell silent, listening to the crunch of the horses' hooves on gravel, then the creak as the gate was swung open, and finally the clatter of stones and the driver's encouragement as he urged the horses into a trot along Whitcombe Lane.

"Well." I sighed out the word, feeling my shoulders slump a little with the relief of Blanche's departure. From Broadmere, she would travel straight back to Tunbridge Wells, where Dederick planned to join her.

"Well, my lady." Guttridge grinned. "Might I suggest a walk to work up an appetite for luncheon? I could have you in your walking dress and boots in a trice."

"A walk." I almost groaned out the word. "The perfect suggestion. Yes, Guttridge, I think I'll walk a very long way rather fast to burn off my aggravation at my sister. I hope that scheme is agreeable to you."

"Most agreeable, especially on a morning like this." Guttridge sniffed the sweet, fresh spring air appreciatively. "That lady's maid of Lady Hastings talked my ear off this morning. I wasn't sorry to see her go."

I laughed but said nothing as we made our way indoors and upstairs. Family loyalty prevented me from remarking that I felt exactly the same about Blanche, who had been even more full of herself than usual since receiving the news of Deddy's visit. With her son in residence, Blanche would be able to live as expensively as she liked for a few days. My nephew never stinted on his comforts, and the understanding between them was that he would foot the bill while he stayed with his Mama. Or at least he would order the bills to be sent to him. How long the purveyors of Tunbridge Wells had to wait for their money was another matter, but Deddy was a marquess, and they could hardly refuse his custom. And Blanche would summon her dressmaker immediately upon her return, at my expense. No wonder she had taken her leave in the manner of a cat who'd just polished off an entire bowl of cream.

Within half an hour, we were proceeding down Whitcombe Lane through a perfect spring morning. Guttridge easily adjusted her long stride to my quick, impatient steps. Around us, the sweet, liquid tones of the smaller birds were occasionally interrupted by the cawing of rooks in the high trees or the far-off mewing of the seagulls that constantly circled Littleberry. The daffodils, planted years ago at Justin's behest, that had brightened the lane a few weeks earlier were now withered, their heavy seed-heads bent to the ground. There were still plenty of violets, dandelions, and fritillaries in the hedgerows. The salty scent of hawthorn blossoms was carried on the breeze, and the new leaves on the trees showed semi-transparent in the sunlight. A few ewes with early lambs wandered the high field, keeping to the shade of the huge oak that had somehow withstood the wind for centuries. Their tiny offspring explored their new world on uncertain legs, never straying far from their mothers and returning often to butt their heads vigorously into their source of nourishment.

We turned onto the main road and headed inland. There would be time enough, as the weather grew warmer, to walk out over the marsh to the shingle beaches where sea kale and samphire grew. For now, our delight was in the fresh green of the trees and the cool dampness beneath them, the smell of new growth alongside the straggling footpath atop the road's high bank. A vigorous and easy walk downhill would bring us to a farm in the valley where the farmer's wife would oblige with a glass of fresh milk and perhaps a small jam tart for a few pennies. Thus refreshed, we could tackle the harder walk over the fields and the steep climb back up the hill to home.

It was I who finally broke our companionable silence, which hitherto had only been interrupted by casual remarks about the beauty of the day and the plants we came across.

"Now that Lady Hastings has gone, I'm going to tackle my workroom properly. I want to ask Taylor about building a separate shed for drying herbs so that they won't create too much clutter."

"Wouldn't the conservatory do?"

"Some herbs are better dried in the dark—although now you mention it, Taylor might let me have a little space in his hothouses as well."

"Or you could have a—well, I suppose you'd call it an arbor, on the sunny side of the shed."

"That's an excellent idea." For a few moments, I was heedless of the day's magnificence as I sketched a plan in my mind. "And I suppose I'll have to set about finding a new assistant. How does one find such a person? Put an advertisement in *The Lady*?"

Guttridge had removed her hat to neaten her hair, and now repinned it with an economical movement. "I can think of someone who'd be excellently suited."

"Who?" Puzzled, I stopped in my tracks and stared at my lady's maid.

"She stands before you."

I almost laughed. Guttridge's manner of speaking was always very proper, as befitted a superior servant, even if the traces of a Cockney accent lingered beneath her refined speech. But she delivered this line in the grand manner of Ellen Terry in one of her more dignified roles.

And yet I didn't laugh. That would have been cruel, and besides, the notion of Guttridge working beside me was appealing. All the more so after our joint travails in Susan's bedroom, where we had labored together in perfect harmony. There was one worrying aspect to her proposal, however.

"Do you mean you want to cease being my lady's maid?" I reflected that I would probably survive the experience, but hiring a new lady's maid was a task every lady naturally dreaded. "Wouldn't that be a step down for you?"

"I was thinking more along the lines of additional duties. I'm not afraid of a bit more work. I sleep better when I've had a busy day."

"So do I." I smiled at Guttridge. "So you'd be my—my right-hand woman? Almost like a lady's companion."

"I'm not genteel enough for that." Guttridge looked alarmed. "A companion eats upstairs instead of in the servants' hall, and I'd miss the chatter below stairs. My young man would think I'm too grand to walk out with him."

"Not a companion, then. So I wouldn't have to call you by your first name." I couldn't resist a giggle.

"Heaven forbid."

"Just as well, really, because 'Albertina' doesn't exactly trip off the tongue."

"It's not *my* fault my parents worshipped the Prince Consort." There was laughter in Guttridge's voice. Of course, she knew that *I* knew very well that she was called "Bertie" by her intimates—but that wouldn't do at all upstairs.

"I suppose you'd want higher wages?" I raised my eyebrows at Guttridge.

"For more duties, of course I would." Guttridge threw back her shoulders. "And Tilda Brenzett would like to move from Hyrst to work at Whitcombe instead of Julie Pococke who wants to work at Hyrst because she's walking out with that dark-haired footman of his lordship's, although I hope they hurry and put the banns up before something happens. Anyway, Tilda would be happy to oblige in the workroom from time to time when there's dirty or heavy work—she says she likes all the bottles and smells. So I'd be doing the preparations and keeping records, that kind of thing. Nothing that would make me look like an under-servant."

I nodded as gravely as I could manage. It was odd how servants loved to weigh their own status and that of others by the ounce. They were far worse than most of the gentry with, perhaps, the exception of Blanche.

"I agree to all points of your well-thought-out scheme, Guttridge. Name your price."

She did, and I suppressed a grin. Guttridge clearly knew how much I paid Dunnam and Mrs. Eason. She had calculated a sum that would definitely increase her status and yet not make her any enemies.

"It's a deal, as the Americans say." We were striding briskly downhill as our conversation unfolded. I halted and held out my hand for Guttridge to shake. She did so without hesitation.

"And now, Guttridge, let's see if the farmer's wife can provide us with the wherewithal to celebrate our new partnership. All this upheaval is giving me an appetite."

26

A SUMMER FRIENDSHIP

*A*s spring gradually drifted toward early summer, my life appeared to be taking an upward turn. The approach of the end of June marked the eight-month anniversary of Justin's death, and it seemed not unreasonable to begin a tentative return into society. So despite my widow's weeds, I regularly ventured into Littleberry on foot, with Guttridge for company. This was a most pleasant variation on my almost-daily walks to Hyrst to see Mama and a rapidly burgeoning Julia. I could usually find some little excuse to visit the shops on the High Street, and of course I visited Gerry.

Gerry's house was uphill from the main thoroughfare, and the views from the upper part of the town were magnificent on a bright day. It was quite natural that Guttridge and I should walk up that way often. We passed the Dermody house most days, but the massive front door was invariably shut. If I did occasionally catch a glimpse of a huge black horse, it was generally at a distance. The increase in my heartbeat when we reached the top of the steep cobbled street and passed the Dermodys' door was obviously due to the strenuous climb.

Such was the case one Thursday afternoon. I had decided to visit an elderly lady who happened to be a tenant of mine. I carried a small wicker basket lined with straw, in which nestled three ripe peaches, and their heady sun-warmed fragrance was a sensuous delight that brought a smile to my lips.

We had just turned the corner toward the church when I heard my name being called.

"Lady Helena! I was hoping I'd see you one day."

I turned to see Gabrielle Dermody waving from the top of the broad stone steps that led up to the Dermody house's grand front door. I stopped, lifted my veil, and smiled.

"I'm delighted to see you too, Mrs. Dermody. I see you are in excellent health."

As I approached, I could see the details of Mrs. Dermody's dress, which had struck me from a remove as very smart. I particularly admired the pattern of marguerites and berries in deepest crimson on a cream ground, and the complicated swag at the front. Indeed, she would not have looked out of place in a far grander house than Whitcombe.

We shook hands, and Mrs. Dermody's eyes widened at the contents of my basket.

"Heavens, I haven't seen peaches like that since I last visited Provence. How did you manage to find them—and so early too?"

I laughed. "We have one hothouse that, according to my head gardener, was designed by God's angels specifically for the growing of peaches. These are for one of my tenants, but you must allow me to send you some."

"Politeness would dictate that I beg you not to, isn't that so? But I would never refuse such an offer." She had run down the steps to meet us and now gestured toward the great windows that loomed over the corner of the street—a building I knew to be the summer house. "Let me make anticipatory repayment by inviting you to tea in my garden. Miss—Guttridge, is it not?—is welcome too."

Guttridge and I looked at one another. Did she mean Guttridge was to take tea with us or with the servants? Such situations could be awkward. But Guttridge knew what to do.

"I should get over to Mrs. Holling with the fruit, my lady. She and I can have a nice gossip in the kitchen—she'll like that."

It was true that without my noble presence Mrs. Holling would not feel obliged to take off her apron and entertain us in her tiny parlor, most of which was taken up by a large cage containing a gray parrot who liked to repeat phrases from hymns. She and Guttridge could enjoy the sunny afternoon through her open kitchen window, which had a view as magnificent as Whitcombe's.

"Very well. Do you have the tin of biscuits?"

Guttridge patted her large reticule. "Right here, my lady."

"Then give her my compliments and best wishes and tell her I'll be sure to drop by soon."

Guttridge took her leave of Mrs. Dermody with a blend of cordiality and deference that perfectly acknowledged the latter's kind invitation yet displayed an understanding of their different stations in life. If she'd been a man she could have entered the Diplomatic Corps.

"When our mulberries are ripe, I'll send you some," said Mrs. Dermody, opening the stout wooden door that led into the garden. "Unless your gardener grows them too."

"He certainly doesn't. We'd never get a mulberry tree to do well with the wind we get up at Whitcombe." I looked admiringly at the massive, spreading tree in the middle of the lawn. "I've rarely seen such a fine specimen. And this garden is wonderful."

It was indeed. Enclosed by a high brick wall over which scrambled roses and wisteria, its borders were a riot of color amid billowing clouds of forget-me-nots, many of them white or pink instead of the usual blue. The door to the large summer house was open wide, revealing a white-painted space enlivened by rows of colorful paintings and containing an easel, a drawing table, and blue-painted bookcases full of books and bibelots. Blue-and-white printed curtains hung around the huge windows, and a soft indigo rug sprawled across the floor.

"It's an artist's garden," I realized. "Is this where you draw your inspiration for your pottery, Mrs. Dermody?"

"Of course." Mrs. Dermody picked up a silver bell from the wrought-iron table under the shade of the tree and rang it. "Would you like to take a stroll?"

By the time the tea arrived, I had inspected every corner of the pretty garden. Mrs. Dermody and I had enjoyed a most stimulating conversation about the plants contained therein. There is nothing the English do better than talk about their gardens, and no better topic exists for avoiding social pitfalls since flowers are available to poor and rich alike. By the time we sat down, I felt very much at my ease.

"I hear you're engaged in making your own herb garden," said Mrs. Dermody as she ensconced herself behind the teapot.

"Now that Guttridge is a sort of all-round assistant as well as my lady's maid, matters are proceeding much faster." I accepted a cup of tea and looked with delight upon a plate of tiny, delicate edible cups each containing a swirl of thick cream and a fresh strawberry. "She can twist Taylor—my head gardener—around her little finger. And she doesn't have my social obligations, so she works when I can't. We fail at our experiments frequently, but at least I have someone to laugh with over the failures. We're learning fast."

"Do you have many social obligations?" Mrs. Dermody's fine brown eyes were fixed upon me.

"You mean, should I have as a widow?" I looked down at my dress with a grimace. "Most of my sociable life is spent with my sisters or sister-in-law. I do get visitors at Whitcombe—friends of my late husband, of course. And then there's Mama."

Thinking of my mother threw a cold shadow over the warm day. Mrs. Dermody must have seen my expression.

"Is she terribly ill?" she asked softly.

"Belming—that's her attendant—has trouble getting her out of bed most days," I replied miserably. "She just lies there, staring. And when she is active, which is generally at mealtimes or in the evening, it's almost worse. It's as if my mother has vanished inside a . . . a sort of husk of herself. Something that spouts gibberish and screams when you're trying to help her."

"I'm sorry for you." And Mrs. Dermody looked as if she meant it.

I made an effort to smile. "But at least visiting Mama means I see Lady Broadmere almost every day, and we're good friends. I play with the children too, of course, and that cheers me up tremendously."

"Is Lady Broadmere well? Her confinement will be in July, I've heard, and it's almost that already."

"She's blooming, thank you. Impatient for the baby to be born—as am I."

"You like children?"

"Very much."

"Then I hope you won't mind mine. They've been enjoying a story in the house with their uncle, but I imagine they'll be here any moment." She rang the little bell again. "I will need more tea and some more robust fare for the little ones. Or the not so little—my oldest children eat like horses." She laughed.

"Their uncle?" I supposed, for a moment, that some brother of Mr. Dermody's was visiting. Mrs. Dermody's next words sent a hot wave across my face that had nothing to do with the warmth of the day.

"Armand, of course."

"But isn't he with his patients?" I asked, trying to stamp firmly on my confusion.

"He does take *some* time for himself. He was up till dawn with an old man at the workhouse. He slept till luncheon and says he will only visit two patients today."

A commotion inside the house announced that the arrival of the children was imminent. I braced myself for the first real sight I'd had of Fortier since March. It wasn't long in coming. A tall girl and a pudgy, belligerent-looking boy burst out of the French doors, followed by Fortier with a small boy on his shoulders. Behind him was another boy who walked slowly, his attention on the book in his hands.

I had been alarmed at the notion of meeting Fortier so unexpectedly, but when I saw him I found myself suppressing a giggle at the look of utter astonishment on his face, mingled with a dawning dismay—not, I rather thought, at my presence, but at his own appearance. He was in shirt-sleeves, the areas around his beard were unshaven, and his hair and cravat showed a degree of disarray. The state of his hair was perfectly congruent with the activities of the little boy, around four years old to my eyes, who clung around his neck like a monkey and gave me an impudent grin, large black eyes wide with mischief.

"*Tu aurais pu m'en avertir,*" Fortier admonished his sister in a tone of well-controlled exasperation.

"If I had warned you," said the latter, motioning to her

youngest to leave her brother be, "you would have stayed inside the house and the children would not have been able to take tea with their uncle. And how often does that happen? I would not deprive them of their treat. Besides, you have worked together in difficult circumstances. I don't think Lady Helena requires you to stand on ceremony with her."

"No more I don't." I was determined not to be rattled by a chance meeting, if this could be called chance. After all, Littleberry was a small town—our paths were bound to cross eventually. "Please do not trouble yourself about—anything." I felt a grin tug at the corners of my mouth but fought it off. I didn't want Fortier to think I was making fun of him.

Fortier caught at the small boy's arms to prevent the little fellow landing in the teacups. The children were followed by two maids with fresh tea. They also brought large plates of bread and butter, plain cake, jam tarts, and a squat ceramic pot of anchovy paste.

"This is Sebastian," Fortier informed me as he lowered the child to the ground. Gesturing at the other children, who were waiting with well-trained courtesy to be introduced and regarding me with the same black eyes as their little brother, he reeled off their names: "Mariette, Constantin, and Hugh. Children, say how-d'ye-do to Lady Helena Whitcombe of Whitcombe House."

The children chorused, "How do you do?" with the confident air of those used to society. Mariette made me a pretty curtsey and the two older boys bowed in a rather Continental fashion. Little Sebastian stepped forward and gravely held out a tiny hand. I shook it with as much ceremony as I could muster and then resumed my seat, which Fortier was holding ready for me.

The next few minutes were devoted to the absorbing matter of food and drink. The children, having filled their plates, retired to a blanket spread near the summer house and made a picnic there in the company of a young woman who'd emerged a little belatedly from the house. I thought she was probably their governess.

Fortier, I noted, took his tea without milk or lemon. He eschewed cake and tarts in favor of bread and butter thinly spread with the anchovy paste. He had apparently recovered from his discomfiture and seemed perfectly at ease.

"How go your studies?" he asked me after a few bites of bread.

"They go well. I was telling Mrs. Dermody that Guttridge has been a great help."

"Miss Guttridge is a remarkably sensible and cool-headed woman." Fortier drained his teacup and passed it back to his sister. "She'd do well in the Army Medical Department."

"You told me Lady Helena also evinced a large measure of courage and level-headedness," Mrs. Dermody said, smiling sideways at me.

"She did," Fortier said simply, but the look he gave me made me lower my eyelids and hope fervently that my cheeks weren't reddening. I took a deep breath and quickly diverted the conversation away from my own qualities.

"Guttridge's help has allowed me to make an index of those of Mama's journals I've already read. We've cross-referenced them to the books on herb lore that I've acquired. I've come across quite a few useful volumes by now, and the index means I don't have to keep searching for the information I need."

"A very scholarly work." Mrs. Dermody's expression was encouraging and friendly.

"That's the first time in my life I've been called scholarly." I couldn't help grinning. "My sister Blanche—the Marchioness of Hastings, you know—would be horrified to think I might become a bluestocking. I have to impress on her that I'm still a complete dilettante, albeit an organized one. Guttridge and I found two ladies' writing desks in the attics at Hyrst and have arranged them side by side in the workroom so we can work together on a volume. One of us calls out page numbers and dictates extracts while the other writes—usually Guttridge because her handwriting is clearer."

This led to a prolonged discussion of the difficulties of note-taking and the tendency of handwriting to become untidy as the writer became tired. Fortier then held forth on the subject of typewriting machines, in which he appeared to take an interest.

"I take it, then, that you haven't finished your mother's notebooks?" he asked after a while.

"I don't feel the need to hurry." By now, I felt as if I were among friends. The voices of the children, who were playing games on the lawn, gave the sunny afternoon a holiday feeling, and I felt expansive and confiding. "I'm up to the 1850s, when Lady Odelia was old enough to be given lessons." I paused, but there seemed no reason to withhold what I'd found. "For a while, there was a feeling of happy domesticity to Mama's journals, and she frequently mentioned entertaining. At the point I've reached, though, she's far more like the mother I knew before she became ill."

"The formidable countess?" Mrs. Dermody suggested softly. She was clearly well informed about my family, but that wasn't surprising. I was used to people knowing far more of my business than I knew of theirs.

"She *was* formidable," I agreed. "A no-nonsense whirlwind of efficiency and activity."

"Upon whom the poor of Littleberry and its district relied far more than on the town's doctors." Fortier, having disposed of an impressive quantity of food, also seemed relaxed, his head resting on his fist as he listened to my account. "I've seen the workhouse records that show how often she attended."

"Yes." I looked away, up to the roof of the house where three seagulls sat, squawking with desire for the food they dared not try to reach.

"Was she unhappy?"

"What makes you think that?" I was startled, and my voice sounded brusque to my ears.

"Intuition." Fortier ran a thumb along the underside of his beard, where unshaven hairs showed instead of the neatly trimmed separation of hair and skin I was used to.

"We don't gossip, Lady Helena," Mrs. Dermody said as if she, too, understood my hesitation.

"Then you're the only people in Littleberry who don't." But I knew I would continue. The brittleness, almost cynicism, in some of Mama's writings had perturbed me of late. I was reluctant to discuss the matter with Julia, my usual confidante. She was heavy and slow with advanced pregnancy and the June warmth. I somehow felt I should keep melancholy topics away from her, however distant the past.

"I don't know if she was exactly unhappy," I said. "But she wasn't happy either. I wonder if it had something to do with the Crimean War. I've got as far as '54, and at that time Papa was doing something political or diplomatic and was frequently in London. She must have missed him. She often mentions Miss Florence Nightingale and her nurses, wishing she, too, were attending to the sick in Scutari." I shrugged. "Impossible, of course. She was a married woman, a mother, and a countess—all effective disqualifications from professional nursing."

"She must have felt frustrated, especially with her husband absent on work that I suppose was vital to the country." Fortier frowned.

"I'm glad you realize that," I said. "Most men would refuse

to believe that a husband, a house, and children did not provide enough gratification. We women are expected to be entirely consumed by such matters."

"Not I," said Mrs. Dermody, grinning at Fortier. "When I have an artistic bee in my bonnet, all household concerns fly out of my head. My children would go in rags, uneducated and unfed if I didn't have servants. Quinn would leave me, and Armand would suddenly find that lodgings and meals at the chophouse were far more pleasant than living with his slatternly sister." She smiled affectionately at her brother.

"Don't listen to her, Lady Helena. She's an excellent wife and mother." Fortier leaned over to kiss Mrs. Dermody's cheek, but she waved him away.

"You're too bristly. And you smell of anchovies," she said, laughing as Fortier caught at her hand and kissed that instead. "Ah, Lady Helena, these little brothers! How they plague us."

A pang went through me as I imagined Michael ever plaguing me with affection, but the momentary sadness was lost in the confusion I felt as Fortier's gaze fell unreservedly on my face. His striking, amber-green eyes held laughter, but also something else—a yearning, perhaps. I felt my breath catch in my throat before his lashes fell and the moment passed. He turned from me to his sister.

"I must shave, and then I shall walk to my patients. Thank you for the tea, Gaby."

Mrs. Dermody gave a regal nod. She watched as Fortier bowed in my direction and then moved quickly away to take a noisy, affectionate leave of the children, who were being ushered indoors by their governess. When I turned back from watching them, I saw that Mrs. Dermody was, in her turn, watching me.

"I think you are very sad about your mother," she said.

"And no wonder. Do you read her journals as a way of finding her again?"

I considered the question for a moment before answering. "At first, I simply read them to look for remedies. Now—yes, I suppose I can find the real Mama in their pages. Such glimpses are as precious to me as—" I hesitated again.

"—as if she had passed away," Mrs. Dermody said quietly. "I understand. My mother died when I was nine years old. If she left any writing or drawing behind, it was probably lost or discarded when we moved to London the next year. Our father has a miniature of her. I would give much for a letter written in her hand." She smiled, a little sadly.

"Yes, I suppose in a sense I'm fortunate. Only—you see, I always thought of my parents as happy people, and now I'm beginning to find they weren't."

"Is anybody happy all the time? I think you're finding out that they are and were human, that's all."

I shook my head. "Perhaps. But I'm going to talk to my sister Gerry about my parents. After all, she's known them for a lot longer than I have."

27

BEHIND CLOSED DOORS

"Why this sudden curiosity about Mama and Papa?"

Gerry and I were sitting at tea in the drawing room of Four Square, the house in which she and Ned had lived for twenty years. Like the Dermody house, it was situated in a quiet corner of the upper town, away from the bustle of the High Street. Littleberry was so small a town that the commercial establishments could be reached by a three minutes' walk, and Ned had not much farther to go to reach his warehouse by the river.

The room was elegant yet comfortable, filled with the touches of family life that Whitcombe now seemed to lack—an embroidery hoop of Maryanne's, Petey's stamp collection, and a stack of books that might have been Ned's or Thomas's. Framed daguerreotypes of the children and grandchildren were everywhere.

Gerry looked well. Her heavy mass of corn-blond hair, streaked with white glints that made it look even richer in hue, shone in the golden afternoon light. Her eyes were an unusual shade of pale blue, much prettier than Blanche's, and her strong, straight eyebrows were still as impressive as they'd ever been. She could curve those eyebrows into perfect arcs when she wished to indicate disapproval. That expression—so well known to the women of Littleberry—was trained on me.

"Am I not permitted to be curious?"

I tried my most winning smile. Since my earliest memories, I had been in awe of Gerry, who was twenty-two years my senior; we had never lived at Hyrst at the same time. Besides, most people were in awe of my oldest sister. I supposed that was a quality to be desired in the undisputed leader of Littleberry society, but it did rather keep one at a distance.

"Curiosity is vulgar." Gerry secured a single lump of sugar in the silver tongs and dropped it into her tea. "The past is sometimes best left in the past."

That remark was guaranteed to pique my curiosity even more. To give myself time to ponder my best approach, I took a sip of my tea. Gerry served tea in the most wonderfully fine china, the porcelain so thin it was almost transparent, the tea itself fragrant and delicious. I still remembered the first time I'd been allowed to drink from one of these wonderful cups, on my twelfth birthday.

I set my cup and saucer down carefully and searched my mind for the most diplomatic approach.

"I'm reading one of Mama's journals from the time of the Crimean War. You know I've been going through her journals looking for her herbal recipes. But there's more to them than that. I keep catching glimpses of Mama at a time when I wasn't even born. I'm fascinated by them. Right now, for example, she seems somehow—well, unsettled."

"What do you mean?" Gerry spoke a little sharply, and I looked at her in surprise.

"I have no idea. That's why I've come to you, to see if you

can fill in some of the gaps. There's no harm in that, is there? It was a long time ago. Right now I'm in the years of your marriage to Ned and Lydia's birth. It occurred to me that a young bride, about to become a mother, would be close to her own mother. Especially as Papa was clearly away a great deal."

"Yes, he was." Gerry turned to look out of the window so that her profile—which, Ned had once told me, had turned every man's head during her first Season—was clearly outlined. A little weakening of the skin around her chin perhaps detracted from its former perfection, but the thoughtful, almost dreamy look on her face could have been that of the young woman she had once been.

"You've never really spoken to me about the past," I said softly, watching the memories flicker across her face. "Nobody does. I sometimes feel as if I were a doll born into this family, not a real person. Michael was always a real person—wasn't he?—because he was the longed-for son and heir. But I was a little pet to be fussed over and made much of and then put away in the nursery until you had time for me again."

I said this without rancor. A sixth daughter is accustomed to being overlooked. I had benefited from a great deal of relative freedom, not to mention a bevy of servants who could always be relied upon for food, drink, and comfort. All in all, I had little to complain about.

"You were always so quiet." A smile curved Gerry's lips. "We never so much banished you to the nursery as allowed you to escape there when you were tired of playing behind a chair or sitting on someone's knee, lost in your own thoughts while we all talked. Michael was so horribly noisy and diffi-cult that you seemed a little angel by comparison."

She turned to face me. "It amazes me that you didn't hear more than you were supposed to. Nothing ever seemed to touch you, not until Daniel died, and then you simply became withdrawn. Before that, you were—" She stopped to consider her next word. "You were self-sufficient. Until you and Daniel began to fall in love, you never seemed to need anyone. You never seemed unhappy. You never seemed to think other people might be unhappy. Except for Michael, of course. I don't suppose even you could have missed Michael's signs of distress."

"I think Michael was the reason I learned to ignore other people." I grinned. "When the nearest person to you is noisy and disruptive all the time, you build a wall and retreat behind it." I took another sip of tea. "Are you trying to tell me there *was* something I missed?"

"Not always." Gerry ran the fingertips of a beringed hand over her immaculate coiffure. "There were years when they seemed perfectly happy together. Those years inevitably resulted in more children. I've occasionally wondered how many of us there might have been if our parents had always been in harmony. You could easily have been the sixteenth daughter, not the sixth."

"Heaven forbid. And in the years they weren't happy? What happened?"

Gerry shrugged. "The usual sort of thing, I suppose, when people are bound together for life. Papa strayed a little, here and there. Never close to home, and never for long."

"Strayed?" I stared at her, the meaning of her words gradually sinking in. This was not at all what I'd expected to hear. "You mean other women? *Papa?*"

I felt cold all over. My handsome, charming, kind father had always seemed to me like some princely ideal of a husband. Truth be told, it was an ideal that had made it easier for me to accept Justin's proposal at a time when I had felt little more than affection for him. Daniel had gone and my youthful passion with him, and if I couldn't have that passion

I could at least found the rest of my life on fidelity and trust —as I thought my mother had.

Gerry took the teacup out of my unresisting hand. "Don't look so shocked, Baby. Mama bore it well, as a lady of breeding should."

I felt a brief stab of anger. "*Should?* Have *you* ever had to bear it?"

For a moment, Gerry's blue stare resembled Michael's. "I have not. Not that I know of anyway. But it's common enough; you must realize that. Mama might not even have told me if I hadn't been upset when Ned was so terribly preoccupied with his business, just after we married. I was already expecting, you understand, and rather fragile. I suppose Mama sympathized—or perhaps she was bracing me for the worst or reassuring me. I don't know. She said something along the lines of men having other interests than their wives and then said something about other wives. Then it all came out—how Papa had strayed in the early years of their marriage and yet returned to her in the end."

"I know it's common. Justin had a sharper ear for gossip than most people realized. But I never imagined . . ." I shook my head.

"I know you didn't, Baby." Gerry's voice held an odd tenderness.

I felt my shoulders slump. "So that explains the . . . the unhappiness. She wouldn't admit it fully, even to her private journals."

"And she certainly wouldn't have confided in anyone else in Littleberry. She knew I was safe—I'd rather die than let anyone else know my father had a mistress." Gerry sat up straighter. "But it passed, Baby. I deduce from your existence that a reconciliation took place shortly after Lydia was born, but I had a baby of my own to distract me by then. The world seemed to be full of babies in that season of my life—first

Lydia, then you, then Michael, then Thomas and Maryanne. And Thomas was such a worry, of course—so was Michael."

"Did Papa—stray—after Michael and I were born, do you think?"

Gerry's lips tightened. "Don't speculate, Baby. Mama never said another word to me about Papa's peccadilloes. Not directly anyway."

"What do you mean?"

Gerry frowned at her hands, running a finger of her right hand over the skin of her left. "There were occasions when Mama made a remark that referred, I think, to the distant past. As if she were warning Papa that she had told me about —the other women. She would do it when we were *en famille* so Papa could never reply to her directly. He would react as if she'd made a private joke and turn the conversation. I imagine it all went over your head. I used to find it oddly jarring. In fact, I've often wondered whether Mama's illness started well before Papa died."

"Or perhaps she was still deeply wounded, and all the more so because Papa dismissed her feelings." I frowned. "I always thought of Papa as a kind man, but that would be cruel."

"Hmmm." Realizing she was fidgeting, Gerry laced her fingers together primly. "Baby, they'd been married a long time. I'm dreadfully sorry your marriage ended so tragically after just three years, but at least you were spared the . . . the *pettiness* that can steal into a marriage after a while. The hurtful things you say to one another behind closed doors. Papa was far from perfect in that respect, you know. But by the time you came along, he had perfected the charming façade he wore every day. He *was* kind to you—more so than to his older children."

Gerry gathered her blue silk skirts together and rose to her feet, a signal that she considered our conversation at an end. "Don't think too much about the past. If you're trying to find Mama in those journals of hers, don't look for signs of unhappiness where there may be none. After all, what's the point? Really, Baby, I never thought you had such a deal of imagination."

~

My first instinct upon returning home was to seize the journal of Mama's that I'd been reading. I pored over every page or fragment where there was some mention of her family life, in particular Papa. I ate my solitary dinner without even noticing the food, trying to square my image of my parents with the new one Gerry had presented to me. Afterward, I went back through some of the journals I'd already read. I paged back and forth until my eyes were sore and my head ached.

I barely slept that night. How could I have gone through life with no inkling of anything wrong in my parents' marriage? Was Gerry right that Papa's infidelities were just "the usual sort of thing" to which any wife in our social circles needed to resign herself? Had Mama really not cared all that much, knowing the impossibility of divorce would always bring Papa home to her? Or had she hugged her pain to herself, unable to stop it from occasionally leaking out through her pen onto the pages?

The dawn brought little counsel except the commonsense realization that fretting was futile. I hooked and tied myself into my riding habit long before the breakfast hour and went to find Mank—who always rose early—at the stables.

By the time I returned home and found a surprised Guttridge waiting for me, I'd been all the way down to the sea on Sandy. Mank and I had thoroughly blown away the cobwebs with a good long canter along the water's edge. The salt-laden air, the fresh breeze of the early morning, and the bright June sunlight had combined to tire me out in a delightful way. I welcomed my hot bath and large breakfast with enthusiasm.

I had promised Taylor I would go over the changes we'd decided on for the herb garden, so it was mid-morning before I walked into my workroom. I found Guttridge carefully straining herb-infused olive oil through a sieve.

"I've ordered coffee," I informed her as I almost fell into one of our two Morris chairs. "I feel like I've done a day's work already."

"I hope you're not going to be too tired to walk this afternoon, my lady. I want to show you that patch of comfrey I found by the field gate in High Lane. It's got much bigger leaves and flowers than usual. I think we should dig some for the shady side of the garden."

"Slave driver." Yawning, I stared stupidly at Guttridge as she stoppered bottles and wrote carefully on their labels before pasting the same onto the glass. I should join her in her work, I thought, but instead I reached over to the small bookcase that held Mama's journals and selected the next one. There were only three left—were some later ones missing?

With the help of coffee, I managed to remain awake while I read steadily onward. The notes in this volume were even more fragmented than usual, as if Mama was too busy to write much. She mentioned the Crimean conflict and the inevitable committees to aid serving and injured soldiers and their families. Workhouse patients and Ned—he was a young man then and still had his knighthood in the future. I was pleased to see how often he and Mama worked together. He was then as now a great organizer of schemes to benefit the poor of the district and to improve those parts of the town that were falling into decay. Notes on remedies that seemed to become ever more subtle and complex. My own skills and knowledge were too limited to understand what Mama was doing; I skipped over many of the pages with a promise to myself that I would revisit them during the long winter evenings.

As the war drew to a close, there were hints that Papa was now at Hyrst more often again. With my new knowledge, I thought I could detect a note of reconciliation. That would accord with Gerry's theory since I had been born quite soon after the war ended. And here indeed was a new remedy for morning sickness and a poignant little note: "Perhaps this time it will be a boy." She was to be disappointed again.

Pages of records pertaining to the herb garden and remedies for heartburn—Mama was clearly dosing herself. And then, pleasantly, my name, and my mother's note that I was a dear good little baby and very pretty. That ended this notebook, and my morning.

After luncheon, I went with Guttridge to see the comfrey and agreed it would do very well for the herb garden. Upon our return, I tackled the next journal. Disappointingly, this one mostly comprised copies of earlier remedies that Mama had clearly decided to collate in one volume. There were no dates save on the cover, but I surmised that several months had elapsed during its composition by the last few pages. Here Mama referred obliquely to the discomforts both she and Gerry were experiencing and to her "shape," which she remarked was different this time. The only time Mama and Gerry could have been *enceinte* at the same time was—I spent a few minutes counting on my fingers—the latter part of 1857, as Michael had been born on Christmas Eve. The last page of the journal held a drawing of a star above a snowy field.

It was a warm day, and I found myself dozing until Guttridge, who had disappeared to tend to my clothes, returned to the workroom with an armful of tender rosemary shoots she'd cut from a large old bush that grew by the side of the house.

"Are you finished with those blessed notebooks?" The sharp, pleasant smell of rosemary filled the air as Guttridge began sorting through the sprigs for spoiled leaves, dirt, and insects.

"Just one more. I wonder if some have been lost or if Mama gave up writing them after Michael was born." I pulled the journal out of its shelf and began turning its pages. "Come to think of it, I don't remember her writing in journals when I was a child. I do remember her sketching and painting in watercolors though—she was always in the garden painting her flowers."

"Perhaps she grew fonder of painting than she was of writing. I used to love knitting, but I can't be bothered with such things now."

"I suppose so." I turned the pages in a desultory fashion. "There are dates here and there, and I can see there are big gaps of time between the entries."

"There you are, then. She was losing interest, or maybe she was just too busy to do her writing."

"Hmmm. Oh look, here I am again—good heavens, I did suffer from croup as a small child. No wonder my nursemaids were always giving me elderberry and rose hip syrups."

"Now that's something I'd like to make, my lady." Guttridge smacked her lips. "Nothing better than a bowl of rice pudding with rose hip syrup on it."

She picked up the cleaned sprigs of rosemary and bustled off to the stillroom, no doubt to wash them. I turned the pages of the journal rapidly, noting that nothing seemed amiss. Mostly children's remedies, often calming or soothing preparations for Michael, which was hardly surprising. He must have absorbed much of her energies, as he did everyone's. The entries were now months or even years apart: 1859—1860—1862—1863—

And then I came to the final ten pages and woke up completely.

2 8

MRS. BATCH-CROCKER

y twin sisters' eyes, always almost
preternaturally round, seemed even more
spherical than usual as they considered my request.

"Mama's notebooks, Baby?" asked Annette. "Why, I
thought you had all of them."

"So did I, but now I'm afraid I might not. The last one I
have covers the years '58 to '65—Mama didn't write in
it much."

Until the end.

"What makes you think there are more?" The corners of
Alice's small mouth tweaked upward in an encouraging little
smile, as if she were addressing a child.

"Because she suddenly began writing every day. Long
passages—something had clearly upset her terribly. She talks
about her pain and her distress and asks why she should be
used so. She talks about being trapped—there's one passage
that describes Hyrst as a prison. If she didn't sound so rational, I'd think it was the start of her illness, but in '65 she was
quite—normal, wasn't she?"

I clenched my fists, waiting for an answer as the twins

gazed at each other. As so often happened, I had the impression they were somehow communicating without speaking. Could they read each other's expressions? The seconds lengthened until a full minute must have passed, and I lost patience.

"Eighteen-sixty-five," I said slowly and with emphasis. "The two of you were about the age I am now. I was nine or ten—and heaven knows, I don't remember noticing anything wrong. But from what Gerry told me last week, there was a great deal in our parents' lives about which I was entirely oblivious—which all of you hid from me."

I saw their eyes narrow for a moment in mirror image. A lump rose in my throat so that when I continued speaking my voice sounded thick and hoarse. It was frustration, I told myself—else why should I be emotional? Michael would say it was most illogical.

"You *must* know," I insisted. "You were living here with them—with us—and you were grown women by then. For goodness' sake, tell me. What was it that upset Mama so?"

"What did Gerry tell you?" asked Alice.

"It's not like her to be indiscreet," said Annette, as if continuing Alice's thought.

"It's hardly an indiscretion." Furious with myself, I whipped out my handkerchief and dabbed at the corners of my eyes as surreptitiously as I could. "I'm a member of this family. I'm a grown woman, a married—a widow. I'm old enough to know the truth about the past, so don't try to hide anything you know. Was Papa unfaithful again in '65?"

"What good is it, Baby?"

"To bring up the past—"

"—when he's been gone for years and years, poor old darling—"

"—and Mama's as good as gone—"

"—and why should it matter to you anyway?"

"It matters because it's the *truth*," I wailed. A sudden memory of Fortier telling me how much our sort of people liked to keep unpleasant things hidden crept unbidden into my mind. "It matters because I feel as if I barely knew my own mother and father. I'm sure you're hiding something from me. I know you'd probably have gone to the grave hiding it, but now I can see Mama's distress right there, there on the page. I want you to stop hiding whatever it is and treat me like a responsible member of this family."

I stopped there, fighting back my tears. They already thought of me as much younger than I was; acting like a child wouldn't improve their opinion.

There was another long pause while the twins looked at one another and I fidgeted in my seat. Quite apart from my unexpected descent into emotion—why *did* I allow my family to upset me?—I had to admit I found all this secrecy infuriating. I began to have some sympathy for Fortier's point of view.

At long last, Annette and Alice reached out simultaneously and linked hands, their dry skin making a whispering sound as it met.

"Mrs. Batch-Crocker," Alice said and pinched her rosebud mouth tight. Annette let go of her sister's hands and put an arm around her waist.

"That horrid woman." She leaned her head against Alice's shoulder.

I frowned. "I know that name. An American, isn't she? The one who caused a scandal two—no, three—years ago by running off with a guardsman."

I remembered Justin poking his head out of his study and shouting, "Scandal ahoy!" with a wide grin. By the time I'd entered the room, he was hidden behind the newspaper, which hitherto had lain in its usual neglected position on his desk, chortling over the salacious details of the affair.

"Justin knew the Batch-Crockers," I continued. "He said the husband was dreadfully dull but important in his own county, especially with the money he got from marrying the American woman. I suppose she was one of those heiresses we all hear so much about." I sat up straighter, discarding my reminiscences as the realization hit me. "Are you telling me this woman was—well, was involved with Papa? How old was she then?" In 1865, my father must have been nearing sixty.

"Terribly young," said Alice. "Young and wild and shameless."

"Younger than we were." Annette's brows drew together. "So horrid of Papa."

"Did you know at the time?" I looked from one identical face to the other, feeling the blood drain from my face as the answer to my question became apparent from their silence. "You're not telling me Papa didn't even bother to hide it."

Alice sighed heavily, one hand lightly rubbing her twin's shoulder. "*She* didn't hide it. So of course people knew, and that meant gossip, and Mama got to know about it."

"And she was rapacious, that Batch-Crocker woman," said Annette. "She made demands on Papa—financial demands, I mean. Her family cut off her allowance because of her behavior—"

"—and of course her husband controlled her dowry, so she couldn't get her hands on that—"

"—and she just wasn't used to not spending whatever she liked, being from such a rich family," continued Annette.

"She had Papa make her a present of the most dreadfully expensive carriage horse," Alice said. "Snow white and quite the prettiest thing you ever saw, they say."

My head began to ache. Justin must have known about the affair too—how could he not?—and he hadn't troubled to tell me either. The miserable thought occurred to me that my behavior after Daniel's death had made people think my nerves couldn't stand bad news.

"She made Papa look a fool," Alice continued. "He was fortunate Mr. Batch-Crocker lost his temper when he did, otherwise he might have been challenged to a duel."

"What happened?" I said faintly.

"It was the horse," Alice said. "Of course Mr. B-C knew at once where it came from. His wife positively taunted him with her *amours*, by all accounts. Until then, he'd behaved with a certain—how should we say it, Netty?"

"Indulgence," said Annette firmly. "He was much older than his wife. Almost Papa's age. He had perhaps been *too* complaisant."

"Maybe she wanted him to be jealous." Alice nodded. "Well, she had the horse hitched up to a tilbury—she was a good driver, and always a fine horsewoman—"

"—and drove round and round their park so her husband could see the animal. Just to enrage him."

"And it worked." Alice's words ran over Annette's. "He waited until she drew up in front of their house and went for her with a whip."

"She jumped out of the carriage and ran off screaming, and he—" Annette looked helplessly at Alice, shuddering.

"He shot the poor dear horse." Alice raised her hands as if in horror at the memory. "It was the talk of the Season."

"And then he took Mrs. B-C to *Chicago*, my dear, the dreadful place in America where she came from, and left her there with her *family*. With such threats, she didn't set foot in England for ten years, by which time one hopes she had learned a little discretion."

The guardsman would seem to indicate Annette's hope was in vain. But that cynical thought flew straight out of my head, ousted by an overwhelming sense of shame. My Papa, involved in such a scandal—

"It was the fact everyone *knew* that Mama hated so much." Alice bit her dry lips. "You know what Littleberry's like. All the good she'd done, and now people were talking about *her* as if she'd done something wrong."

"We went to great lengths to ensure you children didn't hear about it," said Annette. "You were such an inquisitive little thing back then."

The room was tilting slightly around me, and I realized I was holding my breath. I let it out with a great sigh and tucked my hands—which were strangely cold—under my arms.

"You all knew," I whispered. "You, Gerry, Odelia, Blanche . . . And nobody has ever told me. Even Gerry, when she admitted Papa hadn't always been faithful—" I stopped short. "Gerry *lied* to me."

"Don't blame Gerry," Alice said quickly. "She's never let a word about the whole Batch-Crocker business pass her lips. Never. She doesn't believe any good can come of bringing up the past."

"And Blanche—well, you know Blanche." The ghost of a smile flitted across Annette's face, then was gone. "Who does she think of except herself? And Deddy, I suppose. She let it be known that anyone who even *hinted* at the affair in her presence would lose the regard of the Marquess and Marchioness of Hastings forever."

Alice laid a hand on my arm. "And O was clever enough to use the scandal to her own advantage. Papa and Mama would *never* have let her move permanently to London at the tender age of nineteen in the normal way of things. But with the household in disarray . . ." She shrugged. "And I believe she pointed out to Mama that if she lived at Scott House, Papa could not . . . well . . . have private guests."

"Oh, good grief." I shook Alice's arm off and put my hands

over my face, only to pull them down as another thought struck me. "Do people *still* talk about it?"

"Knowing Littleberry—"

"—I'd say yes—" said my sisters simultaneously.

"—but it was a long time ago, and nobody will mention it to our faces."

"And all families have their secrets," finished Alice. "And with poor Mama so ill . . ."

"How did she cope back then?" I asked. "How did she live it all down?"

"She held her head high and looked people in the face, as a lady does." This time Annette did smile, a strangely triumphant expression. "She said at the time it was the final straw, but it wasn't, of course."

"I suppose she forgave him eventually," said Alice. "For the sake of you little ones as much as anything else. Besides, what could she do? Our sort of people don't divorce."

I closed my eyes, shaking my head. "Of course they don't."

"But I think you're wrong about there being more note-books, Baby." I did not see which twin had spoken.

"Why?" I opened my eyes and looked hard at my sisters, attempting to read their identical expressions.

Another moment when my sisters seemed to be communicating by thought alone, and then they both turned to me as if they had reached a decision.

"There *was* another one," Alice said. "But Papa read it, you see. There was something we heard—it was wrong of us to eavesdrop, of course."

"He put it on the fire, you see—"

"—and forbade Mama from writing any more journals."

"And she accepted that?" My eyes must have been as round as the twins'. "After all that had happened, Mama meekly agreed to remain silent?" I knew I could not have held my tongue had it been me.

"Noooo." Alice breathed out the word, an odd expression of remembered pain on her heart-shaped face. "She made a scene. It was the one and only time I've known her to lose her dignity—except for that horrible day with Susan Hatherall."

"It was as if the loss of the notebook were more important than what had happened," Annette said. "She sounded so . . ." She looked helplessly at her twin.

"Insane." Alice supplied the word, and once more my sisters' hands entwined. "She wasn't herself at all. But then Papa began talking to her, very softly." She shuddered violently.

"What did he say, Ally?" I could hear the dread in my voice.

"We had no right to hear." Annette looked evasive, but I held up my hand to forestall any attempt at dissembling.

"You *did* hear."

"We heard some of it." Alice looked suddenly very old. "He said he'd take you away if she made a scandal. You and Michael. That he'd have her declared insane and—and locked up."

"And eventually we stopped trying to hear because it was so awful, the way Mama was crying. Quietly—whimpering."

"Dear God." I felt sick and cold. Of course, those were the powers and privileges of a husband, and I didn't suppose Papa was the first to use such a threat—but that meant he hadn't been altogether the kind man I'd thought him, and that was hard to encompass.

"There were no more notebooks after that," said Annette. "Mama wasn't right for a long time after that day. She kept to her garden a great deal, sketching and painting. She neglected her workroom and didn't even visit the poor people of Littleberry."

"That's when Netty and I began to offer what help we

could." Alice smiled fondly at her twin. "We gave out that Mama was ailing, which was true, really."

"We didn't want people to talk even more."

"And the house was so horrid for such a long while. Such an *atmosphere*. It was better to be out of it."

"But in the end Mama seemed to cheer up—"

"—and Papa kept such a brave face," said Alice.

"You sound as if you had more sympathy for him than for Mama," I pointed out. "How could you?"

The look that passed between the twins confirmed my suspicions, and I closed my eyes again. "Because a lady isn't supposed to make a fuss."

I was still for a few moments, thinking. In the world in which I was raised, Papa would automatically have the right of it. But my whole being revolted against the years of betrayal and reconciliation and then enforced silence. Was it the stifling of her voice that had driven Mama out of her mind?

"Well." I rose to my feet, aware that my legs weren't quite steady. "Now at least I know there were no more notebooks. And why." And it would take me days or even weeks to recover from what I'd learned in the last half hour.

Alice smiled up at me as if a thought had struck her. "But just think, Baby. There were such lovely pictures. Don't you remember them? If Mama had still been scribbling in her notebooks, she wouldn't have done all that painting."

Annette put her head on one side. "Wouldn't you like them for your workroom?"

I considered her question, looking down at the two women I hardly felt I knew. They were still pretty, with their large eyes and heart-shaped faces, if you overlooked a certain weakness of chin. They were looking up at me with an encouraging expression, as though willing me to forget the unpleasant revelations of the last hour and turn to brighter subjects. Perhaps that's exactly what I should do, for their sakes. I forced a smile to my lips.

"If they're still in good condition, I suppose I've more room for them at Whitcombe than you have here. Are they in a trunk somewhere?"

"Oh no," said Alice. "They're in Papa's map chest, quite nicely preserved. In fact, would you like the map chest itself? You always enjoyed playing with it when you were a little girl."

"Michael dislikes it," added Annette. "He says all the little compartments under the glass lid are crooked, and he doesn't like the way the glass reflects. You know how fussy he is."

I certainly did, and the twins were right, I'd always liked the map chest. Papa had bought it from a sale in Folkestone, where a ship was being broken up. As a child, I'd loved to put conkers, fir cones, and other small treasures into the display compartments and hide objects in the "secret" compartment, which was not at all secret since everyone knew about it. My smile became less forced.

"I'll take it, and gladly, if Michael and Julia agree," I said. "It'll look well in my workroom."

29

AB IRATO

*T*he map chest was duly brought to Whitcombe and set up in my workroom, where, to my surprise, Michael visited me only two days later. My mood by that time was better than I'd expected. There were moments when I even convinced myself that Papa's words had only been words, after all, and that we all said things to each other we didn't mean. Truth be told, I simply couldn't square the threat he had made with the warm, kind man I had known for the first nineteen years of my life.

"I wish you'd brew some potion for Julia's heartburn," Michael said without greeting me. He was followed by the inevitable Brandrick, who, to give him his due, didn't look entirely comfortable about Michael's reference to his countess's indisposition.

"Certainly. Mama's journals appear to contain some fine remedies. Julia should have asked me sooner." Heedless of the look on Michael's face, I stood on tiptoe to kiss him on the cheek. Since his apology three months before, I had felt more kindly toward my infuriating little brother, who was definitely making an effort to be less critical of my every word and action. And besides, his child was due in two or three weeks, and the poor man was beginning to fuss over Julia like a hen with one chick. He did so in his own way, of course, without visible affection, but I—and his servants—understood him well enough to interpret correctly his strictures about exactly how his wife's comforts must be managed.

Michael twitched and hunched his shoulders to ward off any more demonstrations of sisterly feeling. As a further evasive maneuver, he crossed to the map chest. He ran a finger across the gleaming wood of its hinged top and squinted at the glass as if looking for signs of bad housekeeping. Since my servants were as well trained as any in the county, he would find none.

"I suppose I should be glad you like this ugly thing," he said. "I should have given it to you years ago."

"I'm surprised Mama didn't have it placed in her workroom after Papa died," I said. "After all, she clearly used it more than he did. I suppose he insisted on it staying in the library out of sheer perverseness."

As I pronounced the words, I realized a note of criticism had crept into my thoughts about my father. That would pass, I supposed, because of course I had loved him dearly. A child could not stop loving its parents, not even when they turned out to have feet of clay.

"He liked the look of it," Michael said bluntly. "Are you coming to Hyrst with your remedy today or tomorrow? Julia can hardly eat."

"I saw Julia yesterday evening, Michael, and she's the picture of health. I'll take my time to find a good remedy. Now—"

I stopped, remembering Brandrick, who was lurking in a corner of my workroom watching Guttridge put labels on jars.

"Brandrick," I called, "Would you like to adjourn to the kitchen with Guttridge? It's nearly time for the servants' luncheon. You'll be a few minutes early, but nobody will mind."

I watched in satisfaction as Brandrick, with no more than a murmured, "Certainly, m'lady," followed Guttridge out of the room. My lady's maid twitched her eyebrows at me as she passed, while Michael regarded me with a cold eye.

"Brandrick is not a servant. I have told you that before."

"He's not one of us either. Guttridge will make him comfortable," I said airily.

"Your prejudice against my steward—*our* steward—is entirely illogical." But Michael clearly dismissed Brandrick from his mind as he turned toward the large marble-topped table.

"Are these Mama's paintings?"

"They are, and I'm glad you're here. I wanted to ask you about them." I gestured toward the seven large paintings laid out on the table, the largest and most beautiful of all the treasures contained within Papa's map chest. I had spent the last two days in open-mouthed admiration at Mama's work, which I didn't remember as having been so beautifully executed. I realized she had, in fact, found her voice again after her writing had been stifled, and I was glad of it.

"These are the ones I'm thinking of framing for this room." I fingered the one nearest to me, a magnificent study of a purple foxglove complete with separate illustrations of the leaves, seeds, and seedlings. "They're all roughly the same size, you see, and could be nicely spaced across the back wall. Only this one has a title—do you think I should ask the framer to cut it off?"

"But that would make its proportions different to the others." Michael looked horrified.

"The title makes it different. I prefer it without." I brushed my fingertips over the paint, feeling the way the paper had stiffened as the watercolors dried. "But maybe you're right. I could put it in the middle, make it into a focal point. Mama must have taken more care over this drawing than anything else she ever did—it's breathtaking. I wanted to know if you'd like it, though, since they really belong to Hyrst."

Michael shook his head, picking up one corner of the large watercolor. "No, they don't. I gave them to you. What does this say?" He squinted at the exquisitely lettered wording, which read, *"Sola dosis facit venenum."*

I grinned, pleased that Michael hadn't contested my right to the paintings. There were many more of a quite astonishing quality. I would have some of the others framed and offer them to Julia.

"I'm as in the dark as you are about what these words mean. I know some botanical and medical Latin, but Mama never taught me any more than that. This looks like a phrase rather than a name."

"Don't you have a Latin dictionary?"

"Justin had one, of course. But I daresay I'll find someone who can tell me their meaning. Thomas, perhaps, or that tutor of his. Except Thomas has gone to Chichester to meet with some clergyman or the other, and the tutor has left on a walking holiday." I shrugged. "Plenty of time to find out."

Michael put the paper down and traced a long, elegant finger along the finely delineated leaves. "What about *this* writing?"

"What writing? There isn't any."

"Yes there is. In the leaves. Mama's special writing."

"What are you talking about?" I stared at the leaves. "There's nothing there. And you can't read, so how do you know it's writing?"

"I can read *patterns.*" Michael sounded sulky. "And I know well enough what writing looks like. Heaven knows I've spent enough hours staring at it, trying to will it to make sense. Do you have a pencil and paper?"

"What do you mean about Mama's special writing?" I asked as I went to my desk to rummage in the drawer.

"Mama showed me once, when I was little, how she hid our names in her flower pictures. She said it made them more special. She thought it was very odd that I could see them, even though I couldn't read. But they're easier to see than the way writing usually looks. The letters don't move around."

"Letters move around?" I looked curiously at my brother.

"They do for me. They wiggle and slip away when I try to look at them. But this writing is in a picture, so the picture holds it steady for me."

I peered over Michael's shoulder.

"All I can see are beautifully painted leaves and flowers."

I handed him the pencil and paper, rather fascinated at the notion of seeing Michael write something. I knew he could produce a clumsy but serviceable "Broadmere" in cursive for the purpose of signing documents. I also knew that the process embarrassed him and he had Brandrick sign for him wherever possible.

"I don't suppose you've ever seen the watercolor on my dressing room wall." Michael paused, pencil in hand. "Mama painted it for me when I returned from Somerset. It's an apple and a pear. The apple has 'Michael' in it, and the pear has 'Broadmere.' That's how I learned."

"You can write 'Michael'?"

"In cursive."

Was that the faintest smirk of satisfaction on my brother's face?

Michael poised himself to write, staring hard at the foxglove picture as he put pencil to paper. He held the pencil very oddly in his left hand. His forefinger and middle finger rested on the pencil, while his thumb stuck up and outward as though it wished to have nothing to do with the process. But he was definitely producing letters of the alphabet, albeit slowly and painfully.

"Do the other pictures have writing in them?" I asked.

"No." Michael carefully joined up an *O*.

"You haven't even looked."

"Of course I have. I don't have to stare at things to know they're there. I can see everything at once. Besides, this is the only picture where the leaves are big enough to make it work." Michael left a space, then wrote *L*.

"There are separate words?"

"If words are separate, and I suppose they are. I don't see spaces very well when I look at writing. I used to argue with my tutor that people don't leave spaces when they speak. There are four leaves with special writing in them, so I'm making a space here as there are spaces between the leaves."

"Oh." And in fact, when I looked again I could see Michael was spacing out the words into the same positions as the leaves.

"There." Michael straightened up and put down the pencil. He had written:

AB

IRATO

LEX

TALIONIS

"The only word I recognize is 'lex'," I admitted. "It means 'law' as far as I know. I don't have a clue about the others." I shrugged apologetically. "I'm not terribly bright about words myself."

"You're cleverer than you think you are." Michael looked away from me as he spoke. "You just didn't get much education. Girls don't, do they? Mama had to teach herself a great deal."

"Blanche has already warned me against becoming a blue-stocking," I said.

"You're fortunate." For the fraction of a second, Michael's blue gaze met my own. "Education just made me unhappy. I'm not making *my* sons learn any more than they want to."

"Poor Michael." I frowned. "But I could do with someone educated right now. On the other hand, the thought of taking this to just anyone makes me uneasy somehow."

"You have to show it to someone you trust completely," said my brother.

And oddly enough, I could only think of one person who fit that description.

❧

"I am in equal parts surprised and delighted at your summons, Lady Helena. Thank you for putting your trust in me." Fortier bowed as he said the words.

I blinked. "Actually, my first thought was to turn to Sir Edward, but he's in London. I need someone with an education, you see. And obviously someone I can trust to be discreet."

Was it my imagination, or did Fortier's face fall? I bit my tongue at my tactlessness. But he recovered quickly and turned to Guttridge.

"Miss Guttridge, I haven't had the opportunity to express

my happiness upon learning that you've become Lady Helena's assistant. I can't think of anyone more suited to the task in terms of intelligence and aptitude."

I was amused to note that Guttridge, not given to outward displays of emotion, actually blushed. I invited Fortier to sit on one of the Morris chairs.

Guttridge, seated at a stool at the large table, industriously pulverized orris root while simultaneously performing the valuable office of chaperone. The heady raspberry and woody notes of the orris root soon mingled with the aroma of strong coffee, which I had ordered to be brought up as soon as the French physician arrived. Scotty, having greeted Fortier with a great many wags of his plumy tail, settled down near the Frenchman with an air of contentment.

I poured the coffee myself, handing a cup to Fortier before placing another next to Guttridge's elbow along with a few of the thin almond biscuits we both loved. I offered the same to Fortier, who took some with a smile. Once again, I experienced the odd feeling that he was substantial and solid while the rest of society lacked reality. I could still feel the tiny brush of his carefully trimmed mustache and beard against the back of my ungloved hand. I took a rather too large sip of my coffee, which, although well improved with cream and sugar as I liked it, was still hot. I coughed and put my cup down.

"I have something I must ask you in strict confidence, Monsieur Fortier. But first, let me reassure myself as to the main point. Are you conversant with the Latin language? I thought you might be, as a medical man."

Fortier relaxed into his chair. "I am. My acquaintance with the Romans and the Greeks long predates my medical studies. I had what you English call a thorough grounding in the classics. You wish me to translate something?"

"Precisely. Guttridge, how are you getting on with your work?"

This was our prearranged signal for Guttridge to make herself scarce, and she didn't miss it. She slid off her stool.

"I need some more almond oil, my lady. I'll go and get some from below stairs."

"As long as you've finished your coffee."

"I have, and very good it was too. I'll be back soon."

She would be back in exactly twenty minutes, as arranged. I waited until she had left the room, leaving the door ajar for propriety's sake, and I'd heard the telltale creak that meant she'd reached the corner of the passageway. Then I took from my pocket the piece of paper on which I'd noted the Latin words. The drawings were piled on my desk, awaiting the visit from the framer.

I'd had Michael look through the rest of the watercolors and sketches in the map chest, but, although he'd found one or two hidden dates and the full name of his oldest son James, nothing more of any import seemed to be contained in Mama's illustrations. We had also found the date 1876 in pencil on the back of the foxglove painting, but that bore little significance to us other than being the year of Michael's marriage to his first wife, Cecilia. Some of the other drawings were also dated 1876 and 1877, but there were none dated later than 1877.

"The first line is the title of a painting," I explained as I handed the paper to Fortier. "The other words were discovered by Lord Broadmere in the painting itself."

Fortier frowned. "May I see the painting?"

"Of course." I fetched it from my desk and gave it to him, noting the lift of his eyebrows as he took it in his hands. "You don't see the words my brother found, do you?"

"Not at all." Fortier turned the watercolor this way and that in an evident attempt to find them. "Where are they?"

"Lord Broadmere says they're in this leaf here, and this one—there—and these two." I pointed, standing close to Fortier. "It's quite the finest thing Mama ever produced. Apparently, she amused herself by hiding names and dates in some of her pictures. She discovered upon Michael's return from his tutor in Somerset that he could see them."

"The science known as steganography—literally, concealed writing. I certainly can't see anything other than a picture. Your mother must have been exceptionally talented." Fortier's face was grave. "Can you tell me why you wish this consultation to be on a confidential basis?"

"Not really. An instinct, perhaps."

I could have said a feeling of dread. When I looked at the words, I felt like the heroine of a chilling ghost tale, confronted with a door that almost certainly held something unspeakable on the other side, but obliged to open it notwithstanding. Fortier was wrong about me—I did not wish to turn a blind eye to all unpleasant things. Or had I changed since the day of Susan's death?

Fortier was silent for a few moments, clearly ordering his thoughts.

"Well," he said eventually, "the title is a familiar enough Latin tag that most doctors know. It's generally attributed to Paracelsus, who was a great botanist with a particular interest in toxicology. '*Sola dosis facit venenum*' simply means that some poisonous substances are only dangerous if a large enough dose is administered. That's certainly true of foxglove."

"Mama used foxglove as a remedy for heart trouble," I said.

"Quite so. It's a valuable drug if used with care."

I took a very deep breath. "But it's played all too prominent a part in my recent history, hasn't it?" My voice was a little unsteady. "I think that's partly why I took so much notice of this painting in the first place."

I raised my eyes to Fortier's, and what I saw in his expression was—confirmation. He had the same suspicion I had.

"Susan learned about foxglove from Mama." I could feel a slight tremor in my limbs. "More specifically, she learned how to poison with foxglove—from Mama." I closed my eyes, trying to still the thudding of my heart. "And she learned it when she was a *child*. Dear heaven."

I could feel Fortier close to me, feel the warmth emanating from him but also the concern for me.

"A large dose may slow the heart to the point where the result is a fatal attack." His voice was low, but it, too, held a tremor. I heard him swallow. "The plant is also an emetic. An accidental poisoning often leads to vomiting, thus ridding the body of much of the toxin."

"That's what happened with Justin. She said she got the dose wrong. Which means she had been taught about the *right* dose. One that would remain in the stomach so that the poison would be efficacious." I opened my eyes. "Tell me what the other words say."

He hesitated.

"You know what my suspicions are," I said. "You have them too. Tell me."

I could see the reluctance in Fortier's eyes, but his voice strengthened as he spoke. "'*Ab irato*' means, literally, 'by an angry man.' It's a phrase used in law to refer to an unreasonable action brought on by anger."

"Because anger can override common sense and caution and—love." I whispered the words. "And '*lex talionis*'?"

"You will know that one, in its biblical form. An eye for an eye. The law of retribution."

"But that's *not* fair. It's not an eye for an eye. When someone causes you pain, I would understand the instinct to hit back—but not to *kill* them." My throat was hurting me, and I coughed to clear it. "I'm sorry. I don't suppose I'm making sense to you."

"I do understand. At least I'm almost certain I do. I haven't forgotten the sketchbook with the many poisonous plants, you see. I thought then of the power the dowager countess must have once held in her hands. And she was not bound by the ethical and moral principles that we physicians regard as axiomatic."

"And do you understand whom she killed?" My voice was just a thread of sound.

Fortier nodded. "By deduction, yes. You believe she may have killed your father."

"On the very last day of 1875," I said miserably. "I don't think it's by chance that Susan used a cup of cocoa in her attempt to poison Justin. Mama and Papa always took a cup of cocoa together before bed. The pleasant evening ritual of a devoted couple."

I was glad to note I was not going to cry. Anger had begun to course through me, drying up my tears and cutting through the rawness in my throat.

"This painting is my mother's confession."

30

ARRIVALS AND FAREWELLS

I would have avoided Hyrst if I could, but by the next morning I had a more than pressing reason to visit my family home. I found Julia sitting up in bed with my new nephew in her arms.

"No wonder I couldn't eat a thing." Julia grinned broadly as she handed the small bundle to me. "Now I'm ravenous. I ate breakfast at four o'clock and another at eight."

"When was he born?" I put my lips to the baby's head, so warm under his silky hair.

"At one in the morning." Julia smirked. "I didn't even feel any pains until late in the evening. I went to bed at seven, quite downcast from having no appetite and fiercely uncomfortable. At nine or so, I awoke from a doze to discover my waters had broken and I was well on my way to giving birth. Fortunately, Mrs. Kenny was at home, although she said she had almost nothing to do to help me along. Like shelling peas, my dear. I'm rather pleased with myself."

"I can see that. What are you going to call him?" I smiled as the baby opened his eyes for a moment, screwed up his face, and sneezed twice in quick succession.

"I wanted Michael for a boy, but *my* Michael won't hear of it. He doesn't want the baby to turn out like him. Although he might in looks—Gerry was here a short while ago and swears this little man's a true Scott-De Quincy in every respect. I don't know how she can tell since newborn babies are always such puckered little things. He does remind me a bit of Annabelle Alice though. Definitely not like Quentin, who took after me from the beginning. Anyway, Michael favors Julius. He says it's a logical name for a baby born in July, just like his Mama."

"Julius. Well, it's a noble name for a *very* sweet little boy." It was such a delight to feel the solid, warm body of this child wriggle inside his blanket, his tiny face contorting as he dealt with some intestinal struggle or other. One small hand waved in front of his face, and I put my finger into it, thrilled to feel the miniature digits grasp at my flesh, relax, then grasp again. Knowing that there was little hope of having children with Justin, I had tried—rather unsuccessfully, I realized—to distance my emotions from Julia's children, but now I felt once again the visceral longing for my own baby. I sighed.

"He's a little earlier than expected, of course, but he's such a good size I think I must have gotten my dates wrong." Julia shifted a little in her bed and groaned. "Helena, darling, ring for the monthly nurse, won't you? By the way he's fussing, he's going to cry soon, and I need help straightening up my pillows and sheets. I do so dislike bed rest."

A movement at the door made me turn around. I stood up, Julius still in my arms.

"Help is at hand from another quarter. Michael, I thought you'd be far too busy with the estate to dote over your wife and son. But since you're here, can you take the baby?"

"With pleasure." Michael took the small bundle into his arms with practiced ease, shushing the baby while I helped

Julia to get comfortable. By the time I had arranged the pillows properly, the Earl of Broadmere was standing at the window, rocking gently with the tiny blanket-wrapped form tucked tightly into his shoulder in a manner that seemed to please both parties immensely.

"You're rather good at that, little brother." I cast an approving eye over the tall form of the earl as I went to ring the bell.

"I like babies. They're very easy to understand."

"I suppose you'd like to see your Mama now, Helena." Julia yawned and rested her head on the pillows. "Belming brought her up here very early this morning to see Julius. She seemed to enjoy him, although I don't think she has the faintest idea who he is."

"No—I don't think I'll visit Mama today." Moving back toward Michael, I caught the surprised look on Julia's face, but my sister-in-law had a sharp instinct for knowing when she should refrain from a comment or question. A good trait in a countess.

"Michael," I said softly, standing as close as I could to him without making him restless. "You know that thing we found out the other day? The words?"

"Of course I do." The baby twitched a little at Michael's harsh voice, and he modulated his tone. "I don't forget things."

"That's the point. I want you to forget it. To not tell another living soul."

"Why should I tell anyone?"

I looked hard at my brother's handsome profile but saw only complete indifference as he stared out of the window at the marsh. The land was green and vibrant in the sunshine; the river, approaching high tide, reflected the sky's blue serenity in its fast-moving waters. Knowing Michael, he would still be able to write down the letters he'd found in those leaves twenty years hence; but although he approached some topics with a minuteness amounting to obsession, this did not appear to be one of them. I sent up a small prayer of gratitude for the vagaries of my sibling's mind.

I would have to visit Mama again soon. Julia's tact would not prevent her from gently probing for a reason if I, hitherto an almost daily visitor, suddenly abandoned my attendance at my mother's side. I could cite Mama's increasingly eccentric and downright unpleasant behavior as a reason for staying away, but that wasn't like me, and Julia would know it. No, I'd have to overcome my anger fast or risk having to explain myself. And that I didn't want to do.

"I'd better go." I planted a gentle kiss on the baby's head and another on Michael's cheek before he could move out of the way. "Congratulations, my dear."

"Hmph." Michael cradled his youngest son more firmly with his long-fingered hands.

"And you too." I bent over Julia and hugged her. "Send a note if you need anything, and I'll be back in a day or two regardless."

First, there was someone I needed to talk to.

The walk from Hyrst to the cemetery was less than a quarter of a mile, but by the time I arrived I was hot in my bombazine walking dress and heavy veil. Also, I had a headache, and guilt at not visiting Mama wasn't helping. I tried to think pleasant thoughts about my tiny nephew, but instead all I could see in my imagination was Susan, handing a poisoned chalice to Justin. And, much farther back, the ghostly figures of my mother and father settling down to drink cocoa together, one of them bent on murdering the other.

"Hello, Justin." I sighed as I contemplated the rectangle of clay before me.

My husband's grave was still only distinguished by a temporary marker. The ground had settled almost to the point where the large monument I'd ordered could be installed, but the stonemason was a cautious man and preferred to wait another month. Today's wreath was orange lilies rather prettily set off by small sprays of roses. The plot was carefully trimmed and free of weeds.

"We have a new nephew, my dear." I spoke to Justin about little Julius, trying as hard as I could to imagine I was talking to the real man and not think of the corruption taking place six feet below. Such a feat of deliberate ignorance was becoming harder to accomplish. Perhaps that was part of the process of releasing Justin into death that had been working itself out in me for the last nine months.

But I kept talking behind my veil, frustrated at not being able to see clearly down the hillside to where the opposite side of the valley rose up, green and fertile. Far down the path, I could make out two women in black, tending a grave. A breeze gusted from seaward at intervals, pushing my veil against my face and bringing the sound of the women's voices to me. They were matter-of-fact, conversational voices, suggesting that their dearly departed had not recently quit this life.

Before long, I realized that, almost without volition, I had passed on to the subject of Mama.

"Did she give the cup to Papa herself?" I asked my dead husband. "Or did she have the footman bring it? But I would think she'd be afraid he'd mix up the cups, wouldn't you? She'd have to have the cocoa brought up and then pour the poison in herself."

Or have someone else do it, rose the thought in my mind, and there was only one candidate.

"If she had an accomplice, it was certainly Susan." Who would have been about twelve years old, I believed. But it had been New Year's Eve, a cold night for a little girl to be out. Had it snowed? Had Susan been staying at Hyrst? I had no idea. I remembered absolutely nothing about Papa's death except for going to see him laid out on his bed, silver-haired and dignified, his hands neatly crossed on his chest with a prayer book tucked under them.

My father wasn't buried in this new necropolis, of course. Like all the more recent Earls of Broadmere, he had been afforded a place in the crypt of Littleberry's great church of St. Michael, sealed in a niche behind a tablet engraved with all of his names and titles.

A memory from several months after Papa's death surfaced along with my recollection of the crypt. I was standing next to Mama staring at that tablet while ancient Mr. Victor, a sexton now long dead, held up a lamp so we could read the writing. He was weak, and the light trembled and wavered, but we didn't insult him by refusing his help.

"I wish there were a place to lay flowers," I heard my younger self say.

"Flowers are vulgar." And Mama took my arm, gently turning me away from my father's last resting place. She began talking briskly about the dinner we were to give to mark Michael's engagement to Cecilia.

"It's not at all proper." Her voice was both deadened and magnified by the crypt's stone walls. "But sometimes mourning must give way to celebration."

I hadn't cared much about whether we were observing mourning properly, sad as I was about Papa's demise. I was simply glad to get away from the dreadful musty smell of underground decay and return home. I wanted to look once more at a certain nosegay sent to Hyrst by the pleasant baronet who lived at Whitcombe House. He was much older than me, to be sure, but Daniel had been dead for almost three years, and I had begun to find some enjoyment in Justin's gentle attentiveness, especially now that I had lost the second most important man in my life.

The pain of that loss suddenly stabbed me, fresh and sharp once more, made sharper still by the new knowledge that Papa had it in him to be cruel. I felt the slide of tears down my cheek, cooled by the breeze. The two women passed me, still talking, one of them holding a basket containing gardening tools. If they heard me sniff, it would have been understandable. They nodded their sympathy as they passed, addressing me as "m'lady" in hushed tones.

"Dear God, Justin," I whispered. "Do you know now what happened? Is it true the dead see all? Did Mama corrupt Susan, or did Susan corrupt Mama?"

My tears flowed faster as I thought of the day when Mama, screaming incoherently, had banished Susan from Hyrst once and for all. What had the child said? Had a terrible, shared secret lain between them? I couldn't reach it—couldn't reach them—I had set out to find the truth and had only found a shadow of the substance. I had failed.

"Lady Helena."

I gave a small shriek and turned, but what with the veil and the crying could only make out the vague shape of a man looming over me. My heart leapt into my throat.

"How *dare* you approach me without warning—whoever you are—I—"

"It's Armand Fortier, and I've already spoken your name twice. I'm sorry to find you in such distress, although I suppose it's to be expected."

I fumbled at the strings of my reticule, realizing my face must be wet and slimy. I couldn't possibly use my veil to wipe it. If I had a handkerchief at all it was probably of inadequate size for the gargantuan task of restoring my countenance.

And then, mercifully, a large and very serviceable square of clean linen was pressed into my hand. I turned away and effected the necessary operations, blowing my nose as quietly as I could.

"Thank you."

My headache had now assumed abominable proportions. I was doubly grateful for my veil, which cut down the harshness of the noon light as well as disguising the state of my face.

"I apologize profusely for intruding on your grief." Fortier held up his hands in a gesture I found hard to interpret. "I have absolutely no excuse for being here either. I wish I could say I just happened to be passing by, but the truth is—I followed you. At least I waited at the entrance to the cemetery hoping to see you come out—and then cursed myself for a fool when I remembered you could just as easily have gone on down the hill by the other gate. I wanted to see you, so—here I am." He let his arms drop by his sides, his whole demeanor more uncertain, less confident than usual.

"I don't know whether I should object to that or not." I assumed an arch tone in an attempt to cheer myself up. "I'm unaccustomed to gentlemen accosting me in cemeteries. Were you worried about me? Being alone, I mean?"

"Not particularly. Littleberry has the advantage of being a safe place for women. Although I admit I was concerned about what your frame of mind must be, given yesterday's revelations. I've been thinking about you ever since I left Whitcombe."

"I've been thinking too." I tried to keep the bitterness out of my voice but failed. "Discovering that your father was faithless and manipulative and that the woman who bore and nurtured you is a killer certainly merits deep thought."

"Faithless and manipulative—was that the motive? You seemed so sure we were looking at a confession and that the crime was murder. I'm sorry Miss Guttridge came back when she did."

"And that our conversation ended in polite nothings? I suppose I could have continued it in front of Guttridge." I sniffed and applied Fortier's handkerchief to my nose. "She certainly realizes something's up. I don't think I spoke a word for the rest of the day. But as confidential a person as Guttridge is, this is too deep and terrible a secret for *anyone* to bear."

"Except yourself. And Lord Broadmere?"

"He doesn't have the information that allowed me to put two and two together, so to speak. He didn't hear Susan's words about getting the dose wrong, which is what makes me sure she learned to poison from Mama. I don't think he knows about Papa's affairs—that was Mama's motive, by the by. My sisters know, but they *don't* know about the picture, and I will never tell them. I've asked Michael never to mention it, and I believe he won't."

"Affairs, in the plural?" I heard the note of revelation in Fortier's voice. "Excuse me for asking—how old was your father when he died?"

For a moment, I didn't understand, but then my mind caught up with Fortier's. "He'd had his seventieth birthday in the summer—but I don't know if there'd been any recent case of infidelity." I hesitated, then plowed on. "There had been something that had upset Mama terribly a decade before. That's when she stopped writing in her notebooks and took up painting more seriously. The sketchbook you saw when we first met dates to around halfway through that period. I can't help wondering if Mama wasn't in her right mind by the time she—did what she did." I swallowed. "There might have been something else that triggered it, of course.

Something Papa did or said—who knows? That's one of the awful aspects of this whole business—not knowing the whole story."

I could see Fortier nodding as the breeze once more blew my veil back against my face. How odd I must look from Fortier's viewpoint, I thought, the black net molding my features like one of those statues of grief. Yet aside from my headache, my mood had lifted simply from the relief of being able to discuss the whole business with a rational human being.

"You're right though," I said quietly after a few moments' thought. "There should be an explanation for the ten-year gap between the worst incident of betrayal and my father's death, and I think I know what it was. Michael. Mama waited until he was old enough to cope with inheriting the title. She waited until he had turned eighteen—just—and wanted to marry Cecilia. I don't think she opposed the match as Papa did—I *wish* I had been paying attention back then—and she must have thought Michael would be all right with a wife at his side. And by then he also had Brandrick, I suppose."

"It's a sound theory."

I shuddered. "It is. And if it's true, that means my mother spent ten years plotting to kill my father." I took a deep breath. "Ten years in which to get the recipe right and all those workhouse patients to practice on."

I could hear the hardness in my voice, the cynicism, and Fortier certainly didn't miss it.

"Helena." He stepped forward and then stopped. "Good God, I wish I knew what to say."

"You don't have to say anything." I stepped back from Justin's graveside and turned to Fortier. "Oddly enough, I don't feel I need comforting. I don't need sympathy. I have the truth now, or at least as near to the truth as I can possibly get, and . . . I have the strength I need to deal with it. I've learned the worst about my parents and I—I find I still love them." I turned back to Justin's grave, looking down at the clay that held his bones. "And I did it all without you, Justin. I must be growing up."

And with that, I turned on my heel and held out a hand toward Fortier. "Would you take me home, please? It'll be time for luncheon soon, and I don't want to keep my staff waiting."

I couldn't read his expression from behind my veil. He said nothing as he let me take his arm and we turned to walk uphill.

As we neared the main road, the breeze died down, and my veil hung heavy and stifling over my face. Thick hedges of hornbeam and hawthorn hid us from view. Over us towered the cedars of Lebanon planted when the cemetery was new, already grown to a great height. The path underfoot was dry and dusty and scattered with debris from the trees. The only sounds I could hear through my veil were the clicks and rattles of small stones dislodged by our feet.

"Do you realize," I said after a long stretch of silence, "that the truth has come to light with very little investigative effort on my part? This isn't how it happens in novels."

Fortier made a small sound that might have signified laughter, but when he spoke his voice was grave.

"If you doubt your qualifications as an investigator, you're quite wrong—although your methods are unorthodox. You elicited the confession about Sir Justin's death because you were gracious and kind to Susan Hatherall. And it was your persistence in using your mother's journals and paintings to tell her story, to find her again, as my sister says, that led you to this latest discovery."

"And what revelations." I kicked viciously at a stone. "The woeful degeneration of a noble English family."

"Perhaps." I felt Fortier's arm pull me in a little closer. "But I wouldn't dwell on it, if I were you. The tragedy of your mother and father belongs to the distant past and is perhaps better left there."

"You say that? I thought you wanted all things out in the light of day."

"I was an arrogant idiot to talk about the importance of truth as if it were some kind of dogma." I thought I heard Fortier sigh. "When I think of the horrible repercussions that the revelation of your mother's actions would lead to, I would carry this secret to my grave—for your sake. And I had no right to insist on truth from you when I couldn't offer you my own."

He stopped walking and turned toward me.

"Helena, I'm going to have to leave for France again soon. I don't know how long I'll be gone. That's why I was waiting for you—there's something I want to say. Something that was best not said across your husband's grave."

"You make it sound terribly serious." I was suddenly very conscious of my heartbeat.

"Love is always serious." But there was an edge of laughter in his voice—and then, suddenly, a tenderness that turned my legs to jelly. "You must know by now that I love you, my dear. That truth, at least, is best laid bare to the daylight."

I did know. I had known at least since the night of Susan's death. But I had turned my back on Fortier's love then, as I must do now.

"You know I can't." I spoke rapidly, looking down at my toes. "Not yet. I loved my husband, and it's been too short a time since I lost him. Leaving all other considerations aside."

"Such as the social gulf between us?"

Impatiently, I pushed back my veil, heedless of the fact that my eyes were surely still red and my face blotchy.

Fortier suddenly came into sharp focus, his face earnest and drawn.

"No, not that," I said. "I daresay we could get around that. Ned had no title when Gerry wed him, and you're a gentleman—aren't you?"

Lines of amusement creased Fortier's cheeks and puckered the tender skin around his eyes. "I am, indubitably, a gentleman." His face became serious again. "Helena, do you know what I love most about you?"

I took a deep breath, realizing how impeded my breathing had become. "I shouldn't be listening to this."

"It's the contrasts. The sensible countrywoman and the wide-eyed innocent. The imperious aristocrat and the hard worker who's perfectly ready to get her hands dirty. The confidence and the uncertainty in you. I could spend the rest of my life studying your character."

I took a step backward, certain he was about to grasp my hand. "I definitely shouldn't be listening to this. Look, Fortier, I'm—what's the phrase?—flattered by your regard for me. More than flattered. But—"

"And your beauty. Your sweet, perfect face, your elegant little figure—"

"Now you are really going too far." I could feel myself flush up to the roots of my hair.

"I am." The corners of Fortier's mouth turned down, and his arms, which he had raised a little as if he wanted to take me in them, fell back to his sides. "Because even if, when you're done mourning your husband, you could marry me and make that right with your family—and I do understand, my dear, how much your family means to you—I'm not a free man."

"You're not?" I asked faintly.

"I haven't been since I was very young. And I can't explain everything to you because these are secrets that aren't mine to keep or reveal as I wish. I will tell you as much as I dare—and please don't hate me for what I'm about to say."

"It will make no difference. I told you, it's too *soon*. Don't you understand that, Fortier? I've only just begun to learn who I am as a woman alone."

"I do know that. And I'm grateful for it because it means you won't walk into the arms of the next available nobleman for the sake of the child you long for."

"You know that?" My voice was a whisper.

"Yes, I know that. And I wish you knew how much I crave the honor of satisfying that wish. But—" Fortier shook his head. "No, there's no easy way of saying this. There is a woman in France whom people believe to be my wife."

"What?"

Fortier raised a hand in a pleading gesture. "Listen, please, Helena. I swear to you, this is only an outward appearance. We play the part of husband and wife before the world, but there was never any marriage. She and I are in no way bound to each other by anything greater than friendship." He took a deep breath. "As a young man, I agreed to a pretense without ever thinking of the lasting consequences. Without thinking that one day I would stand before the woman I love and feel myself unable to explain the circumstances because I'm bound to secrecy. All I can tell you is that this is no lighthearted circumstance. The matter is of the utmost seriousness." He hesitated. "Can you trust me, Helena?"

I looked at him, long and hard. Once again, his face was drawn, the only animation residing in his large, luminous eyes—which bore an expression of deep earnestness I could not resist.

"I'll have to trust you, won't I?" I said eventually and saw his entire body relax. "Despite my family's predictions that you're a complete scoundrel, I've trusted you since—well, not the beginning, but I think I've trusted you since you came posthaste to my house from the ship, completely exhausted and smelling of vomit. A duplicitous man would have made an effort to look better."

I couldn't help laughing as Fortier's eyes rounded in shock, and soon he was laughing too. He offered me his arm again, and we stepped forth, our footsteps beating time evenly on the rough dirt of the lane.

"I'm going to take you home, Lady Helena Whitcombe," Fortier said briskly. "And I won't importune you with my romantic French notions again until I've found some way to extricate myself from the mess I'm in. But when I have, I hope you're prepared to be wooed in earnest."

31

A NEW BEGINNING

For once, Mama was in a quiet and pleasant mood when I arrived at Hyrst. She sat calmly in her bed, her back well supported by several pillows, her long white hair tidily braided and her clothing neat and orderly. Not for the first time I sent up a prayer of thanks for Belming.

"Hello, Mama." I leaned well in to kiss my mother's cheek. The bed was a large, ancient four-poster with intricate carvings on the posts. Mama smelled pleasantly of lavender and clean clothes.

"Have you sent for the gardener?" Mama's eyes, which had been focused on nothing as if she were listening to a voice in her own head, fixed on me.

"Why, yes, Mama. Of course I have."

It had been a long time since Mama had asked that question, once the prelude to any conversation with her. Of course, my recent discoveries had changed my perspective on many things, not least the significance of Mama's herb garden. Presumably that's where the foxgloves that had poisoned Papa had come from. Perhaps that was why concern for her garden was one of the last vestiges of her old self. Or perhaps I was entirely wrong, and her mind had simply settled on a random mania.

"Would you like to come and see your garden, Mama?" Maybe I could get my mother talking about her plants and satisfy my own burning desire to know I was right about the foxglove poison. Even now there were moments when I thought—I hoped—I had gotten the whole thing entirely wrong and Papa had, as I'd believed for the last few years, died of heart failure following an attack of pleurisy.

"No, dear." My mother gave a tremulous smile but then wrinkled her brow. "Do I know you?"

"I'm Helena, your youngest daughter. I live at Whitcombe House."

"I wouldn't like to know what you could do with that fork. It's grand and pretty, and I smell the onions all over the place."

I looked up and met Julia's amused eyes. She had quietly entered as Mama and I talked, baby Julius in her arms. The little boy was starting to fill out, changing quickly, as all newborns do, and I held out my hands for him immediately. Julia nestled him into my arms, and I cuddled him close to my bosom, crooning as I brushed his hot little head with my lips.

"Contrary to sycamore, I do not have rabies." At least I thought that's what Mama had said, and there was no point in asking for clarification. Mama had started talking entire nonsense lately, generally when she was in a good mood, and I welcomed her babble. I felt sometimes as if she were telling herself stories—happy ones.

"Mama, I've been meaning to ask you something." I drew aside the blanket around Julius so my mother could see her grandson's face. "Would you like to come and live at Whitcombe with me?" I looked at Julia and then back at my mother. "You'd be just as comfortable, and Michael and Julia would like some more space for their family. Belming could have her own room again. I can easily put the night nurse in a little dressing room off your bedroom, which would be so much more convenient for everyone."

"Of course, if you wish to stay here, you're more than welcome, Mama-in-Law." Julia leaned forward to pat Mama's arm. "It's entirely up to you."

"That would be quite nice," said my mother. "But no more prunes. I cannot countenance prunes in the, ah, the boot boy. You understand me?"

"Of course," I said airily. "No more prunes in the boot boy."

If I had intended to have some kind of confrontation with my mother, the moment had passed as soon as Julia entered the room. Never would I allow even the merest hint of my suspicions to pass my lips in front of any member of my family. Besides, I looked at my mother and what did I see? The husk of her former self; an old lady in a sprigged night-gown and a blue candlewick dressing gown; her memories, if she still had them, buried deep down somewhere none of us could reach. What lesson could I learn except to guard myself against the heady power of knowledge as my own skill at herb lore increased? And of course I would not have a venal child as a helpmeet. I would have Guttridge, whose sober honesty and common sense were my best guarantee against mishaps of any kind.

"Naturally, my offer to house you at Whitcombe is entirely dependent on Belming being satisfied with the arrangement." I smiled at my mother's attendant, who had been quietly refolding clothing from a drawer Mama had disarranged. "What do you think, Belming?"

"Well, I'll miss Hyrst, m'lady," Belming said with a glance at Julia. "But Whitcombe's rooms are spacious, to be sure, and the house is airier than Hyrst because it's not so crowded in by trees. I think we'll get on very well there."

I grinned at Julia, handing her son back to her. "I'm thinking of extending the same offer to Thomas. The poor boy is so cramped in one room at Four Square, and I do enjoy his company."

"Goodness," Julia said mildly. "As long as you don't marry someone who intends to give house parties every weekend."

"I wouldn't marry anyone who didn't welcome my family into Whitcombe with open arms." I thought, of course, of Fortier, but immediately tried to banish the thought to the darkest recess of my mind.

"So you *are* thinking of marrying again." Julia looked smug. "I thought as much."

"I'd like one last chance at a son or daughter of my own," I admitted, peering at the small bundle in Julia's arms. My new nephew slept sweetly, the tiny movements of his mouth as he dreamed revealing the milk blister on his upper lip. His ash-blond hair peeped from under his cap, and one tiny hand stuck out from his wrappings like a small pink star.

"And love? Wouldn't you like that? Devotion such as you and Justin had for each other; a lasting love, like your parents' marriage."

I shifted uncomfortably on the seat I had taken so as to be closer to Mama. Julia knew nothing about the real nature of my parents' relationship. She naturally trusted the lie my sisters had built up so convincingly that, until recently, I had believed it implicitly. She didn't know how uneasy references to their supposedly happy life together now made me.

"Of course I'd like love," I said a little testily. "And when the time comes, I will choose with the greatest of care. After all, my new husband will have a great deal of control over my person and property, so he'd better be truly devoted to me."

"Are you sure he'll control your property?" Julia held

Julius so Mama could see him better. My mother said something about a cheese pie falling under leaves and put a forefinger, frail but elegant still, against her grandson's soft cheek.

"What do you mean?" I asked.

"You need to ask Michael about the property thing." Julia lifted her head to look at me, a small frown creasing the skin between her brows. "I could swear he's mentioned some new legislation, and I've seen references in the papers from time to time. Some of my friends think it's rather important."

"I have to admit I've not looked at the newspapers much since Justin died." I shrugged. "And the way they're passing new laws these days, they could have rewritten the whole thing by the time I marry. But I'll make a point of asking Michael and Ned—which reminds me, Julia. It's been a long while since I gathered the family together. Why don't I host a luncheon or dinner to celebrate Julius? Perhaps we can tempt O to leave London—I'd love to see her."

32

THE GLITTER OF SUN ON SEA

"You've made some changes around here."

Michael banged his glass down perilously close to a pretty gold-on-white vase I had placed on a Georgian lowboy I'd had moved down from Justin's bedroom.

"Yes." I signaled to the footman who was circulating with cups of coffee. "I'm trying to imagine this house differently. I don't think I'll be giving any more grand entertainments, so I'm making the rooms less formal. I've moved over to the east wing so Thomas can have a suite of four good rooms. His tutor can stay here overnight now, to save the poor man from trekking back and forth from Eastbourne."

This change had meant dismantling Justin's bedroom and distributing his clothing. I'd not removed my late husband's presence from the house—in fact, I'd made sure that mementoes of Justin were in every room—but I had, in a sense, accepted that he wouldn't be coming home.

Thomas, who had been plundering the tray of marzipan sweets, heard my remark and approached us. We'd all eaten a stupendous Sunday luncheon featuring a baron of beef, but my nephew never seemed to achieve a state of repletion.

"I h-have the most generous Auntie in the entire w-world. And the prettiest. When I'm a bishop, I sh-shall invite you to my palace and show you off."

I laughed. "By that time, I'll be old and gray and not worth showing off at all."

"You should have provided the lad with a private chapel." Odelia, whom nobody had seen for quite a while, looked resplendent. All my sisters had abandoned mourning, but the others were wearing subdued colors nonetheless. O was in a gorgeous confection of crushed raspberry damask, her hair in a sort of Grecian style that suited her admirably. I wondered fleetingly where she got the money for such magnificence, but I wasn't about to pry. One Blanche in the family was quite enough.

"Very funny, A-Auntie O." Thomas made a face at Odelia, a piece of marzipan bulging out his cheek. "J-just you wait till I-I'm ordained and you want me to preside at your w-wedding. I'll step on your toes."

"If I ever indulge in anything so foolish as marriage, you have my permission to hit me on the head and bring me to my senses." O sipped her coffee, wrinkling her nose at Thomas in a playful manner. "I think Baby's perfectly lovely to give house room to you and Mama."

Mama had made a brief appearance before luncheon but had become agitated over the presence of so many people. Belming had led her back to her rooms, where they would enjoy the same feast we were having but in far more comfort.

"Send the boy back home if he gives you any trouble." Ned's face was split by a wide smile underneath his beard, and he clapped Thomas jovially on his shoulder as he passed. Ned and Gerry had Four Square to themselves. Petey had already left for London to become accustomed to city life before he began school, and Maryanne was in Shropshire staying with friends.

"He's no trouble at all. In fact, I'm delighted to have Thomas around to escort me to dinners and suchlike. I have some invitations for September—I won't be avoiding society completely."

"You should be thinking about getting a new husband, not gadding around with Thomas." Michael was fussing around behind Julia, shoving a small cushion behind her back, as she'd strained a muscle picking up Annabelle Alice.

"Rather good news about the Act, eh, my dear?" Ned turned back from the window, where he'd been watching a group of seagulls hovering on the updraft from the hillside. "Just hold on till January the first and you'll no longer have to hand your property to your husband. Keep it in the family, eh? You can have your cake and eat it."

I shrugged. "It'll cut down the number of fortune hunters, that's for certain. Although I daresay I'll still be plagued by men who fancy the idea of living in style and ease on their wife's money."

My thoughts flew to Fortier, somewhere in France in the company of a woman people thought was his wife. I didn't for one moment think he had any interest in my money, but the Married Women's Property Act, now the law of the land, would protect him from accusations of fortune hunting. After all, he already lived in style and ease. The Dermody house wasn't on the grand scale of Whitcombe, but it was smart and comfortable.

I had no illusions that Fortier's devotion to me would remain a secret in Littleberry. And I had decided not to care. I was a grown woman, a widow, not some idiot girl who had to be protected from gossip. I would do what I wanted with my property and my life.

"Which reminds me," I said, raising my voice so everyone

could hear. "Everyone," of course, included my footmen, who would carry what I was about to say below stairs; so much the better.

"I do wish you'd all stop calling me Baby. I'm much too old for such a silly nickname."

The moment of silence that greeted my request gave me time to study my family. Gerry, who had been talking children with Julia, arched her eyebrows and made a little moue of amusement. Blanche, who had been reclining on a sofa trying to look gracious while no doubt reckoning the cost of her son's trip to Scotland for the grouse shooting, waved a hand as if shooing away a fly. The twins, who'd been whispering together in a corner, merely looked blank.

But I was surrounded by allies. Ned smiled broadly and raised his coffee cup to me; Thomas said a quiet "hooray" from his seat near his mother; and O drifted elegantly over to lay an arm across my shoulder. But to my surprise, it was Michael who spoke first.

"I agree. After all, I've never called Helena anything but her proper name, and I *am* the head of this family." He nodded at me. "You've a right to be treated as a grown woman."

"Weren't you telling her she needed a husband not five minutes ago?" Blanche's tone was acid. "It's all very well for you—you've exploited the situation nicely. Don't think I didn't notice you've been able to pay to have the front façade repointed and painted. I bet that came from Baby's—Helena's —sheep."

"In a sense, yes, of course." Michael looked puzzled at the accusation, as well he should since he was incapable of duplicity. "Combining our operations has given both Helena and me more farming income. I've been able to sell a small piece of my land, and I don't have nearly as much interest to pay. It's a great relief. I still think Helena needs a husband though. One with children. She won't be happy on her own."

"I assure you I'll seek a new spouse in my own time and on my own terms," I said. "In the meantime, I'm perfectly happy with Michael's management of my land and livestock. I'll admit I had my doubts at first, but my new tenant appears to be a most proficient farmer. I'm satisfied with the proposals for next year."

And although I wouldn't admit it out loud, Brandrick did seem to be a talented manager and devoted to our family's interests. I still found him annoying in a way I couldn't quite put my finger on, but I was finding it easier to tolerate his presence at our monthly meetings.

"It's going to be rather hard to remember not to call you by your pet name, *Helena*," O put in. "But I'm delighted to see you making a bid for independence."

Michael frowned. "I hope you're not going to start behaving like Odelia though. Papa should have put his foot down—"

"*Michael.*" Julia rolled her eyes as she twisted round to flap a hand at her husband, then winced as the movement pinched her back. "There are some opinions you really need to keep to yourself. O's way of life may seem a little bohemian to the rest of us, but she never causes you any trouble, does she? And Scott House would be horribly neglected if nobody lived there."

"It'll be a positive hive of activity soon," O said airily. "I intend to invite Helena up to Town and inveigle her into helping me entertain. She's a much better hostess than I am, and she'll look charming in second mourning once her year and a day is over."

I saw a spasm of annoyance cross Blanche's face and wondered if she'd had plans to invite me to Tunbridge Wells at last. It occurred to me that my status in my family was rising now that I was, apparently, independently wealthy for life. I decided to regain control of the conversation.

"You're all very kind, and no doubt acting in what you consider my best interests," I said as loudly and firmly as possible. "But I'll thank you to leave me to order my life in the way I think suits me best."

I paused, looking at the room full of handsome Scott-De Quincys and their spouses—a pride of lions if there ever was one.

"When Justin died," I went on, "I thought I had lost the meaning to my life. I'd never really conceived of myself as a single human being, you see. I've always been attached to someone—Mama and Papa, Daniel, Justin, this family as a whole—and never really able to cope with loss. But this last year has taught me otherwise. As much as I grieve for Justin —and I still miss him dreadfully—I feel I have more to interest me now than I've ever had in my entire life. I love you all, but I can stand on my own two feet now."

"Hear, hear," growled Ned from the armchair that had once been Justin's. He was beginning to look sleepy, but a flurry of activity announced the arrival of the children—all eight of them, since seven-week-old Julius was in the arms of the new nursemaid. Scotty, who was on a leash held by James, sounded his high-pitched bark as he saw me.

I picked up Annabelle Alice and carried her to the window, followed by my dog and a group of giggling children. Outside, the August sun shed its golden afternoon light over the fields, verdant still but stippled with the long, pale-gold stalks of the grasses the sheep didn't care to eat. Little-berry's red-brown jumble of houses baked in the heat, their windows flashing points of light in the distance. Beyond the town's distinctive silhouette, the sea was pure turquoise, glittering and lovely.

I cuddled Annabelle Alice close to me, grateful for a

chance to be alone with my thoughts as the children scattered throughout the room. She was tired, and as her head went down on my shoulder I heard the tiny noise that meant she'd put her thumb in her mouth and was sucking it vigorously.

I had plumbed the depths of the Scott-De Quincy family's worst secrets and survived, I thought, straining my eyes in the hope of seeing the French coast. I had, unwittingly or not, brought the truth of my husband's death into the light of day and seen his murderers slain, not by the process of law but by the ineluctable forces of natural justice. I had gained the love of a man I could respect and perhaps one day love in return. And I alone of all those in the room knew that there *was* hope for me to have a child of my own. At that moment, the future shone like the glitter of sun on sea.

AUTHOR'S NOTE

Lady Helena Investigates ends the day after Queen Victoria granted royal assent to the Married Women's Property Act 1882, which came into force on January 1, 1883. The new law marks Helena's entry into that rare sector of Victorian society—women with economic power.

There's a reason why lady sleuth novels so often feature a widow. In the latter part of the nineteenth century and even before the passage of the Act, upper-class widows could end up with greater social freedom than their unmarried peers, because they were less hedged about with rules about chaperonage and behavior (the correct behavior that would make you attractive to the Victorian male and thus rescue you from spinsterhood).

And until 1883, widows could, in the right circumstances, hold infinitely more power than married women. In law, a married woman was a *feme covert*—her property rights were covered over, subsumed, in truth smothered by those of her husband who, upon marriage, would assume ownership of all his wife's assets. Including their offspring—a woman who wanted to leave her husband might never see her children again. Of course, a widow's economic circumstances would depend on how her husband wrote his will . . .

Did you loathe the nickname "Baby?" You were supposed to. It doesn't just refer to Helena's position in her family; it's a symbol of the infantilization of women that became progressively worse as the Victorian age entered its first and second decade. The ideal of Victorian womanhood was childlike, clinging, trembling in breathless adoration of her husband-god. In the twenty-first-century idiom, it was so messed up it doesn't even compute. And it still influences our thinking to this day because of its persistence well into the twentieth century. Remember *The Stepford Wives*?

Even Queen Victoria, probably the most powerful woman of the nineteenth century, was her husband Albert's *kleines Weibchen*—little wifie. Much as she deplored her long widowhood, it probably saved her from a catastrophic transfer of power to her foreign spouse, which could have had constitutional implications. Read Helen Rappaport's superb *A Magnificent Obsession* to learn more about Victoria's marriage and her withdrawal into seclusion and misery after Albert's death, a withdrawal I've mirrored in Helena's backstory.

And yet on August 18, 1882, Helena becomes a powerful woman—independently wealthy and fairly near the top of the social scale. The counterpoise to her rise is her mother's story, which is essentially one of powerlessness, and I invite the reader to consider the poisoner's art in the context of this imbalance. Poison, it is often said, is (or was) a woman's weapon—perhaps because they had few others. I plunged the Dowager Countess into madness or dementia—you choose—because there again was that theme of powerlessness and withdrawal from, or loss of, responsibilities.

And then, of course, there are Michael and Thomas—men with disabilities that shake the foundations of their empowered male world. Yes, Helena is the heroine of this series, but the other characters are extremely important to the tale I wish to tell.

ACKNOWLEDGMENTS

A novel has many stages as it works its way toward publication, and I'll try to put these acknowledgments into chronological order. Every bit of help I've received, whether I've paid for it or not, has been precious to me.

First and foremost, thanks go to my first draft reader and critique partner Katharine Grubb. There aren't many people I'd entrust a first draft to!

Then there's my writing group, who have held onto me even though I've moved far away: Tonja Brice, Sherri Gallagher, Cathy Harvey, Maureen Lang, Judy Knox, and Myra Wells. Some of them have been there for me since I was a new writer, and I can't begin to estimate how much encouragement and advice they've given me over the years.

As I neared the end of the self-editing process, I received absolutely invaluable help from a group of beta readers located all over the world. They are: Sharyn Bellville, Carol Bisig, Carmela Corvato, Margaret Delahoy, Teri Donaldson, Audra Friend, Karen Green, Joan Greening, Judy Johnsen, Maureen Lang, Julie McCarrin, Susan Meikle, Pamela Pond, Toby Shaw, Shirley Stephens, Tracey Stewart, Andrea

Stoeckel, Kit Tunney, and Jacomien Zwemstra. I made many changes for the better on the basis of their sharp-witted and forthright opinions.

No book would feel finished without help from a professional editor and cover designer. Many thanks to Jenny Quinlan of Historical Editorial, who put the essential editorial polish on my words; and Rachel Lawston of Lawston Design, who created the most beautiful cover from my vague ideas.

Special thanks to Ellen Hills for taking over several marketing tasks while I scrambled to get this book out. I couldn't have asked for a more efficient assistant.

And finally, thanks to my family for leaving me some time to write! And edit. And produce. And market. And generally let my writing business take over my life. I love you all dearly for being there with me every day.

ABOUT THE AUTHOR

The most important fact you need to know about me is that I was (according to my mother, at least) named after Jane Eyre, which to this day remains one of my favorite books. I was clearly doomed to love all things Victorian, and ended up studying both English and French nineteenth-century writers in depth.

This was a pretty good grounding for launching myself into writing novels set in the nineteenth century. I was living in the Chicago suburbs when I began writing the *House of Closed Doors* series, inspired by a photograph of the long-vanished County Poor Farm in my area.

Now back in my native England, I have the good fortune to live in an idyllic ancient town close to the sea. This location has sparked a new series about an aristocratic family with more secrets than most: *The Scott-De Quincy Mysteries*.

I write for readers who want a series you can't put down. I love to blend saga, mystery, adventure, and a touch of romance, set against the background of the real-life issues facing women in the late nineteenth century.

I am a member of the Alliance of Independent Authors, the Historical Novel Society, Novelists, Inc., and the Society of Authors.

To find out more about my books, join my insider list at www.janesteen.com/insider

facebook.com/janesteenwriter

twitter.com/JaneSteen

amazon.com/author/janesteen

bookbub.com/authors/jane-steen

pinterest.com/janesteen